JUST LIKE OLD TIMES

In the next instant, with the simple act of pulling on a doorknob, all the oxygen seemed to get sucked from her lungs. Jessie tried to catch her breath, but couldn't. She should have known. His dark hair shining under the porch light, hands shoved deep in his pockets, he stood whistling softly to himself, looking right at home, looking as if he'd never left Carran, or the farm . . . or her.

"Nick," she mouthed, but no sound came out.

—

527
1762

Also by Leigh Riker

Morning Rain

Available from HarperPaperbacks

Harper
Monogram

Unforgettable

Leigh Riker

HarperPaperbacks
A Division of HarperCollinsPublishers

This is a work of fiction. The characters, incidents, and dialogues are products of the author's imagination and are not to be construed as real. Any resemblance to actual events or persons, living or dead, is entirely coincidental.

HarperPaperbacks *A Division of* HarperCollins*Publishers*
10 East 53rd Street, New York, N.Y. 10022

Cover illustration by Jeff Cornell

First printing: April 1993

Printed in the United States of America

HarperPaperbacks, HarperMonogram, and colophon are trademarks of HarperCollins*Publishers*

10 9 8 7 6 5 4 3 2 1

With love,
For the men in my life:

Don, who really does make it possible
Scott
and
Hal

For my father-in-law, Wally
In memory of my father,
Robert Andrew Bartley

And for my littlest love,
Timothy James Riker . . .
Welcome, barefoot boy

Acknowledgments

This book has been a joy to write, in no small part due to the support of all my friends in Connecticut RWA, who've shared the dark moments and the bright. My heartfelt thanks, especially, to Linda Wolter Carlson, who saw immediately where the story really began and set it on the proper path toward home.

Prologue

Charleston, South Carolina
September 1989

In the hurricane's aftermath, devastation had its own smell, stronger, sweeter than he remembered. Yet it wasn't in the humid air that lingered from the storm. To Nick Granby, surveying his ruined garden, the updated memory of destruction would always smell like crushed flowers.

Nick frowned at such waste. It was everywhere.

Three days ago Hurricane Hugo had thundered across South Carolina like General Sherman's troops more than a century before, and, shifting his gaze now from a bed of flattened asters, Nick could only stare at his favorite palmetto, leaning like a drunken Union horse soldier against the house. Sure, he'd seen other roofs caved into attics; the main bearing beams were still solid, his practiced architect's eye kept noting; structurally, his home was sound. Then why did he keep feeling like a ten-year-old boy again, on that cold Connecticut morning when he had cried over his family's flooded fields? The day Nick had decided he wouldn't become a farmer like his father and his father before that.

At twilight he stood in the open doorway leading from what his Gullah housekeeper called the drawin' room and thanked God for the Low Country's warmer weather. More rain was predicted for tomorrow, though, like a voodoo curse heaped upon a curse, and he'd have to replace the shattered glass in the French doors before then.

Squaring his shoulders, he went inside. The blush pink single house he'd bought five years ago on Charleston's famed Rainbow Row had suffered little severe damage, none that couldn't be repaired. Personally, he knew he'd been damn lucky in the storm. Professionally . . .

He shrugged. He'd think about bankruptcy, about his coastal resort complex, which had been three-quarters finished when the hurricane hit, and which now sat three-quarters under water; but he'd think about it later. He almost smiled. Born contrary, his father always said, though Nick preferred to call himself determined. Somehow he'd save Seaview, too.

His boots crunched over glass shards on the Tabriz carpet, coated with a glaze of coastal lowlands mud. It was beginning to stink, not of flowers. Just now the entire room bore scant resemblance to the elegant, watered, silk-papered, pecan wood-trimmed, antique-filled space he'd come to love. Even Carran, after spring flood, hadn't looked this bad.

At the Sheraton sideboard he poured himself a shot of whiskey, neat, knowing he'd find no ice in the refrigerator. There was no electricity in the house, or, in fact, in all of Charleston. In swift gulps he downed the warm scotch. It burned like acid but, oddly, cleared his head.

Then lifting his gaze, he wished he hadn't as he met his father's disapproving stare among the family pictures on the sideboard's mahogany top. His parents. His grandfather. The farmhouse where Nick had been born, where he was still considered a traitor for leaving. A traitor, almost three decades after the flood. A traitor, twelve years after he'd finally moved away. He picked up another photograph, one of his best friend, Ben, holding his son, a pudgy toddler then. Ben's wife, smiling in the old picture, had died six months ago.

Nick's gaze darkened. Something else was missing. *Someone.*

Catching the glint of bright brass against the muddy carpet, he bent down. The missing frame had been dented, its glass smashed into sharp diagonal lines. Without thinking, he ran a finger over the face he had loved so well and cut himself. He didn't see the blood. He pried the glass pieces away, feeling as if he'd hurt her again instead of himself.

What would she think of him now, his gut still twisting at her smile, the white cap and gown, ash blond hair hanging to her waist, blue eyes bright with hope that graduation day? His pulse beat heavily. She probably wouldn't care—just like his father at his mother's funeral.

Nick's stomach clenched at the memory, and he swigged more scotch. "Don't bother coming back here again on my account," Tom Granby had said two years ago.

Suddenly the house seemed stifling, and he needed air, needed to walk. Yet the warm sea air didn't help; and neither did picking his way along the debris-littered Battery overlooking Charleston harbor's Fort Sumter, where the first shots of the Civil War had been fired.

In the soft, sunset breeze off the water, he tried, but failed, to repress the harsh thoughts of Tom, and the more tender memories triggered by a broken picture. He tried to forget the helplessness he'd felt for the past three days, the restlessness that had plagued him . . . for how long?

Not only since the storm, he realized. Years, he thought, glancing back at his house, then across the street toward the prestigious yacht club where he'd attended so many balls and parties, squiring the city's magnolia-skinned beauties, young women he knew he couldn't marry. He'd always known he'd never really belong in Charleston, but that didn't bother him. He'd never belonged in Carran either.

And hell, he didn't care. Almost a thousand miles from his father's farm, he had what he wanted, what he'd worked hard to get, what he just might lose after all. His mouth tightened. Like hell he'd lose it. He had made his choices—but so had Tom—and he was staying right here. Besides, trying to make peace with his father would mean going back to Carran.

She wouldn't be there, he knew. She had married someone else. With the thought, he stopped walking, leaned against the seawall and, for a long while, stared out across the harbor, his gaze unfocused, remembering, regretting.

Ah, Jess . . . I didn't want to leave you.

1

Carran, Connecticut
Six months later

"I suppose I ought to warn you," her brother had said, hesitant as ever when the subject came up. "Nick Granby's back in town."

Only hours ago those few words had seemed to chase Jessica Pearce Simon from a highway telephone booth, along the curving two-lane road that fell and rose and dipped again into Carran. Home, Jessie had thought, before Ben's warning turned anticipation into dread; now, stubborn as Nick himself, the words still followed her around Ben's dining room table, like footsteps echoing a past she hoped she'd forgotten.

Setting the table for dinner, she felt her fingers tremble on a plate that had been her grandmother's, and hastily put it down. She'd come here looking, hoping, to find peace, and ordinarily the familiar china would have been enough to make her feel serene. Now she noticed that the gold had worn from the plate's rim.

Perhaps she shouldn't have come.

If only she'd let Ben know before this afternoon that she was on her way, but . . .

"Leaving Scottsdale was an act of bravery," she'd explained, just inside his front door. "If you'd uttered one word to discourage me, I'd have stayed in Arizona and let the ink dry on my divorce decree."

"If I'd mentioned Nick, you mean."

Jessie's pulse had lurched then, and it lurched again now. Ridiculous, she thought. Too much time had passed for Nick to pose a threat to her peace of mind, for any hurt to remain. She wasn't an adoring child, or a trusting adolescent, but a grown woman. She wrote fiction—when she could—but she didn't live the fantasy, not any longer. She even smiled faintly, admitting only to some curiosity. Maybe in twelve years he had lost his hair, his muscle tone, his charm . . .

Though she wasn't that curious. Nick might be in Carran for whatever reason, but he wouldn't stay, and while he was here, she'd simply make sure she didn't see him.

"Dad?" The front door slammed, startling Jessie from her determined reverie as a male voice called out, "Whose BMW's in the drive?" Then her nephew poked his head around the dining room doorway, his brown hair windblown, his lithe frame looking as if it were still in motion. "Jessie! When'd you get here? I didn't know you were coming."

"No one did. A couple of hours ago," she said and held out her arms. Laughing, she had to look up into his blue eyes. They were the exact shade of Ben's, but on her last visit she'd met them on a level. "My goodness, you've grown."

"Aw, you always say that." He'd barely hugged her before he stepped back, red-faced. "Hey, I was sorry to hear about you and Uncle Peter, splitting up. Raw deal."

Jessie agreed but didn't get to answer.

"Greg, is that you?" Ben yelled from the kitchen. "It's after seven. Where have you been?"

"Tell you later." As if he'd been shot from a cannon, Greg bounded for the stairs. "Gotta wash up for supper. I'm starved."

By the time Ben stopped dead, halfway through the kitchen's swinging door, Greg was splashing water in the upstairs bathroom. "He certainly has energy to spare," Jessie said, delighted.

But Ben's tone was sour. "Why shouldn't he? He doesn't have a job to drain it off." He handed a surprised Jessie a fistful of silverware. "Here . . . I forgot. Set another place for dinner."

"Company?" Jessie traced a finger over the fluted handle of a fork, her tone softening. "This is Gran's too, isn't it? Like the china?"

"Her wedding china. She gave it to me, remember, and the silver, when Beth and I got married."

The swift pang of memory made Jessie's eyes fill. Her grandmother had loved to entertain. She'd loved people, and she'd loved good food; the combination had always seemed irresistible, and she'd set an elaborate table, especially for Thanksgiving dinner. Was her house, so full of happy memories, still there?

Jessie wished she hadn't resisted the urge to stop at the abandoned farm on her way into Carran. But she'd known that, early in spring, the old farm lane would be thick with mud and treacherous ruts, so she'd driven on, telling herself that her life had enough ruts just now: her shattered marriage and self-esteem, a stubborn writer's block. As soon as she could leave Arizona, she'd needed to see Carran and her only nephew, and Ben.

He smiled a little. "On holidays Gran's whole house would smell like cinnamon. She had a heavy hand with it."

"Um, the spices." Jessie's stomach growled. "Cloves and sage and ginger. Her sweet potato casserole, with brown sugar and marshmallows crusted on top. Mom's chestnut stuffing. Gran's pumpkin pies."

"And Dad, complaining that the house was stuffy—then throwing all the doors wide to let the air in." He paused, his gaze meeting hers. "The cold air, and Nick."

Jessie bit her lip. She'd have been watching for him then, for hours. "As if Nick's mother didn't cook like Julia Child on holidays herself."

With brisk motions, she set the fourth service beside a plate. Years ago the ornate silver pattern had moved with Ben, from the farm where he and Jessie had been raised, the six miles into Carran. But here or there the memories had stayed the same, and Jessie treasured them. Most of them, anyway. "It's good to be home, Ben," she finally said.

"It's good to have you." He gave her a long, steady look. "Jessie, I . . ."

"What?"

"Uh . . . nothing."

Then he scooted back into the kitchen as if to escape some impending disaster. Or his own feelings? Ben had always been closemouthed, but since his wife's death a year ago, he had apparently become even more taciturn. Jessie's conversation with him since her arrival had been sparse.

Frowning with concern, she used the last napkin to polish a water spot from a glass. A fourth place at a table set with company china, good silver, etched crystal? Ben hadn't said who their guest would be. Greg's girlfriend? Ben had mentioned one, not in glowing terms, but Jessie didn't have time to wonder at her growing sense of unease.

The doorbell rang. Jessie fumbled the red taper she'd been trying to jam into the glass candle holder. The bell chimed again. "Ben?"

"Get that, will you? I'm up to my elbows in meat loaf and chili sauce."

Her frown deepened. Ben wasn't a panicky cook, not like Jessie, for whom the microwave must have been invented. She started toward the front door, dread following her as, a few hours ago, her brother's warning had chased her the last miles into Carran.

In the next instant, with the simple act of pulling on a doorknob, all the oxygen seemed to get sucked from her lungs. Jessie tried to catch her breath but couldn't. She should have known. His dark hair shining under the porch light, hands shoved deep into his pockets, he stood whistling softly to himself, looking right at home, looking as if he'd never left Carran, or the farm . . . or her. He'd even rung the bell twice.

"Nick," she mouthed but no sound came out.

His whistled rendition of "Dixie" stopped in midphrase as he took a step backward. "My God," he said. "How did Ben arrange this?"

"I didn't. Jessie did it for me. Hi, Nick." Coming to the door, Ben gripped her shoulders to hold her in place. "Her coming was a surprise. She arrived this afternoon. I'm afraid I didn't tell her you'd be here for dinner."

"Didn't trust her with your loaded shotgun in the house?" Grinning, Nick let his gaze travel over her, warming every inch from head to toe. Jessie looked away.

"Come on in," Ben said. "You look out on your feet."

Nick stepped inside, and Jessie's accusing gaze met Ben's.

"Nick's father had a stroke two days ago," he explained gently. "Nick's been at the hospital day and night."

"Oh, Ben." Shock raced through her. Shock, and sorrow. The Granbys had been like family to her once, as dear as her brother and Gran. "Why didn't you tell me?"

"I wanted to. I tried," Ben said, "but . . . I thought you wouldn't listen."

Jessie felt ashamed of herself. Poor Tom, she thought, and before she could stop herself, poor Nick. "I'm sorry. Is there anything we can do?"

Nick shook his head. "It's a matter of time. The doctors don't know yet how he'll come out of this. His right side's paralyzed. His memory's touch and go. He can barely talk."

Ben cleared his throat. "When Nick called this morning—before I knew you were coming, Jessie—he said there wasn't much food in Tom's house, and I knew he wouldn't want to shop after all day at the hospital. I thought he could use some home cooking tonight." Ben smiled. "Even mine."

In Jessie's opinion he could have bought a frozen

dinner and nuked it, but she didn't say so. "It'll be a change from some five-star restaurant in Charleston."

"A welcome change," Nick said; then Ben drew her aside.

"If you were five years old, I'd spank you. I still might. No matter what you think, Nick's a good guy. Take it easy, he's feeling pretty bad—guilty—about Tom."

Ben was right, of course, but Jessie resented that, too. If Nick felt so guilty, why hadn't he stayed to run the farm with Tom? The question was rhetorical; she already knew why he'd gone to South Carolina. She had learned that the hard way one night in Gran's apple orchard twelve years ago.

"I'm leaving you two to sort things out," Ben said. "No violence." He clapped Nick on the back. "Come out to the kitchen when you've signed the truce. I've got a cold Molson ale with your name on it."

"Thanks, Ben."

Nick's quiet tone made Jessie look up, and for the first time since she'd opened the door, she really saw him. He'd stopped smiling. The fatigue Ben had noted made his broad shoulders slump, pulled the corners of his mouth tight, deepened the shadows in his eyes. She'd been wrong. Nick had changed, but not as she'd hoped.

He seemed taller than she remembered, more solid than in his high school football days, but the thick, dark hair was the same, she told herself. The red chamois shirt, navy down vest, and faded jeans looked familiar, so familiar that Jessie could feel her fingers tucked into his back pocket as they strolled together across a sunset pasture. She could smell sweet fresh-cut hay and hear cows lowing near Tom Granby's barn.

But his somber brown-eyed gaze bothered her. It seemed more than fatigue, more than worry over Tom's illness, and Jessie couldn't seem to look away. Nick couldn't either.

"Come here," he said at last, opening his arms, obviously expecting her to walk into them. When she hesitated, a slow smile spread across his mouth, the smile she'd once loved. "Leave the guns at the door and say, 'Welcome home, Nick.' "

Her pulse pounded but she didn't move. "Welcome home."

Nick shook his head. Then he took a step, toward her, and so did Jessie, a step aside, misjudging the distance between them. Nick's body brushed hers, so close that she could hear the discreet tick of his watch.

"Not so fast," he said, and when he moved again, she stopped counting seconds, heartbeats. "Not so easy."

Grasping her upper arms, his touch gentle, he tilted his head. His smile fading, his eyes holding hers until they drifted shut, Nick bent to her mouth, meeting it lightly, softly, in a grazing surprise of a kiss, his mouth just barely on hers; but the kiss sent blood coursing through her veins and Jessie went limp.

"That's better," he whispered. "Welcome home yourself, love. You sure are a sight for tired eyes."

Then, as quickly as he'd kissed her, he pulled back, touched her cheek, and left her standing near the door. Stunned, speechless, Jessie watched him walk through the dining room to the kitchen doorway, where he said something to Ben, their rich male laughter a buzz of memory from her girlhood. Jessie stared blindly down at the fourth table setting.

Nick Granby's back in town.

♦ ♦ ♦

Despite the sad circumstance of Nick's return, nobody had been happier than Benjamin Pearce to see his closest friend. He and Nick had been friends from the day nine-year-old Ben and his parents moved in with his grandmother, six months before Jessie was born.

Theirs hadn't been an auspicious meeting, Ben remembered, nor the move one he'd had much enthusiasm for. He hadn't unpacked his baseball cards before he got the urge to explore his new, unwanted surroundings, which seemed preferable to feeding his grandmother's nasty-tempered Rhode Island Reds at the henhouse. Instead, he climbed the hill behind her barn, skirted the family cemetery at its crest—in case there might be ghosts—then plunged down the slope to the barbed wire fence that defined the Pearce farm boundary. Gazing at the herd of Guernsey cattle in the adjoining pasture, and daydreaming about the friends he'd left behind, Ben leaned on a fence post.

"That's our line," someone said, startling him. He watched a boy roughly his own age emerge from the cow herd and pick his way across the meadow. "I stretched wire last week, I won't do it again." He scowled at Ben. "Are you Caroline's grandson?"

Ben jumped to attention. "Yes." The other boy stood half a head taller; his hands looked hard, and tough, like the rest of him. "I'm sorry about the fence."

"You knock it over, and you'll plant it yourself next time. I don't need any more chores. 'Be a help or you're a hindrance,' my pop says."

"I didn't know."

"You'll learn." Then he said bluntly, "Your mom's pregnant, isn't she?" and Ben flushed. His mother's growing stomach embarrassed him, though the baby wasn't due until May. Suddenly the other boy grinned. "I heard it from Caroline. She wants a girl. But if your dad's going to try farming, you'd better hope your mom has another boy. Take it from me, I used to pray for a baby brother. But my mom can't have more, so I guess I'm stuck, Pearce. What's your first name?"

"Ben."

The boy stuck out a hand. "If you can climb this fence without tearing those brand-new overalls, I'll show you my pop's cows up close." He helped Ben clamber over the wire. "Watch where you walk. There's cow flops. We got a horse, too," he continued, "and I got a dog of my own. When she has pups, maybe I'll give you one. My name's Nick. Nick Granby."

Soon joined by their common loathing of farm chores, Ben and Nick became inseparable. Ben's quiet nature soothed Nick's more rebellious streak. And as they grew, Nick's stubbornness lent Ben some backbone, much needed according to Caroline Pearce, who doted on Nick. If he hadn't liked Nick too much to feel jealous, Ben would have hated him on sight.

There'd come a time when he did hate Nick, he admitted, for hurting Jessie, and apparently there'd been no truce tonight. Ben couldn't blame her now for holding a grudge. Always so open and loving, Jessie'd had to learn to guard her heart, and Ben knew that her divorce hadn't helped. But she wouldn't even look at Nick.

Glancing across the dinner table, Ben sighed. He

could only hope they reached dessert before Jessie fired one of Gran's crystal glasses at Nick's head.

If only Beth were here . . .

He sighed again. He wasn't the greatest conversationalist, and since they'd sat down to eat, nobody else had said a word. Taking the meat platter from Nick, Ben brought up the dark circles under Nick's eyes. "You're starting to look like a raccoon," he said. "Getting any sleep at all?"

"Not since Pop got sick." Nick buttered his peas. "And it's not just worry over him. His house is a mess, the barn looked like a pigsty when I got there, and his herd's too big. Every night when I drive back to the farm, they're waiting for me, standing hipslung in the corner of the fence by the top gate. Over a hundred of 'em, like a damn punishment." He reached for the bowl of potatoes. "Today I spent eight hours talking to doctors and trying to talk to Pop—as usual, he wouldn't listen—then raced back to milk. Poor damn cows, their udders were on the ground by the time I got there."

Ben grinned. "Sore udders once you finished with them."

"I never did have the touch," Nick agreed, "even just hooking 'em up to a machine."

"That's because you never practiced," Jessie said, addressing her plate. "You always made Ben do your milking, or me."

Nick tried to catch Jessie's gaze. "Yeah, whenever I could con you into it. How about six A.M. tomorrow?"

"A penny doesn't buy what it used to." She looked at her lap. "Or a killer smile. I'm not that gullible anymore."

Nick studied his meat loaf. "And maybe I'm not as selfish as I used to be," he said. "Right now all I am is tired, overworked, and strung out."

Ben wanted to squirm. Long ago, he and Gran had hoped that, despite the ten-year difference between them, Nick and Jessie would someday share their lives. Seeing them now, across the table from each other yet so far apart, made his throat ache. Dammit, if Beth were here, he wouldn't squander a minute. Shoving his milk aside, he reached for the wine. He'd wanted this dinner to be special.

"What will you do with the farm now?" Greg asked, breaking the silence.

"Wait, I guess," Nick said, "to see what happens with Pop."

Ben welcomed the change of topic. "I'm selling real estate on weekends," he said. "If you decide to list his place, let me know. I need the commission."

Greg's fork clattered onto his plate. "Mr. Granby won't sell. When he can talk, I bet the first words out of his mouth will be, 'Who's puttin' in my spring crop?' "

"Well, it won't be him," Nick murmured.

"It won't be you either," Ben said to Greg, who was getting up his foolish hopes again. He'd nip those in the bud. "When would you find the time? Your whole life's off track." He glanced at Nick. "My kid drops out of college after one semester, spends half the day sleeping when he should be looking for—"

"I am looking for a job."

"Doing what?" Ben asked.

Greg shrugged. "There isn't much around. Busing tables, pumping gas—but even the guy at the Mobil station said 'Come back next week.' I'm trying," he said, "but you know what I really want."

"A job on some farm?" Ben speared another slice of meat loaf. "How many times do I have to tell you? The small farmers are in the worst shape of anyone in this economy, and that's saying a lot. You're spinning dreams, Greg."

"At least I have them."

Nick cleared his throat. "Maybe you could come stay with me in Charleston. There's enough hurricane cleanup from last fall to go around. I'd be glad to add you to my crew at Seaview."

The luxury coastal resort, designed and built by Nick's firm, had sustained heavy damage, Ben knew, which reminded him that Nick not only had his father to worry about; he had his own business problems, too. The last thing he needed was a surly nineteen-year-old to look out for.

"Greg won't leave town," Ben said. "His afternoons are spoken for. You should see the piece of jailbait he's dating. Any job he gets will take second place to that twitching little miniskirt in the tight sweater." He saw Jessie's shocked expression and dared her with a look to say something. "Fifteen years old," he went on, "with a body like that—"

Jessie set her glass down. "Ben, for heaven's sake."

"Look, Dad—"

"Jailbait," Ben repeated. "The two of you alone in her house while her mother works. I don't know what in hell's happened to families in this country." He scowled at his whipped potatoes. "God knows, you'd be better off pumping gas sixteen hours a day—I know it's too damn much to hope you'll go back to school—than risking whatever future you have left, and on what?"

"Heather's a nice girl."

Ben's eyebrows lifted. "I see more messed-up kids in my office every day than I care to admit. You think she hasn't been among them? Why Amy Stone can't stay home instead of playing professional woman at the historical society, or fix her schedule for her daughter's sake—"

"Amy Stone?" Jessie echoed. "Wasn't she in your class, Ben?"

He only grunted. She wasn't going to divert him now.

"Head cheerleader," Nick said and smiled faintly. "She had quite a figure herself—which never escaped your notice, Ben."

"Heather's mom was home today," Greg said, "but we were at the library. That's why I was late. Heather doesn't need a pass from your office to go to the public library, does she?" He paused. "I sure don't. I quit being the high school principal's kid at graduation."

"You could use a refresher course."

A heavy silence followed. Greg glared at the wall behind Ben's head. Jessie picked at her salad. "I think your father's just jealous," she said.

Nick chimed in. "I'll bet your girlfriend's terrific. Amy was an A student, in the top third of our class. Everybody liked her."

"Everyone likes Heather, too," Greg said.

Ben pushed his plate away. Even though, together, they'd tried to defuse the situation, Jessie still wouldn't look at Nick. Ben glared at his son. They quarreled more than they agreed these days. "Why can't you just take my advice? Stop worrying about that girl, and start worrying about your own life?"

Greg jumped to his feet. "You're just jealous of me

with Heather 'cause you haven't been laid in a year!"

"Well, I wish I could say the same for you, god-dammit—"

"Why can't you say what you really mean? What you feel, for a change? Why can't you admit, you miss Mom?" His eyes wounded, Greg clicked his glass on top of his plate and headed for the kitchen.

"Jesus, Ben," Nick said.

Ben's heart was racing. "Sorry."

"You used to have a sense of humor, some perspective with young people," Jessie said.

"Yeah, when I was a teenager myself." He felt sick. "I'm still a regular Bill Cosby at school. But my own kid"—Ben glanced toward the kitchen, where he could hear food being scraped into the garbage—"my own kid makes me crazy."

Jessie touched his hand to soften her words. "Don't you remember? 'Suspension of hostilities during mealtimes.' " It had been their grandmother's firm reminder whenever Jessie and Ben squabbled at the table.

Nick remembered, too. "Looks like this place could use a civilizing influence, Caroline Pearce style." His gaze snared Jessie's at last, but Ben looked away. "Aren't you glad your baby sister came home? I know I am."

Then Nick got up and carried his plate into the kitchen, leaving Ben with his guilt and Jessie, who looked equally pale and shaken. There had been no smashed crockery after all, he thought, no broken crystal.

Why don't you just admit, you miss Mom?

Ben pressed both hands to his eyes. No love, he added to himself.

◆ ◆ ◆

An hour after dinner, in the dark, Jessie stood shivering on the back porch. She'd left Greg inside with Ben, and more angry words, but she soon realized there would be no escape. Nick had come after her.

"The sounds of battle," he said. Harsh male voices flooded outside with the spill of light from the house before he shut the door, trapping Jessie outside with him. Feeling embattled herself, she didn't respond. She glanced down at her ringless hands and felt Nick looking at them, too.

"I wanted to say that I'm sorry about your divorce." He shifted his weight. "I didn't know how to bring it up before. At dinner your brother . . ."

"I'm sorry about Tom," she said when he didn't continue.

"More battles," Nick murmured, then held out his down vest. "Here, take this. You'll catch a chill."

"If I take it, you'll catch one instead." She wanted him to leave her alone.

"Put it on." He slipped the vest around her shoulders and, in only his shirtsleeves, leaned against the porch railing, facing her. Nick folded his arms, drawing the shirt taut against his shoulders and biceps, which Jessie tried not to notice.

He regarded her solemnly. "You'd freeze to death before you willingly took anything from me, wouldn't you? Is that why you're out here? To keep away from me?"

"Actually, I was wondering whether I made the right decision, leaving Arizona." But he'd guessed the other reason, all right. "In Scottsdale the mercury was hovering in the nineties." She glanced at the splash of stars overhead. "Here, even the sky looks cold."

Jessie looked down in time to see Nick's features tighten. He knew she didn't mean the weather. "Dinner wasn't very pleasant, was it? Your brother's a hard case sometimes."

"He's worse since Beth died. Maybe I shouldn't intrude on his privacy now." And you shouldn't intrude on mine, she thought.

"Ben reminds me of Pop and the years at the farm when all I wanted was to get out."

"Well, you did," she said. "Are you happy in Charleston?"

Nick was frowning, as if he knew he'd said the wrong thing too late to take it back. "Away from Carran, you mean? Sure, it's a great city. Gracious, beautiful, well-mannered."

"Like a fine southern lady," Jessie said, ignoring the edge in his tone.

"It has a different tempo, a gentler one. And yet, since last September's hurricane, there's been a new air of excitement." He shrugged. "But I didn't come out here to discuss Charleston, I—"

"How did your property survive the storm?" Inching away from him, as she'd been doing since he'd stepped onto the porch, Jessie retreated to its far end, twining one arm around a sturdy post to anchor herself.

"The biggest tree in my garden went through my roof," he said, "but the attic's been fixed. The mud in my oriental carpet has been lifted out, so I'd say things are back to normal.

"Other people weren't so lucky," Nick continued. "We had more than thirty-six thousand homes de-

stroyed or severely damaged. My construction foreman's new house got knocked clear off its foundation,
and that wasn't unique by any means."

Jessie's tone was dry. "All those homes lost must
mean business is booming." Business, and Nick's
profits.

"More or less. But let's not get into a gloomy re-
hash of my liabilities versus assets." His dark eyes
looked troubled. "Granby Design's been the top firm
in Charleston for three years running. I own a house
the local bluebloods would kill for. But the banks still
have a problem with Yankee carpetbaggers, and as far
as they're concerned, I'm still from up north." He
gave the word a soft southern drawl that made Jessie
want to smile in spite of herself.

"Don't they know the Civil War has ended?"

"No more than anywhere else south of Philadel-
phia." His frown faded. "Of course you have to understand. Down there, belonging's a matter of birth.
The story's told of a man whose family had moved to
Charleston when he was three days old. He lived
there all his life. Married well. Made money. Pillar of
the community et cetera. Finally, when he was well
into his nineties, he died and was buried—with all
due respect and ceremony—in the cemetery still re-
served for 'outsiders.' "

Jessie gave in to the grin.

"Seriously," Nick went on. "It's across the street
from where they bury the 'natives,' those who were
actually born in Charleston."

"What if you married a local aristocrat?"

His answering grin flashed white in the darkness.
"We'd end up on opposite sides of the street in eternal
rest."

Jessie relaxed her grip on the porch post. He'd always told a good story, not that Nick had won her over now, she thought—and in that instant saw grim determination overtake his grin.

"Enough stories," he said, taking a step toward her. "I didn't come out here to talk about South Carolina, or your ex-husband or Pop. I want to talk—"

"About what?" She couldn't retreat any farther but refused to shrink into the porch corner like a seventeen-year-old virgin.

"About everything else," he said, then stopped walking as if he sensed her withdrawal. "Your books, for one. I've read them both. They're great. You don't know how many times I almost wrote to say how proud I was."

Jessie flinched. Above all, she didn't want to talk about her work. "But you didn't write," she said.

"You hadn't exactly accepted my apology for the last time I saw you. You wouldn't take my calls or answer my letters."

"There was nothing more to say."

"Then you married Peter, and were living another life, far away. It didn't seem right to dredge things up."

"Then let's not dredge them up now."

She hadn't seen him move again. He stood only a foot away, his nearness reminding her of a warmer spring night, smelling of apple blossoms, the chorus of spring peepers singing near Gran's pond, the rustle of fabric, the taste of his mouth . . . so long ago.

"Twelve years," she said.

"A long time," Nick agreed. "Are you going to hold that night against me for another twelve years? Hell, I made a mistake." He gestured toward the house and the rumble of voices inside. "Who doesn't? Your own brother with Greg tonight—"

"You're right." She'd been a mistake. "We all make mistakes."

"Well, I've paid for mine," he said. "Dammit, I have, *Jess*."

And with that one word, tears welled in her eyes, and she lost the battle. No one had ever called her Jess, except Nick.

"Oh, Nicholas," she whispered past the tightness in her throat. It had been her grandmother's endearment, usually in exasperation. Pushing away from the porch corner, Jessie started for the kitchen door with Nick at her heels. Such an escape was a childish gesture, she knew, and cowardly, and she shouldn't run; but her footsteps hurried faster.

Since her divorce, she'd felt shattered. She'd come to Ben's to rest, to put her life together, to work if she could; after publishing two successful novels, and despite a contract deadline in six months, she couldn't seem to write a third. Not a chapter, not even a line worth putting on paper since she'd left Peter.

How did life get so convoluted? How, Jessie wondered, when she'd wanted such simple things, ordinary things: a good marriage, children, her career going well. Now she slammed into her brother's kitchen, her heart thumping in panic, with Nick right behind her.

"Jess, don't hate me."

Not so simple at that, she realized. She had wanted it all. Perhaps the real problem was that she'd stopped believing in happy endings, and, seeing Nick again, had just been reminded of that.

She hadn't wanted to see him. Now that she had,

she'd have to avoid him. When he called her name again, Jessie kept moving, through Ben's kitchen, his dining and living rooms, and upstairs to bed. She knew she wouldn't sleep, but she also feared the novelist had been right when he said you can't go home again.

Or had she simply come to the wrong place?

2

"*You want to* move—*where?*" Across the breakfast table Ben poured another cup of coffee, which he drank black, while Jessie watched.

"To Gran's," she repeated, fighting a smile, and he groaned.

"You can't be serious. That old wreck of a farmhouse has been shut up for years. It's run-down, dilapidated. God knows whether the wiring's even safe."

But she could already feel excitement humming through her veins. "I'll have it inspected."

"The house is haunted," Greg announced around a mouthful of cereal and milk. "Everybody says so."

"The kids say so. The boys, mostly." Ben glanced at her. "The notion adds an extra spark of danger when they take the girls parking there at night. Keeps 'em cuddled up close."

Now Jessie groaned. "You can't be serious."

"Perfectly. Caroline's place is a great attraction for the macho element, football players and their girls."

Jessie briefly envisioned Ben, and then Nick, as high school heroes themselves, before she pushed the thought away. "Cheerleaders," she scoffed, remembering that had included Amy Stone once; that Ben had briefly dated her. What had happened between them that he now criticized her daughter—and Amy—so freely? "You'd know all about that. Well, it shouldn't take long to discourage them once I'm living on the property again."

"You can't go back, Jessie."

Unknowingly, Ben had repeated her own conviction of two weeks past, the night Nick had come for dinner, the same night she'd realized she didn't belong inside Carran's town limits.

"I'm going to try," she said.

"It won't work. And all I'll do here is worry about you, alone out there, at the mercy of vandals—or worse." He placed a hand on hers. "Listen, Greg and I will be on our best behavior, how's that? I know we've been driving you nuts. We'll keep our arguments to a dull roar just for you."

"That's my point. You shouldn't have to accommodate me. Besides," Jessie added, mentally crossing her fingers that he wouldn't hear the truth in her tone, "I need to get the book going. That requires space and silence. I don't want to keep you up nights while I prowl the house struggling with my plot."

"You'll be keeping me up nights if you're out at the farm."

She smiled. "I'll call you, big brother. Every hour on the hour. I promise."

"There's no phone there," he said.

Jessie fought not to groan again. "I'll have one

installed." That, at least, she was serious about; not that she worried for her safety, and certainly not about ghosts. Knowing that she could communicate at a second's notice with town, and her family, would be a convenience, that was all.

But as she'd guessed he would, Ben played his trump card. "Put in a telephone? You'd be wasting money. I didn't want to remind you, but as half owner of Gran's property too, I think we should sell."

"Sell? We grew up there." Alarmed by his flat tone, as if the decision was already made, she poured more coffee to brace herself. "That farm is where our roots are. Our parents and Gran are buried on the hill. How can you even think of selling?"

"You know I need the money. It may sound crass, but Beth and I had debts, and without her job . . ." He shrugged. "Since she died, it hasn't been easy making ends meet. We have parent loans for Greg's college." Ignoring his son's frown, he held her gaze. "Jessie, you haven't seen the farm in years. That old place is falling down, with weeds everywhere—"

"It was home, Ben. The only one I've ever really had." She paused, realizing how true that was; she'd never felt at home in the house she'd shared with Peter. Like so many other things in their marriage, it had been his choice, his style, not Jessie's, like the farm. "I think I have to go there," she said, "to see where I came from, before I can decide what should come next in my life, my work."

"Jessie, don't give me that creative-artist-head-in-the-clouds routine. This is real life."

Greg interrupted. "I don't know why Dad's so worried. I don't want you to move out either, Jessie, but if you do, at least I could come to see you."

' "See the farm, you mean," Ben said, but Greg hadn't finished.

"And you'd be safe there, close to Nick—right next door at Mr. Granby's."

Jessie felt the color drain from her face. She knew Ben couldn't miss it. Leaning back in his chair, he asked coolly, "Reconsider?"

"I'll think about it."

Jessie was still thinking when she reached the hospital that afternoon to visit Nick's father. In fact, she was ruminating like one of Tom Granby's cows chewing its cud. One minute she knew how right it would surely feel to return to her grandmother's house; the next instant she felt doubtful again. Nick wouldn't spend much time at the farm, she assured herself. She'd hardly see him, and she needn't worry about running into him at the hospital; since his father's condition had stabilized, Nick had spent most of the past week in Charleston, according to Ben. Yet on Friday it was possible that he—

"Well, there you are, girl. At last."

Tom's voice had stopped her cold. His bright gaze took in her cream-colored sweater dress and gold chains, her dark tweed coat enlivened by a green wool scarf. Giving him a quick smile, she felt glad she'd dressed to please him.

"Good afternoon." She bent to kiss his cheek. "You look chipper today."

"I'd be fine if my doctor'd let me have my favorite pipe."

Nick's father sat propped up in bed, where he'd been perusing the newspaper, his bifocals riding the bridge of his nose. Unlike Nick, who'd had help from his mother's genes, Tom had just missed being a handsome man; yet his dark hair turned to salt-and-pepper had given him a distinguished air in his later years, and in his strong, now weathered features she could still see something of his son's. But the sparkling blue eyes were Tom's alone.

As he dropped the paper onto the blanket, giving her a smile, vaguely lopsided, she had to remind herself that he was ill. The stroke's effects were there, but his paralysis had faded, and each time she saw him, Jessie noted improvement. Today his speech was only slightly slurred.

"What's it like outside? Warm?" Tom glanced toward the window. "That sun looks like it's startin' to bake things a bit."

"The temperature's above fifty. Spring's definitely here."

The smile tilted some more. Nothing could have been better news to a farmer. "Busy time of year," he said. "I ought to be gettin' ready to plant."

"Forget the crops," a familiar deep voice drawled from the doorway. "And the pipe. You're a sick man."

Startled, Jessie turned. Giving her only a curt nod, Nick entered the room, wearing a three-piece gray pinstripe suit that looked custom-made. More used to seeing him in jeans, she found his air of professionalism, of success, more surprising than his entrance. He said, "I've just seen the doctor. He wants you to spend a couple of weeks more—"

"In this place?" Tom said. "By God, I won't!"

"Not here. At a rehabilitation center outside Litchfield." Nick held up a hand when Tom would have spoken. "They'll move you tomorrow by ambulance."

"I want to go home."

"Pop, the doctor's in charge of your case, not me. We discussed the alternatives, and the rehab center makes the most sense. You don't need to stay here. That's good news, isn't it?" His smile was weak, cajoling. "But you can't go back to the farm either. You'd be alone too much."

"I could help," Jessie put in before she knew she was going to say anything. "I'll be at Gran's." Looking into Tom's eyes, which had filled with tears, made her decision easy. "I can look in on him, Nick. Take meals over."

"Great," he muttered, "but he'd still be there by himself most of the time, and I can't be here. I'm up to my eyeballs in construction problems almost a thousand miles away—"

"Then go back to them!" Furious that he'd put his work—and Charleston—before his father's welfare, which shouldn't have surprised her, Jessie turned away. "I'm sure that, in the aftermath of Hugo, there's money to be made."

Nick spun her around, his voice deadly quiet. "He can't even walk. What would you do when you tried to get him to the bathroom and he fell?" Nick ran a hand through his hair. "Jess, he must outweigh you by a good fifty p—"

"Don't talk about me like I wasn't here!" Tom wrestled his sheets to sit straighter in bed, his gaze bright and blinking.

"I'm sorry," Jessie said instantly.

"Hell, I'm sorry too," Nick said, looking shamefaced.

Then a nurse appeared in the doorway, and he colored even more. "Nick Granby? There's a call for you. You can take it in the lounge."

"Thank you." Before he left the room, he threw Jessie a look that clearly said *I'll talk to you later*.

She took a moment to compose herself before going to sit beside Tom, whose work-roughened hand seized hers. "You're a good girl, Jessie. So you're going to Caroline's, hmm?"

She nodded, glad that her decision pleased someone.

"They put her away too, didn't they?" Tom said. "Remember Ben packing Caroline off to that nursing home near Danbury?"

"He—we didn't have much choice," Jessie said sadly, taking her share of the responsibility. "That summer she began living in the past too much, ignoring the present. I couldn't help her." Jessie had left for college that fall, three months, she remembered, after the night with Nick in her grandmother's apple orchard. Three weeks after her grandmother had moved, Gran had been dead. Now Jessie said defensively, "Her physical health was frail and getting worse. She couldn't have stayed alone."

"All of us live in the past, Jessie. The past is a part of us, like the land." Tom paused. "Even Nick would have agreed, once. When he was a boy, too young to be much good around the place, he seemed to love the farm."

"Until he learned to milk cows," she said, but Jessie was surprised. She had only known Nick when he wanted to leave.

"Sure, he grumbled like any other kid about doing chores." Tom frowned. "Maybe I shouldn't have let him pick up a hammer one day and finish fixing the henhouse. I think that's when he started to get unhappy with us, to dream big dreams about those buildings he puts up everywhere."

The bitterness in Tom's voice surprised her even more. Nick's rift with his father was worse than she'd imagined. "He's been milking your cows for the past two weeks," she pointed out.

"That's just protecting an investment." Tom's words slurred again. "That farm's my life, Jessie. I been workin' that land for fifty years. Every springtime, diggin' bare hands into those three hundred acres of dirt, greasin' up the tractor, draggin' that four-bottom plow . . ."

"I know," she said, squeezing his hand.

"These last few years I've seen too many of my neighbors go broke. I've got loans, same as they did. What's going to happen to me if I can't plant seed this spring?" His tone hardened. "What's goin' to happen to the only thing I have, when I die?"

Her eyes fixed on his. "Don't worry, Tom. You'll live to be a hundred. You'll finish getting well, and . . ." She trailed off. What, then? In a few weeks, it would be too late for spring planting.

"Then you'll look after me for a spell?" His look was sly.

"As long as you need me," Jessie said.

"Won't make you popular, understand."

She smiled. "I don't suppose it will."

"That's my Jessie." Tom's grip relaxed. "But I shouldn't leave a square foot of that ground to Nick, just let the bank have it. I know what Nick'll do with the place as soon as he's thrown the first spadeful of dirt on my coffin. He'll sell."

Jessie suspected Tom spoke the truth, but she'd heard the hurt in his voice; hoping for the right words, she took a calming breath. She'd been pretty rough on Nick herself two weeks ago at Ben's. "Maybe if you tried to understand *his* side," she began.

"Why should I? Years ago, he left me flat."

"He must have had his reasons." Did she still hope for one she could believe, too?

"One reason. He wanted off the land." He hesitated. "And I wanted him to stay where he belongs."

"Well, Pop," Nick said from the doorway, "you don't get everything you want in this world. I wish you could."

Tom set his jaw. "Just get me out of here. Nobody else is goin' to do the work. As I see it, it has to be me."

"You stubborn old fool." Nick took a step. "Why can't you get it through your head that you aren't capable of working that farm?"

As she watched their exchange, Jessie felt her cheeks grow hotter. How long had Nick been standing in the doorway, listening, before he spoke? Not that her weak defense of him had done much good; not that he deserved it after all.

"Nick," she said.

"You keep out of this." Advancing to the bed, he trapped Tom between his braced arms. "Now listen up, and listen good. I've made the reservation at the center. I've paid for the two—"

"I don't want your money, big shot!"

"—two weeks, then you can come home. But don't think for one minute that you're going out in those fields as soon as I turn my back, or so help me—"

Tom's face turned purple. "Don't you tell me what

to do with what's left of my life, or with that piece of land!"

"Don't you understand? I don't want to come home some night and find you facedown outside in a ditch. I don't want that antiquated piece of junk you call a tractor on top of you. And I sure as hell don't want . . ." He broke off, straightening. "Oh, damn, why do I bother?" He turned to Jessie in mute appeal.

"You're upsetting him again," she said, and Nick's shoulders sagged.

"Right." Turning his back, for long moments he stared at the floor, then, "Cram it," he said. "Stuff it."

"Nick—"

He stalked past her, into the hall.

"Nick!"

Jessie tore after him. Just outside the room he stopped, and she ran straight into him, her soft breasts barely bumping against his harder chest before Nick set her away.

"I've got to make a call," he said hoarsely. "Then I need to tell you something. Wait here for me."

It hadn't been a question. Fuming, Jessie leaned against the wall in the hallway, pressing her palms to the cool tile, knowing it was just as well he'd given the command, and that she'd chosen to obey it. But when Nick came back, she'd tell him a thing or two about unnecessary bluntness, about cruelty.

When he returned five minutes later, Jessie simply stared at him, not moving, making him come to her, not wanting to see how pale he was, how bleak his eyes looked. And because of both, she remained silent.

"I can't go back in there," he told her. "Give him a message, will you?"

"If it won't hurt him."

"Tell him he's getting what he wanted." Nick put his palm against the wall just above her head, but she could hardly hear his words. "I'm staying here, Jess. I'll hire a man to help me. I'll grease up that old International Harvester of his, then buy some seed. Tell him he'll have his goddamn fields planted before he gets home."

Pushing from the wall, Nick strode down the corridor without looking back. Stunned, Jessie couldn't say a word.

In the waiting room at the end of the hall, Nick sprawled on a tan vinyl couch, his hands jammed into his armpits to warm them; to stop their shaking. His heart thudded loud enough to wake the corpses in the hospital's basement morgue. Look at this another way, he ordered himself. Don't lose it. Don't think about Pop.

His gaze fixed on the bowl of picked-over fruit someone had left on the Formica coffee table. A yellow cellophane wrapper and red ribbon lay crumpled beside it. The single banana's brown speckles reminded him of the age spots on the backs of Tom's hands, and the apples . . .

His vision blurred. Dammit, think about Jess.

But his thoughts, his memories, of her were hardly less troubled than those about Tom. His fault, Nick silently admitted. The memories had been happy enough until that night. . . .

She'd been almost grown then, but he'd known her

all her life; he'd known her since Jess was a five-day-old baby, wearing crocheted lace, lying in her grandmother's antique black walnut cradle. Her wizened little face had scrunched up, her tiny hands fisted. Then she'd opened them, grasping his grubby index finger, holding on for dear life; and she'd opened her eyes to Nick's first glimpse of dark, compelling blue. Going on ten years old, he hadn't known it then, but he was a goner.

As proud of her first step, of her first word as Ben had been scornful toward his baby sister, Nick had thought that was all she was to him—the sister he'd never have. With delight, he had watched her grow from baby to toddler to young girl, while he passed through boyhood into adolescence then manhood with Jess's hand firmly tucked in his. Then the spring Jess had turned seventeen, she'd started dating a boy from her senior class, and Nick, already living in Charleston, estranged from his father, had begun making weekend trips home.

That soft June night he'd sat in Caroline's kitchen for hours, waiting for Jess. He'd grown sullen, then ashamed of himself for sulking. She had every right to date whomever she pleased. She was young, beautiful, more so each time he saw her. By the time she got home, cheeks flushed and blue eyes shining, his stomach had tied itself in knots.

"What's wrong, Nick?" Jess had led him out to the orchard, and turned in the cover of the blossoming apple trees. He had never been able to hide anything from her.

"Nothing." He tore a fragrant blossom from a low-hanging branch and tucked it gently in her hair. His hands were shaking.

In the shadow of the trees, her blue eyes were dark with confusion; her bare arms in the button-down-the-front white sundress looked satiny, sleek. If that *boy* had tried to . . .

"Come on," he said, "let's go back to the house. Caroline made peach ice cream while we waited for you and that"—he couldn't help himself—"that gangly, red-faced . . ."

"Why, Nick, you're jealous!" With a soft cry, she twined her arms around his neck, pressing her body the length of his, before he thought to stop her.

"Jess," he said. And then he stopped thinking at all.

He'd never really touched her until then, never even realized he'd been wanting to, that she wanted him to, that the crazed demon inside him for weeks had been jealousy. Possessiveness, he'd thought; protection, no more than Ben would have given her. But some high school boy, pawing her in a car on some lonely road? Maybe even the half-mile stretch of dark road between his father's place and Caroline's?

In the next instant, Nick wrapped her in his arms. With a groan, he dipped his head, eyes closed, his mouth groping for hers in the shadowed orchard like an infant seeking nurture. When their mouths met, she whimpered but he didn't stop.

And soon, kisses weren't enough. He heard her sigh, heard his own breathing change, heard the spring peepers singing from the pond. High-pitched, humming, intense with purpose, it was a mating sound. He'd never know how, but he and Jess landed on the grass, his body, taut and hard, stretched over hers. The buttons of her dress undone, her silky slip pushed aside, her breast . . .

"Don't stop, Nick. Please don't stop."

Dropping his head into the warm hollow of her shoulder, he pressed his lips to her skin. Her name was a helpless moan. "Jess, we can't—"

"I want you," she whispered. "Didn't you know? I've always wanted it to be you."

He smelled apple blossoms, sweet and heady, the scent of Jess's skin . . . he smelled danger.

"Get up," he breathed. "Put yourself together."

At her look of astonishment and hurt, he levered himself off her. He had a thousand reasons, most of them false, but he spewed them out like the physical release he had denied himself. He was too old for her. Jess was too young. She—

"But I love—"

"Nick? Jessie?" he heard Ben call. "Where are you?"

"Damn. You don't love me," Nick said harshly. He couldn't look at her. "At your age, you love the idea of being in love." He flipped the edges of her dress closed, flinging the blue tie belt at her. It landed on Jess's half-bare breast, and Nick tore his gaze away.

"Jessie? Nick?" In the next instant Ben had come crashing through the trees to find Jess, fumbling with her buttons. "What the—" His eyes widened on Nick, whose shirt was hanging from his pants. "I thought you were my friend! Get back to the house, Jessie. And you"—he leveled a finger at Nick—"get the hell out of her life, and mine, too."

Nick had been almost twenty-seven years old then; old enough to know better. It had taken years for Ben to forgive him. Jess never had. And Nick had never been able to smell apple blossoms without remembering that night.

In the hospital waiting lounge, he slowly refocused

his gaze until the fruit on the coffee table became distinct again. One of the apples had a bruise, and smelled cloyingly sweet, decaying . . .

Nick jerked upright, returning to think about Jess.

She hadn't forgiven him. But in Ben's doorway, for an instant, she'd let him kiss her. It hadn't been a wise move on his part, but he could no more have stopped himself than he could have left Ben's house just because she wouldn't talk to him. She'd kissed him back, though.

And let him look his fill. She wore her ash blond hair shorter now, and *beautiful* no longer adequately described her. She was a woman, not a girl; but still, the curves, the planes, the angles, some less, some more, were simply . . . *Jess.* And that dimple in her left cheek? Nick hadn't seen her smile enough to notice, or want to kiss, it. Yet. He rose, rolling the tension from his neck, the clenched fear from his shoulders. Had he been given an unexpected second chance, if not with Tom, then with her?

Somehow he'd change her mind about him, remove the wariness he'd put there from her deep blue eyes. It wouldn't be easy, but he'd give a lot for that. Nick grimaced, certain that, with one telephone call, he already had. Not that he was staying in Carran only for Jess. He'd done it for his father, too.

He didn't relish telling her why.

Jessie found Nick waiting for her by the elevators when she left Tom's room. "Let's get something to eat," he said and, in the cafeteria, chose a quiet corner table, leaving her to save it while he bought coffee and doughnuts. Jessie wasn't hungry.

When he'd settled in the chair opposite, she said, "Your father's grateful," not adding that Tom had cried.

"Grateful but stubborn." Nick stirred his coffee endlessly, and she frowned. Usually he guzzled gallons of the stuff, nonstop, without getting wired as she would.

"He's always been his own man," Jessie pointed out. "Think how frightening it must be for him to lose control. Like anyone else, he wants to be in charge of his life again."

"And mine," Nick murmured.

"Gran always said stubbornness is a Granby trait."

"Me too, huh?" He made crumbs out of the uneaten doughnut on his plate. "Did you ever hear, I was a breech baby? I came ass first into this world. Pop's always said I was born contrary."

She grinned. "He should know."

But Nick didn't smile. "Jess, I didn't mean to rile him before. That's the last thing I wanted, to raise his blood pressure. But I'd just talked to his doctor, then I walked in and heard him, planning to set seed." He looked away, and her pulse tripped.

"What's wrong, Nick?"

"I think . . . I mean, his doctor said . . ." He stared at the blank green wall behind her. "Jess, he's going to die."

His voice had been so low, she couldn't believe she'd heard correctly. "But you said—"

"He shouldn't even think of getting out of that bed he's in, not that anything might make much difference. Maybe not even putting on overalls and mud-caked boots and climbing on that tractor himself, hell, who knows?"

She still couldn't comprehend what he was saying. Tom seemed so much better.

"He's pretty good today, but a few days ago," Nick said, pulverizing the doughnut crumbs, "while I was in Charleston, they did another CAT scan on him." His gaze was bright when it met hers. "He's got an aneurysm that didn't show at first. They won't operate, it's in too delicate a spot. He wouldn't have much function left if they did."

"Nick." Instantly, she covered his hand. "I'm so sorry."

"Me, too. God," he whispered, "me, too."

"He doesn't know," Jessie guessed, and Nick shook his head. "Do you want me to be there when you tell him?"

"I don't want him to know."

Jessie insisted that knowing was Tom's right, that it was his life they were discussing, but arguing with Nick was like arguing with his father.

"You know how he is," Nick said. "He wouldn't believe me anyway, he won't believe the doctors. Why not just let him go to the center for a couple of weeks, get some strength back, maybe start walking a bit? Then come home." He stared at Jessie's hand on his and blinked. "If he stays lucky, he'll have another spring, see his crops sprout one last time." He blinked again and said, "Won't he just love seeing me on that damn tractor? That's all he ever wanted from me. Now, that's all I can give him."

"Nick. Nick, I'll . . ." What could she do?

He must have heard the tears in her voice; Jessie saw that he was perilously close to giving in to them himself.

Nick cleared his throat. "You're really moving to your grandmother's place?"

"Yes," she said, enjoying the sound of it more and more.

"Ben won't like it."

"I've already told him. You're right. He doesn't."

Nick stood, and waited for her. "I'll talk to him."

Jessie tossed their paper plates and cups into a trash bin. "I'm all grown up now," she gently reminded him, "and you're not my surrogate second brother. I do my own talking these days. Thinking, too."

With a faint smile, Nick slung an arm around her shoulders. "Yeah, I'll bet you do, famous lady writer."

"Hardly," she said, but she didn't feel ready to mention her terminal writer's block. She just let him hug her, because she needed that, too.

In silence they rode a packed elevator to the lobby and went out, by themselves, into the parking lot. "I suppose that's your BMW with the Arizona plates," Nick said, pointing.

Jessie smiled, weakly. "My Beamer, my baby."

He walked her to it. "I never took you for the upwardly snooty type, Jess. Amazing. That's a yuppie-mobile if I ever saw one."

"And what are you driving?" She looked around. "A moped?"

Nick waved a hand, and her mouth dropped. It wasn't the Ferrari or Porsche she might have expected with his three-piece suit, but close. Sleek as a bullet, the dark blue Jaguar gleamed showroom-new in the space next to hers. "Nicholas Granby," she whispered, shaking her head, unable to stop the smile that grew. "Conspicuous consumption."

"It's not mine." Holding her door open, he

managed a grin. "But I say if you're going to lease a car, then lease a *car*."

After she'd slipped inside, he bent to her window and touched her, his fingers grazing her cheek, his eyes still somber. "Thanks for making things easier today. For volunteering with Pop. It'll make a difference."

Fighting the warm sensation his touch was causing, Jessie looked away. "I'm happy to help."

"At least you always loved it here. I can't say I'm looking forward to sore muscles or a stiff back or blisters on my palms. But I've just turned millions of dollars' worth of renovation projects over to an assistant I'm not sure is ready for the responsibility, and whether you believe it or not, I don't care. If I could change things for Pop . . ." He straightened but didn't finish.

"I know you would, Nick," she said. "So would I."

"Jess?"

"What?" Her voice was husky.

Their eyes met, his dark and bright. "I'm really glad you're here."

The statement made her heart lurch. The words were simple, honest enough, but Jessie couldn't say the same about Nick. Since that first night, when he'd told Ben much the same thing, she had been avoiding him; it wouldn't be that easy now. When he'd told her he was staying to plant Tom's fields, he could have knocked her over with the proverbial feather. She knew how much he disliked the farm—and how quickly he would leave when he could. What she didn't know was why it mattered to her now whether he left or stayed. "I'm glad I'm here, too," she said at last.

"When are you going to Caroline's?"

"Probably tomorrow. Two weeks may not be long enough to straighten things out before Tom comes home."

"Let me know if you need help."

"I just may do that," she murmured, remembering what Greg had said at breakfast that morning. "God knows what I'll find there."

Not ghosts, Jessie promised herself. Oh, there'd be ghosts all right. She didn't doubt that. But they'd be ghosts from her own past—hers and Nick's—and, she feared, still very much alive. Jessie didn't want to believe in or confront them, either.

3

A hundred and ninety years ago the Pearce farm, toward which Jessie drove the next morning, hadn't even existed. Its three hundred acres, New England rocky-soiled and deep-gullied where they didn't roll with the green, wooded Litchfield hills, had flowed into another parcel of equal size. At the nearby crossroad, a weathered board sign, its hand-painted arrow pointing east, away from Carran, had read simply, Granby. Nick's ancestors had farmed their unforgiving six hundred acres with staunch Yankee grit and determination. They'd done it through spring flood and summer drought. They'd even done it successfully.

Then, at the turn of the century Nick's great-great-great-grandfather had suffered, in the parlance of the times, "reverses." To survive, he'd been forced to sell half his land, three hundred acres east of the second, newer house and barn he'd recently built, to Caroline Pearce's father, with a typically terse comment.

"No sons of your own, you'll be lucky to last the season. Let me know if I can be of help pullin' you through."

It hadn't been long before Caroline Pearce, just three years old and sassy as a farmer's day is long, hiked herself for the first time over the fence to call on the former owner. Soon, the towheaded little girl had cracked the ice around an old man's bitter heart. He'd taught her to milk cows and gather eggs before she was of school age; he'd sifted warm spring soil through her fingers, and taught her when to plant; finally, he'd admitted how wrong he'd been. Her father wasn't going anywhere, and he didn't need a son. He had Caroline.

Caroline had stayed right where she was, and so had her family. When she'd married—a third cousin also named Pearce—thirteen years after the old man had died, she brought her husband home to farm. Three years later she bore him a son, and a decade after her husband had passed away, in 1960, she coaxed their unemployed, only child of thirty-seven back home again. He'd brought his pregnant wife, and nine-year-old Ben. Jessie's birth the following May had been a sign to Caroline, to all of them, that the farm would thrive—as it had, in one form or another, for nearly two centuries.

Slowing now for the right-hand swing onto the dirt farm lane that she found predictably thick with another early spring's mud, Jessie felt the smile on her lips expand.

The Pearce farm at the end of the lane lay fallow, as it had since her parents had died when Jessie was twelve; but Tom Granby, on his three hundred acres closer to the main road, still planted corn in May and harvested hay in July and milked one hundred dairy cattle twice each day. At dusk she would see the fawn-and-white Guernseys edging their way toward his big aluminum barn. Its gleaming silhouette topped the sloping meadow from the road, the white farmhouse off to its right on the same crest of hill.

Her pulse picked up as she hurried her BMW along the rutted road. Home. Had she come home at last? Easing the car to a stop in the weed-choked driveway, she leaned back, waiting, hoping, and it happened, as she'd prayed it would. Like a calming hand, the warm rush of gladness swept through her, as always when she came to Caroline Pearce's house.

The house was ancient now, peeling white, its paint coming off in sheets and fingers, and the front porch sagged, down in the center, up at each end—like a smile to welcome her. Jessie smiled back. Getting out of the car, she picked her way through the mud and climbed the steps. How many times had she burst through that door, shouting for Gran or her own mother? "I'm home! What smells so good? Tollhouse cookies, Mama?"

The silence told her how much time had passed, how much had changed, and a glance toward the side orchard made her blink back sudden tears. Without their burden of autumn fruit or springtime blossoms, even the apple trees looked barren, like her grandmother's land.

Jessie tore her gaze away. She'd have to ask Tom whether the orchard still bore fruit on its own or would need pruning, fertilizer. Tom, next door again. Any day now she'd hear the rough rhythm of his tractor, or should she say Nick's, filling the air between the two farms. His plow would bite into dirt, flinging clods of rich earth and clouds of dust behind. And Jessie would be sneezing her head off again.

Her nose twitched at the thought, but over the years she'd developed an air of fatalism about something she couldn't cure, or escape. She'd always teased Peter that she'd married him to get away from her grass allergies, then followed him west only to develop a new allergy to cholla cactus.

Smiling, she turned back to her grandmother's house but didn't go inside. Instead, she walked around it, noting the rope swing that, although frayed, still hung from Gran's old maple tree, the broken second-story window in what used to be Ben's room, the sagging porch roof. Her brother had been right in one thing: she had her work cut out for her here.

Then, in the backyard she found flowers, blooming.

"Oh, Gran." Jessie dropped to her knees in the soft dirt. She let a handful run through her fingers, felt the first warmth, smelled its rich fertility. Trembling, she touched the upthrusting stalks of yellow daffodils, the striped leaves of snow crocuses that had finished blooming, the first tulips that had just broken through. This garden had been her grandmother's joy. How astonishing to find it still producing from bulbs Caroline had buried long ago.

Jessie bowed her head and prayed without words, only silence, for her parents and for Gran. Unlike Caroline she'd never been very religious, but the thought came anyway.

If there is life everlasting, it should be like this—a patch of garden, a bed of flowers.

Embarrassed by the sentiment, she rose to her feet.

Treacle, her editor would say and strike out such a phrase. If she ever wrote again.

Jessie dusted off her hands as if to be rid of self-pity, which wasn't like her. Yet tears threatened anyway, tears of gratitude—for the flowers, the springtime earth, this very house. If Nick had always loathed it here, Jessie had always been a farm girl at heart; and she'd just been reminded that this land would soon bring forth life again in the ages-old, comforting repetition of sowing and harvesting and reaping.

She stepped gingerly over a broken plank on the back porch and eased her key into the door's rusty lock. Later, she'd pick daffodils for the pale-scrubbed deal table in the kitchen. As she'd done a thousand times before, she'd eat dinner there—even if she had to nuke a frozen burrito in the microwave she'd packed. As the door swung open and cool, musty air rushed out to greet her, she could feel the welcome again, the love.

The next day Jessie was up early and out in the orchard, wielding a huge pair of garden clippers, snapping off apple tree branches when Nick came by. He didn't seem to have an excuse for his visit, which irritated Jessie though she couldn't say why exactly—until he spoke.

"What do you think you're doing?"

"Pruning my orchard."

"A little late in the season, Jess."

"So your father told me."

"Did he tell you not to bother fertilizing, too?" He inspected the nearest tree. "Look at all these suckers. This orchard's been abandoned for twelve to fifteen years, easy." He looked at her, his eyes dark and full of something she chose not to understand.

"An orchard can last a hundred years."

"With proper care," Nick said. "Any good farmer would replace stock in half that time, vary the species—"

Jessie clipped off the branch that Nick had been fingering and let it fall. "I'm sure your grandfather or mine did exactly that. I'm no expert on apple tree varieties, but it seems I remember my own father planting young trees for Gran one autumn."

Nick looked around the orchard then at Jessie again. "It seems to me you remember only what you want to—what pleases you."

She whacked off another branch near Nick's head this time. "Think what you like. I don't need your advice, Nick, and I sure don't need your disdain—for Tom or for myself. He's a good farmer and I—"

"Don't tell me. You're planning to open a roadside produce stand and sell apples to the leafpeepers next September."

"I don't have to sell apples." She stomped toward the next tree, trying not to remember another spring when the orchard had been loaded with blossoms, when she and Nick had . . . Jessie stopped herself. "I have a small settlement from Peter, which I deserve, and we made out all right on the sale of our house. I have royalties and an advance coming—"

"Hold on," Nick said right behind her.

"I don't owe you any explanations, but I'll give you one anyway." Jessie turned so fast that the pruning shears jammed against Nick's stomach. "I'm also living rent-free in Gran's house, which I happen to own with Ben, so I'm hardly destitute."

"I'm glad to hear it." Stepping back, Nick seemed to be fighting a smile, which enraged Jessie.

"I can take care of myself," she added.

"I never doubted it." Nick paused. "Still, you won't get any apples this year, that's for sure, no matter what you do." He was halfway to Tom's truck when his voice drifted back to her like the faint, sweet smell of old apple blossoms. "But it wouldn't surprise me if you did."

Jessie didn't watch him go. She turned back to her pruning. It might be useless to Nick, but to her at least it was therapy. After all, she had come home. With luck, and time, could she, like the flowers in Gran's garden and the trees in the orchard, experience her own rebirth?

Plenty of time, Jessie thought as she flapped her rag against a lamp shade in the front parlor, and choked. In three days she'd barely made a dent in the amount of dirt in Gran's house—one reason she'd hired Greg to help for the afternoon.

For another, she had begun to dislike solitude. Last night she hadn't slept well, just dozed fitfully over a best-selling novel that, on the previous nights, had failed to put her to sleep but had kept her light on until the wee hours.

Irritated, she flicked the rag at a tabletop and sneezed. If her nose wasn't streaming because of the dust she'd stirred up, it was stopped shut. All day Nick had been churning pasture next door.

Nick was working hard, she'd give him that. Last night she'd seen lights blazing in the barn at eleven o'clock. This morning he would have been up at dawn, she realized, remembering the gruesome daily schedule her father and Nick's had kept. Even at that, he'd be lucky to finish planting before Tom came home.

"What's the matter, Jessie?" Greg asked. "You're frowning so hard there's a line right between your eyebrows."

Startled, she dropped her rag. "Nothing, just daydreaming."

"I thought maybe you were worrying about tonight."

"Tonight?" Her pulse thumped, but she could hear the lazy amusement in his tone.

"When all the kids in Carran come roaring up the lane past the Granby place to neck here like Dad says."

"And will they?" Jessie asked. *Would Greg?*

But she'd met Greg's girlfriend several times over the past two weeks and decided Ben was wrong. Slender, long-legged, with a shy smile and big, dark-lashed green eyes, Heather looked, like most girls these days to Jessie, both more mature than her fifteen years and, at the same time, innocent. The combination would be dynamite to someone like Greg, and the obvious attraction between them couldn't be missed. "Hot blood," had been Nick's wry assessment.

Greg sighed. "I wouldn't dare come up here and have Mr. Granby see Dad's car. Jeez. Dad always says I should be careful I don't 'get some girl in trouble.' " He rolled his eyes. "I guess he thinks I oughta go to prison or something just as a precaution. The Benjamin Pearce No-Fail Method of Birth Control."

Seeing the flush on his cheeks, Jessie hid her smile.

She picked up her rag to polish a minuscule spot from a tabletop. She wanted Greg to keep talking.

"Maybe he's right." His voice lowered. "Not about Heather being trampy, and not about having problems at home—her mom's really great—but he could be right about Heather and me, being alone."

"What do you mean?" Jessie asked carefully.

"It's all my fault," he said. "Heather won't even let me in her house when her mom's not there." He paused. "And I'd never bring her out here to neck, not just because of Dad's car."

"You're afraid you couldn't stop with necking?"

"I could," he murmured, "but I wouldn't want to." He looked away. "Did you ever feel like that, Jessie?"

"Yes."

"With Uncle Peter?"

"Yes," she lied, wishing her marriage to Peter had been that emotionally driven, that intense. "Yes. Once. Everyone's entitled," she said, "but don't tell your father I told you so."

"Tell him?" Greg glanced at her, with a slow grin. "He'd croak. He even thinks your books are steamy. When your first one came out, he ordered me not to read it."

"Oh, Lord." The complaint, though unjustified, was common enough—but from her own brother? Ben made the Puritan Cotton Mather seem like a libertine.

"I read it anyway," Greg went on. "I think you write great men . . . heroes."

"Thank you."

"You know, the guy in your first book reminds me of Nick, with that same dark hair and eyes and smile." His grin widened. "Why's your face turning red, Jessie?"

"I meant no such connection, though it's true, readers often ascribe to fictional characters parts of people they know. Sometimes writers do, too. Perhaps you did see a similarity, but I hadn't seen Nick in a dozen years until recently."

"But Dad always says he was your first love, and when Mom was alive, she agreed. Then Dad would say all the women loved Nick, and Mom would say he only wanted to think they did, that Dad was jealous because he married so young." Greg frowned. "Then sometimes they'd start fighting. Did you and Peter fight?"

"Not often enough," Jessie admitted.

"I never fight with Heather."

Her expression softened. "Greg, sooner or later any two people in a relationship quarrel. Argument clears the air."

"Does it? All Dad and I seem to do since Mom died is argue, and it never clears anything."

"Your father misses her. You said so yourself."

"Well, I miss her, too." His jaw tightened. "But I try not to take his head off every time he says something I don't like—which is almost every time he opens his mouth."

Jessie touched his arm. The muscles were taut. "Your father's lonely. He sees you drifting away, as all kids do when the time comes. Cut him a little slack, Greg."

"Yeah, I guess. If only he wasn't so . . ."

"Prickly?" She refolded her dust rag to find a clean spot.

"Yeah."

"Like a porcupine," Jessie added, and he smiled a little as she'd wanted him to. "Come on, let's finish up or we'll both hear Ben screaming all the way from Carran that you're late for dinner. Maybe before you leave, we'll have time to scrape more grease off my kitchen stove."

"Jeez, I'd rather—" He broke off. At the same instant, Jessie heard a truck's gears whining up the driveway. "Nick! It's his father's pickup!" Greg raced for the back door, in a blur of yellow T-shirt and stone-washed jeans.

He worships him, she thought, not having to wait long before her nephew returned with Nick in tow.

Jessie tensed. She could swear she'd seen that denim jacket years ago, not to mention the disreputable Dunham work boots now tracking mud across her clean kitchen floor. What was he doing here, again?

"Hi, neighbor." Nick headed straight for the refrigerator, reached for a can of Coke, and popped the tab.

"Help yourself," Jessie murmured. "Make yourself at home."

He did just that, straddling a chair at the kitchen table where she'd seen him so many times, drinking a glass of Gran's lemonade. "Greg," he said, "run out to the truck, will you, and see if my wallet's on the seat."

The door banged shut, leaving them alone.

"What's the matter, Jess?" Nick's gaze held hers. "You're wearing your I-can't-stand-Nick-Granby expression again."

"It's not you," she lied, as she had to Greg. Jessie waved toward the old iron stove. "Gran kept a spotless house, but Ben rented it out for a few years, and his tenants weren't so meticulous. I've had enough dusting and scraping for a year."

"I've had enough farming for eternity."

His weak grin didn't fool her. Neither had Nick's excuse about the wallet; when he'd opened the refrigerator, she'd seen its bulge in his rear pocket. Jessie could also see that after four days Nick looked even more tired than he had at the hospital when he'd told her about Tom, more overworked than he'd mentioned the night at Ben's.

"Your wallet's not in the truck," Greg said, slamming through the back door again, oblivious of the fact that he'd been sent on a needless errand.

Nick drained his Coke. "Jess, do you have a socket wrench I can borrow? Pop's got everything else over there. I know he has one, but I'm damned if I can find it."

"Socket wrench?" She saw his eyes were cast down, a typically Nick evasion that told Jessie he wasn't telling the complete truth. "I don't know anything about tools, but the shed's open. You're welcome to look."

He came back holding up a piece of chrome, which of course she didn't recognize. "Got it."

"Fine." She clipped off the word. "Then hadn't you better use what daylight is left? It's supposed to rain tonight."

"Yeah, I'll be plowing mud in the morning." Nick leaned against the sink. "If I'm plowing at all. The Harvester's on the blink again. I wish Pop had let me put a down payment on a new one when I was here last. Everything's back ordered now."

Greg frowned. "Dad says the small farmers are doomed. All the land's being sold for housing."

"He's right," Nick agreed. "They're a dying breed."

He and Jessie exchanged looks, but she saw pain

flicker in his eyes and sensed that he was thinking, as she was, of Tom. Nick slapped the socket wrench into his palm. "Well, I'd better go. The parts guy at the Ag Co-op is holding what I need."

Greg's eyes lit up. "Then forget your wallet, Nick. You can charge there, or at the feed store."

Nick winced. "Take my advice. Stay away from credit. Personally, I carry plastic, but I pay the balances every month. And shop around when I need a loan for my business. Pop's in hock to his eyeballs. If you really want to farm some day—"

"I really do." Greg refused to be discouraged. "Give me a ride home now, though? It would save Jessie the trip to Carran." His car was being repaired, and she'd picked him up.

"Altruism lives," she murmured. "You wouldn't be trying to avoid my greasy stove, would you?"

"Well . . ."

Nick laughed. "I can spring you from your aunt's clutches, if you don't mind being dropped off last." He glanced at his watch, slim and gold, incongruous with his clothes, like a vestige of a former life. "Forty-five minutes till the store closes." He looked at Greg. "Actually, I've been wanting to talk to you. You go ahead, get in the truck. I'll be out in a minute."

Jessie's pulse thumped in the awkward silence.

Nick cleared his throat. "Speaking of time—a hundred years back or so—your shed door's rusted, coming off the hinges."

"Darn. I'll see what I can do." Everything seemed to be rusted, or dirty.

"I'll send a man over as soon as I hire one."

"No, really, Nick." She hadn't been hinting. She didn't want to be obliged to him. "I can manage."

He sighed. "You don't take orders worth a damn these days. I said, I'll send someone over, as a neighborly gesture. Think you can handle that?"

"Why not?" Then she met his gaze, squarely, and saw what she hadn't seen before in his evasion. Vulnerability. The wrench had only been an excuse. He wanted something else, and like his downcast eyes, the overly casual tone was a dead giveaway.

"Taking Greg home, fixing your shed. Two favors in one day, don't you think you could ask me to dinner?"

"I'm a lousy cook."

"How could I forget? You made biscuits as hard as hockey pucks." He grinned. "Ah, hell, we're both tired. We'll warm something up in your microwave, how's that?" He added, "Tacos."

Damn him. Jessie groaned in frustration, her mouth already watering. Mexican food had become a passion long before she moved to the Southwest. And Nick knew it.

"I'll pick 'em up on my way back. Refried beans?"

"You remembered," she said, inordinately pleased. And more than a little scared.

Afraid she might come out of her skin, Jessie stood on the porch, watching Tom's truck rattle down the drive. Then, with a last wave for Greg, she turned into the yard and began yanking weeds from her grandmother's flowers, weeds that had barely begun to sprout. *Why so frightened, Jess?*

She could have sworn she'd heard Nick's voice, or had it only been the breeze? In the next instant, she even imagined she could hear her pet calf of years past, bleating from the old barn for a good-night treat. Goosebumps on her arms, Jessie stopped weeding and walked across the grass, which had overgrown the dirt tractor path in front of the paint-blistered barn door. There was nothing here to be frightened of, she told herself.

The big door stuck, shrieking back at last on rusted rollers. But inside, it was dark and cool, still smelling of hay and animals . . . and the memories of a night long ago.

Jessie had been barely eight years old the night her brother and Nick graduated from high school, and Caroline, who loved a good party, had put on a bang-up, two-family celebration. Allowed to stay up late, Jessie had eaten too much cake.

Feeling queasy, she'd wandered toward the barn to look for her brother, who would surely be with Nick. Seeing neither of them, she slipped into a stall to say good night to Sunbeam, Nick's 4-H calf, which he'd given her for her birthday and helped her name. Moments later, she heard Ben's voice.

". . . can't farm by himself, with two hundred—"

"I know his herd. I know how much work there is. That's not the point." Jessie heard Nick sigh. "Ben, I don't want to hurt Pop, but how can I spend the rest of my life here when what I want . . . ah, hell."

Her heart was suddenly racing. "You aren't going to leave, are you, Nick?" Jessie stepped from the stall. "You'll go to college, like Ben, then come home, won't you? Won't you, Nick?"

"Hey, squirt, why are you up so late?" he asked.

Ben made a disgusted sound. "She's been following us again. Go on now, back to the house. This is man talk."

"My stomach doesn't feel so good," Jessie said with a gulp.

"Oh, dammit."

"Jess, are you—" Nick began, then his strong hand clamped the back of her neck, rushing her out into the clear air. At the side of the barn, he held her while she retched, and even in her misery, she knew Ben had left them alone; he was never good about illness. "Are you okay now?" Nick asked her.

After cleaning her face, he carried her home, Jessie's arms clamped tight around his neck, her own throat aching with unshed tears. In her room, with its forget-me-not-patterned wallpaper and white eyelet curtains, she felt a little safer. She'd always known that Nick hated the backbreaking farm labor his father loved, hated his father's incessant worry over weather, outdated equipment, overdue loans. Because she loved everything about the farm, Jessie didn't understand that, but she knew what Nick wanted. She'd known for years. When he offered to read her a bedtime story, she asked him instead to build something for her.

The marvelous buildings Nick could deftly fashion, using Jessie's plastic bricks, always amazed her, but that night his skill only made her stomach knot again.

"This one's a skyscraper," he told her, his voice husky, his eyes glowing. "Like in the city, New York or Chicago. Maybe some day you'll see the real thing."

She swallowed. "Some day you'll *build* the real thing, Nick."

His fingers stilled. Then his head came up, and his gaze held hers for a long moment. "Maybe," he said. "Thanks, Jess."

At his intense look, joy had flooded through her, yet the faint nausea remained. The fear. What if his dream took him far away, took him from her?

She'd never thought about that before. She didn't want to.

Standing in the barn twenty-one years later, Jessie blinked away the memory. The fear was still with her, but at least she knew why. She hadn't wanted to see Nick again. After she had, she'd decided to avoid him. Then she'd agreed to help with Tom, and told herself she could minimize her contact with Nick somehow, that they could be polite but distant. But the house and this barn were too full of memories. Living ghosts, she thought.

She hadn't wanted to confront even one of them. She'd certainly never expected to remember something bittersweet and loving about Nick, whose eyes had looked so dark and warm and gentle then . . .

Frankly, the memory terrified her.

Later, and very much in the present, Nick hauled Jess back against his chest, and she screamed. His hands with scraped knuckles met at her eye level.

"Take a whiff of that, woman." A large white bag emblazoned with the logo of a Mexican fast food chain dangled in front of her. "Satisfaction in a paper sack."

"Nicholas Granby, you scared me!"

"What are you doing in the barn?" He cast a jaundiced look around. "It just might fall down around your ears, you know. What's so fascinating?"

"My own thoughts. I'm . . . working out a plot problem."

"Must be the grandmother of them all. You were off in another world."

"That's what it takes." Snatching the bag, she strode from the barn. Nick followed. In the kitchen, while he watched, she pulled out containers of food as if each held precious jewels. "Ummm, good. I hope this house can survive the technological intrusion of a microwave oven into a 1930s kitchen." She grinned. "Gran will spin in her grave, but I like my refried beans hot enough to burn my tongue."

"Yeah, Caroline was a stickler for things as they were. She could make a coat of paint last forty years. Look at that barn."

"She liked what she knew."

"Just like Pop," Nick said.

"Just like me."

Nick dug into his first burrito. "Don't get me wrong, I loved that lady as much as you did."

They ate in silence, and when they finished, Nick sorted trash into the garbage while Jess washed their plates. He kept his tone casual. "It's been a long time since I was in Caroline's house. Mind if I look around?" Not waiting for an answer, he added, "Come with me, Jess."

She shook her head. "I've seen it. I live here."

He didn't argue. Nick simply took her hand, lacing his fingers in hers, which were stiff, resistant.

"I'll give you a free architectural inspection. You wouldn't want the ceiling to cave in on you some night, would you?"

To his relief she said no, and let him lead her through the parlor and Caroline's sewing room on the other side of the hall, then up the stairs. The same third step from the bottom creaked, just as Nick remembered, but it only needed a couple of nails. The wood was solid.

On either side of the upstairs hall, he found the first bedrooms empty, only a stray ladderback chair with a weakened rush seat in one, a scarred pine dresser in the next. "What happened to the furniture?"

"Most of it's packed away, I suppose. In the attic, probably. Some in the barn loft, I imagine."

"You haven't gone exploring?"

"No." Her fingers were trembling now.

Nick soon realized that he and Jess were on a different kind of treasure hunt. When he opened the door to her childhood room, where the white eyelet curtains still hung, yellowed, at the windows and the forget-me-nots on the wallpaper begged for brighter blossoms, it hit him.

A strong, strange feeling washed over him. Warmth seemed to flow from the walls and ceiling, to embrace him like a loving woman, as if he had touched her again after so many years. Nick's gaze met hers, and softened. Her hand had tightened in his. Did she feel it, too?

"Oh, Jess," he said, remembering the nights when she was a child, when he'd tucked her into that white spindle bed, when he'd had her trust, her love. "This brings back memories."

"Memories?" She tugged her hand free. "This house has become the height of fashion, as you must know. The country look is in." She ran a hand down one of the plainly turned bedposts that still supported the worn canopy, and disappointment swamped him. She'd deliberately misunderstood.

"Is it? I didn't do that much residential work until the hurricane hit Charleston."

"I assure you that, given time and elbow grease, I could call in the photographers for *Architectural Digest*."

"You'd have to raid that attic first, and the loft."

"Sometime," she said. "I'm in no hurry."

Her thin tone made him smile. "Not spooked, are you, Jess? Out here alone with Greg's ghosts?"

"He told you that?"

"All the way into Carran."

He watched her spine stiffen. "Of course I'm not 'spooked.' "

"Then why was the light burning in your room at four-thirty this morning?"

"Yours must have been burning too, or you wouldn't have noticed. I was working," she added.

"Are you working now, Jess?"

She took a step backward. "I don't know what you mean."

Nick's smile disappeared. He'd allowed her enough distance. "I mean that you're the writer and I'm the architect. So don't try to build walls between us. You're lousy at it."

When she started for the door, he caught her, his fingers firm but gentle around her upper arm. Her profile to him, she shook her head, eyes lowered so he couldn't see them, and guilt flashed through him.

But even if she struck him, he couldn't stop himself. Nick pushed gently, pressing her spine to the wall beside the open door, his fingers trembling on her arms.

"We shouldn't have come upstairs," she murmured brokenly. "I feel things in this room too strongly, old things, dear things." She gazed at him imploringly. "I can't seem to help how they make me feel."

"Jess, for God's sake. Just feel them then."

Letting his hands drift upward, he cupped her shoulders. They felt slight, easily breakable. He made small caressing motions, soft fabric rubbing against her softer skin. Madness.

He could feel her resistance like another presence in the room, one he wouldn't permit. He wouldn't have it there. But she kept her body rigid, her eyes closed. Slowly Nick's fingers feathered along her shoulders to her throat, her chin. He tipped it up. "Open your eyes," he said. "Stop fighting."

To his surprise, even astonishment, her head dropped back against the wall, as if it had been connected to a spring, and the spring had snapped. When he lowered his head, she didn't move. Her eyes stared, wide and lost, into his.

"Jess," he whispered, his heart hammering, "sweet Jess."

"Dear God."

She kept her arms at her sides, but her lips parted slightly, her mouth went slack, and he took it, his arms braced against the wall behind her, his whole body shaking. As on the night at Ben's, they were scarcely touching. When Nick let his mouth graze hers, he could hardly have called it a kiss. Then, as if she couldn't help herself either, her arms lifted to his neck, her fingers sifting through the thick darkness of his hair, and with a groan, he covered her mouth completely, the slow glide of his tongue seeking hers.

Lazily he shifted angles on the kiss, deepened it, played her mouth with his as if he were molding warm clay into a masterpiece, until she cried out. Until she cried his name with all the pent-up yearning of a dozen years and sent his heartbeat soaring.

Bending his knees, Nick held her firmly in place, pressing against her now, wanting, letting her feel how much. The bed loomed three feet away.

"Jess." He turned the kiss hot, sensing the very instant when he drew her under too, completely. "I missed you. Tell me you missed me, too."

No sooner were the words out than she was pushing at his chest, dragging her mouth from his. Nick drew her back again.

"Nick, *don't!*"

Breathing hard, he finally heard her through the haze of arousal and dropped his forehead to her shoulder. "I'm sorry, God, I don't know what came over me."

"I suppose the same thing that came over you in the orchard one night," she murmured, and pushed hard at his hipbones.

Stung, Nick let her go. He knew he'd been out of line, but damn, she could pour ice water on the flames faster than any woman he'd ever met. The warm, heady rush of feeling in the room was gone. And in the next instant, so was Jess.

Intent on saving his male pride, he followed her downstairs. In the parlor doorway, he shoved his hands deep in his pockets while she perched on the horsehair sofa, twisting her fingers together. "Nick, I think you'd better go."

Crossing the room instead, he knelt down, his hands covering hers. He'd really blown it this time.

She'd never let him near her again. "Jess . . ." He didn't know what to say.

"I've had enough heartache. I don't want any more. I can't bear any more right now. And that's what you bring me."

"That's not true. We brought each other joy. We did," he insisted, stroking her knuckles with his thumbs, and feeling grateful when she didn't pull away. "Years ago, Jess. Years ago and now, upstairs."

She shook her head. "I shouldn't have come back. After the divorce, I wanted somewhere safe and simple, where I belonged without question. I tried Carran, and Ben's, but that didn't work. I hoped Gran's might . . ." She trailed off. "I wasn't telling the truth before. I wasn't working in the barn, or last night. I was lying awake, unable to sleep. I have a deadline in less than six months, but I can't seem to write."

"You will," Nick said. "Give it time." He paused, knowing he had to say the right thing. "While you were married, I stayed away, Jess. But Peter's gone now, and we have something here."

"We never had anything."

"We could, if you'd let us."

Her gaze darkened. "Nick, I was a foolish adolescent girl who worshiped the air you breathed, but that's all I ever really had, air and empty dreams."

"I had dreams, too, Jess. One of them—"

"Yes. I know. You dreamed of leaving."

His gut clenched. Anger, hurt, guilt, and Jess's distance. He was sick of them. "I didn't hold yours against you. Why in hell are you holding mine against me? I left Carran because I had to, to become what I wanted."

"And you'll leave again as soon as Tom's fields are planted."

"Yes," he said, "because I've got a business to run. A business that's not all gravy and profits as you seem to think it is. Yes, I'll leave. What's the crime this time, Jess? What do you want from me?"

Freeing her hands, she stood. "I want you to leave this house. That's all. And not come back."

"Bullshit. You lie to yourself if you want," he said, "but you'd damn better not lie to me."

"And you can forget about fixing my shed."

"Like hell. I said I'd fix your goddamn shed and I will. I haven't seen hand-filed screws like those in anything under a hundred years old—before automatic screw machines were patented the middle of the last century. It'll be a challenge, all right?"

"Whatever."

He was shaking with the urge to rattle her teeth. And Tom called *him* contrary. "I promised I'd stay to help Pop and I'll do that, too. You got that?" When she nodded, he said, "Good. As for tonight, I have no excuse for what I did except that I'm tired, bone-tired, and my judgment stinks. Every muscle in my body aches. I've been working twenty-hour days for the better part of a week, with more to come and—"

"Don't expect sympathy. You made your own decision to stay."

"You think I want to be here in Carran? For more than two days? On that stretch of rocky, useless farmland? Well, think again. Every time I come back, I can't wait to leave."

"Obviously," she said, her blue eyes wounded.

The fight went out of him. "Goddammit, Jess. I'm no farmer." He looked deeply into her eyes for the understanding she wouldn't give. "I never was," Nick said.

4

June 18, 1856

Aaron brought me to the farm today. No,
Aaron brought me home. Already I think of it
that way, as if we've always lived here. As if we
always will. . . .

Jessie stared at the computer screen, pondering
the next word she would type. The trouble was, she
didn't quite remember typing what she already saw
there. After Nick had left the night before, she'd felt
edgy, tense, and known she wouldn't sleep. She'd
also known that dozing again over the same best-
seller wouldn't help her overcome the memory of
Nick's kisses. Hot, persuasive kisses. At midnight she
had decided to try breaking her writer's block, spent
the rest of the night setting up her computer, and now
her story opening blurred in front of her eyes.

She blinked at the steadily winking cursor. The
sentences she'd typed made a surprising start. Her

book had been planned as a contemporary, but she looked at the date she'd written, then the first word. *Aaron*, a good old-fashioned name, strong and beautiful.

Staring out the window, she hummed to herself, about tying a yellow ribbon on an old oak tree, to set the mood. She envisioned a book about basic values, about love and loyalty and laughter with a little heartbreak thrown in to leaven things, as long as the heartbreak was fiction and cathartic.

At last Jessie began to smile. Last night and Nick were already fading from her troubled thoughts. Her mind whirled, her excitement grew. Yes, she decided, Gran's house would provide the perfect setting. Shifting her gaze from the side yard and the orchard below her bedroom window, she faced the keyboard again.

Later, she'd drive into town to see Amy Stone at the historical society, where she worked as assistant director. Still, Jessie knew she would need little help researching her new hero. Her fingers flying over the keys, she was already half in love with Aaron herself. It was always a good sign.

Today we drove out from town after the wedding—oh my, but it seemed short, only a handful of words to bind two people together for eternity—and Aaron was so sweet, wanting to show me everything at once like a little boy with a new litter of puppies. He handed me down from the wagon, and taking time only to unhitch his beautiful matched bay geldings, Sugar and Spice, nearly dragged me to the barn. . . .

The sharp thud of a hammer against wood snapped Jessie's concentration an hour later. She swiveled on her desk chair to glare out the window. Down in the yard stood a man in blue jeans and plaid flannel shirt. Immediately she recognized his youthfully broad shoulders and the gleam of brown hair.

"Greg?" In seconds she was outside, striding across the overgrown lawn to the shed.

" 'Morning, Jessie."

"Good morning. You gave me a start." She gestured at his hammer. "I thought Ben had sent someone to tear the place down."

"Sorry, I should have knocked first before I started bashing things. But there's so much other work to be done, I wanted to finish this shed before I drive into Carran for—"

"Other work?"

He grinned. "I got a job. We want to finish spring planting by Friday, that is if the tractor's fixed before sundown today, then we—"

"Spring planting?"

"You sound just like Heather when I told her Mr. Granby'd hired me for the summer."

"Mr. Granby," Jessie repeated. Tom was still at the rehabilitation center.

"Nick sent me over as soon as he could, to replace the hinges on this door."

Her heart tripped. "Ah, yes. The hinges."

"These are a mess all right. Real museum pieces." Greg's grin widened. "Nick says he doesn't know which is worse, your place here or his pa's. Everything's old as the hills or broke or both. Nick says that old tractor of Mr. Granby's has half killed him more 'n a hundred times and now it's fixing to kill Nick before noon."

"I take it he's having mechanical problems."

"Man, I never saw anything stop running so fast. That thing went belly up out in the west pasture, just like cardiac arrest, Nick said."

Jessie couldn't help laughing. "Nick's a smart man. I'm sure he'll figure it out."

Greg gave the rusted metal hinge a few raps with the hammer, then applied muscle to a large screwdriver that, in seconds, had unfrozen the ancient fittings.

"He'll figure it out," Greg agreed, "or Tom Granby'll climb out of bed in that rehab hospital and come fix the tractor himself." He pried the last screw from its hole. "Aha, there it comes. Anyway, Mr. Granby's been giving plenty of advice."

"Unasked for, I assume," Jessie said.

He propped the unhinged door against the shed. "Yeah, he's pretty free with his words but he knows a lot, too. He's a hell of a—excuse me, Jessie—a good farmer."

Jessie grinned. She'd been feeling tuned in to another time, a slower pace. She was glad she'd been forced to take the break. "That's what my father always said."

Greg gazed toward the barn. "I sure wish someone could say that about me some day. But at least I get to work one season."

Jessie knew about ruined dreams. "I won't keep you then."

When she turned to go, Greg caught her arm. "I didn't mean for you to run off. I wanted to thank you for listening to me grumble about Dad yesterday."

"My privilege as your doting aunt." Her tone was gentle. "Feel free to come talk to me anytime. And I know you don't mean to send me away, but I do have to get back inside. I'm working myself today."

"Another book?" When Jessie nodded, he said, "Awesome. Well, hey, good luck."

"The same to you. If you want a cold drink, just come inside and help yourself." Halfway across the yard, she called back. "I hope Nick gets that tractor repaired, with or without Tom's advice."

Greg laughed. "Tom says what we really need's two mules and a plow."

"And what did Nick say to that?"

"That it was like talking to the old *Farmer's Almanac*."

Jessie was still smiling when she headed into town. She doubted things would ever change between Nick and his father, both stubborn men. Nick kept surprising her, though, and she'd decided to make amends for last night. His hiring Greg had changed her opinion of Nick yet again, just as she'd been forced to do when he agreed to stay and help Tom.

She would apologize for overreacting last night to a few kisses, which meant nothing. But when her BMW bumped down the lane by the Granby gate, she saw Nick's legs sticking out from under the tractor by the barn—and drove on. Did she only imagine it, or was the air around him turning as blue as his jeans?

. . . The barn is enormous, much bigger than Papa's house in Carran on Prescott Street, just off Hector and the square. Aaron's barn—our barn now, I should say—is low and brown, with sheds added on at the sides and back. It seemed to me at first sight to go on for miles, though Aaron thinks it's small, and already inadequate. He's stocked it well with oats and hay, such a dusty, sweet smell there is inside, and the sunlight, shafting through when the big doors stand wide or the hay mow window's open, is full of dancing motes. . . .

Jessie wrote feverishly in the steno pad she always carried. She'd stopped her car at a meter beside Carran's courthouse square, where yellow jonquils and bright red tulips rioted in profusion, to admire the view. It was something she couldn't have done in Scottsdale, where she'd frequently parked when she hadn't planned to, in the midst of stalled bumper-to-bumper traffic. She snapped her notepad shut; the book was taking her over.

Just inside the brown-and-cream foyer of the historical society, a taller, more youthfully slender Amy Stone than she remembered rushed to greet her, heels clicking on the tile floor.

"Jessie, I was so glad when you called earlier. Let me look at you." Holding her off, Amy laughed with delight. "My, you're not Ben's baby sister any longer. Or Nick's tag-along. All grown up, and famous, to boot."

"Not famous," Jessie murmured but without feeling the panic any mention of her work had caused until today.

The two women hugged. Amy said, "Come into the office, find a seat if you can, and tell me what's new."

"Nick Granby has hired Greg."

Amy grinned, waving Jessie toward a chair piled high with books and papers. "I know. Heather was on the phone no more than twenty seconds after Greg knew himself, I'm sure. That was kind of Nick. I imagine, for one thing, he hoped Ben would cool down a little about the kids being so deeply involved. He gives Greg a terrible time." Her expression hardened. "Heather, too, which makes me mad as a yellow jacket trying to get at a bowl of sugared peaches. That man . . . Ben used to be so sweet."

Jessie dumped the books on the floor. "He still is. He just hides it well."

Amy shook her head, a motion that set her dark, wedge-cut hairstyle swinging. "So many changes," she said. "I know how broken up he was when Beth died, but it's been—how long?"

"Over a year." Jessie grimaced. "Greg thinks his father just needs to get laid—his term."

"Don't we all?" Amy had been divorced, Jessie knew, for some time. Apparently there was no one new in her life. "Sometimes I think the old saying's true—'The more things change the more they stay the same.' It's like high school again, everybody so desperate to . . . connect." She sobered. "By the way, I was sorry to hear about your divorce."

"Thanks. It's been a little bumpy."

"See? We're all in the same boat." She moved papers around on her desk. "Nick, too, I hear. His father's stroke and all . . . still, I was more than surprised to learn he'd come back to Carran, then that he planned to stay." Amy's eyes, green like her daughter's, lit up. "I ran into him yesterday at the co-op. I'd stopped to see when the vegetable seedlings will be in. In school Nick was a great-looking guy, but the man is something else again . . . orders of magnitude."

"He's the toast of South Carolina." Jessie's tone was dry.

"I'm sure. In school, when he and Ben and I were together, Nick seemed so determined to get what he wanted. Girls, or grades. And he could always salvage victory from defeat in a football game—I'll never forget his touchdown pass against Rocky Ridge in the last five seconds—but now, in his work . . . did you see the article in *People* about that luscious resort he's building down south somewhere?"

"Charleston," Jessie said. "No, I didn't." Amy's interest in Nick had begun to irritate her. So, to Jessie's dismay, had Nick's success.

"But now he's home again, another example of things not really changing." Amy looked at her. "Do you see much of him?"

"I'm too busy putting my own life together to tag along after Nick."

"Yet you're neighbors. You must hear more than rumors." She paused. "Is Tom Granby really going to sell?"

Jessie's heart skipped. She had just remembered why Ben didn't like Amy Stone; though she and Beth had been friends, so had Amy and Julie Carmichael, the biggest gossip in town. Ben still blamed both of them for telling tales about him and Beth. "*Sell?* Where did you hear that?"

"Heather said Greg's father and Nick had discussed it."

"When?"

"Recently, I suppose. I understand Ben's working

weekends selling real estate. I imagine he'd like to earn the commission."

"He'd like to sell our grandmother's farm, too. But I don't agree, and Tom Granby wants more than anything to stay," Jessie insisted. "He told me so."

Amy's tone gentled. "Look, I realize you've been his champion ever since Nick decided to bail out for Charleston, but how long do you think Tom can keep farming? He must be seventy, he's in poor health—"

"And sitting on a prime piece of real estate that Nick—and my own brother—think could be used more profitably?" Her pulse refused to settle. Getting up, Jessie stacked books from the floor back onto the chair, the motion hiding her flushed cheeks.

"Where are you going?"

Anger surged through her in waves. Nick had promised Tom, he'd promised *her*. "I'm working on a book," she said, glancing up. "I need to get back to it."

Amy's look clearly said she wasn't fooled by the change of topic, but she walked Jessie without comment along the brown-tiled hall to the society's entryway. "What's the book about?"

"History. Love. It's different from what I planned to do," she admitted, "but it feels right. I wanted to ask your help with research."

"But instead you're going home to nail Nick's hide to the barn door." It wasn't a question.

"I'll try not to shed any blood."

"Jessie, I'm sorry if I've caused trouble between you and Nick. Why don't you just give me your list, and we'll talk some more."

"I really have to go." Fishing in her purse, Jessie pulled out a scrap of paper. "If you could start with this, I'll need information on mid-nineteenth-century farming methods, customs, lifestyle, costume . . . oh, and perhaps an area map of the period."

"My pleasure." They went out the main doors into the sunshine. Amy hugged Jessie. "Seeing you all grown up and gorgeous makes me feel a hundred years old, but it's good to have you back. After all those picnics and parties at your grandmother's, I almost feel reunited with my younger sister. Come get those books tomorrow." She gnawed at her lip. "And say hi to Ben for me."

Jessie started to turn away. Then she remembered something, though Ben would say she was meddling, which didn't strike her now as such a bad idea.

"As a matter of fact, we're having another party at Gran's, for Ben's birthday. It was Greg's idea. Will you come?"

Amy looked away. "Oh, no, Jessie, I—"

"Just to see if he can blow out all those candles?" Her brother was turning forty in two weeks.

"I don't think . . . that is, Ben and I haven't exactly been friends, especially since Greg started dating Heather." She wrung her slender hands. "And I'm so involved in my work here, I don't go out much."

"You're divorced, not dead." Jessie waited for Amy to look up. "Maybe you could talk sense to Ben about the kids," she suggested. "He's not so bad after a beer or two. He might even loosen up and smile." She glanced at Army's trim figure. "Besides, Greg has recruited me to help bake 'the best cake ever,' even though I hate to cook. Please come help us eat it so I don't gain fifteen pounds."

"Well, all right, but I remember your cooking. For Greg's sake, why don't I bring the cake?"

"You're on." Satisfied, Jessie said good-bye and headed for her car. As she drove out of Carran toward the farm, a glance at the sky told her Nick wouldn't get the rain that had been predicted for today after all. Or was he worried about that now? If Amy'd been right about his selling the farm . . .

Then why had Nick said he'd stay in the first place? And why had he been trying to fix Tom's tractor?

"What you need is a good pair of mules and a plow."

Jess's voice made Nick, his jeans-clad legs still sticking out from under Tom's tractor by the barn, jump as if he'd been shot. He hadn't heard her drive up and, instead of answering, cursed again just as she spoke. A wrench went flying to land at her feet.

"Goodness, it must be worse than I thought."

Nick scooted out from under the Harvester, banging his head on its metal frame when he sat up. He'd spent the morning alternately cursing the tractor, then himself for last night, thinking he'd be lucky to see her again. Now she was here. And she didn't sound angry, merely cool. Nick got to his feet. Maybe he had a chance. He gave her a slow smile.

"I'd be better off with a repair manual for this old hunk of junk, wouldn't I?"

"Or the *Farmer's Almanac*." She didn't return the smile.

"*Farmer's*—? Oh," he said, rubbing his head. "Greg's been talking."

"Quoting actually, while he fixed my shed this morning. Thanks for sending him over, Nick." She gestured at the tractor. "What's wrong with it?"

"I thought at first it was the fuel pump, then about noon I decided the carburetor was clogged. Now I'm leaning toward the worn-out starter theory."

Another apology balanced on the tip of his tongue.

"Why fix it if you don't need to plant after all?" She took a deep breath, then said, "Rumor has it, you're putting the screws to Tom about selling out."

"Where'd you hear that?"

Jess told him and he nodded, his mouth tightening, the apology abandoned.

"I'd forgotten how fast gossip travels in a small town, which is a damn good reason for not living in one." He cocked his head and studied her. "So what did you do, Jess? Spend the drive from Courthouse Square, building up a full head of steam? Getting ready to blast me again about how badly I treat my father?"

"I didn't say "

"Well, save your breath. We're not selling," Nick said too softly. "I promised Pop the season here." He pointed toward the two young men unloading feed sacks by the barn. "Why do you think I hired Greg and his friend? I keep my promises, dammit."

Jess folded her arms. "I'm sure Tom's glad to know that."

Nick stared at her maroon Arizona State sweatshirt. "You're not talking about Pop," he said, "are you? Is that all the trust you have left in me?"

She answered with silence.

"Hell," Nick muttered and rubbed the back of his neck. "What did Amy say exactly?"

When Jess mentioned Ben, he frowned. "Sure, he's hungry for commissions. And we've been kicking around the idea of selling for years—nothing new, but that's all it was, an idea. Hasn't he tried to get you to sell your grandmother's place?"

"He tried, when I first mentioned moving there. I cut him off."

Nick said, "Well, I heard him out because I'm careful these days with Ben. Twelve years ago it took a lot of explaining—a couple of years, in fact, and some help from Beth—before he'd believe that I hadn't been about to rape his baby sister in the orchard. I value his friendship, Jess, so I watch what I say to your brother."

"I'm sorry. I'm afraid I was more hasty. It isn't like me to jump to conclusions—"

"Except where I'm concerned." She could hardly deny that, he thought.

"The subject of selling came up by accident," she explained, "when I stopped to ask Amy some research questions."

"Research?"

"I'm starting a book." Though her eyes were still cool, she couldn't keep the pride from her tone.

Nick gave in to a smile. "Way to go, Jess."

"Damn," she said after a silence, and reached up to wipe a smear of axle grease from his cheek.

Nick's pulse shot up. "Damn what?"

"I drove over here expecting to find a farm equipment auction, and instead, you're happy that I'm working again."

"Ashamed of yourself?"

"Yes."

"Good," he said, then dared himself to bend and kiss her cheek. "I told you you'd get back to business, though I didn't think it would be this soon. That's great, Jess. When can I read it?"

"You'd really want to?"

"Sure. I'll insist on it." Why would she think he wouldn't?

Her gaze faltered. "As soon as I'm happy with the first chapter, how's that?"

"It's a deal."

"Thanks." She nodded toward Tom's tractor, much of its engine strewn everywhere. "If I could, I'd help you with that thing." At her feet a can of oil had tipped onto the ground, making a dark reflecting pool, and Nick caught their grins in it.

"Black magic to me," he admitted. "Frankly, I don't know what the hell I'm doing."

"Why should you? You're not a mechanic," she said. "But you could build a new barn overnight if Tom needed one."

"Hell, woman, *you* need one. The wind just whistles through those missing boards, and I'd bet money the hayloft floor has rotted through in more than one spot. By comparison, that shed Greg fixed today is state-of-the-art technology."

She could hardly disagree. The barn on Jess's land, which had been her grandmother Pearce's, and Caroline's father's before that, now listed north. But Nick knew Jess preferred its lopsided, falling-down, ramshackle appearance to the corrugated metal siding and stainless-steel milking stanchions of his father's barn, and she said so.

"Then you're as much a relic as Pop is," Nick said.

"And just as proud of it. Gran would be, too." She kept smiling. "You can hide behind your architectural degree if you want, but I think you're just afraid of Greg's ghosts."

Nick remembered the strange feeling he'd had,

standing in the doorway to Jess's bedroom, and frowned. "I don't believe in ghosts," he said. "I believe in small-town family gossip."

"I said I was sorry."

"Accepted." But Nick also remembered his own behavior the night before, his own apology. "You're still mad at me, aren't you? For kissing you like some sex-starved teenager?"

Jess shook her head. "Actually, I meant to come over here and apologize for overreacting like a panic-stricken virgin, but then I went into town . . ." And Amy Stone had convinced her that he'd broken his promise.

"After I left last night," Nick said, "I couldn't sleep. I know you weren't sleeping either, because I saw your lights on again. I almost drove back to your place. Now I'm glad I didn't, because you were working, but there was something else I did want to say."

"Nick—" He could sense her withdrawal.

"Something that I *have* to say." He caught her hand when she would have moved away. "Jess, for twelve years I've missed you. I missed the girl you were, young and filled with hope for the future and so beautiful." His voice turned husky. "I missed the even more beautiful woman, the stronger woman, you've become without me, the woman I held last night." His tone dropped even lower. "But it wasn't until last night that I realized how much I've missed something more, how much I still miss my best friend."

Jess shook her head, but Nick stilled it, cradling her face between his hands. He never stopped to think how dirty they were.

"Ben and I sneaked away from farm chores, played football, and chased girls, but I don't think he and I were ever as close as I felt to you. We had something different, *special*—until I blew it. We had a pure friendship, and I miss that most of all."

"Nick, please"—her voice broke—"don't say any more."

"Jess, can't we be friends again at least?"

"I'm trying to adjust to being neighbors."

Nick tried not to show his disappointment. She had changed. The girl he'd known and loved would have come freely, openly. But at least she hadn't said flatly no.

"First step," he said. "We have to have learned something in twelve years. What do you say?"

Her pause was brief. "I'll sleep on it."

"You're an unforgiving woman, Jess," he said, managing a smile. Then, with a last brush of his thumbs over her cheekbones, reluctantly he let her go.

Not touching, they walked across the yard toward Jess's car. "Where's the Jag?" she asked.

"Back at the leasing agency." He gestured at Tom's red pickup. "That gets me where I have to go, on less gas."

"Spoken like a true, cost-conscious farmer."

He threw her a dark look. "It's one less machine to fix."

"Maybe you should have Greg look at the tractor. He seems good with his hands."

"That depends. He's already jammed up the electric milkers. It seems we have two"—he glanced toward the boys carrying feed sacks into the barn—"no, three carpenters, including me, but no mechanics. He's a good kid. Ben should look closer at him."

"The whole town's heard that you've given Greg a job."

"Heather, Amy, Ben, you," Nick said. "Greg of course. I wouldn't say that's the whole town."

"It's small," Jess reminded him.

Nick laughed, then quickly sobered. He didn't know how she'd take this either. "By the way, Pop's doing great. He'll come home a week from Friday. If you're still willing, I'll need help with him."

"Of course." She smiled, showing the dimple in her left cheek. It was the first time he'd seen it since he'd come back to Carran. "In return, I'll expect you and Tom at Ben's birthday party. You can help me keep Ben from strangling Amy Stone."

"Deal." Then he said, "Let's begin the celebration early. How about dinner tonight? I can throw a chicken in the crockpot. You could bring a salad." He paused. "I'll even keep my hands to myself."

When she hesitated, he saw that even the brief camaraderie had made her uneasy. Friends, he'd said, and he thought she'd missed him, too; now, he knew he'd need all the determination he possessed to get Jess even as far as being friends again.

"Sorry," she finally told him, "I have to work."

"You have to eat, don't you?"

"Not when the computer's humming. I'm on a roll." And with a farewell tap of the horn, she bounced the BMW down the rutted driveway past his father's barn.

In Aaron's barn the light seems softer somehow. There's magic in that barn, I think. Aaron only laughed when I told him. "The magic's you and me, love," he said, and the way he looked at me made my heart jump, made me wonder what it would be like to become Aaron's wife in more than words mumbled by a preacher. . . .

5

Coming back from the barn to the house, Aaron paused often to hold me close. While we were courting, I loved to get near enough to savor his smell, but mostly didn't dare to. Papa always seemed to be watching. He thinks Aaron is too old for me, though there are only six years between us—Aaron turned twenty-five on Sunday last—and it isn't really years. Once Papa said that, being from the farm, Aaron knew too much. When I told him that, he smiled.

"Animals are different from people."

Still, I kept wondering about the night ahead and my own strong yearning for him, which Mama never said I would feel.

So I tried not to think of Mama's preaching last night, or of this first night in Aaron's unfamiliar house, where I won't find my way in the dark without a candle.

His is not a grand house, I didn't expect that.

But as soon as we stepped inside, I thought it a loving one.

The house is frame, unpainted, with big square rooms and a kitchen twice the size of Mama's. The front parlor has whitewashed walls, calico curtains, and a carpet made by Aaron's mother. I can just see Aaron, as his father must have looked, at the head of the beautiful old cherry table, me at its other end, when my parents come to dinner (I'll have to learn to cook first!). There are eight matching chairs, worn to a satiny wood patina, enough for company.

We won't use the parlor much. Mostly we'll gather in the keeping room across the hall, where the chairs are sturdy rush-buttoms and the table's plain, everyday pine with Aaron's brother's name carved at his place, a deed that, Aaron says, laughing, earned James a caning when he was seven.

I wish I had asked Michael—my own older brother—about the night to come, but I wouldn't have dared. Women don't discuss such matters, Mama says, especially with men.

I wasn't sure I wanted to see the bedrooms. Going up the stairs, I felt Aaron's hand lightly brush the small of my back, sending a fluttery feeling through me, like the touch of butterfly wings, and I kept up a chatter that Mama would have hushed me for all the way through each room.

There are four bedrooms around a center hall, all with carpets and spare furnishings. But the beds, I could see, are ample, with goosedown pillows and patchwork summer quilts. His mother made the sheets, all strong, fine linen, snowy white.

In the doorway of the largest room, our room now, Aaron told me, where he'd been born, he framed my face in his strong hands, making me feel small and fragile. "Stop rattling on, love," he murmured, "or I'll think you're full of nerves about our wedding night."

"Stop fidgeting."

"I haven't done this in a long time," Jessie said, her tongue caught between her teeth.

"Neither had I," Nick observed, "until a few weeks ago. Hey, watch out—"

A heavyset Guernsey cow aimed a rear hoof at its own belly, where Jessie's head rested while she adjusted the electric milking machine. Nick dragged her out of reach, then released her.

"I told you, you'd get cow-kicked. You trust these ornery milkers more than you should."

"It's those big brown eyes," she said, looking into Nick's.

Jessie frowned. She'd always trusted everything and everyone more than she should—him especially. She had to remind herself to be careful; if she accepted his friendship again, she would lose her chief protection against further hurt. If she hadn't been daydreaming, imagining the new camaraderie with Nick to be as genuine as Aaron's with his bride, that cow wouldn't have taken her by surprise. She hadn't been away from the farm that long.

"I've been kicked before," she told him, following Nick to the next stanchion and the cow that stood waiting, heavy with milk. "It serves me right, coming over here at the wrong time."

"The right time, as far as I'm concerned." Nick shoved the Guernsey aside, attaching the machine to its udder with only slight fumbling.

"You've improved at this," Jessie said.

He glanced up. "Yeah, but you're still better. Women have a way with animals. Women make the best dairy farmers," he said.

"Oh, please. Save the flattery for those Charleston girls." At least she could see his obvious ploy more easily than she had years ago. "Greg milks fifty, I do a dozen—what's left, Nicholas?"

He grinned. "Can I help it if Pop has twice as big a herd as he should? We need womanpower, and your touch is gentler than Pop's. You used to know his cows by name too, Jess."

When he turned away, fussing with the rubber tube that led to the suction line, she stared at Nick's back, at the play of muscle in his arms and shoulders. Feeling warmth spread through her, she dropped her gaze. His strong hands, no longer red from the raw spring wind, were beginning to tan, and she glanced away, feeling guilty for thoughts that belonged more to her heroine on her wedding night.

Jessie hoped she'd be able to get to the scene itself. She'd had nothing but trouble with her outdated computer. In Scottsdale she'd promised herself a new system, then the divorce had taken over her life, and since she'd come to Carran, she hadn't found time to shop around. She should have made time. Smack in the middle of her second night's work—the night she'd refused to have dinner with Nick—she'd lost the whole first chapter.

The repair shop had kept her damaged disk drive for the better part of two weeks, increasing Jessie's conviction that she had somehow jostled the CPU during the drive from Arizona.

Or had it been Nick's fault? She'd rather think so.

Two weeks ago Jessie had been happily working away, lost in Aaron's pleasure at showing his new wife their home, when she suddenly heard Nick call up the stairs: "Jess, you there? It's dinnertime."

Her first thought had been that she should have known he wouldn't take no for an answer. Then her mouth watered at the feast he'd brought. The Colonel's best chicken, extra crispy; creamy coleslaw and butter-drenched biscuits; and a man-sized slice of still-warm Mrs. Smith's deep dish apple pie. "You fiend," Jessie murmured, searching the picnic basket for the barbecue sauce she knew she'd find. That Nick would remember she craved.

"Eat," he ordered to her amazement.

Her ex-husband wouldn't have thought to feed her in the first place; he would have sulked over his scientific data the entire evening while Jessie fought her guilt at leaving him to make his own dinner. Nick didn't even offer to share her picnic. He had tied a red-and-white-checked napkin around her neck, set the basket at her side, pointed at the glaring computer screen—without bending to read what she'd written—then left her alone. To sink or swim.

Now, watching him recheck the milker, she'd do the same.

"I only stopped by," she said, "to remind you and Tom about Ben's party tomorrow night."

"We'll be there."

"I'm leaving now. My computer's back from the

shop, and I'm in the middle of a hot scene. You're on your own, Farmer Granby."

"Just like that?"

Nick had been monitoring the flow of milk into the unit. Still hunkered down, he didn't glance at her, but his tone was so low, so mild that Jessie wondered whether she'd only imagined the renewed, though tentative, warmth between them, the new teasing.

With the exception of saving her from that cow kick, Nick had been keeping his distance. Even the night he'd brought her dinner, he had taken care not to touch her. When they brushed in passing, Nick always pulled back first, she realized. He kept their conversation light, and those disturbing moments in Jessie's bedroom remained well buried. Why feel disappointed at getting what she'd asked for?

"Just like that," she repeated.

He unhooked the milking unit. "After all this work, on my own, I thought at least you'd feed us tonight."

At his challenging tone, she shifted like the impatient Guernsey. The night Tom had come from the rehabilitation center, a week ago, Jessie had helped Nick settle his father at home, then provided dinner in the wicker picnic basket she returned. Neither man had complained about the tough turkey or the singed stuffing.

Jessie said now, "I wouldn't want to get the habit."

"Spoil us," Nick coaxed.

He gave her a quick glance, all dark eyes and surprising heat. Jessie's pulse kicked up. Aaron would look at his bride that way. She glanced away but found herself staring at Nick's hands, stripping the last milk from the Guernsey's udder. Her breath caught. The act seemed primitive, sensual.

"You're already spoiled," she said. "Both of you."

Too late, she realized she'd misinterpreted Nick's look. She'd seen that look of pure deviltry before—at five years of age, at ten, at fifteen. In one smooth motion of a strong-boned wrist, he twitched the cow's teat at a near ninety-degree angle, squeezed, and shot a stream of warm milk into Jessie's face.

"Damn you, Nicholas Granby!" Milk ran from her eyelashes, dribbled off the tip of her nose onto her bottom lip.

Nick was on his feet, strolling toward her, his eyes sparked with laughter. "Oldest trick in Farmer Granby's book," he said.

Jessie groaned. "You pulled it often enough when I was a kid. I suppose I should have seen that coming."

"You asked for it." He stood too close for Jessie's comfort. His own fingers wet, he gently wiped her cheeks, her mouth, his touch as light as cream. She felt her lips part, and almost swayed into him. Then Nick stepped back. "Sorry, love. I couldn't resist."

Jessie's heart hammered. "You're not the least bit sorry."

She couldn't look at him. If he was still grinning . . .

After using the handkerchief Nick offered from his rear jeans pocket, she handed it back and, without a word, walked toward the barn entrance, feeling Nick's eyes on her.

At dusk the atmosphere was soft, hazy—like Aaron's barn. Jessie saw motes dancing in the last bright light of afternoon, inhaled the aromas she'd loved all her life, felt a part of this place again. Then she mentally shook herself. She'd become lost, that was all, in the world she was creating, lost in daydreams of another place and time.

When she turned in the doorway, she saw Nick leaning against a stall divider, arms crossed over his chest, the sleeves of his blue chambray shirt, now certainly damp, rolled back over muscular forearms.

"I'll see you tomorrow," she said.

He *was* grinning. "That sounds like a threat of retaliation. You're not mad, are you, because I—"

"Better think twice before you take a bite of Ben's cake. You never know what might be in it," Jessie said, not telling him that Amy Stone was doing the baking.

"Jess?"

"Rat poison, fertilizer." Smiling now, she stepped out into the brighter light of the barnyard, enjoying herself; she'd almost stopped waiting for Nick's announcement that he would leave Carran.

"Not a chance," he said, as if in answer.

And Jessie thought, *almost.*

We were almost downstairs again when Aaron stopped to kiss me. He must have felt me trembling. "You needn't be nervous," he said, his tone teasing. "It's still daylight. And you haven't seen the cellar."

The cellar runs beneath the whole house here, not like Papa's in town, which is a half cellar, all that's needed. Aaron's house—our house—has two barrels still of beef stored there from autumn and two more of pork, so he assured me we won't starve before harvest. There are ten

barrels of cider too, and bins of potatoes, tur-
nips, beets, carrots, and cabbages. I told him
Papa shouldn't worry about me.

"I suppose a man always worries about his
daughters as a matter of course," Aaron said,
guiding me back up the cellar steps. "I suppose
I will, too."

His soft words, like a promise, made me
swallow. Papa had no reason for concern; I was
worried enough about myself and the night
ahead for both of us.

In the kitchen Aaron put the kettle on to boil,
then soothed away my frown, though there was
nothing he could do about the warmth still
staining my cheeks. He looked at me for a long
moment until I had to ask why he was staring.

"Because I want to remember this, today,
when you first belong to me . . . with your dark
hair in ringlets, your gray eyes soft and a little
frightened, my own Elizabeth," he murmured,
"sitting at my table in your wedding dress, sipping tea with me."

"I haven't any tea," I said, my heart thumping.

Aaron flushed. "Oh. I forgot."

We have a real cookstove in our house, and
the water had boiled quickly, but after Aaron
fixed our tea, I could only stare at the steaming
cup.

"Don't you like it?" he asked. "You don't
have to drink it if you'd rather not."

Trying to show him that I did, I burnt my
tongue. "Oh, Aaron, we don't seem ourselves
somehow."

"We don't look like ourselves today," he pointed out, making me laugh. It was true.

I glanced down at white lace over yellow silk, my skirt double-flounced, with crinolines, the most beautiful dress I've ever owned or am ever likely to. My soft kid slippers were mud-spattered now from the trip to the barn.

Then I looked at Aaron in his new dark trousers, waistcoat and frock coat, his white shirt with one of those new, detachable collars looking tight as his city shoes, his handsome face pinched as if the black cravat might choke him.

"I'm scared," I admitted.

Aaron cleared his throat. "If you want the truth, so am I."

How could he not know what the night would bring? I wondered. He has his reputation with the ladies, just as my brother Michael does, and they are friends.

But Aaron's tone grew serious. "There've been a few women, love, but no one like you. Never you before. That makes tonight just as new for me," he said.

And my fears seemed to melt—temporarily at least. Aaron was nervous, too.

"Then we'll learn together," I said.

My own boldness shocked me. I think it shocked him, too. For some time we didn't look at each other. My gaze sought the yard beyond the kitchen window, imagining the rows of squash, cucumbers, parsnips, and beans. But the light had failed, I couldn't see that far, and my heart fluttered. Failing light meant . . . what?

The pleasure I'd only glimpsed in Aaron's

arms before? Or the agony Mama warned me I must endure?

At six o'clock the next evening, Jessie groaned. Aaron's wedding night scene had just ground to a halt, and she had no more time to work. Shutting down the computer, she cast a baleful glance at the sky outside, darkening too early for sunset, and prayed aloud: "Let the rain hold off until everyone's gone home."

She couldn't imagine stuffing Gran's house to its dusty rafters with all the party guests who'd been threatening to show up: Ben's assistant principal, his wife, and four kids; half a dozen high school buddies with whom he and Nick had played football; an ex-girlfriend from Bridgeport; assorted teachers, who felt they "ought to drop by and make brownie points with the old man"; and Jessie's grammar school English teacher, who'd heard she was in town and wanted to talk to her about "the more lascivious parts" of her most recent novel.

And that wasn't counting the invited guests. Jessie was already rolling her eyes. She had no idea how the others had learned about the party.

Jessie wasn't in a party mood. Quickly changing from shirt and jeans to an off-white lacy sweater and linen slacks, she gritted her teeth and went outside.

Soon, cars crowded the drive and bright blankets spotted the front lawn. Along with the gas barbecue grill, one of the football buddies had ignited his cutoff sweatshirt ("The way to a man's heart," it read, "is through his fly"). And someone's two-year-old had stepped on a broken soda bottle. Thank heaven, the cut was small.

Tossing a box of Big Bird Band-aids toward the

distraught mother, Jessie jerked around at a truck horn's blast behind her as Tom Granby's pickup crunched to a halt in the driveway, not six inches from her fanny.

"The best defense," Nick said, climbing from the driver's seat, "is a good offense." He slung an arm around Jessie's shoulder. "This looks like a Billy Graham tent revival meeting. Where'd all these people come from?"

"Tell me," Jessie murmured, allowing herself to lean against him for a moment.

Nick grinned. "Small-town gossip."

"Ah, I should have guessed." The other truck door opened on squealing hinges, and she turned to greet Tom, who was trying to step down by himself. "Careful, there. The yard's uneven. I wouldn't want you to fall and end up in that stuffy hospital again just when your hay's up and the corn's almost rustling in the field across from me."

Nick took his other side, and Jessie snugged Tom's shoulder against her armpit.

"Wish I'd got sick before this," Tom said. "I've never had so much pretty female attention."

"It's gone to his head." Nick planted Tom's foot on the bottom porch step. "Pop, you should save yourself for some of those Southern belles. Next winter in Charleston—"

"I'm partial to Yankee women," Tom said, winking at Jessie, "to cold New England winters with plenty of ice and snow."

"We'll see."

A prickle of irritation crept up Jessie's spine. If Nick wasn't baiting Tom, then his father was goading Nick.

"Could we have a peaceful birthday party, please?" she asked, helping Tom into a maple rocking chair on her grandmother's porch.

"That depends on the big boss, the hotshot here."

"I doubt it," Nick said. Her answering glare swept past him as Nick pointed toward the lane in front of the house where Ben's gray Chevrolet pulled to a stop, nose to tail with a bright red Miata. Amy Stone's, Jessie realized.

"Help me," she said. "You promised."

"And you promised to feed me rat poison, as I recall."

Jessie raised imploring eyes to his. "I was kidding. See?"

She waved at Amy, struggling up the uneven slate walk, one hand balancing a gaily wrapped package, the other a Tupperware cake holder. Ben was already scowling.

"I'll do what I can," Nick said, his tone implying that he meant to extract payment.

Jessie didn't care. When Nick dragged Ben off to help set up the volleyball net in the side yard, she would gladly have milked every cow in Tom's barn, twice each day for a week.

Soon a lively game was in progress, allowing Jessie to slip back into the kitchen to put the finishing touches on a huge bowl of potato salad, and—she hoped—an end to her sour mood.

"Are we having fun yet?"

At Amy Stone's wry tone, Jessie's measure of coffee missed the pot. The volleyball game had paused while everyone ate, and now that it had resumed, she was back in the kitchen, brewing Nick's caffeine high and staring into a sink full of dirty dishes.

"This is supposed to be a party, not a wake," Amy added, bending to peer into Jessie's downcast face. "I realize my cake slid slightly eastward in that gooey chocolate-nut frosting, but it tasted great. And Ben may have looked apoplectic for a few minutes after blowing out all those candles, but he did it. Successful party. So what's the problem?"

"I wish I knew," Jessie said and shrugged.

Glancing out the window, she smiled faintly as a little girl, shirttails flapping and bare feet pounding, caught her baby brother at the out-of-bounds line for the volleyball court. The ball sailed over the children's heads, the baby laughed, and a cheer went up. Nick had scored another point.

"Look at that," Amy said. Jessie followed her pointing finger. Heather and Greg, arms around each other, were sharing Gran's old rope swing in the maple tree, as if observing the game, but frequently they touched, nuzzling noses, then tilting heads to gently kiss. Jessie felt a wave of physical desire, then a fresh one of misery she couldn't explain.

"Ben would have a fit," she murmured.

"Heather's lucky he's too busy to notice."

In a tangle of brawny arms and legs, Nick and Ben had collided at the net. It was almost too dark now, with dusk and the heavy thunderclouds gathering overhead, to see the ball.

"I hope he's enjoying himself," Jessie said.

"Ben?"

"I worry about him. He's forgotten how to laugh, and he and Greg . . ." She shook her head. "But I haven't seen so many other people having such a good time in this yard since my grandmother was alive."

"I hope you had a better time then yourself." Amy turned Jessie from the sink. "Come on, you've done your drudge work for one night. I'll help you clean this up later. While the light lasts, the home team needs your serving arm. Let's play ball."

"Slave driver."

"Party animal," Amy corrected, steering her into the yard.

The sky kept darkening, but the game went on. Jessie and Amy played against Ben and Nick, which suited her lingering mood.

Even victory didn't lift Jessie's spirits. Dread had been dogging her footsteps all night, just as Sunbeam, the cow she'd owned as a child, had followed her everywhere. She glanced at the sea of happy faces all around, at the brief glow of red as Tom lit a forbidden pipe. Why dread? she wondered.

"The kids are gone." Ben spoke urgently at her shoulder, and Jessie jumped.

"Gone where?"

"Damned if I know. They just disappeared." He ran a hand over his short brown hair.

Jessie thought of the tender kisses she'd seen through the window. "I'm sure they're fine. Just kids."

Amy came across the yard. Giving Jessie's brother a long look, she smiled slowly. "You're cute when you're angry. But you worry too much, Ben."

He stared at her, then scowled. "You don't worry enough." His blue eyes dark, he turned away.

"Leave them alone." Amy stepped in front of him. "Benjamin Pearce, you have far too much suspicion in that sterling character of yours. Stop playing high school principal for one night, will you? I'd bet that boy has never given you a serious moment's concern, and Heather is a good girl."

"I'd think you'd want her to stay that way."

Amy made a strangled sound. "Haven't you ever been in love? For the first time? When it's more romance than passion?"

Jessie couldn't miss his dark sweep of Amy's form. She'd seen him sneaking glances during the volleyball game, too.

"I've been in love," he said, his jaw set. "You damn well know it, you tried hard enough to—"

Trying not to smile, Jessie stepped between them. "Ben, Amy, they can't have gone far. Greg's car is still out front. They'll be back soon."

Lightning flashed overhead, and the sky rumbled.

"We're going to have a storm," Ben said, "any minute."

"Looks like we've already had one." Grinning, Nick joined them. "Here, drown your sorrows." He tossed a beer at Ben, and a meaningful look at her. "Jess and I will find the kids for you."

Picking up the cue, she quickly agreed. "Of course we will."

With a quick tug at her hand, Nick set off toward the front of the house, out of Ben's sight. "They're in the barn," he said.

"Then why are we walking in the opposite direction?"

"To give your brother the slip. Amy'd come after him, he'd lecture all the way—like the fine educator he is. Do you really want to hear more of that?"

"No," she said and grinned as he hadn't seen her smile all night.

"We'll give the kids just enough time, but not too much." Jess's hair, worn loose, spread over his shirt front, his sleeve, and Nick's heart went racing. "A few kisses, all lips but no tongue."

She sounded breathless. "I think it's gone beyond that already."

Nick felt his features tighten into the same sharp expression he had just seen on Ben's face. He'd been pretty hot-blooded himself at Greg's age. With Jess, he still was. "Then why didn't you say so?"

"I just did."

Heather and Greg were in the hayloft. Nick heard their soft rustlings, the softer sighs as soon as he and Jess stepped into Caroline Pearce's ramshackle barn.

Nick's voice echoed in the sudden silence. "Greg?"

"Heather?" Jess tried.

More silence.

"Greg Pearce, get your butt down out of that loft or, so help me God, I'll turn you over to Ben and you can consider yourself fired!"

The order, issued in a no-compromise-considered tone, brought a slender, flush-faced girl with tousled honey brown hair and a suntanned but red-necked boy to the hayloft ladder, which was missing two rungs. Nick's earlier acceptance of the romance had vanished.

"Get down here. Both of you."

Greg dared a smile that made Nick want to knock his teeth down his throat. "Hey, listen, we just—"

"Don't bother. You shouldn't be in here. This place is a firetrap. And watch your step, that ladder's not safe."

Eyes cast down, Greg yanked Heather away from a gaping hole that had been half-hidden by straw.

Boards creaked as he helped her climb down to the barn floor. Heather's lips were swollen, moist, and Nick watched her press them tightly together as if to hide the evidence of what she'd been doing. He felt the kick in his own gut.

"I'm disappointed in you, Greg," he said, then not getting a response, hardened his tone. "Look at me when I'm talking to you. Heather is a very young girl. Her mother cares for her deeply and won't see her hurt. Neither will I."

"You think *I* don't care?"

Nick put a hand on his shoulder. "I'm sure you do. But you had no business hauling her up to that hayloft. Caring turns into something else pretty fast in the dark, all alone. Take Heather back to the party and have her cut you another piece of that chocolate cake. And don't disappear again, all right?"

"Yes, sir."

Nick heard the edge in Greg's tone.

"You don't have to like me for it, just do as I tell you. And think about getting home soon. We have cows to milk at first light and one due to drop a calf any minute now. I may need your help, so stay by the phone."

"I don't know anything about birthing," Greg muttered.

Nick almost smiled. "Neither did Scarlett O'Hara. You don't have to. If you want to be a farmer, you'll learn."

With a curt nod, Greg drew Heather toward the barn doors, open only a foot or so on their sliding tracks. Lightning split the sky outside, and the sound of thunder rolled in. As Greg shoved the door wider, Nick called him back.

"Knock that two-by-four off your shoulder before tomorrow morning, kid. Believe it or not, I know what it feels like to be young—and in love."

As soon as Greg and Heather were gone, he turned to Jess with a sigh. "Am I a hypocrite, or what?"

"Excuse me?"

He should have known she'd blame him. "You think I was too hard on them?"

"A little."

"Hell, maybe I was. Young or not so young, control hasn't always been my strong suit either."

Yesterday, he thought. In his father's barn, he'd watched Jess milking cows in her tight blue jeans, her gingham shirttails tied at her slim waist, her hair twisted into a loose knot that begged his fingers to free it, his eyes to watch it tumble down, and he'd come close to losing it again. He'd promised her friendship, nothing more demanding than that. For weeks he'd kept his hands to himself. He'd hunkered by that cow yesterday after he finished milking, not to embarrass himself by standing up and letting her see the erection in his jeans. He'd aimed that cow teat at her in teasing, in friendship, but mainly to keep from grabbing her and kissing her senseless. And he'd been tied up in knots himself ever since. He wondered whether she'd guessed; whether she was still mad at him for almost overstepping the bounds he'd marked himself. And tonight . . .

"The orchard," she said, her tone husky, "was a mistake, one we agreed to forget, Nick."

He saw pain in her eyes. "Ah, Jess, I didn't mean *you* were a mistake. Is that what you've been thinking? Nothing could be farther from the truth." He stepped closer, caught the faint drift of her perfume, soft and flowery. "The mistake was mine," but she only shook her head. Nick stilled the motion with both hands. "I wanted you then. I've never stopped wanting you. The past few weeks . . . ever since he came home, Pop says I'm like a bull with his tail caught in the gate. Christ, every time I see those kids"—he glanced toward the barn door—"with their hands all over each other, Heather's eyes soft, Greg's hard with need plain enough to knock you over . . ."

"Nick." She gripped his wrists with cold fingers.

"I get crazy, Jess, just like those kids. I get so . . ."

Hard, he thought but couldn't say that. He looked at the floor. The scattered straw must have been there since Jess's parents had died, and the farm had gone fallow. Seventeen years at least. The year of Nick's final rift with Tom about coming home, to farm, instead of becoming an architect.

"I'm sorry," he said, then, "Jess, I have something else to tell you."

"You're leaving."

At her flat tone, he lifted his gaze to hers. "I'm flying to Charleston tomorrow. There's a crisis on that coastal development project. The wetlands conservationists are crying destruction of habitat, eighteen months too late, the local population has been circulating petitions. My assistant can't hold everyone at bay by himself. But I'll be back," he said, wondering whether she cared.

"Spring planting's done." She looked away. "Greg and his friend should be able to do the work from now on."

Nick's jaw tightened. "The boys need supervision."

"Tom seems stronger every day. He can tell them what to do."

Maybe she'd just been waiting for him to get out of her life again. "Look, nobody's happier than I am to see Pop doing well—not even you," he said. "But he can only do so much without sapping his energy, risking the progress he's made." He put a finger under her chin. "Or isn't that the point, Jess? You've been down all evening, keeping clear of me. Glad, are you, to see the back of me at last?"

"I didn't say—"

"You're right, planting's done. Why do you think I've stayed after it was finished?"

"You said you'd been overworked in Charleston."

"Yeah, and I've had some vacation here, haven't I?"

"A beneficial change of scene," she said.

"Bullshit." He tipped her chin until she had to look at him. "We agreed to try being friends again, at least. I wanted to make the most of that." With one finger, he traced a feather-light line over her mouth, over the spot on her left cheek where the dimple would be if she smiled. "We are friends, aren't we?"

She didn't answer.

"Aren't we, Jess?"

"Yes!"

Nick breathed again. "And you'll miss me while I'm gone?"

"You can be a bastard," she murmured without pulling away.

"Miss me even a little?"

"Yes, damn you!"

"Then believe me when I tell you that I'm coming back."

Framing her face once more in his hands, he felt the rumble of thunder vibrate down his arms, through his palms, to her cheeks. She took a shaken breath, her eyes fixed on his. Defiant. Then slowly, she laced her fingers at the nape of his neck and pulled his head down, by inches, until her mouth met his.

The kiss stayed light, Nick's hands cradling her face even lighter. Then her lips opened, she slanted her mouth to deepen the contact, and he groaned. "Yes, kiss me good-bye. Kiss me good-bye, and mean it." His tongue slipped inside, tasting, exploring, tantalizing hers. His breathing quickened. His arms tightened around her. Jess's fingers stroked his neck, his shoulders, and he felt himself losing control.

"God, Jess."

But she let him take command, draw her deeper, until thunder cracked again overhead, like caution.

For Nick, that only made things worse. The scent of her skin, its feel as sleek as watered silk, her mouth, hot and loose . . .

"I'm coming back," he said, his hands moving down her spine, then up again, "and when I do, we'll settle this."

His breath rushed in his ears like sea waves, blocking out all other sound. Curious. It started soft, gathering strength and volume and tempo until it became a hard, pelting roar that filled his body and the very barn in which they stood. Suddenly Jess tensed, and Nick's mouth stilled against her throat.

Then he raised his head and his eyes met hers, full of terror. The pounding in his blood hadn't been just his feeling for her, and it wasn't simple rain.

"Hail," he said, already running for the barn door. "Jess, we've got a fucking hailstorm!"

6

"*Jess, get in* the house!"

"I'm going with you!"

Her footsteps pounding at his heels, Jessie raced Nick for Tom's red pickup. The yard was already empty. While she and Nick had been locked in each other's arms, the rain had started and people had gathered blankets, beer bottles, and babies and headed inside. Gran's old house had ended up stuffed to its rafters after all.

"Greg! Ben!" Nick shouted but never broke stride. He ripped the truck's driver door open at the same instant Jessie fell onto the passenger seat, breath heaving.

Hail the size of golf balls thundered against the roof and windshield, which Jessie feared would shatter.

"What do you expect to save?" she shouted above the storm.

Yet she'd grown up on the farm, and knew how

discriminating a hailstorm could be. It might plow a path down one side of a farm lane, destroying everything in sight, but leave the opposite fields untouched.

"The cows are out."

As Nick accelerated, Jessie's door was flung open and Ben threw himself inside, rubbing his head. "Damn stuff's like cannon balls. Greg drove Heather home. I all but tied Tom to the banister. I'm coming with you."

Several other cars were pulling out of the yard behind them, but Nick barreled down the road in the lead, fishtailing the pickup in front of Tom's barn. He hit the ground running. The terrified bawling of cattle filled the rainswept air. Nick, Jessie, and Ben raced for the nearest paddock, their backs and shoulders stinging from the hail that pounded them. They were already herding cows through the rear barn doors when the rest of the men arrived.

"Dammit, I didn't think we'd have rain this soon. Watch his hind end," Nick warned.

"Hell, *God*, sonofa—" Ben hopped on one foot. "I always knew I'd be better off as a teacher. Darn thing stepped on me!"

"This one's pregnant," Jessie said, grabbing a Guernsey's halter. "And bleeding. There's a bad gash in her side."

Nick took over. "Find me some adhesive, the wide stuff." He hauled the cow inside, nudging and yanking her down the barn aisle. "Get the gauze, Betadine wash, iodine and antibiotic cream, needles and gut. You know the first-aid cabinet, Jess."

More than one cow had been hurt. The barbed wire cuts, the anxious milling of frightened animals in their stalls, kept everyone busy until midnight. By then the hail had stopped, the storm had changed into a steady rain, Greg had come from town to help, and Nick sent Ben, their football buddies, and the assistant principal back to Jessie's to collect their families.

Her arms fiery with red welts, her body aching from physical exertion, she stood beside Nick in the barn doorway, watching the red glow of taillights down the drive and sipping at a cup of cold coffee. Without the cream and sugar she preferred, it was still the best she'd ever had, even if she had perked it herself in Tom's kitchen.

She said with a sigh, "Just listen to that gentle rain." Actually it was coming down in torrents, but it wasn't hail and sounded, by comparison, peaceful.

"Skip the optimism," Nick said. "I'm just glad it's pitch dark in the fields, so I don't have to look at things until morning." He rubbed the back of his neck. "I could sure use another cup of coffee, though. Make it strong."

"Is there any other way?" Beyond the glaring barnyard lights, Greg was helping Nick's father from the car into the house. Jessie assessed the dull glaze of exhaustion in Nick's eyes. "Stay on your feet. I'll be right back."

"Thanks."

Letting Tom's kitchen counter hold her up, Jessie was waiting for fresh coffee to brew when Nick slammed through the back door moments later, his color high, his eyes so alert they snapped. "Jess, grab your nurse's cap, and get back to the barn. Bring that coffee pot. Don't let Pop come with you. Where's Greg? Greg!" he shouted then turned to her. "Damn cow with the foot-long slice in her side? The one we stitched? She's in labor."

"Is she due?"

"Overdue. Looks bad. She's down in the stall, but nothing else is happening. It might be breech. And the vet's out on another call, or three dozen. His wife said it seemed everybody in the county'd been calling."

She paled. It had been a long time since she'd helped birth a calf, and never as a child had she been allowed to watch a difficult labor. Too many calves died, too many cows, and Jessie had never been much good at dealing with death. She decided that tonight wouldn't be her first loss, as far as Tom's Guernseys were concerned.

An hour later she wasn't so sure. Crouched across from Nick, she watched his face tighten.

"Easy," he crooned, "easy does it," one arm up to its elbow inside the laboring cow. "Damn." With his free hand, he patted the cow's swollen side. "Sorry, girl. I bet it hurts. It'll be over soon."

Jessie knew that labor should be reasonably quick and uneventful, that under normal circumstances, in nature's fashion, the cow did most of the work. But if the calf faced the wrong way in the vagina, as Nick feared, either a vet's skill was needed, or the devil's own luck. Without either, Nick had finally decided to try an internal examination. "Otherwise," he'd said, "I'm going to have to call Pop out here for a consult." With a wide-eyed Greg holding supplies, Jessie had helped Nick strip off his shirt, then wash, disinfect, and lubricate his arm.

Now he groaned and said, "That's it. Not breech, just caught. Believe it or not, this calf's elbow's snagged on the rim of its mama's pelvis." Frowning, he twisted his arm, then at last withdrew it. Jessie quickly wiped the blood and mucus off his skin.

Then they waited.

On his knees, Greg came to attention first. "Nick, the calf's coming! Look, Jessie! I see both its legs and— Wow! Awesome," he breathed.

Jessie couldn't have agreed more. Lack of sleep, the hours of profanity-filled toil earlier, the too-long wait now, worry—all were instantly forgotten in the age-old miracle of birth. The Guernsey heaved one last time, and a dark, wet mass slid onto the stall's clean hay bed. But then there was no time for joy, or any other emotion. Jessie blinked once, but Nick was already moving.

With both hands, he swept the birth sac from the calf's nose and mouth. "Thatta baby, there you go." With Jessie's help, he cleared the remaining membranes away. "We have ourselves a girl, Jess! Come on, sweetie, breathe."

Silence.

Nick and Jessie exchanged glances. "She's had a rough time," she murmured, frowning.

Prying the calf's mouth open, Nick swept two fingers around inside, while Jessie wiped mucus from its nostrils. "Breathe, dammit." He began massaging the still body.

"She's so limp, Nick."

"Yeah. Greg, get me a rag, will you? A feed sack's fine."

Minutes passed, but nothing seemed to work.

"Aw, shit," Nick finally said, sitting back on his heels. "Goddammit, I hate this. I've always hated it."

"Don't give up." Jessie remembered his gentleness with Sunbeam, the 4-H calf he'd given her; she'd just seen his tenderness with the laboring cow. Things couldn't turn out wrong now. "I thought I saw her take a breath, Nick."

"Want me to try?" Greg asked.

Nick hung his head. "She's dead, stillborn. Forget it."

"No!" The hell she would. Jessie gave Nick a hard shove. She'd buried her parents, she'd buried Gran; she'd even, in a different way, buried Peter. And Nick. "You want to be a quitter, Nicholas Granby, go ahead. With this farm, you were always a quitter. That's how you ended up a carpetbagger in Charleston. But I won't quit! I won't!"

"Jess—"

Ripping the feed sack from his hands, she nudged Nick aside, rubbing the scratchy burlap over the wet form on the hay, and then over again until her fingers oozed blood, but still she kept going.

"Jess, for Christ's sake—"

"I won't stop, just shut up. I won't!"

"*Jess*, she's breathing!"

Jessie stared, blinked, then stared again. "Nick, yes! She's trying to get up!" She touched his arm. "We did it—oh, my God, we really did it!"

With Greg on one side, Nick on the other, and Jessie in the middle, they watched the tiny calf struggle for the first time onto four wobbly legs. By the time it took a tentative step, knees comically buckling then locking into place, by the time it bleated a first pathetic cry and nuzzled its mother's teat, tears were streaming down Jessie's cheeks.

With a murmur, Nick pulled her onto his lap, into his arms. "You're one helluva farmer, love. The doc couldn't have done better."

"Jeez," Greg said, sniffing. "If you're all gonna cry, I'm out of here. And if you're gonna kiss her, Nick, just make sure you keep out of the hayloft."

"Smart-mouth kid." Jessie felt Nick's grin against her hair before she freed herself from his embrace, and stood.

Her throat felt tight. Now that the excitement had passed, Nick's bare chest, his arms around her felt too good, made her remember their kisses in Gran's barn. "It's late. I should go home." She glanced at the cow, nursing the tiny calf. "Do you think they'll be all right?"

"Right as . . ." He laughed. "I was about to say rain," Nick said. "They'll be fine. Let me finish up, then I'll drive you home. Greg, why don't you spend what's left of the night here? You can sleep in my bed, I'll bunk down on the sofa." Jessie mumbled something about washing out the coffee pot, but when she turned to go, Nick snagged her wrist. "Thanks, friend. You saved a life tonight. It's all yours."

"Mine? What—?"

"I want you to have the calf. You can move her to Caroline's when she's weaned."

"What will Tom say?"

Nick shrugged into his shirt. "He'll say, 'Why didn't I think of that?' "

Her hand drifted to his cheek. "You knew I was remembering Sunbeam, didn't you?"

With a half smile, he looked away. "So was I."

They'd shared something special, Jessie thought, and she didn't want to let it go. At four in the morning, she decided she owed him more coffee for a start—and breakfast. She wouldn't take no for an answer.

"Come on, Jess, look at me." In her driveway Nick turned in the pickup's front seat. "I washed my hands, but the rest of me's a mess."

Jessie glanced down at her own clean hands, her bloodstained clothes. "We could . . . take turns showering."

His eyes darkened. "Not a good idea, love."

He had a point. Wondering why she was so willing to court intimacy just when Nick was leaving, she took a breath. She'd been too aware of him all night, even before their kisses in Gran's barn. "I'm a grown woman. And we're just friends, remember? Besides, at your house everyone's sleeping. We brought life into this world last night. On the scale of importance, a couple of showers hardly compares."

"I don't have fresh clothes," Nick protested weakly.

"My father's jeans are still hanging in his closet." At Nick's incredulous look, she grimaced. "I know. Peculiar, isn't it? But Gran would never pack them away. My mother's things, either. Though if you're squeamish about wearing them . . ."

Nick grinned. "You shower first. I'll put on the coffee. My tongue's still curling from that last batch you made."

Jessie let the hot water pour over her, easing her aches and stings, if not the guilt she'd begun to feel. When she'd patted her skin dry and slathered aloe cream everywhere, she dressed in fresh jeans and a navy ribbed sweater against the predawn chill, and went downstairs. If she and Nick were really friends again, she owed him not only breakfast but an apology.

"I didn't mean to call you a quitter," she said, her stomach rumbling at the rich smell of coffee brewing.

He stood at the kitchen sink, rinsing Jessie's favorite mug. He didn't turn around.

"I was wrong, Nick. Caught up in the moment, afraid the calf would die and there was nothing I—we—could do to save it. I shouldn't have said what I did, and I'm sorry."

Drying the mug, he set it on the table, where two place settings of Jessie's sunflower-pattern dishes had been laid. He looked at her.

Jessie frowned. "I'd say tenacious was a better word. When you decide what you really want, you go after it." Amy had said just that.

She watched his index finger play around the rim of the mug, slow and light, like a caress. "I've always known what I wanted, Jess."

She promised herself she wouldn't say it, then said it anyway. "Charleston."

Nick's jaw tightened.

"But right now, you're in need of a scalding hot shower while I fix eggs Benedict." It was his favorite. "Go," she said, opening the refrigerator. "I bought fresh brown eggs yesterday at the farm stand on the highway. I have slices of Canadian bacon as thin as"—she paused—"the premise of my new book. It'll melt in your mouth, so . . ."

Nick sighed. "Don't tell me you make your own hollandaise, Jess. I won't believe you."

"Then I won't tell you."

His boots clumped toward the hallway. "An unforgiving woman," Nick murmured, "but one who knows that the way to a man's heart is through his—"

"Fly, according to your old football buddy."

"Close," Nick said, "but compared to eggs Benedict, no cigar. I'll be clean and hungry in two minutes."

Moving about the kitchen, Jessie hummed to herself. Maybe she didn't really hate cooking; she simply hated cooking for herself. Hated taking the time when she wanted to be writing. In the pantry she found a packet of hollandaise mix. Maybe it wasn't the closeness she and Nick had shared over the calf, the tempting but unwise kisses, or apology that inspired domesticity; maybe it was her newest mini-writer's block. Having stalled just before Ben's party on Aaron's scene, Jessie decided she wasn't eager to face the computer again. . . . *failing light meant . . . what?* How did a young bride feel on her wedding night?

"The sun's dropping," Aaron murmured. Then he stayed quiet for so long that I had to look up and meet his eyes. They're such beautiful eyes, too beautiful for a man, Mama says. Blue, but at the same time, green, and thickly lashed. In the fading light, those lashes made long shadows across his cheek, over the taut, high bones. I could look into Aaron's eyes forever, and I plan to.

"What are you smiling at?" he asked.

"Our wedding day."

"It's not over yet."

"That's why I'm smiling, Aaron."

He grinned. "Ah, I've a trollop on my hands, it seems." He helped me from the table. "Well, we can sit in the parlor if you're not ready to eat those meat pies your mother sent and savories and vegetables, or . . ."

"Or what?"

Aaron drew me near. "We can see how you like my mother's linen-making."

Even I knew what he meant, and my heart sped faster. Aaron's head began to lower, hiding some new, dark purpose in his eyes, and the breath wouldn't come to my lungs. Suddenly I didn't feel so bold. "But it's not dark, quite."

"Dark enough," he said, then kissed me, and my knees went weak. "Farmers, even farmers on their honeymoon, have to get up early. Besides, I can't wait," he told me, his voice husky. "I've waited over a year as it is."

"Aaron," I said helplessly, feeling now like a convict going to the gallows. Would he stay patient with me when he learned how hopeless I was? Could he overcome my trembling? Were my feelings for him shameful, or as right as they felt inside? Was it really a matter of duty, as Mama said, of duty or—?

"Please," he whispered, "now, love. Please."

And because I wanted to learn what it was all about as much as I dreaded the finding out, I let him take me upstairs, holding the lamp high to light my way in the shadowy dusk of our wedding day. Aaron pushed the bedroom door shut and doused the light, and we were alone in the last ribbon of soft, rosy sunset, alone together as we'd never been before.

Whispering my name, he planted kisses along my throat to the neckline of the yellow silk dress. His fingers sought the first button down the back, making my whole body shake with pleasure, and terror.

The button slid free. Moving the fabric aside,

his lips pressed warm, bare skin. "No, please,"
I cried. "Mama said . . ."

"What did she say, love?" Aaron's breath,
warm and fast, sent shudders over my skin.

"That they . . . that she and Papa have never,
in twenty-four years together, I mean, they've
never seen each other . . ."

"Naked?" Aaron murmured in disbelief.

I felt the hot color clear to my toes. "Yes."

"Your mama's wrong," he said. "Naked is
how God made us." The next button eased free,
and the next until, from behind, Aaron's hands
slipped inside the dress, around my corseted
waist, and I wondered why I didn't stop him.
He kissed a soft, moist trail from shoulder to
shoulder. "I *want* to see you. I want to touch
and—"

"Aaron, I don't think I can. Please!"

Would it hurt? Could I bear it? Would Aaron
be angry with me if I couldn't? And in the morning, oh, how would I face him in the morning, in
the light?

Dawn broke over the horizon, promising a sunny
day after the storm. In the kitchen Jessie poured coffee
at both places, and the eggs were keeping warm in the
pan, but Nick hadn't come down. She'd heard the
shower stop ten minutes ago. Perhaps he couldn't
find the jeans and flannel shirt she'd laid across her
bed.

"Jess?" she heard Nick call.

She hurried to the second floor, where the bathroom door stood open, steam wafting out into the
cool hall. Her bedroom was empty and so was her

parents', where Nick might have looked himself for clean clothes.

"In here," he said.

Jessie turned, finding him fully dressed where she'd least expected to: in her office. Her nerves stretched taut. Nick lay on her only concession, other than her computer and the microwave, to modernity here: Jessie's eggshell-linen-covered futon in its lounge position. She loved to sprawl there herself while reading manuscripts. Which was exactly what Nick had been doing.

The pages were still in his hand, his dark eyes intense, and Jessie's pulse skipped several beats.

His gaze holding hers, he stood and walked toward her. Without speaking, he took her in his arms, pressing her tightly to the quick, hard beat of his heart, his mouth against her hair, her cheek. He kissed both corners of her mouth, then lifted his head to stare at her again.

"What?" Jessie murmured.

"You promised me Chapter One."

"When it was ready, I said." Her hands clenched at her sides. "If you wanted to—"

"Why wouldn't you think I'd want to, Jess?"

She shrugged. "Peter rarely read my work. I doubted you'd be interested."

"Wasn't he?"

"Not very."

"Tell me."

"The books—the time they took—were just one of my shortcomings on his list." She tried to step away.

Nick pulled her closer. "I thought as much."

"My work interfered, he always said, with 'more important things.' Like his work, I suppose." He'd belittled her in teasing tones, so Jessie couldn't take offense without appearing overly sensitive, but she couldn't tell Nick about the humiliation she'd felt anyway. Jessie made a wry face. "Let's not talk about it, please. Or I'll get another terminal writer's block."

She glanced toward the futon, still uneasy about letting anyone see her drafts. "Where's my manuscript, Nick?"

"Here." His hands were laced at the small of her back, and she heard pages rustle.

"I—have you read it?"

"Yeah."

"All of it?"

"Yeah," he said.

She looked up into his dark eyes again, then closed hers. Disbelief edged her tone. "And it . . . turned you on?"

"Oh, *yeah.*"

Jessie tried a laugh. "Well. I've never had that reaction before." The laugh caught in her throat. "It's only rough draft, Nick. I did a quick edit right after I printed out, but there's a lot of fixing to do, I'm never satisfied with—"

"Jess, be quiet."

He opened his hands, letting the manuscript pages fall to the old turkeywork carpet, scattering over its surface like seeds blown to the wind. Bending, he kissed her, both corners of her mouth again, then her lower lip, drawing it lightly between his teeth. Finally he let his mouth close over hers, immersing Jessie in magic, in the world he'd borrowed, ironically, from her.

In seconds she'd forgotten her embarrassment, the sense that her privacy had been violated, that she might be hurt again. Nick had read her pages, those imperfect pages she'd fretted over, and he liked them. The emotion there had worked, and she would trust it now. It pulled her in too, sensation after rich sensation drowning her. "Nick," she moaned.

Still kissing, he backed her toward the futon. Nick's hands played at the hem of her sweater, edging along her bared waist, then sliding upward until he found her breasts. Jessie's nipples knotted, at first from the rush of cool air over them, then even more from the warm touch of his fingers, tugging. With a moan, she helped him raise the navy cotton over her shoulders.

The sweater thrown aside, Nick stared at her dusky nipples, at the breasts Jessie had always thought too small. When she flushed under his intent regard, and tried to cover herself, he drew her hands away. "Let me, Jess. I want to see you," he whispered. "I want to touch and—"

Jessie groaned. They were Aaron's words. Did he know he'd even said them?

"I don't think—"

"It's all right," he said and placed her hands on his borrowed shirt. "Please, Jess."

Swiftly unbuttoning it, she eased the soft, worn flannel from his shoulders, her fingers brushing his hard rib cage, a flat brown nipple. Like hers it tightened instantly, and she heard, felt, him suck in a breath.

As Jessie pushed the shirt down his work-hardened arms, her pulse beat frantically, and his next kiss, fierce enough to steal her breath, pushed her last misgivings with it. His erection low against her belly, he nudged until Jessie's legs gave way, and he followed her down onto the futon. She opened her mouth to his, making him groan.

"I want you. I want you. I want you," he chanted.

Eyes closed, his mouth on hers, he jerked at the buttons of his fly. Jessie shut her eyes too. She'd forgotten how beautiful he was, how tender he could be. There was no impatience, no fumbling, no sense that they hadn't all the time in this world, or any other. When she touched him, he groaned again.

"Looks like we're going to settle this right now."

"Love me," Jessie whispered into his mouth. "Oh, yes. Love me . . . *Aaron* . . ."

Even before she realized what she had said, Nick had stopped moving. His braced arms quivered, and when Jessie opened her eyes, mortified, she couldn't help seeing the shock in his.

"I never thought anyone actually did that."

"Nick, I'm sorry."

He eased away and sat up.

When Jessie touched his back, he flinched. "I . . . when I'm writing," she said, "I get lost in a story. I was having trouble with this one yesterday, when I finished the pages you read—"

"Let it go, Jess." She watched him get up, fish for his shirt amid the scattered papers on the rug. "I hoped you were kidding." He shrugged into the shirt but didn't bother with the buttons. "I guess I was waiting to hear you say it—that you didn't really think I was . . . Aaron."

"What can I say, Nick? Except that a writer always falls in love with her own heroes, fantasizes about them as she writes?" It sounded callous.

"Fantasize all you want," he said, pulling on jeans and boots. "The book's going great. But when I make love to a woman, frankly I'm not inclined to make it three in a bed. He may not be real, but that doesn't mean I want Aaron between us." From the doorway, he gave her a long look. "You know, you're hell on a man's ego, Jess."

"Nick—"

"I'll see you when I get back."

Ashamed of herself, Jessie barely heard Nick leave the house. He didn't slam the door, he didn't rev the truck's engine, he didn't lay rubber on the dirt road between their farms. What was wrong with her? Her body throbbed from Nick's aborted lovemaking, yet she'd imagined she was with Aaron.

After a while Jessie wandered downstairs to the kitchen. The eggs Benedict had congealed in the skillet, the bacon had frizzled in its grease.

How does it feel to be a young bride on her wedding night?

Inexperienced, she thought, ambivalent—at once anticipatory and fearful. She hadn't come to Peter an innocent girl, except in the most technical sense. No, her first lovemaking had come years before her own wedding day. She felt the trembling, the sweetness of that other night, and bit her lip to keep from crying now.

She'd hurt him.

Jessie scraped their uneaten breakfast into the garbage. Yes, she remembered how it felt to be young and innocent and eager as well as afraid, to tremble as she was trembling now. Even her pulse seemed not to pound but to quiver.

She had felt just that way, twelve years ago, with Nick.

7

At *seventeen*, *full* of impatience for life to begin, Jessie had always been in a hurry; where it was possible to run, she never walked. That June night the week after her high school graduation, she ran up the porch steps, heart slamming in her chest, gaze already searching for him inside the front entry, then along the dark hallway and into Gran's kitchen. Like the good-night kisses she'd endured just moments before, her date was already forgotten. Seeing Tom Granby's new red pickup out front, she'd been able to think of nothing but—

"Nick!"

He sprawled at the kitchen table, an empty plate by his left hand, one of her grandmother's strawberry-rhubarb pies directly in front of him, two empty beer bottles all but touching his right hand. Jessie stopped in the doorway. "I didn't know you'd be home this weekend," she said.

"Neither did I." His dark gaze roamed over her,

and she felt the same low, throbbing feel it always brought. "It's midnight. Where were you?"

"After the movies we drove to Litchfield to eat. Then . . ." She trailed off. Nick was staring at her white sundress, which buttoned all the way down the front, and Jessie didn't think he'd heard a word. She flushed. "Where's Gran?"

"In bed."

The word seemed to carry more meaning than it should have, as if Nick had slipped into her own dreams. "Are you drunk?" she asked, eyeing the empty bottles on the table.

"Hardly."

He was too angry—for some reason—to be drunk, she decided. But if he wanted to argue, she didn't want Gran to hear. "Let's take a walk. I think we could both use some air." With a coaxing smile, she added, "It's a beautiful night, too beautiful to spend shut up inside. Come on, Nick."

She led the way to the orchard, and he followed a step behind, his hand laced with hers, his shoes occasionally catching Jessie's heels. Maybe he was drunker than she'd thought, or the clean air had forced the alcohol through his bloodstream. But the orchard was Jessie's favorite place, and she hoped it would clear his mood.

Just under the cover of the first trees, Jessie stopped. He hadn't said a word since they'd left the house and she was tired of chattering about last week's graduation, where he'd sat with her grandmother and Ben. He'd even kissed her afterward, a kiss Jessie had tried to prolong; but she hadn't expected him home so soon again.

"What's wrong, Nick?"

"Nothing." He tore a fragrant blossom from a low-hanging branch, tucking it gently in her hair. Jessie noticed his hands were shaking. "This was a bad idea," he said. "Let's go back to the house. Caroline made peach ice cream while we waited for you . . . for you and that gangly, red-faced—"

"Why, Nick, I think you're jealous!"

With a soft cry, she twined her arms around his neck. She'd waited so long for this.

"Jess," he murmured, then said nothing more.

Jessie's heart quivered. Was it really possible? She had prayed that some day he'd see her not as Ben's little sister, not as his faithful pal—the kid he could con into milking Tom Granby's cows—but as a woman. A woman Nick could want.

In the next instant he had her in his arms. With a groan, he dipped his head, eyes closed, his mouth groping for hers in the shadowed orchard like an infant seeking nurture. When their mouths met, Jessie whimpered; half afraid that he'd think it protest, she waited for him to pull away, but he didn't stop.

And soon, kisses weren't enough. Sighing, Jessie heard Nick's breathing change, becoming fast and harsh and shaky, and he was pushing against her.

When Nick pushed harder, Jessie instinctively knew what he wanted. With a glad cry she felt her knees give way, Nick bearing her down onto the grass, his body stretched over hers so that Jessie, at last, could feel every inch of him. "I want to see you," he murmured.

He unfastened the buttons of her dress, eased her slip aside, bared her breast. "Oh," Jessie whispered and felt him tense. "No. Don't stop, Nick."

"Jess, we can't do it." Dropping his head into the

hollow of her shoulder, he touched his lips to her skin.

Her skin burned. Jessie half expected to see it glow, like fireflies, in the dark. "It's all right." She hoped she wouldn't cry, the feeling was that strong. "Didn't you know? I've always wanted it to be you."

As soon as the words were out, she knew she'd said something wrong. Nick took one deep breath, then said, "Get up," his mouth still warm against her skin.

When he finally moved, Jessie gazed up at him, her eyes wide, all her senses open. The scent of apple blossoms drifted on the light breeze; she heard the spring peepers singing from the pond. Mating, she realized. She looked into Nick's dark eyes, the taste of his mouth still on hers.

"Get up," he said again, "and pull yourself together."

He said it as if she'd done something terrible, sinful. Jessie reached out a hand to draw him back. "But I love you, so it's—"

"Nick? Jessie?"

They both froze at the sound of Ben's voice, calling from somewhere between the house and the orchard. Why was he here? He and Beth lived in town with Jessie's seven-year-old nephew; and Ben usually went home after his late shift, second job at a local convenience store. Why was he looking for her now like the outraged older brother? Nick had already played that role, sitting in Gran's kitchen, waiting for her to come home.

Jessie heard Nick swear. "Get serious, Jess. You don't love me," he said harshly. "At your age, you only love the idea of being in love." He leaned over to flip the edges of her dress closed, flinging the blue tie-belt at her. It landed on Jessie's half-bare breast, but Nick looked away, as if he didn't want to see her.

"Jessie? Where are you? Nick?" In the next instant Ben came crashing through the trees to find Jessie fumbling with her buttons. "What the—?" His eyes widened on Nick, whose shirt was hanging from his pants. Then Ben turned his glare on her. "Get back to the house, Jessie. And you"—he leveled a finger at Nick—"damn you, I thought you were my friend! You get the hell out of her life! And mine, too!"

Nick, Jessie thought now in her grandmother's kitchen, had been only too happy to comply. The next day he'd been gone, back to Charleston, leaving Jessie to deal with her pain, her shame, her unrequited love. Had tonight really been an accident? she wondered. Or had she been waiting, unconsciously, for twelve years to pay him back?

Aaron, she'd called him. Hunkered down in the field he'd planted three weeks ago, Nick wrapped his fist around a clump of timothy shoots. Only the day before they'd been tender, fragile, barely growing but green, so green; a few hours ago, in seconds, hail had pounded them into the damp earth, as flat as his garden in Charleston after last fall's hurricane.

Ruined, he thought again, and felt his stomach churn.

Flinging the wet plants down, he stood, wiping both hands on his jeans. He hadn't wanted to leave Charleston, where private restoration work had taken whatever time Seaview's reconstruction didn't. He hadn't wanted to come home. But things had been going all right. Pop's fields thriving, Nick and Jess becoming friends again; he'd even kept his hands to himself. Until tonight in her barn when she'd kissed him first; until later, when she'd squatted with him in the hay, delivering the calf; until she'd insisted on fixing Nick breakfast and, for the first time in a dozen years, opened her heart.

He had no excuse for coming on to her; except that after hearing about Peter, after reading her book, he'd felt . . . driven again, unable to keep from touching her there in Caroline's house.

Then Jess had called him Aaron.

Frowning, Nick lifted his gaze to the horizon. Hell, rather than trust him again, she'd invented a man to love. A farmer, of course.

He kicked a clod of dirt. She wasn't about to give *him* another chance, that was sure, and . . .

"Nick?"

At her voice, he fought his startled impulse to whirl around. When she dropped a hand on his shoulder, Nick stiffened.

"I'm sorry," she said and for one instant he thought she meant sorry for calling him by another man's name. "Is there anything left untouched?" She waved toward the sodden field.

Nick caught the motion in his peripheral vision. "Nothing." He shook his head. "A plague of locusts couldn't have done better."

"What will you do now?"

"Fly back to Charleston, according to plan." He turned, finding the sight of her painful. In jeans and sweater, without makeup, her gaze uncertain, she could have been twelve-year-old Jess again, the day her parents died. "I have an all-day meeting tomorrow." He looked at her. "Nothing to keep me here."

Jess flinched. "No? Greg's awake at your house," she said. "He just called, wondering where you were. Your mama cow feels hot to the touch, he said, and her udder's inflamed."

"Milk fever," Nick replied. Jess could diagnose that as well as he could. "Did you tell him to call the vet?"

"Yes. I also said I'd step outside, see if you were in sight." She paused. "I'd have come looking for you anyway. Nick, I shouldn't have started talking about Peter or—"

"Forget it." Nick dug the toe of his boot into the mud. "I was out of line. Besides, I had no business reading your manuscript." Now he wished he hadn't. He'd learned he didn't measure up.

"Nick—"

"There's nothing here, Jess." And he sure as hell didn't want to talk about farming either. "Not a blade of grass, not a stalk of corn. It's lucky we didn't lose any of the herd, which is about all the assets Pop has left."

Her eyes flashed. "But surely you could—"

"Replant?" He felt his gut tighten. He could barely stand to look at the devastation around him; in spite of himself, he'd felt pride in the simple accomplishment of setting seeds in dirt and watching them grow. He'd forgotten how good that could feel, but— "I'd have to be out of my mind. You think this hasn't happened before? A hailstorm, a drought? Pop would reach this same damn point, everything coming up roses, him already counting profits with harvest three months off, then along would come some three-day rainstorm, the wind kicking up at seventy miles per hour, and he'd lose everything."

"I never thought you were a pessimist."

"About this farm? Hell, yes." She'd just caught a look at his weak spot, Nick thought. "Listen, I've seen this land as dry as the Arizona desert where you lived with Peter. I've seen it under eighteen inches of water, but mostly I've seen it—one way or another—with everything gone. That's what I remember about this place, Jess."

He watched her spine straighten, a gesture he remembered in Caroline. Her tone cooled the same way, too. "Why can't you remember the good years? All those springs and summers with Tom's fields—and my father's—thriving? Green and gold, sheaves of wheat waving in the sun, Gran's apple trees loaded with fruit."

"Don't write a poem about it, for Christ's sake." Opening her hand, Nick slapped wet earth on her palm. "Jess, this field is dead. There won't be any crops this year. There won't be any profit to pay Pop's loans, to feed his livestock, or to put food in his belly next winter. So, even if he wasn't sick, what choice does he have?"

"You tell me."

No. He wouldn't say it, not yet, not the words she wanted to hear so she could keep on hating him.

"You know what else I remember?" He held her troubled gaze with his, realizing he'd never told anyone this. "When I was a kid, ten years old—the spring you were born—we had a wet season. Too much runoff after a winter full of blizzards, too much rain. That April my father's fields flooded out. He couldn't pay his loans, could barely feed us and his cows. We could only stay here because my mother sold eggs from the chickens she kept, some fruit from our peach trees, and a couple of hand-sewn quilts she'd made that brought hundreds of dollars from the city people who drove out for a breath of bucolic air to clear their lungs."

"Nick, you don't have to—"

"Rich people," he added, and narrowed his eyes at the pink blush of morning above the horizon. He could tell the day would be crystal clear, all bright sun with a sky as blue as Jess's eyes, when he no longer needed perfect weather. "That fall Mom took a typing job in town to make ends meet. I used to lie in bed at night and hear her fighting with Pop because he didn't want her to work. Even then, he was stubborn and old-fashioned."

"Traditional," Jessie said. "It hurt his pride."

"Pride was a luxury. That Christmas, it was lucky I didn't believe in Santa Claus, because there wasn't much. Not enough oil to burn for heat, not enough money to buy presents, except new shoes for school. No toys, I mean. I remember Caroline asked us to dinner, but Pop wouldn't go unless she let Mom help cook the turkey, and a tough old goose he slaughtered—didn't want to spend feed money on it anymore, he said."

"Oh, Nick, because he—" She broke off, tears in her eyes. Damn, now he'd made her cry.

"Christmas was all right," Nick said with a shrug. "Because, by then, I'd decided not to stay on the farm. I decided that the morning of the flood. Never to feel poor again."

"You weren't poor." Jessie blinked twice. "You had Tom and your mother and Gran. You had my folks then, too, and Ben—and even me."

"You?" His mouth softened. "You were seven months old that Christmas, all done up in red velvet and white lace. Yeah," he said, "dumped like a present under Caroline's tree when we got there. I remember, you'd just learned to sit up, and your daddy plopped you down in the pile of red and green packages to take your picture."

"See?" she murmured. "You do remember something good."

Nick shook his head but couldn't quite clear the memory. "I remember that, before he snapped the shutter, you wet your diaper. Peed all over Ben's new baseball cards before he'd even opened the package."

"You would remember that." But she was fighting a smile now.

"Christmas was one day out of the year, Jess. The point is, this is a hard life. Harder than it needs to be. So whether Pop likes it or not, whether you agree with me or you don't—" he paused, then gave it to her on a long, expelled breath—"I'm calling Ben as soon as I get to the house."

When he turned to go, she caught his arm. "There must be something else you can do!"

"Go ahead, hate me," he said. "I know I promised Pop this season, and you never thought I'd stick that long, but last night changed everything."

"Only because you want it to."

"Wrong," he said. "My gut's been in a knot since I heard those first hailstones. I came here tired, burned out, and worked my butt off anyway. I did my best, but it's gone. All that work, Jess. Finished. How do you think I feel?" He didn't wait for her answer. "Rotten," he said. "As soon as I shower and pack, I'm going to Charleston for that meeting, then I'm coming back, just like I promised. I have no choice and neither does Pop. We're selling, Jess."

"You know what will happen if you do!" Her eyes were cobalt dark. "Ben will pressure me to do the same."

"You'll have to work that out with him. We're selling," Nick repeated. "Get used to the idea." Wrenching his arm from her grasp, he strode to the edge of the ruined field. Looking back, he told her, "I'm not Aaron, but at least I know when to cut my losses."

Stubborn. Prideful. Arrogant. *Man.*

Hours later, still fuming, Jessie sat gazing at the computer screen on which she'd called up Aaron's unfinished wedding night scene. But how could she work, when she kept wanting to cry?

She'd felt so guilty for calling him Aaron—wondering whether she'd done it on purpose after all?—that she'd walked down the road to apologize. She hadn't expected Nick to cut off her apology, though she should have expected him to sell Tom's farm. At least she'd been warned, and when Ben came running to pressure her, she'd be prepared.

Jessie sighed. She'd almost had the scene's ending before. That morning, still feeling the closeness she'd shared with Nick, even after she'd hurt him, for the first time she'd even allowed her memories of the night in the orchard to surface. The memories hadn't hurt; in fact, they'd felt so good that she'd known she had to tell Nick she was sorry for hurting him—as if she could really think he was someone, anyone else.

Then why the slip of the tongue?

Self-protection? Staring at the green letters on the screen before her, Jessie yawned. She'd had no sleep and knew she should lie down for a few hours. Still, she couldn't shake the feeling that she'd lost something, something precious, the very thing she'd come here hoping to find. Squaring her shoulders, she poised her fingers over the computer keys and began to type. Years ago, Nick had taken something from her—if not her virginity. She'd come back to find it, and by heaven, whatever his decision now, like Aaron's bride, she meant to keep it.

"Aaron, I don't think I can. Please."

I tried to pull away, but his hands only tightened, crossing over my waist inside my wedding dress, as his lips sought the tender place beneath my ear. He rocked me against him, and fire seemed to flare inside me. I remembered Aaron's kisses on the front porch in Carran when we courted, and how, after our betrothal, he had let his hand stray one night to my breast, gently squeezing while the same fire leaped in me. Would I feel like that again if Aaron touched me now, went further than before?

I tried to relax in his embrace, to sway with him, slowly, his mouth teasing my cheek, my throat, the shoulder he bared, nudging the fabric aside with his teeth, taking tiny nips of my skin. I could hear myself breathing now. But still, I felt afraid.

Aaron turned me in his arms. "You're trembling again. What else did your mama tell you?" he asked, and I mumbled the words.

Invasion, blood, pain. Duty.

Shock took over Aaron's expression. "Did she forget pleasure entirely?"

"Pleasure?"

With a groan, he touched his forehead to mine. "I'll try not to hurt you, but if it does hurt, it won't last long—and it's only the one time." He kissed my lips, half-open in surprise, in hope. "I think I'm sorry for your mama and papa," he said. "There's far more pleasure than there is pain, believe me. I'm sorry they've missed that." Then he kissed me again, more deeply, slowly and tenderly, taking his time about it.

With those kisses, as if they belonged to someone else, my arms came up around Aaron's neck, pulling his head down. Our bodies meshed, fitting perfectly as if they were two halves of a mold, and I could feel the swift thudding of his heartbeat like an echo of my own.

Aaron said, "Come to bed, love," the words a coaxing whisper, as light as his fingers at my breast, and just as quickly gone. He lifted me in his arms, then held me there, not moving, and we smiled into each other's eyes.

"I thought you were afraid, too," I said.

"Quaking in my boots. Shoes." He nuzzled my neck. "New ones, and they hurt. Why don't you help me get them off?"

Even as he placed me in the big bed among the cool white sheets and light patchwork quilts, all my fear dissipated. Urgency replaced it.

"I love you, Aaron."

"I love you," he said, then groaned. "God, Lizzie, I do love you."

And so, as we'd agreed, we learned together. Aaron was patient, even when I sensed he didn't want to be. Until *I* didn't want him to be, long after I knew for certain that Mama had been wrong. Has there ever been a feeling in this world like that of two warm bodies pressed together, touching everywhere? Any feeling more wonderful than Aaron's strength, and yes, that single quick, sharp pain followed by long, liquid, luxuriant pleasure?

"Oh," I murmured, staring up into his beautiful blue-green eyes. "This is home, Aaron," I told him. "We're home. Oh, Aaron."

8

Ben Pearce *rolled* his desk chair away from the window, where he'd been peering at the traffic departing the school's lighted parking lot, and stared at the stack of papers on his desk. He had plenty of work, and he didn't want to leave just yet. Because of the ongoing war with Greg, his office at Carran High School had come to seem more like home to Ben, even at ten P.M., than his own living room. Because of Beth, he added. Since Beth had died, so publicly, he'd had no stomach for social events. Frankly, he'd been hiding out in the office most of the evening.

Tonight he hadn't wanted to attend the music department's annual spring concert, to fidget through three hours of Miss Franey's junior chorus, her "gifted" soloists. He had a natural ear for music, and one violinist stroking a sour note was always one too many for Ben. In the middle of the a capella choir's stirring rendition of "Go Down, Moses," he'd faked a coughing fit and left the auditorium.

On his way out he spied Amy Stone in the back row. She'd come late, of course; the dedicated professional woman, whose daughter's soprano solo wouldn't rate that high on her priority list. He knew dozens of such women, none like Beth.

With a glance toward the window, Ben sighed. The stream of car lights had thinned to a trickle. He wasn't about to get any work done, and he really should get home. Greg had been sitting in the front row center tonight; he and Heather had left as soon as she finished singing. By now, God only knew where they were or what they were doing.

Not brooding in an empty office, he thought, and checked his pockets for his keys. He'd lock up, start home, and pray not to find Greg entwined with Heather on the sofa or, worse yet, upstairs. He'd pray not to spend the rest of his night remembering the past, which only reminded him of how lonely he was now.

As luck would have it, Ben stepped outside into the balmy spring evening to find himself staring at the only two cars left in the lot: his own gray Chevrolet and Amy Stone's red Miata.

Under the mercury vapor light her face looked pinched and greenish white, but her sassy brown haircut swung like some kid's in a schoolyard when she whipped around at his approach.

"Ben, thank God."

She didn't say anything else, which only made his frown deepen. Then he saw her right rear tire.

"Flat as a Frisbee," he observed. The hubcap rim rested on the concrete pavement. Next to it lay a dismantled jack.

"I know it's asking a lot, but . . ." Her look was beseeching. "Could you fix it for me?"

"Me, and my 'sterling character'?"

She winced. "I suppose I had that coming." She held up a can. "I tried this stuff that's supposed to seal the leak? It didn't work."

The independent woman pose, he had to admit, suited her better than the helpless female she'd first affected. Ben squatted down, feeling the seat of his dark dress pants strain. He'd picked up a few pounds, had been meaning to try Greg's weight bench or his ten-speed bike. After a moment's inspection of Amy's tire, he grunted and stood. "No wonder it didn't work. There's a cut the size of Rhode Island. Maybe more than one." Without a word, he rounded the car to the trunk. "Keys?"

Amy opened it for him. "I'd be really grateful, Ben, if you could change—"

Swearing, he slammed the trunk shut. "Did you know you don't have a spare?"

If it had been light, he knew he would have seen the color flood back into her cheeks. "Oh, Lord. Now I remember. I chaperoned Heather's biology field trip last week and had a flat. We left the tire at Benson's Garage to be fixed. I'm afraid I never had time to pick it up."

That figured. Did she think he'd give her points for the field trip? No way. Ben's hands rested on his hips. "So now what?"

"You don't have to take that male-superior tone. If it's too much to expect a ride home—"

"Get in the car."

They drove in silence. Amy lived on the other side of Carran, a twenty-minute drive from Ben's house. After her divorce she'd bought a huge old Victorian that always needed work—and always would—just for herself and Heather. As if, Ben thought, she needed to prove she could afford it. She'd always been hard-edged, pushy. No wonder her husband had left her.

"I could use some," she murmured.

"Huh?" Ben had no idea what she'd been talking about. Sex maybe? "Some *what?*"

"Coffee."

They were passing the short string of fast-food restaurants just outside town, not far from her house, and Ben whipped into the lot at Burger King before he realized he meant to. A knee-jerk reaction, he supposed, to Amy's high-handed presumption that he might want to share her company any longer than necessary.

She ordered hot apple pie and a large coffee with double cream and sugar. Ben took his black. Choosing a booth at the rear of the empty restaurant, he hoped she'd eat fast.

"That stuff'll kill you," he said. "What kind of pie comes wrapped in a cardboard envelope?"

Amy grinned. "What's the answer—the kind that's five hundred degrees at its center, guaranteed to burn every taste bud in your mouth?"

"Not mine," he said, grimacing as she took a bite.

"You're spoiled, Ben. You grew up eating Caroline's homemade apple pie, homemade everything else. How do you eat these days?"

He stiffened. "I've learned to cook."

"Actually, Greg says you're not bad." Then she glanced up and saw his face. "I'm sorry, Ben. I didn't mean . . . since Beth died."

Nodding, he looked into his coffee. Little more than a year ago Beth had still been with them, gently teasing Greg about his girlfriends—not Heather Stone, then—chiding Ben when he took a second slice of her apple pie, almost as good as Gran's. Then she'd gotten sick.

Well, not sick exactly. Nearing forty, she'd begun to have difficult menstrual periods, cramps she hadn't suffered since Greg was born. Her doctor finally performed a D&C, a routine procedure. Beth had come home the same day. Then they'd gone to the basketball tournament at Ben's high school.

That spring the team was among the top three in the state, and Ben helped shout the gymnasium roof down. He'd still been screaming when Beth turned to him, her eyes looking into his for one second before they closed, and she crumpled to the floor.

"She died instantly," he told Amy. "The shock . . ."

Amy set her pie aside. He could hear her swallow.

"I couldn't stop screaming," Ben said. "One second I was yelling for the home team, that lanky kid the college scouts were hounding had just sunk an unbelievable basket to tie the score—and the next, my wife was dead at my feet. And I just went on screaming."

A blood clot had reached her brain, they said; nothing anybody could have done to prevent it. These things happen.

"Beth was a beautiful person," Amy murmured. "I know how much you loved her, Ben. How much she loved you."

"Don't," he said.

"She was my friend, and I miss her too, but—"

"If you say 'life goes on,' I'm outta here."

"Well, it does." She bent to see into his face. "Because it has to."

"That's easy to say, Ms. Stone."

Amy drew back. "You think so? When my husband left me, just disappeared and left me to finish raising Heather on my own—me, without a college degree, a job, any skills other than being a pretty excellent wife and mother, if I do say so myself—I wondered whether life goes on, whether it should."

"Divorce isn't the same thing."

"But you've never been divorced, have you?"

He nudged his chin toward her coffee cup. "You finished?"

"No," she said. "No, I'm not."

Ben stared at her.

"You may not be aware of this," she went on, "but people in this town, including your own sister, are concerned about you."

His pulse jumped. Was he in danger of losing his job? "Concerned, why?"

"You keep to yourself too much, more than ever. Like tonight, when you squirmed through the concert, clearing your throat every ten seconds and barking that phony cough. At first I thought you'd left the auditorium because of me. Then I realized that the only time you notice me is when you're about to deliver some diatribe against my daughter, who seems, in your presently demented state, to have become something akin to a scarlet woman. So I knew, because Heather was still singing, that your leaving wasn't my fault."

"Amy, for God's sake. What is this?" Her level gaze was making him feel trapped. "I have absolutely nothing against you—"

"No grudges, Ben?" She shook her head. "Think harder."

He shifted on the plastic bench. So they'd dated a few times when he was still a kid, younger than Greg. The last time, he remembered, they doubled with Beth. The next day, with Beth's soft laughter still on his mind, he'd called her instead of Amy and the rest was history. Two years of trying to keep their hands off each other; one year when they'd stopped trying; marriage at nineteen, Greg before they turned twenty. He'd never imagined Amy Stone had been heart-broken.

Or did she mean the other thing? Her vicious gossip?

"I never meant to hurt you, Ben. Either of you."

"As you said, it was a long time ago. Don't worry about it." Without checking to see whether she'd finished, he stood up. "Ready to go?"

"Yes." The clipped word didn't register until they reached his car. Then she said, "You can keep on disliking me if you want, for whatever reason you need to, but sooner or later, you'll have to give up grieving—and start living again. It really would be best for you, and for Greg, too."

Holding the passenger door, Ben stared at her until she looked away, and slipped into the car. She'd always had a big mouth, he told himself. Forget that perky dark hair, those wide green eyes, a waist he would still be able to span with both hands, good legs, and the best ankles in Connecticut. He turned away. That big mouth, with the tiny mole beside it, that he'd kissed a few times. She'd been a helluva kisser, he remembered.

Slamming her door, he went around to his side. "What Greg needs is a full-time job. He just lost his."

"And what you need is—"

"One good night's sleep," Ben said.

He had her home in three minutes. A quick good night without getting out of his car, and he was headed back toward Carran like a man pursued by spirits.

On the way home he tried to forget Amy Stone by thinking about Nick. His call yesterday morning had lifted Ben's spirits. With the commission check from the sale of Tom's property, he could pay off Greg's college loan—no sense throwing good money after bad. Then, in Nick's absence Ben had taken the appraiser to the farm, where Tom had met them on the front porch steps with a shotgun. His message had been clear, and the quick once-over the appraiser had given the place hadn't brought better news. Nick wasn't going to like it, either.

Ben pushed the accelerator down. He'd be glad when the farm was sold; his grandmother's, too, because holding on to it wasn't wise, though he'd have to convince Jessie of that. Somehow. Ben himself would be glad to escape the memories in that old house. Maybe he should sell his place in town, too; more memories, of the home he and Beth had made together.

Perhaps Amy Stone had a point about picking up his life again, but he still wished he hadn't seen her tonight. He wished to hell he'd never given her that ride.

Nick counted six round-trips between Carran and Charleston over the past weeks, no longer sure which end of the circuit to call home. For two days he'd spent so much time en route to and from airports, on planes that, until he turned the rental car off the highway and into his father's drive, he didn't fully realize he was back in Carran.

He'd barely dropped his leather garment bag inside the front door before Tom shuffled from the kitchen. "Surprised you'd show your face here again," he said, blue eyes snapping.

Nick tugged at his tie. "I'm surprised that, in forty-eight hours, you haven't accepted the inevitable."

"Nothing's inevitable, 'cept death and taxes."

"Pop, that's the oldest saw in the book. And untrue." He rubbed the back of his neck. Lots of things were inevitable. Like his father's stubbornness, and Jess's refusal to forgive.

Tom came into the living room, his gait slow, shoulders hunched for battle. "If you think you've convinced me to sell and that Ben Pearce is going to pound some damn fool For Sale sign in my front yard—"

"Nobody was going to put up a sign. Ben was just—"

"Wouldn't let him yesterday, don't plan to change my mind."

"I shouldn't have believed in miracles," Nick murmured.

His father's voice rose. "He brought some young dandy around, snoopin' through the barn and sheds, stirrin' up my herd so none of 'em wanted to give milk last night—"

"Because you were shouting, not because Ben came by." Nick shrugged out of his suit jacket, dropping it on the sofa. "I'd bet money on that."

"I got no use for that boy, a farmer's son who ought to have some reverence for the land. Mary and David Pearce taught Ben better, so I run 'im off."

Nick followed his father's gaze to the shotgun propped in a corner. He groaned. "Next thing, I'll be bailing you out of jail downtown. Pop—"

"I'll run you off, too, if you don't come to your senses."

"Come to my senses?" Nick stalked to the battered oak desk near the dining room archway. "Just what does that mean? What else do you expect to do with this place except sell?"

"Replant," Tom said, "just like always."

Nick sighed. "For Christ's sake, we've been over this already. You sound like Jess."

"She's a sensible girl."

"She's a dreamer, Pop, and so are you." He flung himself into the desk chair and winced. The seat springs were broken, and he'd hit hard as a sled at the bottom of a gully. Nick yanked open a drawer. "Come on," he said, though he knew he shouldn't upset Tom, "over here, and show me the books. I'm a sensible man. Make your argument."

He slapped the ledger open on the desk. It infuriated Nick to remember the checks he'd sent over the past twelve years, checks Tom had never cashed. The time he'd come back for his mother's funeral, Tom's accounts had been in sad shape but nothing like this. When he'd first returned to Carran after his father's stroke, Nick had spent his time either at the hospital, worrying, in the barn milking cows, and worrying, or trying to get some much-needed sleep. And worrying. He'd paid Tom's current bills as they came in; but until recently, he hadn't really looked at the books, or guessed the extent of the problem. Now, seeing the proof of his father's mismanagement, or sheer bad luck, didn't make Nick feel any better.

"Jesus, Pop." In two years things had gotten worse. His father owed everyone in town, was now clearly in danger of losing the farm his ancestors had owned outright for two hundred years. "Your credit—" Nick was reaching for another bill on the stack as the telephone rang.

When Tom heard who was calling, he turned away.

"Yeah, Ben," Nick said. "The trip wasn't bad, but I hear you had some trouble out here. I shouldn't apologize for my father"—he glanced at Tom, who was studying a shelf of ancient books—"but I am sorry."

Nick listened for a moment to Ben's response. "So, off the top of his head, what does the appraiser think?" Nick stared at the bills. "Ben, I'm looking at twice that in debts. We have to get more."

Nick could feel his stomach knotting tighter with every word. The market was down, prices were falling. Tom's equipment was outdated, his fences in poor repair, the tillable land depleted. Last year's harvest had been poor. The house itself—

"I know, I know." Nick cut Ben off. "But can you get another appraiser out here tomorrow? I'd like a second opinion."

When he hung up, Tom spun around—not bad for a man just out of the hospital, whose speech was slurring again. "Am I goin' to need my shotgun?"

"Not if I have to tie you to a kitchen chair." Which wasn't a bad idea, Nick thought. He grabbed a fistful of bills. "Some of these are thirty days overdue, sixty, even ninety"—he waved them at Tom—"and those are just from the bank. I thought maybe the first dun letter was the only one. How many shutoff notices did you get last winter from Connecticut Light & Power? When were you planning to pay these?"

Tom looked away. "I got a couple of bull calves almost ready for sale . . ."

Nick snorted. "A *couple?* What are they worth? We're talking tens of thousands here, Pop. Your whole herd wouldn't begin to cancel these debts!"

"A good season will help," Tom insisted. Nick didn't like the red flush that crept up his neck. "The price of corn's sure to skyrocket, and I'll have enough hay to—"

Knowing he should back off, Nick swore. "You know, I've always thought of you farmers as conservative, right-handed thinkers, right-handed voters. But I've been wrong. Pop, the guy in a silk shirt and gold chains, stretched out in a complimentary suite at Trump Castle, working the slot machines, the roulette wheel, playing blackjack all night long in Atlantic City or Vegas isn't one-tenth the gambler you are."

Tom's eyes flashed. "Now listen here—"

"You want to replant, do you? How will you buy more seed? Tell me who would give you a loan, owing what you do."

"I've done business for fifty years with the First Agricultural & Mercantile, right downtown in—"

"Give it up, Pop, *now, dammit!*" Nick slapped the bills into the file and shoved it and the ledger back in the drawer. Then he saw Tom's face, all purple splotches now. Sweating, Nick slumped back in the chair. "All right, hey, take it easy, don't—"

"I don't want your advice, city boy!"

"Don't have another stroke." Nick forced his voice lower. "Tell you what we'll do. In the morning we'll drive into town and talk to the loan officer at First

Agricultural. If he'll lend you the money, then I'll replant for you."

Hope flared in Tom's expression, but Nick felt as if someone had bashed him with a two-by-four. Still, they'd come this far, he thought; and the morning after the hailstorm he'd felt keen disappointment himself at so much wasted effort.

"You'll stay?"

Why raise false hopes? Nick asked himself. Yet his father had hung on this long. Just maybe the bank would approve another loan, though he doubted it. If they didn't, his father would have no choice but to sell; but at least he wouldn't have let Tom down. Right now, he had to get out of here.

Getting up, Nick started for the door. "Yeah, Pop," he said, his voice husky. "I'll stay."

"You mean that, Nicky?"

"I mean it." He grabbed his suit coat as he zipped past the sofa. "Listen, I have something for Jess in the car. Her lights are still on, I think I'll drop it off now."

He shut the door on Tom's thanks. No doubt about two things: they were both crazy; and his father hadn't called him Nicky in almost twenty years.

When Jess answered the door wearing a fleecy teal blue robe but no welcoming smile, Nick's spirits sank even lower. As was his custom he'd rung twice, so she knew who it was. Over the last two days he'd spent more time than he liked to admit, thinking about her, regretting their quarrel. Apparently, she didn't.

He'd missed her. He'd even missed lying on the hard mattress in his old room, missed falling asleep with his view of her house lights across the pasture.

"Hi," he said. "I know it's late, but—"

She didn't step aside. "What do you want, Nick?" Then concern shadowed her eyes. "Is something wrong with Tom?"

"No," he said quickly. "No, nothing like that."

She frowned, as if reluctant to even ask. "Your business meeting? How did that go?"

"Great." Lousy, he thought. He'd charmed the wetland conservationists, but his firm was still in jeopardy; he was in hock himself to the banks again. From behind his back he produced a brown paper-wrapped parcel. "Here, I brought you this."

He hoped she'd ask him in, fix him a drink in the parlor.

She stayed in the doorway, the overhead light shining on her ash blond hair, her blue eyes dark. "Why a gift?"

A peace-making present, he thought. "I know your birthday's weeks away, but open it anyway."

She hesitated. Had Ben already told her about the appraiser, about Tom's shotgun? Somehow she'd blame Nick for that, too.

"Go on," he urged.

Nick's heart thudded. He'd never felt comfortable giving gifts, but he wanted her to have this, something of himself. Setting the package on the walnut sideboard in the entry, she slipped off the twine, then the paper.

She lifted the box lid, peeked inside—and gasped. The miniature antique chest of cypress wood, bound in brass, stood a foot high and had six working drawers on center-glide runners. Nick had waxed them himself before he packed it. Now she turned it over and over, examining each side, then the bottom.

Her hair fell, like a swatch of fine silk, to her shoulder as she tipped her head to read the inscription. "This is from Charleston."

Nick looked away. "From my house to yours," he said.

"Nick, I can't accept this."

"Why not?"

"It . . . it must be worth a fortune. Handmade, signed . . ."

"I thought you'd use it in your office, for supplies, paper and such. As soon as I saw it"—years ago, in one of the little shops on King Street—"I thought of you."

"Thank you," she said at last. "It's lovely. I'll treasure it." She turned away, carefully setting the chest in its box, not to scratch the finish.

When she didn't face him, Nick felt dismissed. "Jess, I—"

"It's late, Nick. I was nearly asleep when you rang the bell."

Then in one motion she circled around, her hand finding the doorknob as if magnetized. She opened it, and cool night air rushed inside. He could hear spring peepers, could smell the orchard. "Thank you again," she said, closing the door before Nick realized he'd taken a backward step.

Three more steps and the porch light went out, leaving him in darkness. The hell with it. Nick swiftly crossed the black yard. In the car, he revved the engine to keep it from stalling, he told himself, and realized that neither of them had mentioned their quarrel about selling the farm.

Maybe she was right to keep her distance. Without planning to, he'd come to her tonight looking like a stranger himself in his dark city suit, his reknotted tie, his crisp white shirt. As if he were making a business call, nothing more.

No wonder she'd gazed so dispassionately at him. But dammit, he hated that porcelain-faced coldness, hated her rejection. How many times did he need his brain kicked in before it got the message? She would never forgive him—but she would learn that he kept his promises.

Tomorrow he'd take Tom to see his banker. If— when, Nick corrected—the loan was denied, he'd apply for one himself. The decision made his palms damp. His name, his credit, his risk just when he could least afford it. But he'd replant Tom's fields, and by God, they'd grow this time. And after harvest, when his father's farm was finally sold, he'd stay away from Jess if it killed him.

9

He was *still* here.

I know when to cut my losses, Nick had said, but in the six weeks since the hailstorm, he'd replanted and the weather continued to cooperate. Already new grain was waving, though smaller than that of surrounding farmers, like munchkin crops, to Jessie's west and north, and cornstalks, rich green, crackled in the slightest breeze. Yesterday they'd been shin-high when she walked barefoot between the rows across the road from Gran's front yard.

Inspired by Nick's surprising about-face, Jessie had done some planting herself. Tomatoes, cucumbers, parsnips, and beans—like Elizabeth's kitchen garden. Research, she called it, but the truth was she loved watching things grow, so much that she planted flowers, too—annuals. Despite her allergies, the necessary weeding and watering kept her mind off the guilt that wanted to thrive whenever she thought of Nick.

Which Jessie did every time she glanced at the orchard and saw the few stubborn blossoms that clung to the remaining branches. Sometimes she was right, too.

The argument with Nick after the hailstorm had saddened as much as angered her; a few nights later his gift of the cypress chest had touched her so deeply that she'd turned away on the verge of tears. Yet, along with his city clothes, the Charleston-made antique only reminded her that she needed her own place in the world. She avoided Nick, just as he seemed to avoid her.

After the garden was in, Jessie asked Greg, in his spare time, to help her rig new ropes for the old swing in the maple tree. Then she set to work on her grandmother's house. She painted the kitchen, the front parlor, Gran's sewing room, and the upstairs except for her own bedroom, which Jessie decided to keep as it was.

She still didn't know why Nick had changed his mind about urging Tom to sell now—maybe Tom had changed it for him—but Jessie was here and digging in like Aaron's bride.

There were days, she found, when she didn't need any company other than Elizabeth's and Aaron's, though if she wanted companionship she knew where to find it now. Two weeks ago Jessie had come home from town with a refill for her allergy medicine to find Gran's barn swept clean; fresh hay lining a stall patched with new boards; and a bright red plastic feed bucket hanging on a brass hook. In the stall with its mother, a brown-eyed Sunbeam the Second was contentedly nursing. On her back door, Jessie found a note: "Let me know when you need more feed. Happy birthday. Nick."

Jessie had forgotten her birthday, but he hadn't,

and she loved having the calf around. She'd bonded with it the night of the storm, but she hadn't felt comfortable since then about visiting next door, which meant possibly running into Nick.

She'd called to thank him, of course, but he wasn't home, so Jessie left a message. Nick hadn't returned her call.

On her way to meet Amy Stone for lunch today, if she spied him in the fields, Jessie decided, she would stop. Though maybe Nick wouldn't welcome her gratitude any more than he had her apology for calling him Aaron.

"You didn't actually call him that, did you?" Amy said, swacked back in her chair, sneakered feet propped on her desk. She'd been cleaning files when Jessie arrived, her gamine hairstyle concealed by a blue bandanna. With a streak of dirt decorating one cheek, she looked no older than Heather.

"I'm afraid I did, making myself persona non grata in Nick's mind—which is just as well." Jessie pulled two tuna salad sandwiches on whole wheat bread from the brown paper bag lunch she'd brought, and handed one to Amy.

"Really."

"You bet." Not wanting a discussion of her relationship with Nick, she glanced around the crowded office. "He and I have no more in common than you and Ben."

Except chemistry, she thought. She'd seen that between her brother and Amy at Ben's birthday party.

When Amy admitted, "We went out together," Jessie choked on her sandwich.

"On a date?" she managed.

"Not exactly." Amy explained about her flat tire. "Unless you count having coffee at Burger King. I kept feeling that he had an egg timer in his pocket. Three minutes, and done." She smiled ruefully. "I've never seen a man say good-bye so fast. Zero to sixty by the time he hit the end of my driveway. I'm still choking on the dust."

Jessie laughed. "You know how shy he is. He was probably afraid you'd invite him inside—"

"And he'd have to stop wallowing in grief over Beth long enough to feel alive again himself? To enjoy sex?"

"Amy, you're a fiend."

Her grin didn't touch her eyes. "Just wait. When you've been divorced as long as I have, in a town the size of this one . . . slim pickings, Jessie, believe me. I haven't had a real date, or anything else, in four years."

"Be a nineties woman," Jessie said, not quite smiling. "Feel empowered. Get aggressive. If they don't come to you, don't hesitate to chase 'em."

"You should take your own advice." When Jessie didn't respond, Amy added cryptically, "I think I've already run through my repertoire on that one. Throwing myself at Ben. Besides, I'm not into married men."

"Ben's not married."

"Oh, yes he is."

"Nick's not either."

"Hmm," Amy murmured.

Jessie let the subject drop. Why had she pointed that out? She knew Nick liked Amy; Amy didn't need her encouragement.

"Men," she said. "They're women's universal topic. Listen in on any conversation in a restaurant, on a bus. I don't know why they're so endlessly fascinating when they give us so much trouble." Sweeping a corner of the desk clear of papers, she pulled two strawberry yogurt milkshakes from the lunch bag. "Let's drink ourselves into the next size clothing while we talk about my excuse for being here instead of at the computer."

Jessie needed more information about Carran's history, about area farms like Aaron's. She didn't understand why the safe topic made Amy smile.

"My office isn't the only clutter here," she said. "You should see the basement. We've decided on a major reorganization of the archives, and this morning our director brought me something of interest." A brief search of her desktop produced the file Amy wanted. "This was never catalogued." She handed it to Jessie.

"Oh, Amy."

Granby, the label read. *1850–1900*.

"Take a look before you say anything more."

Nick's family had farmed near Carran for nearly two centuries, Jessie knew. Leafing through the brittle papers, she glanced at bills of sale for cattle, crops, six yards of calico. She read a death certificate dated 1856, the same year her hero's father had died. And then she froze at the name on the next paper.

Her eyes met Amy's. "Aaron?"

"Aaron Granby," Amy said.

"I hadn't thought of a last name."

Shivers ran down Jessie's arms, her spine. Though she wouldn't use it, of course, she shook her head. "This is weird. Like mental telepathy, or something."

But she didn't believe in ESP, in ghosts. "Maybe Tom mentioned him, long ago." She seized upon the possibility.

"Or you might have heard stories from your grandmother. I remember getting stuck on her front porch more than once while she reminisced—for hours. And you did live with her until you were grown."

"Yes," she agreed. She made some rapid calculations. "It's possible Gran knew Aaron Granby," she said, though she didn't remember hearing about him. "If he'd lived to be old enough, I recall she'd moved to the farm as a small child . . . around 1900. It's possible," she repeated.

"Spooky." Amy's feet dropped to the floor and she stood up. "Greg and Heather will love this story."

Jessie caught her hand. "Don't you dare tell. I won't be a laughingstock, and Ben would only use it as ammunition against me in his campaign to sell Gran's property and move me back to town."

"It's a hard opportunity to pass up," Amy teased.

"Blackmail?" Jessie grinned. "What do you want? An invitation to dinner at my house when Ben just happens to be there?"

"That would be even harder to pass up."

"You must be desperate," Jessie said. "He's not exactly great company since Beth died. Greg and I call him the porcupine."

"It fits, but what the hell."

"Desperate," Jessie said, "and impossible." She stood up too, holding the Granby file. "Are there more of these?"

"Somewhere."

"May I study this one? I know you can't release it,

so is there someplace I can park myself for a few hours to take some notes?"

"I'll find you an empty desk."

Being drawn along the corridor outside Amy's office, Jessie said, "You know, every writer has this fear. I'm always afraid that I've stored someone else's terrific bit of dialogue, or plot twist, a character—"

"Caroline's," Amy said.

Jessie frowned. She'd have to think harder. She really didn't remember ever hearing about Nick's dead relatives, which bothered her. "Still," she murmured, "it's just a name. Only a first name at that."

"Hmm," Amy said again.

As she drove back to the farm, Jessie could feel her mind racing ahead. She'd spent the afternoon gleaning every morsel of information she might use from Amy's file and, excited, she turned off the highway, then on impulse into Tom Granby's drive.

When she'd passed by on the trip to town, she hadn't seen Nick, but his father's red pickup had been conspicuously absent. Then she remembered a brief conversation when she'd called to thank Nick—who hadn't been home—for Sunbeam, and asked how Tom was doing. He'd mentioned a doctor's appointment today.

The wind blew gently, scattering pollen. Fighting back a sneeze, Jessie parked her dusty BMW near the front porch. After Nick's mother died the Granbys' lawn had disappeared, like a balding man's hair, and, as she climbed the steps, Jessie noted the withered flower beds. The place sadly lacked a woman's touch;

it lacked fresh paint and the old, familiar smells of furniture polish and bread baking.

Now she smelled the mustiness of a closed-up house, mingled with Tom's forbidden pipe tobacco. "You've been smoking again," she said when he appeared.

His grin was sly. "Nick's had a head cold this week. Shhh, he thinks it's supper cookin'."

Jessie looked around, not finding Nick. Her pulse was thumping. "I stopped to see you. How was your checkup?"

"Checkup?" He looked blank.

"Didn't you see the doctor today? I thought you said—"

Tom's face cleared. "Oh, you mean that young city slicker barely out of knee-high pants. What does he know?"

Nick wandered into the living room. "He knows enough to tell you to quit smoking." He barely glanced at her. "Hi, Jess. What can we do for you?"

Jessie blinked at his cool tone. "I, uh, came to see how Tom was doing."

"He's doing fine."

"Better than fine," Tom said. "Didn't need that snot-nosed kid to tell me I can walk a mile every day to build up my strength." He beamed at her.

"That's wonderful."

"A *half* mile," Nick corrected. He sank onto the sofa, stretching his legs out. His nose raw, his eyes red, he still looked good enough for a layout in *GQ*, which irritated Jessie.

She saw no point in lingering. Clearly Nick didn't want her around. "I won't keep you from your exercise, then, or your pipe." Avoiding Nick's gaze, she smiled at Tom. "But I spent the afternoon with Amy Stone, and I have a question for you."

When Jessie asked it, Tom said nothing.

"He'd have been your great-great-grandfather," she prompted. "He took over this farm when his father died in 1856."

Nick's look sharpened, but he hid his obvious interest by taking a handkerchief from his rear pocket to blow his nose. Her own nose twitching, Jessie tried not to feel sorry for him. She wished he hadn't been here when she mentioned Aaron.

"Aaron Granby." Tom scratched behind his ear.

Getting up, Nick steered her toward the door. "Jess'll talk to you later, Pop. She probably has dinner burning on the stove at Caroline's."

"Caroline?"

Nick looked into Jessie's shocked eyes and said, "You're wasting your time. I told you. He has good days and bad days when parts of his memory are gone."

"I didn't realize . . . I've never seen—"

"You have to be here," Nick said and opened the door.

Jessie held her ground. She'd been trying to catch him for two weeks. "Before I go, I wanted to thank you, for Sunbeam and her mama, for fixing that stall."

"No thanks necessary. They had to have a decent place to sleep, out of the rain. Even Caroline's barn," he added.

"Jessie?"

She turned toward Tom's voice.

"Old Aaron should hit close to home. Way back, these two farms were one, you know. Aaron lived in the old house then," Tom said. "In Caroline's house."

Jessie's knees went weak. "I'm glad you remembered, Tom." The look she threw Nick on her way out
said, *His memory seems fine to me.*

Nick, she decided, just hadn't wanted her asking
questions.

Nick shoved a moldy cardboard carton closer to
the third-floor stairway without bothering to examine
its contents. In his opinion one box of junk looked like
another, and Tom's attic was packed to the rafters.

The day before he hadn't merely been trying to get
rid of Jess; his father's memory loss worried him, and
he couldn't bear watching Tom try to remember
things that had simply vanished from his mind.
Maybe going through these cartons would bring
some of the past back to him.

Besides, Nick thought, while he was here, he might
as well help Tom lighten the load. With the replanting
finished and the crops growing at last, he had time on
his hands. Better to prepare for the autumn's disper-
sal sale before haying time, before harvest. Greg and
his friend Brian could handle the other chores.

Nick paused to wipe his nose, and winced. His cold
was minor and better now, and other than that, he
hadn't felt this good in years. When he'd left Charleston at the news of Tom's stroke, he'd been overworked, overtired, overstressed. Those first days of
milking cows, he'd thought he'd die himself. But the
sore muscles had turned hard again; the June sun had
tanned his skin; and now, in mid-July, he had more
energy than he'd had in years.

Hauling another carton close, Nick kicked it toward the stairs. The box split, and papers spewed

across the rough board floor. "Damn," he said. He'd meant to spend a half hour upstairs, then face Tom's bills again.

Ever since the trip to the bank, Tom's loan refusal—they'd all but laughed him out the door—and Nick's application, which had been quickly approved, he'd been trying to put his father's business affairs in order. A full-time job, he thought, for a CPA.

In his own affairs, Nick worked as much as possible on a cash basis. Paying Tom's creditors sent him to bed every time with a hard stomachache.

The afternoon before, he'd been writing checks when Jess arrived. He'd been glad of the interruption, even happier to see her. He'd hidden it, though, and was still conscious enough of the night she'd kicked him out the door to feel mean-spirited, and glad, at the puzzled expression on her face when he did the same.

He'd also felt guilty. Only moments before, he'd found a folder in Tom's desk, an old one marked Granby/Pearce Development—a residential housing complex Nick and Ben had dreamed up while they were still in high school. They'd wanted to combine the two farms, throw up a bunch of glorified Colonial houses, and make a killing. Kid stuff, he thought. And yet . . .

If Tom had any sense, he'd do just that. Sell out to a real estate developer, like his own son.

Knowing what Tom would say to that, what Jess would think, too, Nick had slammed the folder back into the drawer when he heard her voice at the door. He'd made an unnecessary visit to the bathroom, giving himself time before he saw her.

Now, on his knees, he scooped up papers, thinking

at least they weren't bills. That finished, he turned to the trunk in the corner; covered with cobwebs, its brass latch long broken, it didn't contain bills, either. It contained treasure.

"Trash," Jessie muttered, tipping the saucepan's contents into the garbage. She'd made creamed chicken to go with the now-rock-hard biscuits she'd baked yesterday, then had gone upstairs to work while it simmered and had forgotten to come back down.

She switched on the new exhaust fan above the stove. It had been a necessary purchase for Gran's old house. Peter had always claimed Jessie was a rotten cook; he'd be a rich man, he said, if he had a dollar for every pot of vegetables she'd cooked dry. Maybe she should call to tell him she'd just scorched the last of her peas, too. Let him know how right he'd been about her. Again. Maybe not, she thought.

She'd come back to Carran, hoping to find herself somewhere in the wreckage of her marriage—and despite Peter, despite Nick, she was beginning to. With a determined nod, Jessie climbed the stairs to her office overlooking the orchard and the backyard. Since her visit to Nick's, she hadn't felt hungry anyway.

I don't know what is wrong with me. I've always been flighty, Mama says, and there is so much to learn here each day that perhaps I'm feeling nerves. I never dreamed that there was so much to being married, to running a farm.

Aaron gets up before the sun. It's still dark

when I hear him pulling on his boots. "Sluga-bed," he calls me, not as Mama would, but with love in his voice, his eyes. Then he leans over to kiss me and whisper, "Go back to sleep."

By eight o'clock he has fed and watered all the stock, stoked a fire in the cookstove, and, because I am still afraid of the chickens pecking my fingers, gathered eggs for our breakfast. After he lets the cows and Sugar and Spice out into the pasture, he brings the eggs inside to find me fumbling biscuit dough, or—one morning—carving my own hand with that clumsy, wicked butcher's knife instead of slicing melons. Aaron would fix breakfast for us, but I am determined to be a good wife, so I keep trying.

"You make good coffee," he tells me, trying not to grin. "Strong enough to clean my boots after I've mucked the barn. Keeps a man alert all day long."

My coffee, like the rest of my cooking, is terrible.

At night, in Aaron's arms, I know I please him as he surely pleases me; but in the daytime Aaron needs a wife who can clean and cook, who doesn't mistake the first bean plants in the garden for weeds and pull them.

Perhaps he will lose patience and send me home to Mama. I doubt she will be surprised.

If only I could feel well again. At first, I could keep pace with Aaron all day long, even when my muscles ached from hoeing weeds—or bean plants—even when my feet burned from help-ing him drag cows into the barn for evening milking. But this morning I felt so weary that, when Aaron said, "Sleep," I did just that and didn't hear him come back into the house for breakfast.

I am so endlessly tired, Mama wouldn't know me. I was always her "scootabout," she said. Today I could scarcely keep my eyes open while Aaron made the coffee, pared potatoes, fixed our scrambled eggs. When he told me to go back to bed, I lay there crying until my breakfast came back up. I have been sick, so very sick, all afternoon.

I'll have to tell him. When Aaron comes home—

A glance out the rear window captured only part of Jessie's attention. When she wrote, she entered an altered state of consciousness, experiencing the lives of her characters right along with them—especially her heroine. Now, as her stomach rolled with Elizabeth's, she couldn't ignore the shout from the yard again.

He was home. She'd tell him now.

Seconds later, she pushed open the back screen door and ran down the steps. A broad-shouldered man in worn jeans and a blue work shirt, his head gilded by the sun, its angle sharp enough to blind her to his features, was scrambling down the slope of the hill between Jessie's house and the Granby farm.

Her heart quickened. He was leading a cow, its calf trailing behind. Jessie had her arms open wide, ready to fling herself at him, when reality came crashing into the lingering remnant of her fiction.

Nick, not Aaron, walked past her to the paddock near the barn, opened the gate, and slapped Sunbeam's rump. The calf sauntered inside after its mama. Nick shut the gate, then turned to her.

"You have a hole in your fence as wide as the Housatonic River, at the bottom of the hill."

Jessie grimaced. "I know. I meant to fix it."

"You should have told me. I'd have sent Greg over."

Her cheeks hot, she eyed him. How could she have mistaken Nick for Aaron again? "That's not necessary."

"I guess Sunbeam decided to visit her birthplace," he said.

"Thanks for bringing her back."

"I was coming to get you anyway." When she glanced up, surprised, his eyes warmed. "C'mon, Jess. Let's sign another truce. I have something to show you."

The scarred trunk in his father's attic stood open, and Nick watched Jess home in on it like Sunbeam heading over the hill. "Oh, Nick!" Not waiting for him, she fell to her knees. "Look, a calico dress—and a matching sunbonnet. They're not even that faded."

Looking around, she snatched a canvas tarp from some cartons and laid it on the floor. Then dust and clothes flew from the open trunk. Jess arranged them as Nick imagined Amy Stone might do, as if she were cataloguing them for some museum. "A pair of gray pants—did they call this linsey-woolsey?" she asked.

"Damned if I know. You're the research expert."

"No, I've barely begun." Laughing, she held up an enormous sweater. "This guy must have been a giant. Oh, look, a baby's rattle made of horn or bone. It has little balls inside to make noise. And—what are these? Underpants? Pantaloons?"

Nick held them up. "They don't have any crotch seam."

Jess threw him a look. "Women didn't wear real underpants back then. How would you like to struggle out of six layers of petticoats, a chemise, just to go to the bathroom?"

"What bathroom?"

Her quick laugh made him smile. For a brief moment when he'd found the trunk, he'd wondered whether to show her.

"Here's a medal of some kind." She slapped it into Nick's palm, but the lettering had worn away; he couldn't read it.

"And a Bible." He pulled the small, slim leather-covered New Testament from a bundle of men's ivory white shirts, the kind with no collar and full, banded sleeves. Nick opened the book and his heartbeat faltered. "Jess . . ."

When she reached out their fingers touched, and Nick had second thoughts. He didn't want to give it to her. But she wrested the Bible from his hand.

"Oh, Nick, listen." Her upward glance showed him dark blue eyes, full of tears. Then she read from the flyleaf: " 'Lieutenant Aaron Granby, 8th Connecticut Volunteers, Antietam, September 1862. God keep me, for my son Seth Cochran Granby, and see me home from this terrible place, though my heart, my soul, are forever with my lost, my beloved————' "

The name had been obliterated, washed away. In some Civil War battlefield creek? Nick wondered. By blood? Or tears?

Frowning, he stared at Jess's bowed head. "There's

your Aaron Granby. You didn't need Pop's memory after all."

"I need much more," she whispered, then looked up at him again. "I know it's here somewhere. There must be papers."

"Jess, what's the point?" His heart thrummed. "I'm sorry now that I brought you over here to see this. It's nothing but a bunch of old, musty clothes."

"You're wrong." She held a yellowed shirt to her cheek, her eyes still misty. "I can feel it, Nick. Something, a presence. A story," she said.

Jess mentioned the reorganization at the historical society. "They turned up one file, mostly bills and shopping lists, but even in that, there was a death certificate, Nick. Aaron's father's." She turned away, rummaging in the trunk bottom. "A picture, that's what I need. A big family Bible with everyone's marriage, everyone's birth and death inside."

"Jess, that's maudlin."

"No, it's plot." Her eyes were shining now. Nick felt a chill creep along his spine. "And without plot, I have no book. I've been wondering about my story. There's not enough conflict."

"Maybe you've had enough recently in your own life," he said. "Maybe you don't want to give your characters trouble, too."

"Maybe." She shrugged. "But what if the name, the plot I have so far was real, Nick? Do you remember the night looking around Gran's house when we both stopped just inside my bedroom door? It was as if we'd walked backward, not forward, back into the past. I saw your face. Didn't you feel it, too?"

He looked away. "Feel what?"

"A warmth, gladness . . . I don't know, welcome.

Love," she said. "Yes, that's it. Love. What if that room, long ago, was Aaron's and Elizabeth's? And—"

"I made a pass at you in that room, Jess."

"As if you couldn't help yourself."

Nick swallowed. "You're saying that someone wanted us to make love there?" He shook his head. "I don't believe in spooks. Leave that to the kids, Greg and Heather."

"I don't believe in them either," Jess said. She touched his arm, and Nick looked into her eyes, clear and blue and determined. "But I always have the same feeling in Gran's house, especially in that room. I think that's why I chose it when we moved there. I always thought it was because she loved me."

"She did," Nick said, "and that's all there is."

"No."

She sat, Indian-fashion, on the dirty floor and meticulously examined each item from the trunk. She found no more inscribed Bibles, no papers or family pictures. And Nick was glad.

He'd had that feeling in Jess's girlhood bedroom, and it scared him. Then he'd felt a familiarity he couldn't explain while reading her manuscript; the love scene between Aaron and his bride had made his loins ache, made him want Jess more than ever before. And when she called him Aaron . . .

Nick put both hands over Jess's. In her lap she was holding a baby's nightdress trimmed in handmade lace, and tears were rolling down her cheeks. "What happened to them, Nick? His 'lost, beloved,' he wrote . . ."

He tried to take the dress from her, but she wouldn't let go. "Listen to me, Jess. Peter was wrong. You're a good writer, a wonderful writer. This book may be the best you've ever done, and I hope it will be. But you're too close to it now. Step back a little, give this thing a rest."

"Are you saying not to continue?"

"No," he said.

"Then what are you saying?"

He let his hands drift from hers, up Jess's bare arms, lightly over her shoulders, to frame her face. He brushed the tears away, and she didn't slap him. She didn't move away. "Maybe I'm saying that I'm jealous. That I don't want to compete with Aaron in your book, in my father's attic, or in bed. Jess, I've been trying to keep away from you but I can't. I want you, and I'm tired of hiding it, from myself and you."

"Nick . . ."

"We need some time together. The night you called me Aaron, if you hadn't, we would have made love—and it felt so right."

She said nothing, but she nodded, and Nick took a breath.

"Then will you do that for us? Spend time with me? Come away with me?" he asked, his voice husky.

"Where?"

"Charleston." He felt her stiffen. "You've never been there, have you?" He knew she hadn't. "It's beautiful, Jess. Like we said, quiet and gracious—"

"And in July, hot as hell itself."

He wouldn't be put off by her falsely light tone. "My house is air-conditioned. So's the car and my office and every restaurant in town. At night the breeze comes off the water like a blown kiss in the air, and the stars—"

"Nick, I don't know." She lowered her gaze. "I have a deadline, and the book's not half finished."

"You can do research at the library in Charleston. Sit in my garden while I'm working, and spin plots in your head like spiderwebs." He bent close to kiss the corners of her mouth. "I have to go back on business again, but we could stretch the three days into a week and have plenty of time together. Come with me."

When she lifted her head, he saw uncertainty in her eyes, uncertainty and temptation. But he'd learned not to push any harder than the words, "Please, Jess?"

"I'll think about it," she promised.

10

Ignoring the smell of smoke on his damp shirt, Ben skimmed the grocery cart along the aisles of the local supermarket, tossing canned green beans in here, a loaf of rye bread there. The store would close in ten minutes, but he finished shopping in five. Wheeling up to the checkout counter, he came face-to-face with Heather Stone at the register.

"Hello, Mr. Pearce. Isn't it a nice evening?"

Ben hadn't noticed. With school out for the summer, he'd spent the morning in his office, straightening files, the afternoon washing his car, and the evening as a volunteer fireman helping out at a nearby garage blaze. "Welcome enough," he muttered, "after such a hot day."

He squared his shoulders. The back of his neck was sunburned, and now his ears felt hot. Heather's smile easing from her mouth, she dragged a loaf of bread over the laser scanner, intently watching the amount register on the display. If she asks about Greg, he thought, I'll have my opportunity.

"Well, well. The man of many talents." He turned at the sound of Amy Stone's voice. "I heard from your captain's wife about the fire. She said you'd been a volunteer ever since you married Beth." The words didn't sound like a compliment. "Now I see that even a local hero—even the high school principal—has to buy toilet paper."

Ben's gaze flew toward the blue-flowered rolls in his cart. He mumbled a greeting.

"Mouthwash, too." Amy leaned over the carriage. "Razor blades, steak—your Sunday cholesterol treat?—and I see you've a fondness for frozen dinners. Disappointing, Ben." She let her green eyes meet his darker ones. "Just when you'd convinced me you've become a gourmet cook."

"I never said that." He looked away, trying not to notice how her white shorts clung to long, slim legs, how the yellow-and-white top defined her breasts.

"Mom," Heather said, twin spots of color on her cheeks. She punched up the total. "That'll be $34.73, Mr. Pearce."

Ben had to write a check, and his hand shook. The tips of his ears were really flaming now. Damn her, he thought. Her and that cheeky mouth. Someone ought to shut it for her. He ripped off the check, jammed the cartridge pen back in his shirt pocket, then glanced down to see blue ink spreading like a Rorschach blot over his chest.

"I forgot to put the cap on," he muttered.

"Here, let me." Amy plucked the pen out. "Take your shirt off."

"What?"

"Take your shirt off, Ben." She looked around. "For heaven's sake, we're practically the only three people in the store."

He stripped off the shirt, which had already been wet and smoky from the fire, and slapped it in her outstretched hand. Asking Heather where the ladies' room was, Amy disappeared. The manager was announcing the store's closing when she came back.

"You won't be able to wear it home, but I think the rest of that ink will wash out now. It's not as bad as ballpoint."

Ben wadded the damp shirt into a ball, pressed it to his bare chest like a shield. "Thanks." Then he escaped, pushing his shopping cart through the automatic doors to the parking lot, taking his red face with him.

Ten minutes later, he was home. He'd just doused the headlights when Amy Stone's red Miata buzzed to a stop at the curb in front of the house. Jesus Christ, he thought.

And went to see what she wanted now.

Before he could speak, Heather opened the passenger door and jumped out. The front porch light flashed on, and Greg banged through the screen door. "Hey, babe, ready to go?"

Amy leaned across the seat to look at Ben. "Sorry. Heather didn't mention that she and Greg planned to see a movie tonight. I'm just dropping her off."

The tips of his ears on fire, Ben was glad for the near-darkness. "Too bad, I'd have brought her from the store. Saved you the trip."

"Well, you seemed in such a hurry," Amy said with a smile.

"Hey, Dad." Greg trotted over. "Can I borrow

some gas money? Me and Heather—I mean, Heather and I—want to catch *Ghost* over at the Grand, nine-thirty show. Five bucks?" he said.

Ben fumbled in his khaki pants for a bill. "You ever heard of a budget? This happens every week. I should charge interest."

Handing over the money, Ben saw his son's face fall. "Call me irresponsible," Greg said and, snatching the five, stalked away. "Thanks. I'll pay you back on Friday."

Then Heather came back to the car. "Mom, could you spare a few dollars for popcorn and a soda?"

"Of course." She smiled as the bill exchanged hands. "Enjoy the show. I'll find out tomorrow how you liked it. Don't be too late getting home, honey."

Heather hesitated. "Uh, I know you wanted to see the movie, too. Why don't you join me and Greg?"

"Oh, that's sweet, but—"

"You could come, too, Mr. Pearce," Heather suggested.

Ben's pulse lurched. "Me?"

"Yeah, Dad." Greg's voice challenged him. "I'll bet you haven't seen a movie since . . ." Mom's death, Ben heard. "In a long time," Greg finished. "How about it? At the same time you can show all those Carran kids and parents that set of pretty impressive pecs."

Heather giggled. Ben glanced down at his chest.

"Put a shirt on," Amy said. "Button-down collar, long sleeves. We'll even let you wear a tie."

His gaze trapped hers. "Won't you be surprised?"

He'd thrown the groceries in the freezer, started the washer with the inkblot and stain remover inside, added Greg's jeans to balance the load, and pulled on

a black T-shirt with a Harley Davidson logo by the
time Greg's car backed out of the drive.

"Where are they going?" he asked. Amy Stone was
sitting on the porch steps, waiting.

She gave his outfit an approving stare. "They're
kids. After the show, they're meeting some friends.
We're the oldies but goodies, though Heather invited
us to sit with them during the show."

"Great," Ben said. Some protection.

"So. Do you want to follow me—or shall I follow
you?"

"Do you always speak in double entendres, or is it
only with me?"

Amy's brow furrowed. "I don't understand."

"I'll drive," he said. "But lock your car. A flat tire
last time, I don't need to come home and find a break-
in tonight."

"God forbid."

At the movie, Ben squirmed through the erotic pot-
ter's wheel scene. He was certain Amy had been laughing at him at the house; now, he felt even more aware of
her beside him. His seat cushion sagged, throwing Ben
toward her every time he relaxed his muscles, and he
could smell her perfume, something dark and musky
that made him feel weird. In the darkened theater, he
inhaled her scent through his pores and wished they
hadn't come to see a movie quite so sensual. It would
give Greg ideas, he told himself.

"Sit still," Amy hissed.

"My seat's broken."

"Then move over here." She patted the seat to her
right, which put Ben on the aisle and left the kids
toward the center of the row. He could already see
Greg's hand groping for Heather's.

Then Patrick Swayze, playing Sam, got killed, and Ben's attention focused on the film. Like Amy's perfume, he absorbed it, lived it. By the final, moving farewell scene, Ben had decided he hated going to the movies. Someone always turned the lights on while you were still gripped by painful emotion.

Walking back to his car, he stayed silent.

"Maybe *Ghost* wasn't a good choice tonight," Amy finally said.

Ben opened her door and gestured her inside. "Maybe it was."

The bittersweet love story reminded him of Beth, of all they'd had, of all he'd lost. But in Amy's presence, he needed the reminder. So why did he drive home without saying a word, then ask her in for coffee?

When she hesitated, he even said, "I make a mean pot of decaf, and there's still pie left from dinner."

"Homemade?"

"Well, no." From the driver's seat, he smiled at her. "Frozen. Blueberry. Defrosted."

"Wonderful," Amy said. "I'll need two pieces."

She headed straight for his kitchen, not asking where he kept the cups and saucers, the silverware. She flung open cabinets and set the table. Over pie and coffee laced with brandy—Ben's idea—she asked too many questions.

Ben tried to shut her up.

"Did you see Greg during the movie?" he said. "His hands were all over your daughter."

"And when the ending came, he kissed her. Yes, I saw." Amy cut a bite of pie into even smaller pieces. "I'm sorry that disturbed you, Ben. I envied them."

"You envied—?"

"They love each other. It's been a long while since

I've felt that kind of love for anybody. I miss it." She lifted her gaze. "Don't you?"

Ben shifted. "You get used to being alone."

"At night? In bed?"

"Amy."

She pushed her pie away. "Sorry. Read any good books lately?"

To Ben's surprise, she didn't mention love again. She told him of a treatise she'd read on higher education, which Ben had read, too, and they argued, more amicably than he expected. Grinning, they quarreled about politics. Then it became apparent that they enjoyed some of the same novelists, though Amy preferred thrillers to Ben's favorite horror stories.

"Have you read Jessie's books?" he asked her.

"Yes. I love them. They're full of honest emotion, real people. She has a way with a woman's heart, and I think she understands a man's outlook, too."

"From a woman's point of view," he said.

"You think it's fantasy?"

"Sure. Just look at her, with Nick. She hasn't the vaguest understanding of what he wants from her."

"Which is?"

"I'm not Nick, but I watch his eyes. I'd guess he wishes Jessie could absolve him of what happened between them long ago."

Amy studied him for a moment. "Not only a man could wish that," she said. Then she stood up and began stacking plates.

Ben, watching her back, realized that he'd relished talking with her, even though they disagreed on most issues, such as the kids.

"It's after twelve," he said, helping her dry dishes. "They should be home."

Amy wasn't worried. "You know how kids are. Watches are only ornaments. Relax, Ben."

He walked her outside. He didn't know why. But then, Amy Stone defied his attempts at analysis—or rather, the analysis of his own motives. He'd been happy with Beth. Both shy and quiet, even bookish, they'd made a perfect match. Their lives, probably so routine as to seem mundane to Amy Stone, had fit for Ben like the tongue-and-groove planks of their bedroom floor, which they'd laid by hand themselves. With Beth, he had always known what to expect. Amy Stone's irreverence unsettled him, confused him. Yet it also drew him, which made Ben feel guilty.

"I enjoyed tonight," he said anyway.

Tonight their conversation, her nearness in the dark theater, had energized him, made him feel . . . alive again.

"You surprise me, Ben." At her car, she opened the door, then turned. And ran a finger down his chest. "A Harley T-shirt, black no less. It looks good on you."

"It's Greg's."

"Pie and coffee—with brandy. Now this. You actually had a good time."

"Don't rub it in."

"With me," she added.

"Don't worry. I don't plan to make it a habit."

To his irritation, she laughed.

"Listen," he said, "before you go, I need to tell you something about the kids. Maybe you won't feel so permissive toward them when you hear."

"Hear what?"

He looked down at the grass, already wet with dew. Crazy thought, but he wanted to walk barefoot in it.

"When I loaded the washer tonight, with my wrecked shirt, I threw in Greg's jeans. They were dirty from the farm. Turning the pockets inside out, I found a few sticks of straw, two rusted bolts, twenty-three cents in change . . . and a foil-wrapped condom."

He'd shocked her.

"A condom," she repeated. "Well. I'll talk to Heather."

"I'll talk to Greg."

His heart was pounding. He couldn't seem to block his thoughts. The kids, the obvious sexuality between them that, at their age, he admitted, could be so difficult to control. The movie, with its sad-sweet, fated love affair. Amy Stone's long legs, gleaming in the summer moonlight, the sheen on her dark hair, the challenging sparkle in her green eyes. When she turned to go, Ben clasped her wrist.

"Amy?"

Then he tugged and she was in his arms. Before he'd stopped to think, he'd pressed her back against the car and lowered his mouth to hers. Her lips instantly parted. He tasted coffee on her tongue, still warm and sweet from too much sugar, mixed with the brandy on his, tasted heat and desire. Beth. He could hear his own breathing; but it wasn't Beth beneath his searching hands, not this sleek, compact body, the sweep of breast and waist and thigh. Her arms crept around his neck, holding him close as Ben deepened the kiss, then deepened it more.

The side of the car was slick with dew. It slid across his knuckles as he grasped Amy Stone's slender hips to drag her near and ground himself against her. Her moan mingled with his, and winded, stunned, Ben drew back.

"Jesus, I'm sorry."

He was no better than an eighteen-year-old kid in the backseat of his father's car. No better than Greg.

Warm in his arms one second, in the next Amy had spun away. She started the car with a rush that had him stepping back from the curb.

"I've heard enough 'I'm sorrys' from you, Benjamin Pearce. Don't be sorry for being human after all."

She sped off down the quiet street and left him standing there, his body aching, his mind a blur. Beth, he thought. But it was Amy Stone's eyes he remembered, full of unshed tears.

Last night I cried myself to sleep.

It was late when Aaron came from the barn— late again. Without a glance at me, he banged the kitchen door behind him and stalked to the sink to wash his hands.

"It seems to me," he said, "that it's not too much for a hard-working man to expect a hot meal waiting."

His words stung, all the more because hours ago I'd made his favorites, and he hadn't so much as peeked into the pots on the stove. "Dinner's ready, Aaron."

He didn't even look at me when I filled his plate. "These potatoes are dry, lumpy, the green beans like mush." He pushed a stringy chunk of meat around. "I wouldn't feed this to the pigs."

His voice sounded like Papa's. But I didn't know how to soothe Aaron, and truth be told, at that moment I didn't care to.

"Not good enough for the pigs? I disagree,"

I said and, snatching Aaron's plate, dumped its contents back into the iron pot.

"Elizabeth!"

I went outside and pitched our dinner over the fence to the hogs.

Aaron grabbed, too late, for the pot handle. "What did you do that for?"

"It seems you've made a bad bargain," was all I said.

I am surely not Aaron's mother, talented at her linen-making—the linens we've tumbled in the big bed every night—skilled in her garden, in her kitchen.

I know Aaron's had his troubles, not only preparing for harvest but with his livestock. Aaron has been fretting over two cows due to deliver late calves any day now. He has more work than one man can do, and he must be as tired as I am, but I'm here, too, and can't help feeling neglected.

"I think you care more about this farm, about the animals, than you do about me," I whispered.

"I think you're acting like a spoiled schoolgirl!" The pot thumped to the ground and he stormed back to the house.

When I finally went to bed, Aaron was asleep, but I only lay staring at the ceiling. I have come to dread the mornings, my stomach fluttering like bird wings as soon as I lift my head.

Perhaps Mama is right, that I was too young to marry. I fell asleep at last to dream of home— in Carran.

When I awoke, it wasn't yet light, and Aaron was missing. Ignoring the dizziness when I stood up, fighting the first surge of nausea, I hurriedly dressed and headed for the barn.

The barn lantern glowed like a beacon, guiding my way.

"Aaron?"

"Here," he said, his voice low and husky.

I turned to one of the stalls he'd mucked and strewn with fresh straw for birthing. Head down, shoulders hunched, Aaron was on his knees, his legs spread wide. Between them lay a shiny, wet mass.

I caught my breath. "The calf's been born."

He didn't answer, didn't look up. Apology for our first quarrel was on the tip of my tongue, but the miracle of birth was one of the first things I loved about the farm, and I wanted to share it again with Aaron.

"Born," he said, "and . . ."

His hand moved in a futile gesture toward the dark lump in the straw. Blood covered his fingers, splotched his shirt.

"Dead?" I whispered.

"Breech," he went on. "Stuck like a cork in a bottle. I couldn't turn him round until it was too late. I was lucky to save his mama."

Stunned, I fell to my knees beside him. "Oh, Aaron. I'm sorry."

He lifted his gaze, and I saw tears spiking his dark lashes, filling his eyes. "I'm sorry, too," he murmured.

He meant our quarrel as well, and so did I. Leaning awkwardly over the calf's still body, I wrapped my arms around his shoulders. Aaron rested his forehead against mine.

"Such a waste," he said.

"I love you, Aaron."

A sigh shuddered through him. He raised his head to kiss me, long and lingering, his mouth wet, trembling over mine. "Enough to fix me breakfast?" he asked at last.

"Enough to try," I said.

He shook his head. "Last night was my fault. I was late and I've been worried." He looked at the calf. "Now I know why."

He rose, taking my hand to pull me up, and after Aaron carried the tiny calf outside, we walked back to the house. I knew I couldn't worry him any further.

Aaron still loves me, and I'll keep trying to be the good wife he needs. This morning, sure that my nerves had finally settled, I ate eggs and toast and managed to wait until Aaron went to bury the calf before I lost my breakfast.

Clattering about the kitchen, Jessie hummed to herself. It was either hum, she thought, or cry as Aaron had in the barn. The scene had been difficult to write; Jessie imagined Sunbeam as the calf and Rosie, its mother, nudging the empty straw bed in search of her baby.

Jessie worked to keep from searching herself for the answer to Nick's question. The afternoon in Tom's attic had spurred her to greater effort in her writing, and the novel was flowing well. The clothing Nick had found, the Bible belonging to his great-great-great-grandfather, Jessie's relentless queries about the past—all kept her awake far into the night, wondering, working. How had she stumbled on Aaron in the first place? How much of his story had she already used herself? What more could she hope to find out? What was real and what merely invention?

Maybe Nick was right. She knew he'd found his discoveries in the old trunk as intriguing as she herself did; yet they'd somehow frightened him, too, and she couldn't seem to set that, and what it might mean, aside either. Maybe, as he'd suggested, she should get away.

Time together, he had said. Or did Nick merely want her away from Carran, away from the farm? And her book was only an excuse?

Jessie turned salmon steaks splashed with wine, in the skillet. She sprinkled them with lemon and dill weed.

What did Nick really want from her?

Her bitterness had faded in these few months; but Nick was still Nick, determined to have his way, and Jessie had learned the hard way to be true to herself. Nick might want her, as he had long ago; but he hadn't loved her then, and she doubted he loved her now.

Yet Nick had stayed in Carran this summer to please his father, maybe to please her; he had asked her to be friends again; he'd come close once more to being her lover; he'd invited her to Charleston.

Was she being fair to him?

Nick, who'd left Tom's farm so long ago for his own success. And Jessie, the country girl come home again. What could she afford to give now?

She thought of Elizabeth, trying to please her young husband. A city girl who'd married a farmer, "a harder life," Nick said, "than it has to be." Still, Elizabeth was trying, and Jessie kept cheering her on.

With a sense of purpose all her own, she plunged into the refrigerator, coming up with the fresh broccoli she'd bought the day before. She had enough greens for salad, too. Maybe it was time, on one condition, that—like Elizabeth with Aaron—she tried to see Nick's side of things.

"Greg, see you for a second?" Nick stood, hands on hips, watching the boy lope back across the farmyard. Nick walked him closer to the barn where they wouldn't be seen, or heard, by Greg's friend Brian. The two, with Friday paychecks in hand, had been heading for town. And a couple of hot dates, he assumed.

"Yeah, Nick. What is it?"

He looked down into Greg's serious blue eyes, so like Ben's. Nick still had three inches on the kid. Maybe his extra height would help deliver the authoritative message. Damn Ben, anyway, for shyness—and with his own son.

"Your father asked me to speak to you. He's a little concerned about something he found in your jeans the other night."

Greg flushed.

"You know what I'm talking about?"

"Yeah, I guess." Greg toed the dirt with his work boot. "So?" he said, glancing at Nick, who had seen the manly defiance before and knew how fragile it was.

"So, what about it?"

"Nothing."

Nick cleared his throat. Maybe it was a good thing he'd never had children. "Seems to me you and Heather are getting in deep," he said, "before her time."

"Oh, right. I'm already convicted on circumstantial evidence." Greg sighed, his face burnished like a Red Delicious apple. "We haven't done anything."

"But you're thinking about it."

He couldn't help the half smile. "All the time. So does every other guy my age with his girl."

"What does Heather think?"

"She . . . we . . ." He tried again. "Look, Nick, I care about her."

"I know you do."

"I'd never hurt Heather."

Nick let him off the hook. "But you want each other worse than you've ever wanted anything in your life. And sometimes, no, every time, it gets harder to stop the loving from getting out of bounds." He set a hand on Greg's shoulder. "Does that about sum things up?"

"A-plus," he said, then looked up again. "God, Nick, just holding her, kissing her . . . feels so good. She thinks so, too. And I know one of these nights . . ."

"So you bought the condoms."

"Yeah."

Nick let out a breath. He thought of Jess now, of the girls long ago. "Believe me, I know how you feel. When I was your age, I carried a Trojan in my wallet—the obligatory telltale circle—until it got so brittle it fell apart. The girls I dated then didn't know how lucky they were that I was scared to use the damn thing. It sure wouldn't have provided any protection."

"You never . . . ?"

"Well, I didn't say that." Nick squeezed his shoulder. "But your dad's real worried, you know. So am I. Heather's pretty young, Greg. We hope you'll wait a few years before—"

"*Years?*" It was a groan.

"You're the man here," Nick said. "Try to remember this—anticipation's half the game. Mystery's an underrated factor. Cool things down a little, and I don't think you'll be sorry."

"That's the theory, huh?" Greg grinned at him. "With you and Jessie, too?"

"That's the theory."

He didn't tell Greg that he'd only remembered it at the last second in Jess's office. If she hadn't stopped him with one word . . . Who was he to give Ben's son advice?

"Thanks, Nick."

But Nick stopped him again halfway across the yard. "I'm advising against early sex with a fifteen-year-old girl, but if it happens that you just can't wait, I'm glad you've thought about keeping Heather safe."

He had no idea whether his words had done any good. He watched the two boys sail Brian's pickup down the driveway in a cloud of dust, then with a sigh, he stripped off his work shirt and headed toward the house to wash for supper.

Moments later, at the enticing aroma of lemon and dill, Nick stepped out of the downstairs bathroom to find Jess at the kitchen counter, unloading food. He hadn't seen her since he'd asked her to go with him to Charleston. He was still waiting for her answer. "I didn't know you were coming over. Did I miss something?"

"Not yet." She gestured toward his place at the table, a serving spoon in midair as her gaze met Nick's bare chest.

In the past weeks he'd spent most of his time outdoors instead of at a drafting board or in endless business meetings. Under the hot July sun he worked shirtless, and his tan had deepened by the day, his body had hardened. In Charleston Nick belonged to a health club, not the highest priority in his schedule, but in Carran physical fitness took care of itself. He realized he'd never been in better shape in his life, and took pleasure in Jess's appreciative stare.

"Sit down," she finally said, then called Tom.

"Amen," his father mumbled, dragging the plate Jess had filled for him closer and digging in. "You're an angel of mercy, girl. I wasn't looking forward to another of Nick's frozen pizzas."

"That why you always eat a whole one yourself?" Nick grabbed his discarded shirt from the bathroom before taking his seat. "Fresh broccoli? Real butter?"

"You're a growing boy," she said.

"Baked potatoes and fresh salmon?"

"It's Gran's recipe."

Nick sighed. "I'd know it anywhere." Then he grinned at her. "Nothing's burned, Jess."

She returned the grin. "You're right, I think my book is getting to me. I've written so much about Elizabeth—my heroine—trying to impress Aaron with her culinary efforts that poaching salmon after I shut down the computer seemed the natural thing to do. I even watched the food cook. I couldn't stop myself."

"Amen," Nick echoed his father.

After dinner, with two of Jess's only slightly over-baked brownies under his belt, Nick looked around and decided there were no dishes to wash. "Pop, you must have licked the plates clean, Jess's platter too."

"Hogwash." Then Tom thanked Jess profusely. "I'll clean up here. I miss putterin' in my own kitchen." He looked at Nick. "Why don't you young people find somethin' pleasurable to do?"

"Like what?" Jess asked. "Milk a hundred cows before nightfall?"

Nick ushered her out the door. "No, I'm saving my strength." He turned, backing her into a corner of the darkened porch. His body still hummed from the talk with Greg, and when he'd seen Jess in the kitchen, willingly serving dinner . . .

"Saving yourself for what?" she asked.

The way to a man's heart, he thought. And whispered, "You."

Then, to take his own advice, he decided against kissing her. She hadn't given him an answer yet. From the kitchen he heard Tom, noisily rattling pans, probably so they wouldn't forget he was right inside. For a moment, Nick had; he'd forgotten anyone else existed.

Anyone but Jess.

Dinner had been an excuse, Jessie decided, though she'd enjoyed having company while she ate. Now, in the gathering darkness, she heard Nick's quiet breathing, felt the warmth of his body close to hers. When he reached for her hand, she let him take it. "I've been thinking," she began.

"Yeah?" He glanced at her. "About what?"

"Charleston."

Nick was silent. She didn't think he moved a muscle, even when he breathed.

"I've decided to accept your invitation."

"Yeah?" he said again. "Why's that?"

At the blunt question, which Jessie supposed she deserved, she felt flustered. "I want to see where you live, how you live, where you work." She shrugged. "You said I should get away, but before we go, there's one thing—"

"I said we should get away together."

"That's the one thing," she said. "I want to spend time with you, Nick, but—"

"You don't want to sleep with me."

Hearing disappointment in his flat tone, Jessie drew her lower lip between her teeth. "I don't want to feel as if that's a condition of the trip, no."

"So you're putting one on me instead." Nick dropped her hand. He jammed his fists deep into his pants pockets, met her eyes with a darkened gaze. "Well," he said, "I have four bedrooms. I only need one. You can have the other three, if you want. You can have whatever you need, Jess, as long as you come with me."

11

During Christmas week one hundred thirty years ago, South Carolina had become the first state to secede from the Union, presaging the start of the Civil War. The following April Fort Sumter in Charleston Harbor had fallen to the Confederates. After the war, after General Sherman, the city had lain in ruins on its narrow peninsula between the Ashley and Cooper rivers, and Reconstruction had proved anything but productive. Still, somehow, like a graceful, indomitable lady, its three hundred years of history had survived. The city had outlived wars, both revolutionary and civil, fires, earthquakes, tornadoes, and hurricanes—most recently, Hugo. Now Charleston was thriving again, an easy, elegant blend of past and present, of cobbled streets and church spires, of commerce and concrete.

On first impression Jessie likened the city to Aaron's farm—Tom Granby's farm now, and her grandmother's.

She didn't know what to expect of Nick's Charleston home. Something modern, she'd supposed, multilevel and starkly furnished, all white carpet and walls of glass with a spectacular skyline view; a house that would be the antithesis of his father's; a house that Nick, running from Carran, would have designed himself. But in Charleston such a design would have been distinctly out of place, and Nick's house definitely belonged.

Jessie stood on the sidewalk, inhaling the subtropical sea breeze off the nearby water, the sense of history all around, the scent of gardenias that seemed to waft from the house itself.

Flanked by other narrow homes painted sky blue, peach, and lime green, Nick's three-story house was pink. A soft, weathered rosy pink that made Jessie think of a debutante's blush. Of bridal bouquets. Of all the creamy-skinned, steel-willed southern women she'd ever heard, or read, about.

Nick grinned at her. "Looks like something a hairdresser named Mr. Philippe might buy, doesn't it? This section's called Rainbow Row. Come on inside, I'll show you around."

Jessie followed him into a square, high-ceilinged foyer with a sparkling brass chandelier, a curved mahogany staircase, and a floor of white-veined-with-wisps-of-butterscotch marble. On two walls she saw oil portraits of someone's ancestors. "One was a convicted horse thief, another a prominent slave trader"—Nick pointed at a round-faced, cherry-cheeked man who looked like a choirboy—"and this stern-looking gentleman was, according to my art dealer, one of the area's first rumrunners."

"You're kidding."

"Reprobates all," he said, laughing.

The effect was whimsical, yet to the uninitiated eye one might have been looking at Nick's eminent forebears.

"Not a Granby among them," Jessie observed.

"Right."

There was something about the house that disturbed her, she thought, as Nick led her through the downstairs rooms. From the entry hall they passed into a formal dining room, which flowed into an airy living room that overlooked a lovely walled garden through French doors. He'd knocked out walls to open up the area, Nick explained, and everywhere Jessie saw obviously priceless antiques, rich oriental carpets, gleaming wood floors—and here and there, to shock the eye, small surprises.

A rosewood stand cradled a hide-scarred baseball signed by Mickey Mantle. A burnished gold frame held a child's primitive, colorful drawing. A silk paisley-upholstered wing chair was draped by a woman's delicate ivory handkerchief.

Jessie peered at the initials on the lace. "Was this your mother's?"

"No," Nick said. "It belonged, supposedly, to the wife of the settlement's first governor. She carried it at their wedding, something old. It had been her mother's, and her mother's before that." He paused. "I doubt my mom ever owned a scrap of lace."

With a gesture, he drew her toward the kitchen, which had been added on, jutting into the garden and becoming part of it.

"Tani?" Nick called. "Put that racy novel out of sight and get your apron on. We have company."

Jessie heard a drawer slam shut. Then her gaze

swept the sunny, open space filled with state-of-the-art appliances, green plants hanging everywhere, and settled on the dark-skinned woman who rose from a bentwood chair at the kitchen's rosewood desk. "Why you not call from th' airport, Mister Nick? I didn't think you was comin' till dinnertime. Who's with you, now?" She shook her head, tight black braids streaked with gray flying every which way, like an older version of Whoopi Goldberg. Jessie bit back a laugh.

"Tani, meet Jess, another Yankee carpetbagger who doesn't know pork cracklin's or okra from collard greens."

"She will by the time she leaves here." The housekeeper pulled her into a quick hug. "I'm pleased, Miss Jess."

"So am I. I'm glad to meet you."

Stepping back, Tani gave Jessie a thorough once-over. "Well, yes indeed." Her dark eyes met Nick's. "At last. I see—"

"What, you old busybody?" Nick said.

"See I got to mix you up a potion."

"Don't even think about it."

"A powerful potion to make you irresistible to the right one for a change." Tani grinned, showing Jessie a set of dazzling white teeth. "Welcome to Charleston, Miss Jess. You much prettier than your pictures."

"Pictures?" Jessie frowned. Had she seen the back cover photograph on one of her books?

"Let me show you to your room." Nick took her elbow, steering her from the cheery kitchen. "A word of advice. Don't drink anything she fixes for you, not even ice water."

"Rat poison? Fertilizer?" Jessie asked, smiling.

"Child's play," he said, starting up the long float-ing staircase. "She's a great housekeeper, but we're talking voodoo here, and everybody tells me she knows her stuff."

"And you were badmouthing ghosts? I think you're almost serious. She must drive a hard bargain on pay raises."

"I treat her like a queen." He grinned. "She's ad-dicted to Indian historical romances, reads them when she's supposed to be dusting. I feed her addic-tion. Tani's reluctant to have any of her Gullah rela-tives—hundreds of them—see her buying a book with two people in a clinch on the cover, so she sends me to the store."

Jessie laughed. "Talk about job perks."

The question about her pictures still unanswered, she followed Nick upstairs without pursuing the matter. Maybe, she thought, it was voodoo. After pointing out the other second-floor bedrooms, he ushered her into a large square room with a mahog-any four-poster bed and a matching armoire that covered most of one wall. The silk wallpaper, the bedspread, the quilt folded over the footrail, the pil-lows strewn across the bed, the upholstery of the Empire love seat and twin ladies' chairs—all coor-dinated in shades of peach and cream and a soft spring green.

"It's like an indoor garden," Jessie said.

"An orchard," Nick corrected. Taking a perfect peach from the Limoges bowl on the nightstand, he bit into it. "Sweet. Want some?"

His eyes had darkened, but he didn't move toward her. When she reached for the fruit, Nick's fingers didn't touch hers. In fact, Jessie realized, he'd avoided touching her since they'd stood on Tom's porch the night she agreed to come with him to Charleston.

She savored the succulent fruit, her gaze exploring the elegant bedroom while his eyes inspected her. Jessie's pulse thumped. "This is lovely. Your whole house is beautiful, Nick."

"But not what you expected."

"No." Thinking of Tom's run-down farmhouse, Nick's birthplace, then of her own mistaken expectations, she shook her head. "No, not at all."

"Things aren't always what they seem, Jess." With a last look at her mouth, stained with peach juice, he strolled toward the doorway. "Tani will bring your bags up. I'll leave you to unpack. If you need me . . . for anything . . . my room's on the third floor."

As he gently closed her door, Jessie frowned. Nick's new world surprised her; yet it suited him, too. Maybe he'd been right to follow his dream. She just couldn't put her finger on why that, or something about his house, bothered her so.

Nonsense. She'd come with him to enjoy his company, to see the life he'd chosen, not to ruminate. At the floor-to-ceiling windows that overlooked the garden, she thought: paradise. And with a sigh, decided to spend her afternoon, while Nick attended to business, outside, courting her own Muse.

I can't imagine why, but it happened again this morning. As soon as Aaron disappeared over the hill into the fields, I was sick. What can be wrong with me?

Still, I hesitate to disturb him. While the hot,

dry weather lasts, there is a sense of urgency about getting the hay in, and Michael has come from town to help, much to Aaron's relief but to Mama and Papa's dismay. They think Michael belongs at the bank where he has clerked for the past few years; they think he should marry the banker's daughter and buy a house in town.

Haying is hot, sweaty business, Aaron tells me, so at noon I carried a wicker lunch basket uphill and down into the next field, where I knew he and Michael would be working. By the time I crossed the vast field, I felt hot and damp myself—also nauseated again.

Lifting food from the basket, Aaron said, "Stay, Lizzie, and eat with us. There's plenty here."

My brother, grinning, took his lunch to the edge of the field and sat under an elm tree. He wouldn't intrude, he told Aaron, on a man's time with his bride.

Aaron sank down in the shade of a big willow, its graceful branches nearly sweeping the ground. It made a bower of sorts where we could be alone. Aaron held out a slice of ham on bread, and my stomach lurched.

"I'm not hungry, really. You eat."

He eyed me with a frown. "You haven't been hungry in weeks. You've thrown so much food to the pigs that they're ready to be butchered three months early."

I ran a finger inside the waistband of my calico skirt. "My clothes are already tight. Would you have me as fat as a Christmas goose, when it's still summer?"

He laughed. "I'd have you any way I could get you." His gaze fixed upon my mouth. "Come here," he said, and reached for me.

I went into his arms, clinging, my hands laced behind his head. Poor Aaron. I don't seem to have the energy for lovemaking these days, and it seems I cry all the time lately; I can't seem to help myself.

If I told Aaron how sick I've been, he'd drive me into town to the doctor. But I am afraid to learn the truth.

"What's wrong, love?" His hands light upon my shoulders, he drew back and looked into my eyes. "Why, you're white as hen's eggs and—"

"Oh, no," I said with a groan.

Aaron's strong hand clamped the back of my neck, and he held me while I retched.

At last I sank miserably onto my heels, clammy hands clasped in my lap.

"I'm sick, Aaron."

"Yes," he said gently, "I see that."

"No, I've been sick for weeks," I said and burst into tears.

"Hush, love." Aaron gathered me close, smelly dress and all. He wiped my lips, my cheeks, my eyes with a napkin dipped in watered-down lemonade. "You'll bring Michael from his lunch and scare the horses." He rocked me in his arms, then said, "Tell me about this sickness of yours."

When I finished, he said nothing. Nearby
Sugar and Spice nickered to each other as if to
say they'd enjoyed their lunch bag of oats, that
they were ready now for a nice dessert of fresh
green grass. I looked up into Aaron's face.

"When did you first become ill?" he asked.

"In July, not quite a month after our wedding."

"And when did you have your last . . .
monthly flow?"

For a moment I couldn't remember. "I think
. . . the week before we married."

"And you're tired all the time? Like last
night?"

I nodded miserably. I'd fallen asleep in my
chair, and he'd carried me to bed. "I'd rather
sleep than anything else."

Suddenly Aaron grinned.

"You're not sick, love," he said. "You're
pregnant."

"Pregnant?"

"It's not such a mystery, you know. We've
been giving my mother's sheets a great deal of
attention since mid-June. But then, I don't blame
you for not guessing what was wrong—or
rather, right. If your mama didn't tell you about
pleasure, I'm fairly sure she didn't explain its
consequences."

One more example, I thought, of all the things
I didn't know.

"Are you sure?" I asked.

His hand trailed a fiery path from my cheek
to shoulder to breast, over the tender nipple,

then past my waist to caress my stomach. Still flat, still fluttery. Was it really possible?

"I'm sure," he said. Then Aaron raised his head and let out a shout of laughter, of sheer joy.

· Michael called out, "What's happened?"

And Aaron told him, "We're having a baby!"

A baby.

Rousing herself, Jessie blinked away the scene she'd been composing in her mind and looked around Nick's garden. Stretched out on a white chaise longue, she gazed at his roses, red and pink and yellow and white, at the lush gardenias along one brick wall, at the hydrangeas and hanging baskets of fuchsias. Paradise for sure, but it had taken her all afternoon, and a foray back into her own work, to realize what was wrong, at least with the house.

"Ready to go?" Back from a meeting at his downtown office, Nick appeared at the open French doors. He'd promised Jessie a visit to the Seaview site, and she was suddenly glad to leave the house behind with her scene preparations for Aaron and Elizabeth. *A baby.*

Unaccountably, the thought depressed her.

"What's the matter?" Nick asked. "Too warm out here?"

Jessie stood up, stretching. "No, the heat feels good as long as I can be lazy. Should I change first?"

"You look fine. Great." He smiled. "You might as well add dust to the sweat of a July afternoon in Charleston. We'll shower when we get back, before I take you to dinner."

The shower implied intimacy, the kind Elizabeth might share with Aaron; the kind Jessie had never known with Peter; the kind Nick might want but had promised not to push for. Trying to block out her perverse disappointment, she went outside with Nick to his car, parked in front of the house. Only the front, she had realized, wasn't the front.

"Did anyone ever point out to you that your house is turned the wrong way?" She glanced along palmetto-lined East Bay Street, then toward the harbor. "The gabled end faces the street. Your house is sideways."

"So are all the others." He laughed. "Charleston custom. The piazzas, you'll notice—we don't call them porches or verandas—run front to back as well and usually face south to catch the breeze. But that's also for privacy. Most of these houses were built during the nineteenth century, not quite as old as your grandmother's. Also, at the time, real estate taxes were based on frontage distance, so everybody built the skinny way out," Nick explained. "One or, at the most, two rooms wide. That's why they're called single houses."

"And I thought it had to do with being a bachelor."

Nick's glance was warm. "Apparently not. The man who built my house, one hundred thirty-one years ago, had ten kids."

A baby, Jessie thought again. She couldn't seem to rid herself of the idea. Even after six years of marriage with Peter, who hadn't cared about children, she still wanted a family. Why could she so easily envision the other bedrooms on Nick's second floor as nurseries when she didn't trust him enough to touch her?

". . . so the land around here's largely sand," he was saying. "What are you scowling about?"

If he had his dream, so did she.

"I'm on holiday. I have a right to scowl. At the sandy soil, at your funny one-room-deep house." She stretched her arms over her head, waggling her fingers out Nick's open sunroof at the sky. "It's hot as Hades here, the sun fried my brain half an hour after I went into the garden, the humidity's enough to grow mold on anything that doesn't keep moving . . ." The frown turned into a grin. "But Charleston's gorgeous, Nick. I'm glad I came."

He smiled. "Just watch out for Tani's liquid concoctions—or you may not want to go home again."

For the rest of the day, Nick showed Jessie the city she already cherished. She didn't want to but couldn't help herself. At City Market she bought a huge Gullah basket in which to dump research materials for her book, then, feeling like Elizabeth, hopped a horse-drawn carriage for a tour of Charleston's historic district.

In late afternoon, outside Charleston at Seaview, Nick clamped a yellow hard hat on her head, then introduced her to Rob Griffith, his foreman, who guided Jessie around the yard while Nick conferred with his engineers about a plumbing problem.

If she'd had any doubts about Nick's ability as an architect or an employer, Rob put them to rest. "Nick's great," he told her, pointing out a board with protruding nails before she walked over it. "Watch your step. This place is dangerous, but we have the best safety record of any job in Charleston this year. Nick runs a tight ship, but so do I. After my accident last fall . . ."

When he didn't go on, Jessie prompted him. "You had an accident?"

Rob frowned. "During Hurricane Hugo. Nick had

ordered everybody off site even before the city issued warnings to evacuate, but as my wife says, I'm pretty stubborn. I wanted to finish up, so I sent my crew home and kept working. Next thing I knew, I was in the hospital with a cracked vertebra, a broken leg, and a bad concussion. Damn seawall gave way," he said. "I'm lucky I'm not dead."

"Or unemployed." Nick came back with a rolled-up blueprint in his hand. "Don't let this kid soft-pedal what happened. When that seawall sprang a leak, this place was under water within minutes. Two-thirds of the clubhouse where Rob was working caved in—"

"The old clubhouse," Rob said, grinning.

"The main support beam crashed down but didn't pin him. Rob crawled—or swam—to higher ground and radioed on the company truck for an ambulance. Then he passed out. He came to three days later."

"With one furious Mrs. Rob Griffith bending over my hospital bed—as far as she could bend, six months pregnant."

"And that's not the end of it," Nick went on. "Rob's house just down the road here from Seaview, on the way to the highway, got swept—"

"Clear off its foundation," Jessie said, remembering. Nick had mentioned that the first night she'd seen him again, at Ben's. But she didn't know the rest of the story.

"When Nick learned my insurance wouldn't cover rebuilding, he paid for it himself."

Nick looked at the ground. "Don't exaggerate. A load of lumber, a truck full of cement, a few guys on their day off—it didn't take long to slap things together."

"Nick, you never just slap things together." Rob

ran a hand through close-cropped auburn hair. "Don't let him tell you so, Jess." A shrill whistle from his work crew made Rob break into a jog. "Yeah, coming." Over his shoulder he called back, "Ask Nick sometime about that big bridge loan for the clubhouse and—"

Nick's gaze shifted. "Get moving, Griffith."

"Right, boss." Rob waved back at them. "See you later. Bring your lady to the house tomorrow, Nick. Alaina heard you're back in town, and her nose is out of joint. She says you haven't seen the baby since you moved back north. My wife's talking neglect, and you don't want to be on her bad side. Come early. We'll grill a mess of catfish."

"It's a date," Nick said. "Thanks."

Seaview, Nick informed her as they drove through the site, had been designed as a diversified community/resort with houses ranging from moderate in price to custom-built luxury. The houses, snugged in among mature plantings, made Jessie's mouth water. Each one was unique.

"Home buyers here can bring in their own architect, their own plans if they want," Nick explained. "If they don't, then they hire us—Seaview Ltd., in this case—and we show them fifteen to twenty basic plans. From those, we customize to suit the buyer."

The winding, tree-shaded roads led past a discreet condominium complex, "mostly time-sharing owned by people from up north," Nick said, then around a vast stable and horse training facility catering in part to wealthy Grand Prix jumpers, also from up north, and eventually to a waterfront complex the likes of which Jessie had never seen.

Near dusk, the view was breathtaking. She saw

tennis courts, both clay and grass, several Olympic-sized swimming pools, a sweep of oceanfront, the white sand beach dotted with umbrellas and Adirondack chairs—and then, the ruined clubhouse itself.

"We're in the process of dismantling what's left. After Hugo, there was a lot of concern, particularly from insurance companies, about building on such fragile soil." He pointed toward several shells of smaller buildings, apparently abandoned just off the beach. "You're looking at two homes worth three-quarters of a million dollars each when we built them. All custom. Nobody ever lived in them. When the storm hit this beach, they went under and came up scrap lumber."

He walked her partway down the beach, which stretched for three miles, both of them taking off their shoes in the sand.

"Those home owners weren't the only ones hurt," Jessie said. "Nick, you must have lost a fortune."

"At least one," he agreed. "Just shows you where feeling cocky gets you. Last September I was sitting pretty. Great house in Charleston, best architectural firm in town, more work than we could handle. If I walked into a bank, the loan officer wanted to fill out my form for me, write the check himself. Then came Hugo."

"And no more loans," Jessie murmured.

"Oh, I have loans. Too many of them. All new, and at interest rates you wouldn't want to hear." Then he touched Jessie's shoulder briefly, directing her gaze around the next bend of the shore, and she gasped.

"Oh, Nick." His new clubhouse hugged the coastline, flowing around the sweep of oceanfront like another wave off the Atlantic. In shades of driftwood, white foam, and the blue-green sea, it blended perfectly with the environment. "That's the most beautiful building I have ever seen. Anywhere," Jessie said.

"Thank you."

She could hear the pride in his voice. Her ex-husband hadn't shared the details of his work with Jessie, and Peter had no interest in hers. She stepped closer to Nick.

"Why is it built on stilts?"

"Well, some people—like me—think it's an expression of the sea around it, like moving water. Others, like Rob, call it The Big Bird. There's some bitterness in that," Nick said with a half smile. "We've had a battle here with the conservationists. I'd have rebuilt at the old clubhouse site, but it's not well protected from the sea, and we'd only face the same problems—not only insurance—when the next big storm comes through. After Hugo I had a chance to buy the next parcel of land downshore, which is where we're standing now. We were ready to pour concrete when the environmentalists started flapping their wings."

"They tried to block construction?"

"They'd have buried Seaview completely if they could—not that I have anything against the group who signed petitions against us. They have valid points, and in my work I try not to harm the environment. I try to blend with it."

Jessie glanced at the clubhouse. "Not a bad try."

He smiled. "Anyway, the new site seemed even worse to them, not because it's unsafe but because the tidal marshes are a breeding ground for shorebirds and crab."

"What did you do?"

"Went back to the drafting board. Slashed out the

marina I'd planned, moved that, with a proposed new yacht club—half a mile up the beach, and designed an entirely new clubhouse. Which is what you see."

"That's the reason for the stilts," Jessie said.

"And the colors," Nick said. "The building materials too. They blend with the marsh grasses, the water flowing."

"Do the birds still nest? The crabs thrive?"

"By God, they'd better." Nick grinned. "I think the last problems have been worked out, but this may be the most expensive nursery any proud papa ever built."

"You love the wildlife, too."

"Yeah," he admitted. "So now you know what some of those Charleston meetings have been about, the trips here from Carran."

"Now I know."

Jessie walked closer to the water, away from Nick. He'd left Carran long ago to follow this dream. It hadn't been easy, she knew; not easy to pursue, and not easy to keep. After Hurricane Hugo, before next spring's target date to finish, he was still deeply in debt, putting everything he had at risk to save this resort.

Nick's home was equally lovely, but though he'd shared that with her too, it somehow excluded her just as much. Why? she wondered.

At his soft voice, saying, "Jess," she turned. And for the first time saw Nick as he really was now. Not in jeans and a blue chambray shirt, riding Tom's tractor—reluctantly. But barefoot, wearing expensive pleated beige linen pants, an oyster-colored silk shirt open at the neck, sleeves rolled to his elbows, and a yellow hard hat. He was a handsome man, charismatic and darkly compelling, but in that moment, Jessie wished he were a stranger.

If she'd never known him, been hurt by him, she could easily love Nick now. Looking into his dark eyes, instead she felt sadness wash over her like the waves that lapped the shore at her feet. How could she blame him for leaving Carran, and Tom, so long ago? After seeing his home and Seaview, she couldn't, yet she'd only made another mistake. Because long ago, with his memories of Carran and the farm, he'd left Jessie, who didn't need the reminder, behind too.

Twelve years older, wiser, still she shouldn't forget that. In spite of herself, Jessie knew, she could easily love Nick's world here, but it was a world in which she didn't belong.

"Let's go back," she said. She shouldn't have come here.

12

Ben had been feeling smug about Jessie's trip to Charleston; she and Nick would swelter there. And what else? he wondered, though Nick had called him a prude when Ben objected to the week's vacation with his sister.

"Lighten up," Nick said. "Jess is old enough to take care of herself."

"Don't forget it, then." Don't hurt her, he'd thought.

Nick had asked Greg to stay with Tom at the farm while they were gone, and as soon as he and Jessie left, the heat had moved in, too. In Carran, summer temperatures rarely soared above eighty degrees, but on Ben's front porch the thermometer had edged past ninety-five by ten that morning, heading for the century mark by midafternoon. He wasn't feeling so smug now. It didn't appear that things would cool off before bedtime.

Nursing a second beer, which had replaced his

unwanted dinner, Ben slouched in front of a TV sit-com rerun. The laugh track was driving him crazy, but he couldn't find the energy to turn it off.

"No big date tonight?" Greg slammed through the screen door, which bounced twice on its hinges.

"Take it easy, for God's sake," Ben said, not referring to the door. He held the lukewarm beer bottle to his forehead. Greg hadn't let up about Amy Stone since the night they'd seen *Ghost*.

"As soon as she's done work, me and Heather are going to the high school—"

"Heather and I," Ben corrected.

"Whatever. There's open swim night at the pool. You look real hot," he said. "Want to come along?"

"No, thanks." He straightened in his chair. "I thought you were baby-sitting Tom Granby."

"We had dinner—frozen pizza—then he started watching a cop show. He said to spend the evening with my girl, then come back there to sleep." At the stairway, Greg paused. "That's okay, isn't it? Tom seems fine, he ate a whole pizza himself. And helped me milk cows tonight."

"Great," Ben said. "Nick would have a fit."

"Tom says he hates being babied. He can walk a mile and a half now without even puffing, and he checked his blood pressure this afternoon after his hike. It was almost normal."

Ben waved a hand. "He's your responsibility. The night out's between you and Tom."

Greg, apparently satisfied, raced up the stairs two at a time. When he came back down, in fresh jeans and a U Conn T-shirt that made Ben wince for his son's lost opportunities, Greg's eyes were shining with excitement.

He held out a hand. "Want to see? Take a look, Dad."

His pulse suddenly heavy, Ben popped the lid on a wine-colored jewelry box. "You kids today rush everything—" His mouth snapped shut. Inside, on ivory velvet, nestled a gold ring set with diamond chips and a small ruby. "What does this mean, Greg?"

"It's Heather's birthday. She's sixteen." His jaw hardened. "Does that make it okay for me to see her now?"

Ben didn't answer directly. He shut the box, slapping it into Greg's hand. "Did Nick talk to you before he left?"

"Yeah, he talked to me. I don't think he wanted to, but he did—because you wouldn't."

"Now listen here—" Ben was on his feet.

"No, you listen, Dad." Greg charged toward the front door. "Nothing's happened between Heather and me, not that I don't want it to. I have to wonder, though, why you're up my ass about us all the time."

"Greg!"

"It wouldn't have anything to do with you, would it?" he asked, the screen door half open. "With your feelings? Mom's dead, Dad. She's gone. She isn't coming back. And Amy Stone's probably sitting by the phone right now, wishing you'd call."

"I doubt that." Ben remembered the angry tears in her eyes.

"She likes you," Greg insisted. "She really does."

"That's her problem."

"Yeah, right. Some problem. She's hot for you, Dad. I mean it," he said. "She's got it so bad she knifed her own tire just so you'd change it for her."

"How do you know that?"

"Because she borrowed my Swiss Army knife to do the slashing." He paused. "She didn't give it back yet. Why don't you get it for me?"

Ben's skin felt hot. "Have Heather do it," he muttered.

"What's with you, for Chrissake? You've put Mom on some pedestal, like a damn saint or something. She wasn't, Dad. She was pretty and smart and we loved her, but she had flaws like everyone else. You think I never heard you two fighting?"

Ben looked at his watch. "The store closes in five minutes. Don't keep that girl waiting outside."

"Give Heather's mom a call, Dad. It won't kill you."

It might, Ben thought. He stood listening to the throaty roar of Greg's car, which needed a muffler, until the engine sounds faded in the distance. Then he went out onto the porch and sat on the steps, trying to cool off. He'd never seen it so hot in Carran. The usual breeze through the house had stilled, and sweat trickled down his neck.

Amy Stone.

I envy them, she'd said of Greg and Heather. Well, he didn't, Ben told himself. The kid was getting himself in deep—spending his pay on fancy rings, squandering his freedom—and he had a father who didn't know how to dig him out. Hand-holding, long, intimate looks that shut the rest of the world off, romantic movies, late-night swims . . .

At least there'd be a crowd at the high school natatorium. A lifeguard, Ben hoped.

With a sigh, he heaved himself off the front steps, walked around the side yard to the back garden. He couldn't exactly call it a garden anymore; only Beth's roses were blooming, and the Japanese beetles had made lace of all the leaves. In the darkness the creamy blossoms looked phosphorescent. Ben turned away.

In the garage he puttered at his workbench, organizing screwdrivers in ascending order of size on the pegboard, sanding rust off his favorite hammer. He didn't work with his hands much anymore; but he didn't miss it. In the early days of their marriage, he'd fixed everything around the house, even made furniture for Beth. Like his marriage, the house was finished now, and more and more he thought of selling. Escaping.

Happy memories, he thought . . . but not all of them. Dammit, not all.

Stalking back to the house, he considered a cold shower. Another beer. The news special at ten o'clock. Sleep—in his hot, lonely bed—if he could. And rejected them all. Minutes later, in his sweaty shirt and shorts, he'd headed the gray Chevy toward the other side of Carran.

Checking traffic behind him, he caught his image in the rearview mirror. A faint smile warmed his eyes. She'd flattened her own tire? With a laugh, he jabbed a button on the tape deck, but Greg had borrowed his car earlier, and instead of the Chopin prelude he expected to hear, the Rolling Stones blasted forth. "I can't get no satisfaction." Ben left it on, his finger tapping against the steering wheel.

Amy Stone wasn't home.

The house was dark and so was the yard. Ben slouched against the driver's door of his car and tried not to feel disappointed. Maybe she'd gone shopping, late. To the Danbury Mall. Maybe she'd taken herself out to Burger King for one of those scalding-hot apple pies packed in cardboard. Ben dragged his arm across his forehead. On a night like this?

Maybe she had a date.

Ben pictured him. Some guy who smiled all the time, who treated her right. A history professor from Yale, someone she'd met at the historical society doing research. Tall, dark, handsome. Smiling . . . kissing her. Amy kissing him back, her tongue light and quick over his.

With a curse, he wrenched the car door open. The overhead light flashed on, making the darkness all around more impenetrable. Then he heard the sound.

Splashing. Water, cool and enticing.

Ben eased the car door shut. He followed the sound, around the side of Amy Stone's Victorian monstrosity, past her flagstone patio with its white wrought-iron breakfast table and chairs, gleaming in the dark. The darker green foliage of plants seemed to guide his way, their white cachepots like lamps set along a path. His heart thumping with each step, he stopped to slip off his shoes and socks. The cool grass made him want to groan with relief—or anticipation? The path led him, barefoot, through a line of trees to a pond.

Modest in size, elliptical in shape, it would be Amy Stone's treasure, he guessed, perhaps even the reason she'd bought the crumbling house and so lovingly restored it.

His eyes had adjusted to the dark, and he had no trouble spotting her. Ben's pulse beat thundered in his ears. Ten feet from the grassy shore, she stood in water to her thighs, her shoulders glowing in the moonlight. Naked.

Ben swallowed but didn't look away. Didn't blend back into the trees and disappear. It was too late, and he never considered it. She'd already seen him.

"Ben?"

I'm sorry. The words flashed through his mind, though he didn't dare say them, and desire slammed low through his gut. He hadn't stopped to think she might not be alone here, like this. Thank God, she was.

"You look beautiful," he murmured, "like alabaster." His throat felt tight.

"Ben?" She slipped back into the water, up to her neck. "Is that you?"

"It's me." She hadn't heard him, but he'd heard the tremor in her voice. "Don't be afraid, it's just me."

She laughed, triumphant. "I'm not afraid."

In the next instant she drew her hand back, a slash of white in the darkness, then skimmed a sheet of water at Ben. He didn't yelp in surprise; it felt good, wet and refreshing. All around him, heat shimmered. A mosquito took a chunk out of his bare forearm, but he didn't slap at it. His hands were already at the zipper of his fly. He shucked his denim shorts, dragged the damp T-shirt over his head, and made a running flat dive into the cool, waiting water.

He surfaced ten feet out. Amy Stone laughed again.

"You caught me," she said.

"Skinny-dipping."

She sounded breathless. "You could have killed yourself, you know. This pond might have been two feet deep. You do surprise me, Ben."

"Uh-huh."

He wrapped his arms around her and sighed. Or groaned. Then, getting no resistance, he bent his head to kiss her, their mouths wet and slick and cool against each other, their tongues rough and hot. "God." Slowly, impeded by water, he ran his hands over her naked body, her back and shoulders, her breasts, her hips and thighs. Raising his head to take a breath, gasping, he changed the angle on the kiss, slanting his lips over hers, sliding one hand between her legs, stroking. "God help me."

Amy moaned into his mouth. "I never guessed you were such a fast mover."

Ben pulled back. "No, I'm sor—"

Her fingers covered his lips. "Shhh, it's all right."

Slow down, he thought. In a few minutes more, he would have embarrassed himself. She couldn't help but feel his erection, harder than he'd been in years, and he rocked against her, his loins throbbing, his throat so constricted he couldn't say a word.

It was Amy of course who drew him from the water, her smaller hand tucked in his, both shaking, Amy who led him up the bank and gently pushed him down on the long, soft grass.

A few light kisses, one sweep of her fingers through his wet hair, and he rolled her beneath him. Amy's hand found its way from his water-slicked chest, his wildly pumping heart, lower to his abdomen, then lower still, brushing lightly over the briefs he still wore. He heard amusement tinge her voice. "I don't think you really need these."

"Amy, Amy." He lifted his hips, letting her bare him completely to the night, to her searching hands.

"Ben . . ."

"I want you," he whispered hoarsely, seizing her face in his hands and tilting it up. "I want you so damn much."

"I'm glad." She smiled, green eyes dark. "I want you, too."

He kissed her again, then paused. "I . . . I haven't done anything like this in a long time."

He wondered whether his ears were red; they certainly felt hot. At forty, he was still the closest thing to a male virgin Amy Stone was likely to encounter; unlike Nick, he'd had only one woman in his life, the woman he'd married. Beth. A few earlier girlfriends, some light groping in his father's car, once with Amy . . .

"Done what?" she asked. "Gone swimming, without your clothes on—most of them anyway?"

"Made love," he said, wishing for some of Nick's experience, Nick's freedom. "I wouldn't . . . wouldn't want you to be disappointed or . . ."

Amy drew his head down and smiling, whispered, "It's like riding a bike, or a horse. It comes back to you."

"What about you?" Ben asked.

"Me?"

Hours later, he lay beside Amy—sloshed, really—in her king-sized waterbed, her attic bedroom bathed in moonlight, starlight, and wonder. He still had no idea how they'd gotten from the side of the pond into the house or up three flights of stairs. Ben was certain he hadn't let go of her for a second, her body or her mouth. After two explosive climaxes, he wondered why his heart was still beating.

He tried again. "Do you . . . since your divorce, I mean . . . date much or—"

She turned in his arms, one finger tracing his kiss-swollen mouth. "Do you want me to let you off the hook here, or what?"

"I want the truth."

"It comes back to you," she murmured, "like a wonderful song. Remember the night you and I went dancing at that college mixer over in Storrs? And they played 'Moon River' three times?"

"It was an old song, even then."

Amy ignored him. "But you said it was our song? Then later, we drove to the lake and parked, the road dark as pitch, no stars."

"You kissed the same way tonight, near the pond . . . in this bed." Ben grasped Amy's shoulders, kissing her again and feeling the same hot spill of desire through his body. "God, your kisses . . . the best I've ever had."

And guilt replaced desire.

"Why did we never take it farther than that, Ben?"

He pulled back. "Because I'm a prude . . . shy . . . whatever. Nick says so, and Greg, you—"

"You're also very dear." She kissed him. "Honest and sexy."

"Yeah?"

"Very." She said, "I always envied Beth."

"Don't."

"Don't envy her, or don't mention her?"

"Both," he said.

Ben sat up, the bed rocking beneath him. "How do you ever sleep in this thing? It never stops moving."

"That has its advantages."

But he wasn't in the mood for more teasing, especially sexual banter. "The reason I never, we never, went farther than a few kisses and some petting—"

"What a quaint term. I haven't heard that in years."

"That's what we called it. I'm not as world-weary as you or Nick. I haven't been around the track so many times." Amy made a sound, but he wouldn't look at her. "We never went farther because I met Beth."

"And you still think I tried to destroy your relationship with her?"

"Well, you didn't," he said. "We got married, the next day or so it seems. And I never cheated on her, was never even tempted to leave her. Does that make me boring? Or some kind of jerk? I don't care," he went on without waiting for an answer. "I loved my wife and my kid and the home we had together. I liked having the respect of people in Carran who put their trust in me, first as a teacher, then as high school principal, and I wouldn't let them down. To this day, I won't."

"No one's asking you to. Are you trying to ruin this, Ben?"

"No," he said. "I just need you to understand who I am, what I am. A plain, ordinary guy—"

"With absolutely no self-esteem, obviously," Amy said. "Believe me, I know all about that. I earned a college degree in putting self back together, salvaging ego, when my husband took a walk and left me with Heather. Maybe I deserved his betrayal, who knows? But whether I did or not, I've built a new life for myself and my daughter, one you don't approve of, I'll say it for you"—she jumped up off the bed—"so what am I doing here, naked and vulnerable, with a guy who still blames me for some silly mistake I made twenty-some years ago? Where the hell are your clothes?" she asked, looking around.

"I think we left them at the pond."

"Well, find them. And get out of here. My husband walked on me for twelve years as if I were some rubber doormat, and I let him. But by heaven, no other man is going to wipe his feet on me for the rest of my life—and that includes you!"

"Amy, wait a minute." Ben padded across the large room toward her. She whirled away, arms folded, gaze staring sightlessly out the attic window. "I didn't mean—"

"Yes, you did, Ben. Don't stop being blunt and honest now."

Silent for long moments, he cleared his throat. "Tell me something."

"Why should I?" He heard tears in her voice.

"Because tonight was, well, special." Magnificent, he thought, not only the sex. They'd teased and laughed and played, and he'd stepped out of himself for a few hours. Not even Beth had ever drawn him out like that. "And because I've been thinking . . . You say your husband . . . Did you fight much, or were you afraid to fight?"

Amy turned around, looking puzzled.

"Fight? Doesn't everybody?"

"Beth and I didn't. Or I never thought we did. I always felt we had smooth sailing, even felt superior about how well we got along. Then earlier tonight, Greg said he used to hear us quarreling, and I started remembering that the memories weren't just happy . . . or perfect. That *we* weren't perfect." Ben frowned. "The last years especially, when Greg was a teenager, Beth and I had more than a few words, on more than one occasion."

"Just say it, Ben. You scrapped like hell."

"Several times," he said.

"And how did that feel?"

He had to smile. "Damn good. Almost as good as making up."

"Well, then." She was smiling, too.

"Like now," he said, and cupped her face in both hands. "Let's not fight anymore tonight. Tonight I don't feel like just some forty-year-old, washed-up widower who can't communicate with his only child. I feel . . ." He shrugged.

"Like more?" Amy ran a finger lightly over his lips, and Ben caught her hand. He kissed her fingertips.

"Like much more," he said.

Back in bed, he held her close but didn't want to make love again, just yet.

"Can I tell you something else?"

"Whatever you want," she said, his head cradled to her breast, her hand sifting through his hair.

"The night Beth died, we had a fight. The worst fight we ever had. I realize now that for a couple of years she'd been restless, wanting something in her life that she didn't have—a different job maybe, to go back to school, I never found out what—and I'd been getting pretty bored. Same thing, I suppose. Nineteen years of marriage, the routine gets stale. That night Beth didn't want to go to the basketball game, but I insisted. My duty as principal to support the team, and so on. When we reached the gym, we weren't speaking to each other."

Amy's hand stilled. "And then she died."

"And then she died," he repeated.

"Oh, Ben . . . she would have understood."

"But I don't," he said. "I never even said good-bye. Never said"—his voice cracked—" 'I'm sorry,' and now it's too late. It will always be too late."

Amy's arms came around him, tight, and he dropped his head onto her shoulder.

"I never said good-bye to my husband either," she admitted. "I know it's not the same, but now I say good riddance. We never had what I thought we had. I'm glad you and Beth did, but you have to let go, Ben, you have to let go."

He hadn't cried since the funeral. He wasn't an emotional man, or overly sentimental. The tears embarrassed him, though not as much as he might have expected, and by sheer force of will, Ben soon stopped them. Lifting his head, he closed his eyes and searched for Amy's mouth, which she obligingly offered.

"Ben?"

"What?"

"I haven't had a man since my divorce."

Ben smiled against her lips. "It comes back to you," he said.

Their soft kisses, soft touches made, oh yes, made him want more. His hands went seeking, finding.

"So," he murmured after a while, "without your ex-husband, without Beth . . ."

"What do we have here, Benjamin Pearce?" Amy gazed soberly into his eyes.

"Just you and me," he finally said.

13

Jessie considered leaving Charleston, leaving Nick, but her grandmother had raised a polite child. As an adult, she remained so. Rob Griffith and his wife had invited them to dinner, and Jessie would go.

Gazing out the car window, she felt grateful for air-conditioning. Heat wavered off the pavement, and, in the stop-and-go traffic streaming out of Charleston at five o'clock, more than a few motorists had broken down by the roadside.

The land was flat, the two-lane road between the highway and Seaview washed with sand, as if some giant artist had painted it with a huge brush, and Spanish moss dripped from ancient, gnarled live oak trees.

Jessie couldn't believe the heterogenous neighborhood in which Rob Griffith had built his house. Cheek by jowl, she saw expensive ranch homes, some behind brick walls, next to tar-paper shacks built on stilts the same as Nick's much more costly clubhouse at Seaview.

"Hugo was no aberration. This area floods out whenever it rains," he told her. "Even a light storm can cause havoc. Not long ago, some strange confluence of the moon and sun produced unusually high tides, and Kiawah and Seaview became just like moated castles. Nobody could get in or leave until the tide went out."

"People pay good money for that?" she said.

The few neutral words were the first she and Nick had exchanged since leaving town. Jessie felt his gaze upon her, but awash in her own misery—ashamed of her mixed feelings about Nick's life here—she couldn't make conversation. She only hoped she could get through the dinner with his foreman.

But, as she suspected most people did, Jessie liked Rob Griffith, and as soon as Nick pulled the car off the road onto the short, blunt grass where there would one day be a driveway, she found herself smiling.

Rob emerged from a low brick and clapboard ranch house typical of the area. He wore a broad grin and a coarse apron, and in his arms he carried a chubby, bright-eyed baby.

"Miss Jess, meet Delilah. Not a year old and about to take over the world."

Jessie touched the baby's hand. "She's beautiful, Rob. She looks as if she just may do it."

Rob plopped the dark-eyed Delilah into Nick's arms, then headed for the house. "The grill's smoking fit to kill every mosquito on this coast. I'd better throw the steaks on."

"I thought we were having catfish," Nick called after him.

"I have a slave driver for a boss. No time to be just gone fishin'."

Nick laughed. "Hey, 'Lilah, where's my kiss?"

"Da-da," Delilah crowed, flailing out with both arms to swat Nick's face.

A woman slapped the screen door shut behind her, gliding down the three steps to the yard. Tall and regal in bearing, one of the most beautiful women Jessie had ever seen, she had sleek dark hair, glowing dusky skin, and snapping black eyes full of humor. Her drawl was soft, southern. " 'Lilah's having an identity crisis. Hi, Nick. It's good to have you home." She draped one arm around his neck and kissed him heartily on the cheek. "Our savior. Has Rob shown you the new patio? Your concrete finally set."

Nick kissed her in return. "Not yet. I was hoping he'd offer me a beer before we talk business."

"Follow him around back." Smiling, she arched a brow. "And this must be Jess. Hi, I'm Alaina. Welcome to our humble abode. If you like wet diapers and burned steaks, you'll feel right at home."

"Jess is queen of the burned steak department."

At his grin, Jessie made a face. "Only when I'm feeling absentminded. Hello, Alaina. Thanks for inviting me."

"We wouldn't have missed it." Alaina gave Nick a speculative look. "Nice going, boss."

Nick set off across the yard, and Jessie followed. On his broad shoulders, her pudgy legs drumming against his chest, perched Delilah, babbling in some language no one else understood—except possibly Nick, whose rich laughter floated behind them. His dark hair shone in the late afternoon sun, and Jessie's heart turned.

As a girl, she'd considered Nick somewhat rebellious, had always seen him fighting "his wild side," according to Caroline. Now she realized, from a fresh perspective, that in twelve years he'd settled, if not where she would have seen him stay. One suntanned hand strayed upward to tickle Delilah's belly, sticking out from its striped tank top, and as the baby giggled, Jessie thought what a wonderful father he would make.

After her latest scene with Aaron and Elizabeth, the thought depressed her.

"Beer, Jess?" Alaina asked. "Or we have white wine."

"Wine, please. Thanks."

Alaina followed her gaze. Nick had collapsed on the grass at the edge of the patio, Delilah on his lap. Delilah offered Nick a rattle. When he tried to take it, she grabbed it back. The game went on, Delilah substituting a small stuffed bear, a rubber duck, a soft foam ball—always with the same result. Rolling over the grass, she and Nick dissolved in laughter.

"She's missed him," Alaina said, taking a seat beside Jessie on the patio. " 'Lilah's seven months old, but already in love. Rob says we'd better start saving for the wedding."

"She does seem to adore him."

Had she spoken sharply? Alaina looked at her and said, "Nick's easy to adore. But then, I don't have to tell you that. When Rob had his accident, while I was pregnant with 'Lilah, Nick couldn't have been more helpful. He sat with me at the hospital, made sure Rob had the right specialists, picked up the bills our insurance wouldn't pay." She waved a hand. "And then, this house. With Seaview to resurrect and dozens of homes to restore in Charleston, at cost, Nick still found time to bring a crew out here and set this place back on its foundation. He put up his own money—an open-ended loan, he said, to Rob and me—to save our home. I'd say my daughter has excellent taste. Half this town's in love with Nick Granby."

"And he seems to love it here," Jessie murmured.

Alaina's eyes darkened. "Well, we're kind of a sub-culture, I guess you'd say. Take it from me, belonging's not easy, but Nick's managed somehow." Her gaze met Jessie's. "Are you two . . . ?" With a significant glance toward Nick, she left the question hanging.

"No," Jessie said, squeezing her wineglass. "No, we're not."

"That's funny, I thought—"

"Hey, sugar," Rob called from the other side of the patio. "This meat's perfecto, how about some plates? And another beer for Nick and me?"

Jessie helped Alaina serve the meal. When she handed Nick his second beer, he caught her hand. "Jess, you okay?"

"Fine."

"You look pale. Are your allergies kicking up?"

She hadn't sneezed since coming to Charleston, Jessie realized. "I'm a little tired from the heat, that's all."

"Alaina, let's move inside to the air-conditioning. Jess—"

"No, I'm fine. Really." She took a seat at the picnic table. "There's a good breeze here, and the sea air smells wonderful. I'd like to eat outside."

She held Delilah while they ate. The baby's laugh-ter, the insistent demands for more of Nick's baked potato with sour cream, for a taste of Nick's beer, echoed in the peaceful stillness. The easy jokes between Nick and Rob, his gentle teasing of Alaina had Jessie's throat closing long before she finished the last bite of medium-rare steak. Cuddling the baby close as the sun dropped low, she swallowed.

She liked these warm, unassuming people; disliked herself for resenting the hold they had on Nick. As for Delilah, Jessie had lost her heart, too. Would she ever have what Rob and Alaina did; what Aaron and Elizabeth shared?

After dinner, Alaina carried Delilah into the house for a bath. Following a quick round of good-night kisses from the group still on the patio, the baby went inside to bed and darkness fell, like an intimate caress, among them.

Alaina served coffee and rich apple torte, and Jessie tried to hold up her end in the conversation, which largely concerned local events and people, and of course Delilah.

"She's grown so over the summer," Nick said. "I'm surprised she remembered me."

Rob snorted. "How could she forget her own godfather? The guy who bribes her with toys when she's cranky, cutting teeth, who bought out the store at Christmas—two days before she was born? Who loves her even with a dirty diaper? And offers to change it?"

"Thus endearing himself forever to one Rob Griffith of the queasy stomach." Alaina leaned her head on her husband's shoulder.

"I'll change the next one, I promise."

Her eyes lit up. "The next diaper?"

"The next baby."

"Let's not work on that just yet," Alaina said, faking a groan.

Nick and Jessie laughed, but hers felt as false as Alaina's protest, and she had the most ridiculous urge to cry. She felt Nick's gaze on her, and a few moments later he stood up, drawing Jessie to her feet. "I think the humidity has done Jess in. We—"

Alaina jumped up. "Oh, I'm sorry. We're used to sitting around out here—on our lovely new patio—half the night. But let's go inside. It's cool there."

"No, we'd better head back to town," Nick said.

Jessie barely heard the good-byes. In the car, her voice husky, she said, "What a beautiful family. Delilah's a charmer, Rob's solid and funny, and Alaina . . . Nick, she's gorgeous."

"A helluva woman. Inside too," he said. "Worth bucking the system for."

"Bucking the system?"

"Rob's family is old plantation stock, though penniless now. He's the family success story in this generation. Of course they didn't want him to marry Alaina, cut him off completely. He told me the other day his folks still haven't seen Delilah."

"How unfair. But they love each other so," Jessie said around the lump in her throat. "They'll make it."

He looked away. "If I have anything to say about it, yes. They will."

"You've been good to them." She turned toward him. "You're happy here, aren't you?"

Nick stopped the car. In the green dashboard glow, he looked at her, frowning. "Is that what's wrong? Ever since we toured Seaview, you've been up and down."

"I'm a writer," she said. "By nature we're moody."

Nick ignored her. "I keep waiting for you to announce you're on the next flight home. Is it so bad?"

he asked. "To see me happy? What did you hope to find? Me living in a tar-paper shack"—he waved toward the darkened roadside, where Jessie knew such houses could be found—"scrabbling to put up $30,000 tract homes, hoping to come out with a $500 profit? Why, Jess?"

"No," she said. "No, I—"

"Dammit, why? Because I turned my back on Carran years ago? I was never meant to be a farmer, you know that. Pop and I would have killed each other before the first year was out."

She didn't want to say it. "You could have been an architect in Carran, too."

"No, Jess." He stared grimly at the dark road ahead. "I had to get away, to be my own person. Had to . . ."

"What?"

"Nothing," he said and slipped the car into gear. "Nothing."

Jessie curled into the corner of her seat. She had her pride. She wouldn't beg him for the words. Nick had made his choice, the right choice. His beautiful home, the stylish suite of offices on Meeting Street, which he'd shown her that afternoon—how could she even hope to hear that he hadn't wanted to leave her?

Even his secretary looked perfect. When Jessie had remarked on the slim redhead, who couldn't have been more than Greg's age, Nick smiled. "Her father's a financial mogul. She's marking time here, hoping to drag my assistant to the altar."

"You mean that still-wet-behind-the-ears, sandy-haired boy you introduced me to?"

"That 'boy' graduated first in his class from Rhode Island School of Design. He's thirty-one, older than you are. He's up for an award for the low-income housing project he designed for us last year. The guy who's been running Granby Design while I've played tractor jockey in Carran."

"The one you're not sure you can trust," Jessie said.

"He's inexperienced, not dishonest. He's done well in my absence. A major talent clawing his way up my back. Guess I'm the old man now."

"Yes, right." Jessie grinned at him. "And you'll probably be asked to stand as best man at his wedding—when he steals your secretary."

"Not likely," Nick said. "In confidence, he took her to dinner the other night and told me in the morning that she's a serious airhead."

"A Stepford wife in the making."

"Yeah, maybe." He looked at her. "I like 'em with a lot more brains."

Nick had taken her to lunch at the same restaurant his assistant had previously picked for the banker's daughter-cum-secretary, and they'd shared a fine meal. Continental cuisine, in perfect harmony with Nick's lifestyle.

Now, to the quiet hum of the car's engine, the whisper of air-conditioning, she straightened in her seat. Beautiful secretary, beautiful office. A sublime restaurant. Devoted friends. His exquisite house. But among its precious antiques, its oil portraits of someone else's ancestors, there wasn't a single reminder, or memento, of the years he'd spent in Carran.

That's what she'd sensed was wrong.

He hadn't just left. Nick had made a new life for himself, and buried the past.

Buried her, too.

◆ ◆ ◆

Back at the house, without another word having
been said between them on the drive to Charleston,
Jessie watched Nick rip the seal from a fresh bottle of
twelve-year-old scotch. Waving it, he offered Jessie a
nightcap, which she refused. She watched him splash
a crystal tumbler half full of amber-gold whiskey.

And couldn't keep from asking, "Don't you ever
miss Carran, or the farm, Nick?"

He gazed into his drink. "My life is here," he said
and took a long swallow.

"But your roots—"

"They're here, too."

"Transplanted," she said, "in this sandy soil? How
deep can they be?"

"Deep enough." He edged away from the mahog-
any sideboard toward the French doors. Jessie stalked
him.

"I think it would take very little to pull them free
again, set them down somewhere else, anywhere else,
then tear those out—"

"And plant them where, Jess?" In the doorway he
turned, too close to her. "Back in Carran? No," he
said. "That's not where I belong." Then he murmured
a dismissive good night, and disappeared into the
dark garden with his drink.

Good night? she repeated silently. Sleep? Every
nerve inside her was screaming like a high-voltage
line. Jessie marched toward the kitchen, intent on fixing herself a cup of warm milk. She knew her usual
remedy for insomnia wouldn't work this time, but she
didn't know what else to do.

Nick was wrong about belonging, but she

wouldn't change his mind, and the trip to Charleston had only widened the gap between them.

In Nick's kitchen Jessie was startled to find Tani still there, coiled in the roomy chair at the desk, engrossed in a book. "Don't jump," Jessie said, "it's only me."

Tani slapped the book shut, and Jessie saw its cover. Amid the hot pink and lurid purple of some fictional desert garden, a buckskin-clad Indian embraced a blond in crinolines and lace. The lace had been spread away from her ample breasts, her bared leg climbed the dark-haired hero's hip. "I didn't hear you and Mister Nick come home."

Jessie nodded toward the paperback novel. "Any good? I've never read her work before."

"It's wonderful. Spicy. Romantic, of course." Tani sighed. "Absolutely riveting, Miss Jess." Then she added, "Not as good as yours, of course."

"Well, mine tend toward the mainstream. They're different. Not much grab-and-tickle." She took a carton of milk from the refrigerator.

"Sexy enough," Tani said. "Just between us women. I've read both your books. Couldn't put 'em down."

"That's always nice to hear." For Jessie, that was the mark of a superior story, the kind she hoped to tell.

"You know, your first one—that fella on the cover—reminded me of Mister Nick."

Jessie groaned, nearly dropping the milk. "Not you, too. That's what my young nephew said."

She poured milk into a pan, but Tani snatched it away.

"Miss Jess, you just sit down and keep me company while I fix you somethin' to eat with this. No wonder you're so slim."

"My own cooking's the best diet ever concocted," Jessie said.

"Hardly eat anything at all," Tani muttered.

Jessie didn't argue. In Carran she'd developed a proprietary feel for Gran's kitchen. The kitchen in Charleston was Tani's province, her territory, and it had become her personal mission to "feed you up, Miss Jess." Jessie surrendered to being pampered.

"Mister Nick gone up to bed?" Tani asked idly.

"No, he's in the garden."

She frowned. "He spend too much time there, brooding. He brooding now?"

"I wouldn't know." Probably, Jessie thought. He'd never liked hearing her views on Carran.

Her tone must have given her away. Tani turned, pouring the foaming milk into a tall mug, which she set before Jessie with a plate of gingersnaps. "You wouldn't know, hmm?"

"No."

Tani shook her head, dozens of grizzled braids flying. "Strange goin's on in this house. I'm thinkin' of mixin' up a potion sets sense in some people's heads."

Jessie gulped. The warm milk tasted different, sweet and slightly spicy. "What's in this?"

She grinned. "No rat poison, that's sure."

"Oh, no, you heard him—"

"I know everythin' goes on in this house. Been here five years, since Mister Nick bought it. There's only cinnamon and sugar in that milk to give it character," she said. And then, "One spice jar out of place in my cabinets, I know it. One lampshade turned the other way round, I know that, too. And when that man"—

she glanced toward the garden windows—"starts reorderin' this house, I know there must be a reason."

"Reordering?"

"Now you finish up that hot milk, then trot off to bed. Don't worry about him."

"I'm not worried."

"He's like most men I ever knew. Not comfortable with their feelings, you know. Keeps his mouth clamped shut when he ought to open it right up."

"In my experience, Nick speaks his mind."

"Depends on the topic of conversation," Tani said cryptically and shooed Jessie toward the kitchen door. "Git now, I got to tidy up then go on home myself. My man's waitin' for his dinner, and I'm sittin' here while the laundry spins dry, lost in my romance readin'."

"I can't think of a better way to spend an evening," she murmured, then paused. "Tani, I'm still not sleepy." When the housekeeper started to make a suggestion, Jessie added, "I don't need any concoctions. Just point me toward a roll of stamps, if you will. I think I'll send a few postcards home." As if this really was a typical vacation, and she was getting any rest.

"Stamps," Tani said. She thought for a moment. "Used the last in my desk drawer this morning. You might look in that table in the foyer, then the sideboard in the drawin' room where Mr. Nick keeps his treasures."

Jessie smiled. "Thanks. Have a good night's sleep. I'll see you tomorrow."

"Sleep well yourself, Miss Jess. If that's what you want to do."

Lord, she thought. But Tani hadn't finished with her.

"Enjoyed your books," she called after Jessie. "Enjoy havin' you here even more. I been waitin' a long time . . ."

Nick didn't know how long he could cool his heels in the garden. The scotch hadn't helped, but he didn't feel like another. He'd always considered himself insightful, a good judge of character, and maybe his disappointment was out of proportion with the situation, but he'd wanted so much more from this week in Charleston, with Jess.

He'd wanted her away from her book, and Aaron, and Aaron's strange connection with the things in the attic trunk he'd found. To be honest, he had wanted to get away from that himself. And he'd wanted Jess away from her fixation with Carran and her grandmother's farm.

But he'd also hoped to tip her over the edge from friendship into . . . what? Love? he wondered. Or simple trust? Would that be enough? He didn't think he had a chance at either now, especially after their argument about where he belonged.

Nick sank down onto a Charleston Battery bench under a palmetto tree in the deep corner of his garden. She'd never stop drawing that line between them; he even knew when she'd first drawn it, though she wouldn't have recognized it, the day Jess buried her parents.

Months before, her father had bought a used Cessna. On the way home from an agricultural fair in New York State, the plane had developed engine trouble and gone down—ironically, in a cornfield, or rather, the trees that edged it.

Nick hadn't made it to the funeral. He'd hitch-hiked from college in Ithaca at dawn, arriving at the graveside for the afternoon interment. Still in jeans, he'd made his way immediately to Jess, standing be-tween Caroline and Ben with his wife, and laid his hands on her shoulders from behind. Jess hadn't looked around; her head bowed, she'd simply leaned back against him and, dry-eyed, let him ab-sorb her grief.

When the others started back down the hill toward her grandmother's house, Jess had hung back, Nick's hand enfolding hers. Caroline, ahead of them with Beth and Ben, her white coronet of hair in stark con-trast to black mourning clothes, looked around, and Nick said, "I'll take care of her."

He'd sat with Jess on the grass in the little cemetery that held their families' graves. The autumn leaves blew around them in rustling clouds, the cool breeze lifting her long blond hair. Nick remembered thinking how severe, how prematurely grown-up she looked in the black dress Caroline had cut down for her. He didn't remember exactly what he'd said, but for a long while they'd talked about life and death.

Then Jess said, "It's like the farm, isn't it, Nick? Things grow, then Daddy—someone—harvests, and the earth is dead until spring again."

"Just like that," he agreed, his voice husky.

And he'd held her while she cried.

"I'm here," he said. "I'll be here as long as you need me."

But he hadn't stayed, and that's what Jess in her twelve-year-old heart still remembered. Nick sighed. He could understand that. In this garden last Septem-ber he'd felt like a ten-year-old boy again himself, afraid of poverty, afraid to stay where he was. Just as Jess was afraid to let go of Carran.

What more could he do? He'd brought her to see the life he'd made for himself here; his house, his business, his friends. Tani, he added, and couldn't help the smile. Perhaps he should ask her for a potion—for Jess.

Or he could charge upstairs to her room, rely on the old chemistry to eventually change her mind about them, but the victory would be hollow. Tipping his head back, Nick stared up at the black sky, the stars. He wanted all of her, but she had to come to him this time. Only, he didn't think she ever would.

There were no stamps in the foyer table. Jessie paused to study her reflection in the long mirror above it; pale face, hair in wisps on her cheeks, eyes dark and lost. And Tani, talking in riddles. Voodoo, she thought again. Maybe she preferred Greg's ghosts.

In the drawing room Jessie couldn't help glancing toward the open French doors. From outside she heard crickets chirping, the soft splash of water in Nick's fountain, but nothing more. Perhaps he, at least, had fallen asleep in the cool darkness. After searching the small drawers of the sideboard, she tugged at the center one—and caught her breath.

No stamps there, either.

But she'd found Nick's treasures, and pulled out the first photograph. Tom Granby, with his wife. Tom's father, she remembered from a picture on his mantel in Carran. Ben with Beth, holding Greg, a chubby toddler then, not much older than Delilah. And—

"Oh, Nick." Tears brimmed, but she blinked them back. "You kept this. After all these years . . ."

Her graduation photo showed Jessie as a very young woman, life and mischief in her blue eyes. Her blond hair had been longer then, styled sleek and straight past her shoulders, and the white robe seemed to guarantee her virginity, naiveté.

At a noise, she glanced up. Nick stood in the French doorway, the black night behind him like a nimbus. The room light showed his features clearly, the pallor beneath his tan, the darkness of his eyes.

"I didn't mean for you to see that," he said.

Then he turned and went back into the garden.

Setting the picture down, she went after him, stepping out into a night so dark that she had to stand for a moment, unable to see.

Then she made him out, his head down, standing near the fountain. "Nick, you do care." Jessie stepped closer. "You care a lot. I just didn't see it before. You've even been paying Tom's debts this summer, haven't you? Just as you lent Rob and Alaina money with no expectation of repayment any time soon?"

"Some," he said. "Even Donald Trump couldn't pay all of Pop's bills."

Jessie blinked. "And I'd be willing to bet you took the loan to replant for Tom after the hailstorm in your own name. No bank would have given him the money."

"Yeah," Nick admitted. "But that doesn't mean I love Carran or that broken-down farm, Jess." He nodded toward the house. "Tani steered you to those pictures, didn't she?"

"I think so, yes." She mumbled something about the missing stamps.

"I phoned her from Carran to say we were coming down. Of course she gave me an argument when I asked her to put the pictures in the sideboard."

"Why didn't you want me to see them?"

He turned. "Because I needed you to see this place, my life here, without anything else intruding. Maybe it doesn't make sense to Tani or to you, but it does to me, Jess. All my life I've lived with your love for Carran and that farm. But there are other places in this world, just as good. And I wanted you to see one of them, here."

"I've lived in other places. At school, with Peter. We lived all over the world the first few years we were married, while he completed his doctoral research and I tagged along. Then we moved to Scottsdale, bought a house, tried to dig our own roots there, but it never worked for me. So I came home."

"It's not the place, Jess," Nick said sadly. "Peter wasn't right for you. That's why Scottsdale didn't work, or Africa, or some college campus."

"I think place is everything, and I doubt you can buy that."

"Buy what?"

"The sense of belonging," Jessie said.

"You're wrong." When his gaze met hers, his eyes were bleak, as they'd looked the first night at Ben's.

"Nick, you saved the pictures, saved part of Carran—and yourself. Don't you see?"

"No, I saved you, love." He framed her face in his hands. "Don't you know why? Because you were the best part of me there. The only part I didn't want to leave behind."

"But you did."

"And you can't forgive that," he said hoarsely. "I

don't know how to make you understand that I had to leave, because of who I am and what I wanted to be . . . because of Pop, who won't ever let me be Nick Granby, architect, when what he still wants is Nick Granby, Tom's son; Nick Granby, the farmer who will take his place on that rocky piece of ground. God, Jess, I didn't want to leave you. I sure as hell didn't want to leave you with tears in your eyes, not able to understand why I couldn't stay then."

"Nick, don't. It was a long time ago."

"Listen to me, dammit." His thumbs stroked her cheekbones, and Jessie closed her eyes against the pain she saw in his. "Don't you think I wanted to be with you? That I would have married you—even seventeen years old, with your whole life a clean slate in front of you—that I would have married you and stayed in Carran and become the goddamn farmer my father wanted from the day I was born? Jesus, I used to wish he'd had ten sons so all his hopes didn't fall on me. But they did, Jess. He can't help it, but they did. They still do. And I would have given him his dream in place of mine—"

"We could have been happy."

"No." He shook his head. "I would have stayed . . . and hated it. We'd have had kids, the final bond to hold me there, and I would have turned bitter and mean and in the end . . ." His voice broke. "In the end I would have made you hate me, too. You were the only reason I could have stayed there—a siren song, Jess—but I couldn't have you hate me. I thought I could stand anything but that." His fingers smoothed the tears that had started to fall on her cheeks. "And then, you hated me anyway, for leaving."

The words were whispered. "I never hated you, Nick. Never."

Jessie moved first, drawing him close in the darkness of his garden, the fragrance of roses wafting over them, through them, on the gentle breeze. When she raised her face to his, their first kiss seemed soft and warm and tender, but with something more.

Remorse, she thought. Regret.

"I want more from you than friendship, Jess."

Nick led her deeper into the shadows, urging Jessie down onto a wooden bench that dipped at her slender weight, then dipped again under his. The slight curve of the wood threw them together, and Nick tipped her chin to kiss her again. His tongue met Jessie's, his hands were gentle on her breasts. Through the cloth of her blouse he circled the nipples, hardening them, making her breath come faster. She felt strange now, as if she and Nick were different people, which in many ways they were, and could love freely, without the night in the orchard between them, without her expectation of hurt. Jessie braced herself against Nick's shoulder.

Against her mouth, he whispered, "This bench is made of cypress like the chest I gave you, to bend and take the water in a swamp." His breath, ragged and quick, fluttered over her skin. "It's bending just enough to push you toward me."

"No," Jessie whispered back, "I'm bending."

Soon his fingers were at the buttons of her blouse. One, and then the next. In the nearby kitchen the lights snapped off, and Tani called good night.

Nick's hands stilled. "That's the first time in five years she's bothered to say good night. She knows we're out here." He kissed Jessie, smiling against her mouth. "You sure she didn't fix you something to drink before bed?"

"Only cinnamon in milk, with sugar."

"Hah," Nick murmured, dropping a kiss on her bared shoulder. Then he drew her to her feet. The kitchen was dark, the front door clicked shut, and they were alone, with just each other. No fake Charleston ancestors, no Carran ghosts. "Come on, love. Let's go upstairs. I'm too old to tumble you in the grass with the mosquitoes. And I want to show you something."

14

An enormous carved walnut sleigh bed piled high with pillows drew Jessie's eye the instant she stepped across the threshold of Nick's bedroom. The bed dominated the room, or would have for any other woman. Nick's treasures, Jessie thought again, pulling her hand from his, moving toward the walnut dresser that occupied the opposite wall.

The dresser top held perhaps a dozen photographs in antique frames. Jessie as an infant in her christening gown. As a three- or four-year-old, her face in profile, blue eyes somber. Jessie, laughing, with her front teeth missing. A photograph with her parents. And dressed for Halloween at ten or twelve. Jessie wearing sunglasses, blue jeans, a checkered blouse that covered budding breasts, and perched upon Tom's tractor, which looked brand-new. Her graduation photo from college, in a black robe this time, her blue eyes older, a bit less hopeful. Jessie from her book cover, a thoughtful pose in a blue sweater dress and the

makeup—full, professional warpaint—she had hated.
All Jessie.

Nick stood behind her as Aaron had on his wedding night with Elizabeth. When their eyes met in the
dresser mirror, she felt tears well again.

"You're the first thing I see in the morning and the
last at night," Nick said. "In Carran I miss my gallery.
I had to filch a wrinkled photo from Pop's mess in the
attic and stick it in my bedroom mirror so I wouldn't
feel lonely."

Her blouse was still half unbuttoned from the garden, and he bared her shoulder again, bending to kiss
the soft skin at the juncture of her throat. He trailed
kisses along the back of her exposed neck, then down
her shoulder. Soft, open-mouthed, yearning kisses, or
so they felt to Jessie, who dropped her neck for more.

The kisses didn't come.

Nick touched her shoulder. When she raised her
head, her gaze met his again in the mirror and her
heart turned.

"I love you, Jess," he said, his eyes bright, his voice
shaken. "There hasn't been a day in your life when I
haven't loved you."

Jessie couldn't speak. With a groan, Nick drew her
back into his arms, hands clasped just beneath her
breasts, enlarging the gap of unbuttoned blouse. The
words had stunned her, lowered her last defenses.
She didn't need conditions now, or ruminating. She
didn't think of Aaron.

Turning, she went into Nick's arms and he caught
her close. Nothing else mattered now but his touch,
his kiss, his whispered words of love.

Nick swept Jessie's blouse from her shoulders to
the needlepoint carpet patterned in lilacs and roses.

He knelt to unfasten her slacks, running his hands down her legs underneath them, making her foot tingle when he drew them off and lingered to stroke her arch, her heel.

"Nick."

"In a minute." Then he skimmed a wisp of blue silk panties along the same path, and she was naked. When Jessie would have covered herself, he held her hands at her sides and looked his fill. "You're mine," he whispered. "Everything I need, and I need you now."

Urgency became the keyword. Nick whisked the comforter to the footboard, flicked back the sheets. The pillows flew off the bed. He held out his hand and drew her close, guiding her flat and following her down. Her hands trembled on his shirt buttons, fumbled with his fly. Then Nick was naked too, naked and warm and smelling, as Jessie knew no one else did, of sleek skin and fine soap and faint perspiration after the warm evening hours in Rob Griffith's yard. All male, she thought. And for now at least, all hers.

Nick leaned over her, and Jessie wound her arms around his neck. They kissed some more, their breathing rapid, until Jessie murmured, "I always wanted you to be my first lover," arching toward his mouth at her breast. His rhythm was steady, tugging. "My only lover, Nick," she said on a groan.

"It's the first time now, Jess."

Warm skin sliding over warm skin, he moved back up to kiss her mouth again. His hand slowly traveled the same path downward, then lower, between Jessie's legs.

She cried out.

Frantic now, her fingers slid over the hard muscles

of his chest to his taut waist, closing at last around his erection.

He groaned. "Not yet. Just a second."

The bedroom's air-conditioning chilled Jessie's skin as Nick rolled off the bed. She heard him yanking at drawers across the room, cursing under his breath, then, "Aha," and a tearing sound.

He came back to the bed. "Safe sex," he murmured.

With Nick kissing her, by the time Jessie managed to help him roll the condom on, she was at the point of begging. "Yes," Nick said, "ah, yes, love," and then he was inside her, slow and deep, and Jessie's moans were echoing his.

Twelve years, she thought. Twelve years.

"Oh, Nick!"

"Jess," he murmured. "Jess. Jess. *Jess.*"

She heard him catch his breath. His body plunged deep and holding while he shuddered, his climax came quickly. Jessie went over the edge just after, certain she must be dying of pleasure. Not caring.

With his weight on her, she struggled for breath, too.

"I'm sorry." He ran a trembling hand through her tangled hair. "That was pretty fast and dirty."

"Twelve years," Jessie managed. "You call that fast?"

"Next time," Nick murmured, his mouth nuzzling her throat, "let's not wait so long."

In the middle of another sultry Carran summer night, Ben jerked awake. He lay twisted in the flowered sheets, Amy beside him in her waterbed. His body buzzed with the afterglow of lovemaking, and he turned to her again, pushing himself against her satiny hip, sweeping the damp hair from the nape of her neck to kiss her there. She tasted sweet, salty. He'd never been happier. The last few days . . . Then his gaze, over her shoulder, focused on the brass French carriage clock on her nightstand, and he reared up, his heart pounding.

"Christ, it's five-thirty!"

"Kisses," Amy mumbled, her face pressed into the pillow.

"For God's sake, Heather must have come home hours ago. She'll have seen my car in the drive and—"

"Ben." Amy sat up, plowing both hands through her hair. "Don't panic. It's too late now and besides, Heather has been teasing me for the past three days. She and Greg passed your car on the road the night we went swimming in the pond. It's pretty obvious we're lovers, so why try to hide it now?" She paused. "Unless you're ashamed of our relationship."

Greg had teased him, too. "Get my Swiss Army knife back," he'd said. "You see Amy Stone more than I do." Earlier, Ben had joked with Amy about flattening her own tire, and she'd given him the knife. Their teasing had led to other things.

"I'm not ashamed," Ben said. "I just don't want our kids laughing at us, as if we were some kind of embarrassing porno flick."

"Oh, for heaven's sake."

Searching the dark floor for his pants, Ben sat up and yanked them on. "I should have gone home hours ago."

"Why?" Amy asked dryly. "No one's there."

Greg was still staying nights at Tom Granby's farm. To please Ben he had compromised, though;

Greg fixed dinner for Nick's father and, after work, Heather joined them. They watched television with Tom until he went to bed, then Heather drove back to town herself in Amy's borrowed car. She'd just passed her driving test. If she'd been his daughter, Ben thought, he wouldn't have let her go, and he sure as hell wouldn't have wanted her driving back to Carran alone late at night, but he and Amy never saw eye to eye about the kids anyway, so he'd stopped arguing.

While he finished dressing, Amy went to the bathroom across the hall but hurried back.

"Heather's not in her room," she said.

Ben's head jerked up. He had been hastily tying his sneakers. Amy's green eyes looked so distressed that for once he tried to soothe her. "Maybe she's downstairs, watching a late movie. Or some talk show."

"I don't think so." Amy peered out the bedroom window. "Ben, the car's not here either."

"Maybe she had a breakdown." He tucked his shirt in, grabbed his wallet from the dresser, and shoved it in his back pocket. "I'll make the run from your place to Tom's. If she's had car trouble, she'll be along the road somewhere."

"I'm going with you."

Mistake, Ben thought. He didn't for one moment think that he'd find Heather waiting for a tow truck. Halfway to Tom's, he opened his mouth and said so.

"What do you think, then?" Amy asked.

"You know what I think. She's probably up in Tom's hayloft with my kid, making babies."

"Ben, so help me—"

"You think I'm wrong? Be honest, Amy. It's time you took a good look at your daughter. She's a pretty girl, dancing green eyes, beautiful smile, a terrific fig-ure.''

''I'm so glad you've noticed.'' Amy edged closer to the passenger door. ''And that automatically makes her sexually active?''

''Come on, you've seen the way she and Greg hang on each other.''

Her tone was stiff. ''The same way we've been 'hanging on each other' the past few days?''

''That's different,'' he said.

''You have too many rules, Ben. They change all the time. Whatever suits the situation, I suppose. Whatever makes your point.''

''I'll tell you the point.'' His hands tightened on the wheel. ''They're headed for trouble. Greg's not yet twenty years old, Heather's barely sixteen. They spend every spare minute together.''

''So do most kids their age. So did you when—''

''How many kids do you think I've seen come through my office, panicked because the girlfriend's pregnant? Do you really want our kids to end up shackled for the rest of their lives? Greg will wake up some morning with a wife and three kids, think how much he'd like to go back to school and finish his degree, but he won't have that chance anymore.'' Ben took a breath. ''He'll be trapped, Amy. So will Heather. Before she's eighteen, her life will have been decided for her by a few minutes in a hayloft or the backseat of his car. They'll both be trapped and miser-able and—''

''Like you and Beth?''

He almost ran the car off the road. Ben could feel sweat break out on his upper lip. ''That's a helluva thing to say.'' But guilt flooded him and the years dropped away. "I loved her. Sure, I wish we'd had more time before Greg, but I . . . I didn't feel trapped."

"Then why should Greg, if anything happens?"

"He's so *young*," Ben said hoarsely.

"He's older now than you were."

Yes, he was, but suddenly Ben could see the dark road between Tom's farm and Gran's. He could feel Beth in his arms, his body in hers for the first time. Two weeks later, she'd missed a period.

"What will you do," Ben asked, "when the opportunity to spread the word comes up this time? When it's my son and your daughter having a baby before they're grown up themselves? Tell the whole town? Or just—"

"No!"

"It's not as easy when someone you love is involved, is it?"

"How would you know?" she asked. "Greg doesn't think you love him."

"He said that?"

"More than once. He thinks you care more about his doing the right thing than you care whether he's happy."

Ben swallowed. "You're lying."

"No, I'm not. I'm not lying now and I didn't lie then. I told one person about you and Beth. Just one." Turned toward him from her position against the door, she folded her arms. He tried not to see how bright her eyes looked, how wounded. "I was eighteen years old and, yes, I had a crush on you. It hurt me when you started dating Beth, but it was easy to see—as it is with Greg and Heather—how much you loved her. Beth was my friend, and I wouldn't have hurt her, or you, for the world. But my God, Ben." She shook her head. "I was a kid then, too. We were all kids. I made mistakes but so did you. When Beth told me she was pregnant—"

"She told you that herself?"

"I knew before you did," she said softly. "When she told me, I was shocked. In a small country town, where everybody knows everybody else's business, her pregnancy was a scandal. At least then, it was. You're right that I couldn't keep such news to myself, but telling Julie Carmichael wasn't a capital crime, Ben."

"Julie Carmichael was the biggest gossip in the senior class."

"I thought you'd given me that title."

"Amy, admit it. You like to tell a good story."

"Maybe so, but what about you? No faults, Ben? You're self-righteous, stiff, and priggish all too often. Can you even admit that? We're human, that's all," she said. "We're human."

"Responsible for our actions," he corrected.

"And you've always been responsible, haven't you? Ever since your parents died and left you with Gran and Jessie. By then, you'd been married how long, Ben—three years?—and Greg was a toddler. So you took care of him and Beth and Gran and your sister . . . and six hundred kids in Carran High School, eventually. Oh, and let's not forget your service as a fire volunteer. You've been a model of responsible behavior. Why don't you let yourself off the hook for a change?" Her green eyes flashed in the soft dawn light filtering through the car. "I'd bet money there was more than one day when you wished you didn't have a kid, or a wife, or an orphaned sister to care for. I'd bet solid gold—and win—that you thought at least once of leaving Beth, of running after Nick for a taste of the freedom you must have envied. There's no crime in that. I'd bet—"

He wheeled the car off the highway onto the access road to Tom's farm. "You've said enough, goddammit."

"Don't you try to shut me up! I'm not waiting around for you to notice a crack in your halo. You go on being Saint Benjamin for all I care, and pray that your son doesn't make my daughter pregnant. Because after that his life, with you, would be a living hell—and so would Heather's. Why, Ben? Why do you need to blame Greg for your own mistakes?"

"Go to hell." His stomach felt tight, his ears hot. He felt the hard shape of Greg's Swiss Army knife in his pocket. And in the same instant, saw Amy's red Miata gleaming at the top of Tom Granby's drive. "I wish I'd never caught you the other night, skinny dipping—"

"On my own property?"

"I wish I'd never—"

"Fallen into bed with me, or on the grass by the pond? Or overslept tonight? None of that's a sin, Benjamin Pearce, but you're right this time. I wish none of that had happened, too. They were accidents, a total disaster—"

"Accidents? Like flattening your own tire so I'd look at you, talk to you again?"

"You conceited bastard."

Ben spun gravel to the front porch, jammed the brakes, and wrenched the ignition key out. He was on his feet before Amy opened her door. Jamming his hands in his pockets, Ben scraped a knuckle on the folded knife, and swore. He started for the house.

"No," he heard her say. "Like falling in love."

◆ ◆ ◆

"Marry me."

Nick rocked Jess in his arms, his mouth lingering over the dimple in her left cheek, making her smile, his mouth scattering kisses along her bared throat. In fact, everything was bare and throughout the long night he'd worshiped every inch.

Jess had come to him, he thought in wonder. And with the words he'd just murmured against her fragrant skin, he'd never felt more certain of what he wanted. Like Rob and Alaina, perhaps like Greg and Heather, even like Aaron and his wife, they belonged together, and for the first time in Nick's life, that knowledge didn't scare him.

"Marry you?" She drew back, and smiled. "You don't have to propose. I'll still respect you in the morning."

"It's already morning. I'm serious, Jess."

The smile faded. "Last night, Nick, was the most amazing night of my life. But to make such a somber decision based on one night?"

"Not one night," he said, his pulse picking up speed. She was supposed to say yes, immediately. "You've had twenty-nine years to make up your mind."

"No," she murmured. "I've had twelve."

"Jess, don't start that again. It's ridiculous, after last night, to keep me at arms' length emotionally. I need you," he said. "I want you. I love you, more than I could ever love anyone else. I'm thirty-nine years old, and I want to make an honest woman of you, make babies with you, grow old with—"

She put a hand across his mouth. "It's too soon,"

she said. "I've been officially divorced since March. That's not very long, and I had a rough time with Peter. Please be patient with me. I don't know that I'm ready to get married again."

"I'm not Peter," he said, his voice tight. "I'm not Aaron, either."

Her gaze met his. "I know who you are. You're the man I gave my heart to when I was too young to realize that I have to reserve something for myself. When you left, Nick, no matter how unselfish your motives may have turned out to be—"

"Not entirely unselfish," he admitted.

"—you hurt me. I hurt so badly that I couldn't read your letters, or bear to hear your voice on the telephone. I had to heal myself, Nick. And then what did I do? I turned around and fell in love with Peter. Maybe ours was tepid, compared to what I feel for you, but I wanted it to be right. And I tried, I tried so hard to be a good wife to him, a good companion, a good lover—all the things I thought he wanted from me, that I wanted from marriage myself."

Nick raised himself on an elbow and regarded her solemnly. "The marriage didn't work, but that doesn't mean ours won't."

"I know that." She gently pushed her fingers through his hair, smoothing back a dark strand that had fallen over his forehead. "And I still want a good marriage, a family. But I followed Peter, just the way I used to tag after you and Ben when I was small, trusted him not to destroy my illusions about us, and I ended up hurting again. I don't know that I'm ready to risk a third time yet, so—"

"What you're saying is, you still don't trust me." He drew her fingers away.

"Nick."

He heard the phone ring and considered not answering, but Tani hadn't yet come to work, and Nick had never been able to withstand a ringing telephone. He always wondered who was at the other end of the line. Maybe it came from hoping the caller would someday be Jess. With a sigh, he padded naked across the bedroom to the phone on a marble-topped walnut bachelor's chest. The caller was Ben.

"Calm down," Nick said into the receiver. "Greg what—?"

He listened, his gut tightening a notch at every word. At dawn Ben and Amy had found Greg asleep with Heather on Tom's sofa. All their clothes on, Ben said, but that didn't prove anything. While he and Amy grappled over the kids, and Heather and Greg defended themselves, Nick's father had left the field of battle to milk cows. With his watchdogs out of the way, he'd then decided to fix the old combine before harvest, which Nick would face as soon as he got back to Carran. As he listened to Ben's terse recounting of the disaster there, he felt the blood drain from his face.

Jess, wrapped in a sheet, came toward him. "Nick, what's wrong?"

He covered the mouthpiece. "Pop's back in the hospital."

"Oh no, not—"

"Not ill," Nick said. "He's hurt. Smashed two fingers playing mechanic. Your brother's calling from the emergency room in New Milford." He spoke again into the phone. "Listen, Ben. I'm going to hang up and call the hospital myself, talk to his doctor, okay? Thanks for taking him in. Thanks to Amy, too." He listened. "Yeah, well, that's comforting. He didn't kill himself, but not for lack of trying. Right. We'll see you as soon as we can."

Cursing, he hung up. Jess's light touch on his arm made him want to fly into a million pieces. He wanted to stay here, with her, to resolve things; but he focused his frustration on Tom. "Goddammit, I've had it with him! He's like a kid you can't leave alone for two minutes, and that's the way he deserves to be treated!"

"Nick, give him a break. Why not just say you're scared witless for him? He could have been killed, he—"

"That's the last time he's going to have the chance." Stepping back, he gave her a long look. "Well, so be it. I'm not a patient man, and I'm tired of waiting. From here on, I'm in charge. I'll mow those hayfields of his flat, get his corn to market—and then that damn farm's going on the block. If he can't accept the fact that the whole place is nothing but an anachronism—"

"Like Gran's?" she asked coolly.

"Yes, and if you can't recognize that either, I do. So while I make some calls and get us a flight, you'd better start packing." Nick set his jaw at the flash of blue fire in Jess's eyes and murmured, "The honeymoon's over."

Short and sweet, Jessie thought, her jaw clenched so tightly that her teeth ached as she dumped clothes, shoes, lacy underwear into her suitcase. Nicholas Granby. Stubborn as a Missouri mule. She stripped the hangers in the closet, rolling skirts and dresses into a ball. Ornery as Tom Granby. She squashed the fabric ball into the bag and snapped it shut. Then opened it again.

She'd left her cosmetic case in Nick's bathroom. In the middle of the night they'd wakened, made love again, then showered together. The intimacy, followed by the cozy, shared routine of brushing teeth and drying hair had led to more intimacy, and her body still throbbed from Nick's touch. He was contrary all right, but he was a wonderful lover, too. She didn't know whether to stay angry with him, or to cry. Marching back into the bedroom, she tossed the flowered cosmetic bag into the open suitcase.

How could she marry him?

She closed it again. Hadn't he just proved to her that her fears weren't groundless after all? That her hesitation was fully justified?

"Dammit." For the third time, she opened the suitcase. She'd packed everything; she'd left nothing to wear for the trip home but Nick's bedsheet.

Jessie pulled a wrinkled skirt and blouse from the tangled ball and flung them on the rumpled bed. The action raised a small cloud of scent from the sheets, the smell of herself and Nick and their long night of loving. Oh God, it had been . . .

She stalked into the bathroom. She'd hang her clothes there while she showered; she needed another shower, needed to retrieve herself. Because he hadn't changed. Nick was still the same stubborn, high-handed man she'd loved before and, like Peter, look where that had gotten her. She had gone home to Carran to touch base with her own needs again, and she'd found happiness there, or at least peace and contentment.

In Carran she'd broken a writer's block, which

she'd never had before, a block that terrified her. And with a month until her deadline, the book was going well. What more did she need? Nothing, Jessie thought.

As she turned on the shower, she heard Nick slamming drawers in the bedroom. He was angry with her, she knew; angry and hurt himself. This morning he'd offered her his heart and, like his apology years ago, Jessie had rejected it.

The soap slipped over her sensitized skin, making her shudder. How could she turn her back on last night's pleasure, on the life she had dreamed of so long ago, with Nick? Yet their lovemaking hadn't solved anything; she wondered what could, in fact, resolve their differences.

What you're saying is, you still don't trust me.

With Tom's accident, Nick had the excuse he needed to get out of Carran forever. But Jessie didn't know whether she could leave Carran now. She couldn't make that decision yet. Or any other, especially not about marrying Nick.

She'd wait until her book was finished to decide.

She'd finish, and then, somehow—perhaps with Aaron's help—she'd know.

15

Christmas, 1856

Somehow Aaron knew exactly what I wanted, and this morning, underneath our Christmas tree, I found a large package wrapped in fabric. "I couldn't find the paper," Aaron said, "so I thought after you opened this, you might use the cotton to make a new dress."

My pulse thumping, I hesitated. In Carran, with Mama and Papa and Michael on Christmas Day, by tradition we passed presents round, opening them in turn. How I'd hated being the object of everyone's attention, but Aaron couldn't wait his turn this morning, our first Christmas together. He'd barely given me the blue calico-bound box when he began tearing open his own gift.

"New overalls," he said. "And what's this? A sweater?"

"I made it myself."

"I didn't know you could knit." He held up the soft green heather wool that complemented his eyes. "Thank you, love. Now yours. Go on, open it."

"Oh, Aaron, it's beautiful." I'd been hinting for weeks that I needed a new robe, and the buttery yellow cashmere from the display window at Albert's Mercantile in town was a Christmas dream come true.

Aaron sat at my feet, the love shining in his eyes. "I thought you'd need it, when the baby comes."

"I need it right now, if it will fit over my stomach."

"It's cut full," he said. "The clerk assured me there was plenty of room."

He made me try it on, and was right; it fit perfectly, felt warm and soft over my ever-swelling stomach. With three months left before the baby comes, I am like a huge, round ball with legs, and breathing has become difficult. But the sickness is gone, and I don't tire so easily.

Aaron smoothed the robe over my stomach, his hand lingering. "Have you felt anything this morning?"

I shook my head.

And Aaron pressed his ear against me. "He must be sleeping late today."

"No wonder. He keeps me up all night."

His hand strayed upward to lightly hold my breast. When we married, I felt embarrassed that I didn't possess the charms of other girls at school, but in the past months I have become

. . . voluptuous, though Aaron doesn't seem to mind. He kissed me there, through the soft cashmere cloth, making me tingle. "So beautiful, and when your milk comes in . . ."

His eyes darkened, the need in them so clear that I caught my breath. Without another word, Aaron carried me back to bed, where we celebrated Christmas in a way I hope will become tradition. When we lay at last in each other's arms, happier than I ever dreamed possible, the baby kicked against Aaron's hand, making him laugh.

He planted a kiss on the taut skin of my belly, whispering, "Happy Christmas, my son . . . or daughter," and I thought nothing for the rest of our lives would seem as perfect as this day.

Later, I knew that I was right when Mama came to mind.

Aaron and I shared supper in the parlor on a patchwork quilt—one of his mother's—by our Christmas tree, and he didn't complain about the blackened peas, the stringy turkey ("An old one," Aaron said. "I should have killed it months ago. Nothing you could help.") or the curdled whipped cream on our pumpkin pie. Mama had brought the pie, so that was fine; but I wished I'd left well enough alone and forgot the cream.

"You and Aaron come to us for Christmas," Mama had said. "Michael will be home, with that farm girl he had to marry."

My brother had stopped seeing the banker's daughter at harvest, started courting the oldest daughter at the farm closest to Aaron's. They've been married for two months and are also expecting a child—shamelessly early, Mama always says with a sniff. She feels we have both ruined our lives, but Michael—and I—have never been so content.

"It would do you good to get away from that awful farm," Mama said, "and wouldn't kill that husband of yours to eat a civilized meal with genteel people. You wouldn't have to look at him across the kitchen table in his overalls. I'd make him wash his hands for dinner, that's certain—"

"Mama, he always washes his hands."

"Your father would like a word with him, as well. A good opportunity, to convince your farmer that you should stay with us for your lying-in. Whatever will you do six miles from a doctor when labor starts? Your hips are narrow as a boy's. Believe me, if a doctor's help was needed, you'd scream the walls down before he could get there. The pain—"

"Mama . . ." She'd scared me and I wanted her to stop.

"We've had enough foolishness, Elizabeth. Your father and I will expect you Christmas morning."

"I'll have to ask Aaron. We'll let you know."

There'd be hell to pay, Aaron had said this morning, because we didn't take the buggy into Carran. But he didn't seem to care. He laughed when he said it, and reminded me that we hadn't actually accepted the invitation. Still, Mama's warning frightened me.

She'd certainly known how inept I would be as a cook, a housekeeper, and apparently I am no better at handiwork. Aaron's new sweater sleeves are miles too long.

He tried it on, then pulled me near to kiss me. "No, don't frown, Lizzie. That you made it with love is all that counts," he said.

But tonight, after Christmas supper, while we lay on the quilt and watched the candles softly blazing on the tree he'd cut from our woods, in the gentle darkness I wondered if the morning's happiness could last.

Was Mama right again?

How will I ever deliver Aaron's child . . . how will I know when it is time?

Jessie exited the document on her computer screen and shut the system down. She wasn't satisfied with the scene but didn't know how to fix it. Was it only the usual reluctance to give her characters problems? She'd already increased tension between Elizabeth and her parents. She'd added the subplot about Michael. Was she simply projecting her own confusion onto Elizabeth?

The loving night in Charleston with Nick had soured all too soon. On the way home Nick had been too quiet, and Jessie had felt guilty for her part in spoiling their time together. Ever since, her stomach had been churning with indecision. She couldn't seem to set it aside, to concentrate on finishing her book.

But then again, it wasn't easy to concentrate on writing a Christmas scene when, outside her office window, the temperature was at least ninety-five degrees.

Pushing her desk chair back, she wiped her perspiring forehead. If she couldn't solve her own problem, she might as well drive into Carran and ask Amy Stone's help in solving Elizabeth's.

"I'm sorry, Jessie." Amy shoved a pile of papers onto the floor so Jessie could sit down. As usual, her office overflowed. "We've been buried with the reorganization here, but nothing else has turned up on Aaron Granby. I'm sure the files will surface, it's only a matter of when."

"Well, thanks for trying." She cocked her head, giving Amy, who looked tired and pale, a thorough once-over. "I'm sure your mind can't be on my problems anyway. Just out of curiosity, I'd hoped to find pictures, but not even the trunk in Tom's attic produced any. Nick thinks his family gave everything that far back to the historical society here, so I guess I'll sit back and wait. As long as I can." She sighed. In a few days it would be August, and her manuscript was due at the publisher's office the first of September. "I did want some more textual information. But there's not even an old family Bible at Nick's—if I were really welcome there these days."

"That bad, huh?"

"I'd like to know more than the probable maiden name of Aaron's wife, but—"

"What was it?"

"Cochran," Jessie said. "At least, from the small Bible Aaron carried during the war, I assume that was a family name. Seth Cochran Granby was their son."

Amy wrote on her notepad. "When I said bad, I meant Nick," she murmured.

Jessie shifted in her chair. "We're still speaking, but that's all. What about you and Ben?"

Amy snorted. "After that debacle in Tom's barnyard the other morning? I'm sorry you missed it. Living theater," she said. "Ben shouting like some
evangelical preacher, condemning sin—fictional sin at
that—and me, sticking up for the kids. Heather, crying.
Greg ready to bash his father's skull in with the nearest
shovel..." She broke off. "Is he still staying with you?"

"Greg's sleeping at my place, working at Tom's.
He won't even talk to Ben."

"I can't blame him. If anything could drive those
two children into bed, Ben provides the perfect moti-
vation. How he's ever managed successfully as high
school principal is beyond me."

"And as far as the two of you are concerned?"

"I'm ready for the *Guinness Book of Records*. The
shortest, most combustible romance in history. When
Ben lets his hair down, he's charming and funny and
sexy as hell. Terrific as a lover, but in the human being
department . . ." She shook her head.

Jessie studied her again. "I'd bet you aren't sleeping well."

"Last night I didn't sleep at all. It was hot and
damp, and I took a long swim, but nothing helped. I
keep hearing Ben that morning in the yard. 'You've
always had a big mouth,' he said. So I said, 'Then why
don't you shut it for me?' By then, we'd descended
from the low point of human communication to some
tar pit, but I couldn't help myself." She shrugged,
looking down at her desktop. "I suppose, like some
lovestruck schoolgirl, I wanted him to kiss me and
stop the argument, give us both a chance to come to
our senses before we destroyed the kids, too. But all
Ben did was look at me as if I were some psycho-bitch
and say, 'No wonder your husband left you.' "

"Oh, Amy. But you know how Ben is."

"Yes, and of course I told him—all the bad parts. Maybe he's right. At my age, I shouldn't have expected a happy ending." She smiled ruefully. "I'll leave that to you and your books . . . to you and Nick." Then she grinned. "He really asked you to marry him, after all this time? How did he ask? By candlelight or moonlight?"

"He wasn't so romantic," Jessie said. She still wondered if there were any happy endings.

"You know Nick as well as you do Ben. He likes getting his own way. He probably expected to ask you and have you fly into his arms—"

"I was already in his arms."

"In bed?"

"Yes," Jessie said, exasperated.

"And when you didn't instantly say yes, his male ego took a nosedive."

"I suppose," she muttered. He'd said once that she was hell on a man's ego. "But am I being so unreasonable?"

"No, but Nick's waited a long time for you. And he's got it bad. Why else would a five-star bachelor take the plunge when he's pushing forty? Then again, you've got it bad, too. You think *I* look awful?"

Jessie glanced away from Amy's penetrating stare.

"Look in your own mirror," Amy said. "We could be twins, my bags and dark circles with yours."

"I just don't know what to do. After Peter, after Nick the first time . . . At least I'm content here. Maybe I'm a coward, but I feel at peace again at Gran's—or did until Nick asked me to marry him. Now I'm having trouble working again."

"Join the club." When Jessie stood up to go, Amy caught her hand and squeezed.

"Ben will come around," Jessie said. "He dams everything up inside him, then explodes. But he'll calm down about the kids, and some night you'll find him on your doorstep with red roses, if not the apology you want."

"Ben? Roses?"

"He's as likely to bring flowers as Nick," Jessie said. "The last time Nick wanted to make amends, I found my mama cow and Sunbeam in Gran's barn."

"What's the worst he'll do now if you decide you have to say no?"

Pausing in the doorway, Jessie voiced her fear. "Go back to Charleston and stay there, I suppose."

"I wouldn't underestimate that Granby stubbornness."

"It can work either way."

"So could Ben's stuffy self-righteousness."

"Well," Jessie said, "all I know is, I have to do what's right for me this time."

"Ditto." As Jessie walked down the tiled hallway, she heard Amy say, "Call me if you need a sympathetic ear. I'll do the same—and I'll start picking through the Granby files again. If you want to root around, come tomorrow and wear old jeans."

"Thanks, Amy."

Jessie had just started preparing dinner for herself and Greg when Amy's red Miata buzzed into the drive. Wiping her hands on a dishtowel, she went to the screen door.

"I couldn't wait until tomorrow to give you this,"
Amy said.

Her pulse thumping, Jessie took the faded paper,
unfolding a letter that flowed in bold script from the
November 1861 date to the scrawled signature at the
bottom of the page: Aaron Granby.

"Oh, Amy, where—"

"I've been sleuthing all day in the society's basement. The beginning of the alphabet, from A to F, isn't
in as chaotic a state as the rest. I looked up Cochran,
which you gave me as possibly being Aaron's wife's
maiden name. It wasn't, but it led me there."

"Have you read this?"

Amy's gaze fell. "Yes."

Jessie invited her inside, but Amy refused. "I have
a meeting tonight. The board's deciding on our next
year's allotment for a computerized record-keeping
system, and after plowing through dirty files all day,
I want to speak my mind. But here's part of your
puzzle at least, though not a happy piece."

With Amy's explanation still ringing in her mind,
Jessie waved her off moments later. Then she sat on
the horsehair sofa in Gran's parlor, Aaron's parlor,
and began to read.

Dear Mother and Father Whitney,

*This is a difficult letter to write. As you would be
the first to note, I am not a literary man. I am a man
of the earth, of the fields, more comfortable with birthing a lamb or a foal than using pen and paper.*

*Still, I cannot leave Carran—as I must—or my
farm without telling you what is in my heart. I loved
your daughter. From the moment I first saw her, I
loved her, and I will love her when I draw my last*

breath. There have been moments, whole nights, in the past four years when I prayed for my own death, so that I might be with her again, in God's peaceful heaven.

But if nothing else, as a farmer, I know that life continues. I have a son to raise, her son as well. And for Seth, I do pray to come back from this ungodly war that divides our nation.

I know you would take him and rear him as your own child; that in him you also see her eyes, her smile, her gentle though impatient spirit. How I loved to watch her struggle with learning to cook and clean, to weed her kitchen garden that first, and only, summer. She had no patience with the learning, or with herself it seemed. In Seth, I see her all over again and so, I have never been able to send him to you in town and miss his growing. Now, remaining with his aunt and uncle Michael at the farm, he can keep on growing and smelling the flowers and chasing the butterflies. She would have loved to watch him, too.

I know you blame me for her dying. If the sleigh had not careened around the curve and thrown us both into a snowdrift. If I'd gotten her to town instead of carrying her home. If it hadn't snowed so hard. If . . .

But she did catch a chill. And she did begin her labor before first light in the middle of a March blizzard. And she did deliver Seth into my hands, using the last of her strength, though I didn't guess it then. Even the doctor, when he could get through the snow, said she would be all right.

Pneumonia, he said later. And in three days, I had lost her. Dear God, I miss her, so fiercely that I cannot bring myself to write her name.

Perhaps God will punish me with death on the bloody field of battle, the only field I would never wish to till. And perhaps I deserve it. But that is not my choice. In these last hours before dawn of the day on which I will ride away from this farm, and Carran, with only my memories to comfort me, I want you to know that, whether I return or not, I loved her—your daughter, my beloved wife—with all my heart. And if it eases you to know it, I shall blame myself for her passing unto eternity.

> *Your faithful servant,*
> *Aaron Cole Granby*

In the dim light of dusk, in the parlor of Aaron Granby's home, the room where—in her book, at least—he and Elizabeth had shared Christmas, Jessie read the letter twice. And for the first time since Charleston, she knew exactly what she wanted. Peter would never have understood, but Jessie knew who would. In the kitchen, she dialed a number she'd known by heart all her life.

"Yeah?" he said abruptly.

But the disgruntled voice was like a calming hand to Jessie. "Nick, can you come over here?"

His tone warmed. "Sure. Why?"

"I need you."

"We'll finish milking within the half hour. Can you wait till then?"

"Yes, fine." *Hurry,* she thought.

After a brief stop in the kitchen, Nick found Jess sitting in the dark parlor. He'd washed his hands and face, wiped his boots before walking on the faded carpet, perhaps made by his own grandmother several "greats" removed. But he couldn't do much about his pounding pulse. Had she asked him over to say yes?

No, he saw in her blinking gaze. "What's happened, Jess?"

Her hand trembling, she held out a paper. "Read it."

Scanning the old-fashioned script, he felt his breath rush from him. "Where'd you find this? In Caroline's attic?"

"Amy brought it from the historical society. I'd given her the Cochran name, thinking it was Elizabeth's, or whatever her real first name was. But Cochran wasn't her maiden name; it turned out to be her mother's, though." She sniffed. "She never really let go, did she? She named her only child after the cold-hearted woman who always rejected her."

Nick knelt in front of her, taking her cold hands in his. "Jess, you're confusing fiction with reality again. The only fact you have is Aaron, the rest you made up."

"Aaron was real, Nick. And my story echoes his life, even when I don't mean it to. Why? Why did he take her in the sleigh? Why did they go to town in a blizzard? Elizabeth died," she murmured. "She died after having his baby, and left him all alone. I worried that my characters needed more conflict, but this letter's so sad."

"Hey," he whispered, "hush. It's all right. I'm glad you called me."

She looked up. "Nick, I don't think I can finish the book. I don't want my story to end."

Not knowing what to say, he held her gaze. Since

their return from Charleston, he'd been tied in knots.
If he hadn't been running back and forth to the hospital about his father, if he hadn't been getting ready to
cut hay, he would have lost his mind. Every time he
remembered Charleston, Jess in his bed, underneath
him . . .

The back of Nick's neck prickled. He was feeling it
again—the warmth he'd experienced in Jess's bedroom, and it scared him. It scared him even more that
he knew how Aaron must have felt.

"Come on," he said. "Let's get out of here." He
drew her out into the yard. The air was warm, sweet,
smelling of Jess's bright summer flowers. "Greg said
to tell you he was driving into town, to take Heather
to dinner at McDonald's."

"Okay." Her tone was vague, her movements
those of a sleepwalker.

"Jess?"

"What?"

"You're a writer," he said, putting an arm around
her shoulders. "You can make your story turn out any
way you want."

"Can I?" Nick walked her toward the paddock,
where Sunbeam and her mama were munching grass.
He and Jess leaned against the rail fence, and after a
while she smiled faintly. "That baby's grown so, her
mother will be kicking her away from that milk sup-
ply before we turn around again."

"That's the way it happens."

Night was falling, and overhead Nick watched the
stars come out, a sliver of moon hanging in the sky
like a Christmas tree ornament. When Jess left her
perch at the fence and walked across the yard toward
her grandmother's orchard, he followed.

There were no blossoms now, but stunted apples decorated some of the branches, and a few had already fallen to the bare earth, as if Jess had willed them to grow and ripen. Ordinarily he would have smiled but now, in the shadow of the trees, she stopped.

"Nick?"

"Here, love."

With a small sound, she turned into his arms. His heart pumping hard, Nick touched her cheek, then ran his fingers through her hair. She'd worn it in a loose topknot on such a warm day, and he took delight in pulling the pins out, watching it spill like water to her shoulders. That other night, so long ago, it had nearly reached her waist, but he found her much more sensual now, much more a woman.

"Make love to me," she breathed.

When she drew him onto the dry grass of a late, hot summer, in the shelter of the trees, he went.

"Ah, Jess," he whispered.

She wrapped her arms around him, her legs. She opened her mouth to his, and let him in. When he pushed her T-shirt high, baring her breasts, murmuring his pleasure that she hadn't worn a bra, she writhed under his hand.

A dozen years before, he had bared her to the night like this, run his hands over her breasts, caressed her taut nipples; he'd shoved the skirt of her white sundress to her hips and stared in wonder, in love, at the shadowed blond triangle covered by white cotton panties. He'd bent to her then, his need apparent, his muscles trembling, as he braced himself above her.

And he'd stopped at the last moment.

He'd stopped, and broken her heart.

"Nick," she said. "Please, Nick."

In Charleston, he thought, they'd made love with bittersweet remorse; now, in the place where he'd once hurt her so deeply, they would make love and heal the old memories. With a groan, Nick sank into her and they were one, as they'd briefly been in Charleston, as they should have been twelve years before.

"We're alive," he murmured, "and real. We're here." He kissed one nipple, suckled, and soothed. "We're here, Jess, and I love you. I want . . . I want . . ."

"What?"

He couldn't stop now. "I want to give you a baby, oh, God, *Jess*—"

"Nick, I love you!"

He came in a rush. The world spun away, then back again, slowly, until Jess, also spent and breathing fast, lay cradled in his arms.

"I want you to marry me," he said.

Jessie gazed into his dark eyes. She didn't want to lose the tenderness they'd shared and she couldn't bear to break the mood. He loved her. And she loved him. She'd even said so. For now, it seemed enough.

"Jess, listen to me." Nick raised on an elbow, his look steady. "Pop's coming home tomorrow. I'll cut his hay and get his corn to market. Then we're getting married—and moving to Charleston."

"But I—"

"We're not kids, Jess. I'm thirty-nine years old. I want a deeper relationship with the woman I love. I want the same commitment from you that I'm willing to give. I've been going nuts the last few days. If Amy and Ben want to blow it, then let them. But not us,

Jess." He kissed her eyes closed. "Aaron's letter disturbed me, too. Finish your book. Then we'll leave Carran, together."

Her throat tightened. "I'm not sure—"

"Why not? You can write anywhere. Maybe twelve years ago your love for Carran and this farm was an issue, but that's crazy now."

"It may seem crazy to you, but not to me." She sat up, pulling her shirt down, shaking out her hair.

"We can make it, Jess. We can work it out this time."

But to Jessie, Nick's plea sounded more like an ultimatum.

16

Jessie finished dusting the last picture frame on Tom Granby's living room wall and, burying her face in the crook of her arm, sneezed violently.

"Lost your Kleenex again?" Greg asked, whipping a wrinkled handkerchief from his back pocket.

"Thanks," she said, then blew. "I'll launder this and give it back to you tomorrow."

"No hurry."

Jessie smiled at her nephew. Nick had already left for the hospital to fetch Tom, and after milking, Greg had been assigned to help Jessie clean house. After a frantic few hours of vacuuming and mopping floors, Greg wore an aggrieved expression. "That should do it," Jessie said. "Just in time to help Brian unload the feed Nick's bringing back from town."

"You think that's a worse assignment?" Greg grinned down at the cobbler apron around his waist, one of Tom's. "Give me barn duty any day."

"Well, I appreciate your help. While Nick and I

were in Charleston, you men didn't bother with housekeeping. I thought Tom would like coming home to clean sheets."

"He didn't bother with KP either," Greg said. "I'll have dishpan hands for a month."

"Complain, complain." Jessie swatted her rag against the trim seat of his pants. "You were eating here too, weren't you?"

"Yeah, pizza and frozen chicken patties. Before Dad started World War Three in the yard," he added. "If you see him, tell him not to worry—Heather started her period yesterday."

"Greg!"

"Well, she did," he said. "Not that there was any chance she wouldn't, but don't tell Dad that. You staying here when Mr. Granby gets home?"

"No, I really should try working on my book." Fat chance, Jessie thought. Aaron's letter—and her discussion with Nick—had frozen her creativity. "I'll just put the casserole I made in the oven before I go. Will you be with me for dinner tonight?"

"No, me and Brian and Nick're gonna start haying this afternoon. Rain's due tomorrow night, so we'll work as late as we can. I'd better help Brian finish juicing up the tractor.

"Go," Jessie said. "And about your father—"

The ringing telephone cut off her words. With a backward wave, Greg scooted out the door, and Jessie went to answer the phone. It was Nick.

"A problem with the hospital?" she echoed, then listened to his frustrating encounter with the billing office. An insurance payment credit on Tom's account from his previous stay seemed to be missing.

"I'm sure it's paid," Nick said. "But can you do me

a favor, Jess, and look in Pop's desk? It's still a mess,
but about halfway back in the file drawer, you'll find
a folder on his medical insurance. All the copies
should be there." He gave her the necessary numbers.

The mess wasn't as bad as Nick had led Jessie to
believe; she knew he'd been making order of Tom's
financial life during his summer stay in Carran. In
seconds, she located the folder and the missing in-
voice.

"It's marked paid to the hospital, Nick." She read
him the date, and he thanked her.

"Pop's pacing the hallway by the main doors right
now."

"At least they're not holding him for ransom."

Nick laughed softly in her ear. "Not a bad idea,
though. He's ornery as hell this morning, like a caged
gorilla. I'll take care of this, then we should be at the
house within the hour. See you then. I love you."

"I was just leaving," Jessie said.

His tone cooled. "Then I'll see you when I see
you."

Hanging up, she felt guilty; she took Tom's insurance folder back to the living room desk and, more
slowly than she'd looked for it, riffled through the
files for its proper place. Electricity. Fuel Oil. Farm
Equipment. Granby/Pearce Development, then Insurance.

Jessie paused. The sight of her own family name
made her look back. Inside the folder were notes in
Nick's bold hand, a few in what looked to be Ben's
writing, and a small stack of blueprints. As soon as
she pulled them out, they rolled up tight. Jessie flattened them on the desk, turned them this way and
that, not able to make much sense of the finely de-

tailed drawings, except that they concerned her land, and Tom's, and seemed to be elevations of one sort and another for some kind of housing subdivision.

Jessie's stomach rolled. She sat down to calm herself. But her heart was thudding painfully, and no amount of deep breathing slowed it down.

She was still sitting at the desk, blindly staring at the future Nick had planned for her, for Gran's property and his father's, when Nick and Tom came into the house.

She hadn't even heard the truck in the drive.

"Jessie girl," Tom said, dropping a small overnight bag by the door. One hand was swathed in bandages. "Come give me a welcome home kiss."

"She's my girl, Pop."

Jessie didn't look at Nick. Letting the plans snap into a tight cylinder, she hugged Tom close, careful to avoid his injury. She'd almost trusted Nick again. Almost.

How long had he been planning this? How long before last night in the orchard?

"Nick and me spent an hour in that blasted hospital billing office, getting them people straightened out, wastin' time better spent mowin' my hayfields, but Lord, it is fine to be home again." One arm still at Jessie's waist, Tom looked around the room. "Somebody's been sprayin' furniture polish in here. You know anythin' about that?"

"A little," Jessie managed.

"Pop, why don't you go on out to the barn and see whether Greg and Brian have the combine ready? I'll be there in a minute."

"They'd durn well better have it ready. I watched the weather channel all morning, rain comin' in from the Midwest, movin' like a train . . ." The screen door slammed shut on Tom's monologue.

Nick was still standing near the door, Tom's larger suitcase in hand. "What's wrong, Jess?"

"You lied to me."

"I don't think I've ever lied to you."

"No?" she said. "You lied twelve years ago about your reasons for leaving here." She gestured with the blueprints. "About us."

Putting the suitcase down, he crossed the room. When he pried the smooth paper from her fingers, Jessie didn't look at him. She heard Nick unroll the drawings, heard the sharp intake of his breath. Her tone was accusing.

"When did you draw these, Nick? That day in the hospital, when you told me Tom was dying? Or last night, after we made love in Gran's orchard? Because I didn't jump at the chance to go to Charleston when you snapped your fingers? I've always known you wanted off this farm for good, but this way? To get what you want, I have to give in completely and so does Tom. You'll be shortening his life—or is that what you want?"

"Jesus," Nick said.

"And why bring Ben into it?"

"Jess, no, I—"

"Don't lie to me! That's his writing in the file. I know Ben's handwriting as well as I know yours. I know how his mind works, too. Why wouldn't you include Gran's property in these plans? Then Ben would pressure me to sell, just as you'll pressure Tom."

"And then what?" Nick asked, too quietly.

"We'll all make money from the only place I've ever loved, and you'll move Tom to Charleston."

"As if you had no other choice."

"You'll try to move me, too, so I can't come back again."

"Don't start playing the victim, Jess. It doesn't fit. Who could ever tell you what to do? All I meant twelve damn years ago was for you to try your wings—to go to college, meet people outside Carran. I sure as hell didn't mean for you to marry Peter and run off to Africa, or Scottsdale. I wanted you to have the same opportunity I'd had ten years earlier—at seventeen, to learn what the rest of the world was like before . . . before you married me. But I blew it, Jess."

"I don't want to talk about this. We've talked already."

"Too bad." Nick stepped closer. "I want to talk, all you have to do is listen. I hurt you and you turned away. Temporarily, I thought, and when you didn't answer my letters or accept my calls, when you spent that first Christmas vacation after Caroline's death at your college roommate's house, I tried to give you room, and time, but—"

"I'm an unforgiving woman, Nick, remember?"

"Still true." His gaze held hers. "By the time I realized how hurt you really were, how serious, you'd married Peter. And because of my old fear of getting trapped here, my one attempt at being noble, or telling myself I was, I'd lost you. That hurt, Jess. You'll never know how much."

Jessie briefly closed her eyes. She couldn't weaken now. "So you decided to make sure our old quarrel about Carran couldn't come between us again." When he shook his head, she said, "You told me so the other night, Nick. I just didn't hear the right words." *Twelve years ago, Carran was an issue, but that's crazy now.* "Do you really think I'll let you bully me on this? Just turn my back on Gran's—"

Nick grasped her shoulders. "Jess, that's somebody else's house, somebody else's life! I don't care whether that's Caroline Pearce or Aaron Granby, real or imagined—"

"I'm happy there."

"You're not happy. You're hiding," he said.

"No! I'm putting my own life back together, Nick—here, among my roots, where my father lived, and Gran and her parents before her. I haven't been sure of anything else this past year, but I'm sure of that. *This* is my home, the place where I belong. No questions asked. And if you had one ounce of sense, Carran would be as important to you as Charleston!"

"Wrong."

Jessie shook her head. "No," she said, "you're the one who's wrong, and there's one more thing I'm sure of. You can turn your back on Carran, even spend the rest of your life down south, but you were still *born* here."

"Dammit, Jess."

"You couldn't change that if you turned this farm into a hundred subdivisions." When he gripped harder, she wrenched away. "And some day, if you stay in Charleston, no matter how many friends like Rob and Alaina you have, no matter how many phony ancestors you hang on your walls, no matter how much the community respects your work, they're going to bury you in that outsiders' cemetery."

Nick's jaw tightened. "When I'm gone, I don't care where they put me."

"Well, I do. That's one more difference between us.

I *care*." She drew a shuddering breath. "And I'd rather spend whatever eternity there is in the place I've always cared about." She glanced toward Tom's living room window, in the direction of the hillside that separated the two farms. At its crest were the private plots surrounded by a ragged white picket fence where her parents lay, and Gran. "I want to stay here, to be near the people I've always . . . loved."

Her voice broke on the last word, and Nick took her shoulders again. "Jess, you're wrong. Belonging's not a place, or people long dead for that matter. It's—"

"Churning up Gran's garden and Sunbeam's favorite pasture and your own father's barnyard, his very heart, so a bunch of Litchfield county executives can have a country house with a view? What will their choice be, Nick? Among the fifteen plans you'll offer? A split-level on an acre and a half, or fake Tudor—"

"Will you listen to me, dammit?"

She turned away. "I don't think so."

"Hear me out, Jess." He spun her around and waved the blueprints in her face. "These are more than twenty years old. Ben and I used to kick the idea around when we were still kids, when I'd just transferred out of the ag school into architecture at Cornell, when Ben was a brand-new father with Greg and a wife to support. Jesus, we were both flat broke. It was a daydream, that's all."

"I don't believe you."

"Look," he said, unrolling the paper. "Look at the quality of drafting here. My God, I don't spend an hour a week now at the board in Charleston, but if I couldn't draw a line straighter than that, a floor plan more to scale, I'd hand back my certification. This is amateur stuff, first-year student experimentation. You think I'd try to railroad you with something like this? Or even something better?" He let the blueprints fall to the floor and shook his head. "Jess, when are you going to learn to trust me?"

He started for the door, but Jessie knew she wouldn't call him back. Thoughts tumbling through her mind, she rubbed her forehead as if to order them. The drawings were crude, she saw that now; and she'd seen the new clubhouse at Seaview, but—

"Maybe you can't trust me," he said. "And maybe it doesn't matter who's right or wrong. All I know is this. When Pop's harvest is done, we're selling this farm and moving to Charleston."

"If your father lives that long." Jessie's eyes met his. She was thinking of Gran and made one last plea. "Oh, Nick, *why* can't Carran be as important to you as Charleston?"

"I told you, Jess, my life is there now."

"And mine's here."

"*Fuck.*"

"I can't leave," she murmured. "I can't."

"Ask Ben," he said, banging through the screen door. "Goddammit, you can ask Ben."

The door flapped on creaking hinges twice before Jessie heard rough male voices from the yard, then footsteps on the porch. Tom Granby shuffled inside, his salt-and-pepper eyebrows drawn together in a scowl.

"Damn fool boy," he said, tamping tobacco into a corncob pipe. "Always did have a hot temper. You all right?"

"I'm okay." But she couldn't meet Tom's eyes. Ignoring him as he lit the pipe, Jessie stood at his desk, near the dining room archway. She'd picked up the blueprints and spread them on the desktop. As soon as she let go, they rolled up like a window shade.

"If I was twenty years younger," Tom said, pacing the room, "and he was four inches shorter, thirty pounds lighter, I'd flay the skin off that kid."

"He's not a kid, Tom."

"Then he shouldn't act like one." Sucking on the pipe, Tom made a circuit of the threadbare rug. Considering how fragile his health was, it always amazed Jessie that he could move so fast. "I should have taken a hickory switch to his backside years ago, when he made that fool decision to leave the ag school and spend his life drawin' spidery lines on that see-through paper."

Glancing at a ceiling crack, Jessie sighed. "Tom, his work is wonderful. Have you seen any of Nick's buildings? Seaview—"

"In that swamp he lives in? Too damn hot and humid. I've never been there."

And proud of it, she heard. Why was she always—especially now—defending Nick to his father? Dealing with one Granby male was like dealing with every other, and she'd reached her limit. "That's too bad. Charleston's beautiful. So is Nick's home, his office. His staff adores him, and so does his construction crew. I know he'd like you to see the area."

"He'd like to railroad me," he said. "It's all I hear about, every time we get a little rain."

"Tom, that hailstorm wiped out more than two-thirds of what Nick planted last spring." She paused. "He still kept his bargain."

"And gave me my eviction notice two minutes ago on his way to the barn."

"On his way to the barn," Jessie said, "to harvest your hay."

"What are you askin', girl? My gratitude to that boy? I could have used his help at hayin' time for the past twenty years."

"Nick did what he had to do," Jessie said, surprised to hear herself say it. But even if the truth kept them apart, it was still the truth.

"What, leave me high and dry? Leave the only woman I think he's ever loved? Hell, I know he loves you still, though he's too damn bullheaded to do anythin' about it."

"He's asked me to marry him."

Tom's gaze sharpened. "Has he now?"

"Yes," Jessie said.

"And move to Charleston?" When she nodded, he said, "Well, that don't surprise me. What'd you say?"

"I think I just said no."

"You and me both," Tom said. "Now I'm comin' to the end of my days, Nick can afford to be generous, or look like it anyway. He must've spent his time on that tractor this summer dreamin' about For Sale signs."

Exasperated, Jessie cast a look at him. She hadn't meant to defend Nick, but the sight of Tom's still heavily bandaged fingers made her stomach roll. She glanced at his shock of white hair, the deep lines around his mouth, the age spots on his good hand, and knew Nick was right in that much. His father's strength was mostly in his mind, his spirit. Tom couldn't keep farming by himself.

"Granby men," she murmured, spreading the

blueprints flat again on the desktop, weighing the corners down. "Come here a minute. Have you seen these?"

Tom hesitated. Then setting his pipe aside, and standing at her shoulder, he said, "What if I have?"

Jessie's eyes met his. She'd never noticed before, but his gaze shifted, just as Nick's did when he was being evasive. Or felt uneasy.

Tom edged back from the desk.

"Well, have you seen them?" she asked again.

"Once," he admitted. "Then I tossed them in the desk out of sight because no man—certainly not my own son—is going to carve up this property into a bunch of ticky-tacky suburban ranch houses. Let 'em all live in Carran, like Ben. Let Nick stay in Charleston, for all I care." Tom took another step. "I won't sell, Jessie, never to some city slicker real estate developer. If Nick tries to force me, those plans go to my lawyer as proof."

"Proof of what?"

"That he and Benjamin Pearce have been plannin' for twenty years to take away this farm. Your grandmother's too," he said.

Jessie had no answer. Maybe, as Nick had said, Ben would.

Ben wasn't home. So when Jessie called from his house, hunting for him, he was alerted to her arrival. By the time she stepped into his office, he had his shoes on, his hair finger-combed into some semblance of order, a pale grin on his face.

"What's wrong?" Jessie immediately asked.

He groaned. "That's the trouble with kid sisters.

They think they can spot a phony smile from thirty paces."

"Ben, Labor Day is weeks off. School opens the day after. Nobody else is in this building right now. I figure when you carry dedication to your job this far, there's something else going on."

He took one look at her face and answered, "That cuts both ways. You look like hell. What happened?"

Jessie told him about the housing plans and Ben frowned, unable at first to remember. He gazed past her shoulder at the wall of awards he'd gathered over the years—his own high school diploma, his college degree, a few teacher-of-the-year plaques, a citation from the state board of education honoring his ten years as principal.

"Yeah," he finally said. "I don't remember exactly when we dreamed up those plans. Right after I got married maybe, but Nick's right. You know how long he struggled with himself before he chose architecture for a career, and Tom all but disowned him. Part of our inspiration was poverty, true, but the rest was . . . well, sweet revenge."

"Revenge?"

"Sure, Tom was giving Nick such a hard time, and there'd been a lot of friction at home when Beth and I ran off."

"I'd forgotten that," Jessie admitted.

She'd been nine years old. "Dad was none too pleased, having his nineteen-year-old son elope, then having to pay for me and Beth to live on campus while I finished my degree. He and I had a few words, like Tom and Nick, some shouting. Mom cried a bucket of tears, then Greg came along, and they were grandparents, and everything smelled like roses."

"For a couple of years," Jessie said.

Ben looked at her again. "Yeah, I'll never forget that telephone call after their plane went down in somebody else's cornfield." He shook his head. "God, I wish he'd never bought that used Cessna. But it was his only hobby, so I guess I shouldn't blame him. Dad was never that happy farming for Gran, and I know what it's like to be a workaholic."

"You took good care of me, Ben." She touched his cheek, and his ears began to burn. "Of me, and Gran."

"Until I decided to ship her off to the nursing home?"

Jessie shook her head. "That was the right decision. I know I didn't act then as if it were—I didn't think it was at the time—but she'd have died anyway. Perhaps alone, at home, while I was away at school. She didn't die because she moved from her own house. She died because she was old, and her heart was worn out."

"Yeah," Ben said, looking away. "I guess."

The confession embarrassed him. He'd always felt responsible, as if he'd hastened their grandmother's death. Still, he'd never had Jessie's acceptance before. Perhaps coming home had been better for her than she'd even hoped.

"Our timing was off, that's all," she said. "Three weeks after she moved, we were standing in the pouring rain at the cemetery on the hill, sprinkling flowers on her coffin. A guaranteed guilt trip for both of us."

"She wouldn't have wanted that," he said.

"No, she wouldn't."

Ben cleared his throat. "Jessie, Nick was telling you the truth about the housing plans. Why couldn't you believe him?"

She took a step toward his wall of plaques. Silent for a moment, she appeared to be reading them. "I don't know how to trust him, Ben."

He thought of Amy. "It's hard to trust someone who's hurt you before. Every time you think you have it licked, some little thing happens, and the same sick feeling comes back to the pit of your stomach."

"Fear."

"Is that what it is?" She turned around, and he tried to smile.

Jessie sighed. "As if a Guernsey bull was chasing me across Gran's field and I just knew I was going to fall in that hole near the fence before I reached safety."

Ben knew the feeling himself. He'd felt it every time he saw Amy Stone; felt it most recently in Tom Granby's barnyard.

"Safety is only an illusion, Jessie." He'd learned that with Beth. "For a long time I thought I had the world by the tail. And then Beth . . ." His throat closing, he paused. "I keep remembering things lately. Like how Beth never finished school. She lived her whole adult life for me, and Greg."

"She loved you both."

He faced his desk, puttered through some papers. He couldn't have said what they were. "Yeah, but now I wonder what would have happened if she'd lived. We had our troubles. Boredom, restlessness, I don't know. Maybe she fit my needs so perfectly, there wasn't much excitement left."

"But with Amy there is?"

Ben jerked around. "There's nothing with Amy Stone. We had a few laughs—"

"Which you badly needed."

"—watched a couple of movies . . ."

"Made love," Jessie supplied and he flushed. "Come on, Ben. You're forty years old. Greg's more sophisticated about his love life than his own father. Why hide it?"

"According to him, he has no sex life."

"And you can take it from me, he's telling the truth—technically. I didn't say sex, I said love."

"Well, with Amy Stone, it was just sex."

"Right," Jessie said, trying to hold his gaze.

Ben looked out the window onto the parking lot where he'd seen Amy's flat tire. The one she'd slashed herself. "She tell you any different?"

Jessie sounded self-satisfied. "Why not ask her yourself? Take the lady a bunch of violets and apologize for being such a jerk at Tom's the other day."

"Apologize?" He turned around. "She has an attitude problem."

"*You* have an attitude problem, Ben." She took his face between her hands so he couldn't avoid her gaze. "With Amy, with Greg, but most of all," she murmured, "with yourself."

"Jessie, you always were a pain in the ass."

Her eyes flashed. "Don't be a hypocrite. You're just like Tom, with Nick. You expect too much, impossible things. Today, when I was so angry with Nick I saw stars, I found myself sticking up for him. Nick's sweating like a slave to get Tom's hay in, and Tom still hates him for walking off years ago. Give Greg a break, and Amy, too. She's a terrific woman. I know you're attracted to her."

"A terrific woman with a big mouth," he said.

"One you offered to shut for her?"

Ben winced. "I was angry about Greg."

"You've been bitter too long, and shut inside yourself. Ben, why not let her in? Your son, too?"

"Tell me something." He gently drew her hands from his cheeks. "What makes you trust Greg—about his relationship with Heather—when you can't trust Nick?"

"Nick and I have our history."

"Everybody has a history." He waited for her to look up. "You've just advised me to do something you can't do yourself."

"What's that?" Her voice was low.

"Forgive." With one finger, Ben tipped her chin up. "And I hate to watch Nick squirm. But what really brought you to Carran today when you should be finishing that book of yours?"

"Those blueprints," Jessie said, as if he wasn't very bright.

"Wrong. And it wasn't my problems with Greg. Was it? Or Amy Stone? Or even Tom, hammering at Nick again, either."

"No," she murmured.

When her gaze met his, Ben saw confusion. Just as her blue eyes matched his, he met that same expression in his shaving mirror each morning. Especially since he'd shut Amy Stone's mouth in exactly the wrong way.

"What then, Jessie?"

"A hug, please," she murmured hoarsely and went into his arms. "Just a hug from my big brother."

He held her, rocked her, as he should have done long ago. But she'd really wanted Nick then, and if she didn't realize it now, she still wanted him. As for himself? he wondered. What the hell did he want?

"No free advice, Ben, but I don't think it's Greg you're angry with, or Amy Stone. Do you?" Jessie whispered into his shirtfront. "Who is it that *you* can't forgive?"

17

"*Greg! Brian!*"

Looking out over the west field, Nick cursed. At five P.M. he'd replaced a fanbelt on the always-balky tractor. Now at eight o'clock, with the light fading, the left headlight had blown.

The boys raced back to the barn for a new bulb, but when that one popped too, so did Nick's precarious temper. "Goddammit. We'll never finish haying before rain tomorrow at this rate."

He shoved the one-eyed tractor into gear, and the boys scattered to their respective jobs, Greg making sure the cutting wheels tracked right, Brian feeding stray timothy into the combine. A minute later he was braking to shout, "Greg!"

"Yeah?" Above the roar of machinery, Greg's voice was hesitant.

"Who tied his tail in a knot?" Nick heard Brian mutter. "Had to be either Jessie or Tom."

"My bet's on Jessie," her nephew replied.

Nick leaned on the steering wheel. "Take ten and run back to the house, will you, for a fresh thermos of coffee?"

"Heather and Jessie are making sandwiches, too," Greg said.

"Then bring me a couple."

As the boys trudged back across the field to Brian's pickup, Nick glanced over and saw Ben's gray Chevy coming to a halt behind it. Ben got out. Greg and Brian walked right past him without speaking, as far as Nick could tell. He shook his head, then waved Ben into the field and drove the tractor to meet him.

One look into Ben's face and he had the same feeling he'd had the night Ben found him with Jess in the orchard. The engine idling, Nick said, "You picked a helluva time to visit. You know how bad I hate haying. If not, the kids could have told you."

"Not my kid." Frowning, Ben looked down at his shirt. It had dark smudges across its white front. "I've been at the firehouse. We had a couple of grass blazes out this way. Everything's incendiary. Dry as a fistful of fatwood."

"That works for me right now," Nick said. "I hope this rain holds off till tomorrow about midnight, then you can have Noah's flood if you want." He wiped a hand across his forehead. "What's up, Ben? You look like you could use a beer."

"You look like you could use a six-pack."

"Not until I'm done here," Nick murmured.

Ben shifted. "I stopped by because I have something to say."

Nick's stomach tightened. "I figured that."

The tips of Ben's ears looked scarlet, and Nick didn't think it was a trick of the light at sundown.

"Spit it out, Ben."

"Don't hurt my sister again," he said.

Nick stayed silent for a moment. Small towns, he thought. Close-knit families. Word traveled fast as if by computer and satellite. His quarrel with Jess raced through Nick's mind.

"I bleed too, Ben."

"I know." He nodded. "I don't like that either, and a few hours ago I told Jessie."

"What'd she say?"

Ben snorted. "What do you think? She told me to fix my own relationships." He looked toward the farm lane, toward Tom's barn. "She said I expect too much of people."

Nick knew there was more to it than that, but he only shrugged. Then he shut off the tractor engine, climbed down, and walked along the edge of the field to a stretch of stone wall by the road, stone that Aaron Granby or his father might have piled on the boundary more than a century ago.

Nick flung himself down on the wall, stretched his legs out, and stared at his boots. Earlier at the house he'd heard Tom slam the screen door and supposed that he and Jess had consoled each other over his lack of tact. He'd had words with Tom, too. A bully, they'd call him. Selfish and ornery and hellbent on having his own way, no matter who he hurt.

Raising his head, Nick looked out over the darkening field. Crickets sang in the long grass, in the fresh-cut hay, which smelled sweet and pungent. Overhead stars splattered the sky, standing out as clear as crystal, models for some astronomy class.

He'd tried with Tom, with Jess. He'd stuck out the summer, and in Charleston, Jess had seemed so close to saying yes. What had happened? After Pop's accident she'd withdrawn again.

Arms braced on the wall, he felt the cool, rough stones under his hands. Today he must have reminded Jess of her ex-husband Peter, of the younger Nick Granby who had all the answers. He wanted to take back his angry words—some of them—but it was too late.

When Ben sat down next to him, Nick hung his head.

"I love your sister," he murmured.

"I know that, too."

"I've loved her all her life. From the first moment I saw her. I watched her take her first steps, I was there when she started to talk." He smiled faintly. "Today I guess I wished to hell she'd never learned how, but I still love her, Ben. I loved her when she was six years old and lost her teeth, when she got new ones . . ." He glanced up. "Remember her first day of school, when we waited by this road for the bus to bring her home again?"

"Yeah," Ben said, holding his gaze.

"I couldn't bear the thought that the world might hurt her, change her." He shook his head. "I loved her chasing after us, and milking cows, and with Sunbeam, how gentle she was. And when your folks died." His voice dropped low. "And the night in the orchard."

"It's forgotten, Nick. Let it go."

He looked away. "Twelve years ago I said things to save my own skin, that's what I really did, and all I've had—deserved maybe—since then is a bunch of photographs in metal frames. Until this summer. Then, like a miracle, we both came back to Carran at the same time. Now that I've touched her again, held her, kissed her—"

Ben's tone was wry. "Shacked up with her in Charleston."

Nick tensed. He knew Ben as well as he knew Jess; knew that in the light his face would be flushed; knew he was only trying to avoid emotion. But this was about Jess. "We didn't shack up," he said. "We didn't fuck, we made love. And I asked her to marry me. Okay?"

"Okay. Don't put your fists up. I'm sorry."

"She hasn't said yes." Meeting Ben's eyes again, Nick sighed. "I don't know what else to do," he said. "I love her so much I hurt all the time, I can't even bear to think of not having her in my life again—but I don't know, Ben. I just don't know anymore. How the hell do you make someone care enough in return?"

"You're asking me? I've screwed up with my kid, with . . ." He didn't go on.

"Amy Stone?"

Ben nodded. "So my sister tells me." He paused. "What should I do with that? Take her flowers, Jessie says. And I've come to terms with losing Beth. She's gone and Amy's, well, she's something else, but . . ."

Nick heard the shy tone of voice he'd been hearing for thirty years of friendship, since the day they'd met by another stretch of fence on this farm. "She's worth the try, Ben. Amy's a fine person. Give her a break." Suddenly he grinned. "Besides, she's got a great body, Pearce, always did."

Ben's gaze shifted, and he grinned back. "Yeah, I noticed." Getting to his feet, he said, "Give Jessie time, Nick. Bend a little yourself. I think she'll come around. I know she loves you."

"But?"

"But what?" Ben touched Nick's shoulder, then turned away.

"What else did she say, besides advising you to fix things with Greg and Amy?"

"You're my friend, Nick—"

"What did she say?"

Ben looked at the ground. "She said she couldn't trust you."

Nick was still sitting on the fence minutes after Ben's taillights had disappeared down the farm lane, when he heard the boys coming. Letting out a breath, he pushed to his feet. By the time Greg handed him two overstuffed roast beef sandwiches dripping his favorite honey mustard, he'd schooled his features into a mask, without emotion. Nick swung onto the tractor, settled into the hardsprung seat, and started the engine.

"Greg? Brian?"

"Yeah?"

"Yes, sir."

He glanced at the two boys, their heads down. "I'm sorry. I didn't mean to snap at you."

"That's okay, Nick." Handing up the thermos of coffee, Greg grinned at him. "Jessie just tried to take our heads off, too."

"No problem," Brian said.

Driving one-handed, Nick shoved the tractor into gear and aimed it down the next wide swathe of grass-ripe field. Eager to finish the harvest, he ate and drank while he worked. Despite his deep summer tan, he'd managed to sunburn the back of his neck that afternoon; like any other season, he'd wrenched his wrist manhandling the stubborn tractor's gearshift;

already his back ached and his butt was falling asleep. He was no Aaron Granby. But he'd finish the job with one headlight because he knew this pitch-dark field as well as Aaron had; finish with the satisfaction of knowing he'd kept his promise to Tom.

Then he'd pray Jess made the decision that would keep them together for the rest of their lives. Because he knew damn well there wouldn't be a next time, another chance for him in twelve more years. Just as he knew he wasn't really angry with Jess tonight, or even with Tom. His anger was for himself.

Aaron seemed angry when I told him that I wanted to go home, but I believe his anger masks his fear that I won't come back.

"Mama's right, Aaron. If I should need the doctor—"

"Lizzie, when will you stop listening to that woman? Michael has, and he's all the better for it. I couldn't get on without him. He's a born farmer."

"And she hates you for it." I smiled to soften the words. "But don't worry. When the baby's born, you'll redeem yourself—in Papa's eyes, too, I'm sure."

"Even that?" Aaron asked, looking at the floor. "If Michael's wife is willing to deliver here, why aren't you?"

"I'm afraid," I whispered and glanced away, watching the snow from his boots puddle on the shining wood. This winter Aaron and Michael have kept busy, building a new house just over the hill; after our baby is born and before Michael's comes, Aaron and I will move into the new house, giving my brother this one. Now Michael lives with his in-laws, something Aaron's joked he could never do.

"A blizzard's coming," he finally said. "That's all she'd need, to remind me for the rest of my life that I drove you into town during a March snowstorm that crippled the whole county."

"Aaron, please."

He lifted his gaze. "You're really frightened? You don't trust me to take care of you?"

"I trust you with my life," I said. "It's myself I don't trust." I am so afraid of harming Aaron's child if I stay. "We could take the sleigh," I said softly.

"Spice has thrown a shoe."

"You'd only need Sugar."

"He's never been good in winter," Aaron said, but his tone had weakened. "He's skittish on ice. Oh, Lizzie." Taking a step, he framed my face between his cold hands. "Will you ever be mine? I'd hoped the baby—"

"I'm yours now, Aaron. I've always been yours. I always will be."

When I turned my lips into his palm, Aaron shuddered. "Maybe I should have waited," he said, "until you were older. Not married you before you turned twenty or twenty-two."

I tried to smile. "Everyone would think I was a spinster."

Aaron wasn't listening. "But I wanted you too much. Am I selfish, Lizzie? To want you here, in my house, among my things, in my bed? Burning my meals? Bearing my babies?"

"No, Aaron, but—"

"I can't stay with you there," he said. "I have the animals to tend, and with this snow they won't find forage."

"I'm not leaving you. I'll only be at Mama's until the baby comes. I love you, Aaron," I said.

"All right." He looked at me as if memorizing every feature. "I suppose I can't have my way all the time." And then, at last, he smiled. "All right, love. I'll take you into Carran." Before I could thank him, his hand slipped over my swollen belly. "And then I'll bring you both home," he said.

Frowning, troubled by the scene she'd written earlier that day, Jessie swiped at the coffee stain on her manuscript. Hoping to figure out what displeased her, she'd taken it to Tom's house for the evening while she and Heather manned the kitchen, preparing hefty sandwiches and strong, hot coffee for the men working Tom's fields.

But she'd only yelled at Greg and Brian for refilling a thermos on top of her papers and hadn't accomplished a thing. If Greg and Heather weren't kissing hello or good-bye on Tom's back porch during one of the boys' coffee runs, Tom himself was underfoot, puffing on his pipe and complaining about Nick, whom she hadn't seen since their quarrel that morning.

When Nick finally came back to the house, Jessie had been ready to start screaming. His quiet, self-contained manner hadn't helped. Dirty and smelling of fresh-mown hay, he'd given her a brief nod, a longer look, then headed for the downstairs bathroom to wash up.

Jessie hadn't screamed. She'd begun sneezing again, and having left her medicine at Gran's, quickly gathered up her manuscript. "If you don't need me here, I'm heading home," she called.

Emerging from the bathroom, Nick said nothing, just wiped his face on a towel. Under his tan, he looked gray with fatigue. He walked into the living room, snapped on the TV, which was already tuned to the weather channel, and studied the forecast map.

"We're done here for tonight anyway," he said. "That system from the Midwest has slowed up some. The rain should hold off until late tomorrow, and as soon as I've put the tractor away, I'm ready for some sleep. I've already sent Brian home. You can take Greg and Heather. They're out nuzzling each other in the yard." As if Jessie had done something wrong, he glanced over his shoulder at her. "The sandwiches were great. The coffee, too. But I'm sorry we interrupted your work."

Her manuscript in her crossed arms like a shield, she said, "You didn't interrupt anything. I'm stuck on a scene." She sneezed again. "And if I—I—*achoo!*— had to smell hay all night, it might as well have been here as at Gran's."

Then she let herself out the back door.

As soon as she reached home, Jessie gulped a pill and shooed the kids outside again to say their final good nights. She hoped the heated kisses in the driveway wouldn't last too long. Between Nick's earlier coolness and her book, she felt little tolerance for romance.

When Greg didn't come inside, Jessie sighed. She gave up trying to erase the coffee stains on her manuscript and got ready for bed. Then she decided to glance once more over the troublesome pages she'd written that day, but tonight the words swam in front of her eyes.

Jessie was stumped. Once they took the sleigh out into the storm, what would happen to her fictional Aaron and Elizabeth?

What would happen with Nick? she wondered. If he sold Tom's farm and moved his father to Charleston, if she stayed in Carran, he'd have no reason to come back again.

The realization frightened her as much as Aaron's fear of losing Elizabeth to her family.

Or was it Aaron she'd been writing about?

Curled up on the futon in her office, she felt her heart begin to pound. In her book Elizabeth, a city girl, struggled with her feelings of inadequacy on Aaron's farm; while Aaron, who loved his land, struggled to keep her there.

Earlier that day Nick had quarreled with Jessie about living in Charleston while she fought to stay on the farm in Carran.

Yet this summer, she had to admit, Nick had come back. He'd compromised and kept his promise to Tom. Like his father, Nick could be stubborn; but like Aaron, he was steadfast, too.

There hasn't been a day in your life when I haven't loved you.

Jessie frowned. Shoving aside the pages of the scene that bothered her, she went to her desk and pulled out the rest of the manuscript. Pausing here and there, she flipped through it. The wedding night scene had troubled her, too—until she remembered how new love felt, how *she'd* felt long ago; how she'd felt with Nick in Charleston.

Why hadn't she seen before that Aaron's love for Elizabeth and hers for him mirrored Jessie's own love with Nick? Emotionally, Nick was the basis of Aaron's character. Perhaps unconsciously she had even flipped Nick's and her own views around, hoping through her fiction to better understand their conflict in real life. But did she? Had she ever?

Two years ago, when Nick's mother died, Jessie had been away with Peter on a field expedition. She'd learned of Nick's loss a month later . . . and done what? Guilt washed through her. She'd sent a note, but only to Tom, as if Nick no longer existed.

You're an unforgiving woman, Jess.

Quickly Jessie stacked the manuscript pages. No wonder she couldn't write the ending.

All right, love. I'll take you into Carran . . .

She and Nick had their differences, too. Yet they wanted similar things, ordinary things. Solid things, like Aaron and Elizabeth. A home, Jessie thought, a good marriage, children. Each other.

She'd been writing about him, about them, all along.

And if she had anything to say about it, Nick wouldn't have the chance to leave Carran again without her. Ben was right.

Ben parked his gray Chevrolet in Amy Stone's driveway, then sat there, frowning at his hands on the steering wheel. He must be crazy. The thought of throttling Jessie, even Nick, ran through his mind before he opened his door.

He'd been driving around Carran ever since he'd left Nick, and if he wakened Amy now, she'd just have more reason to slam her door in his face.

She answered on his second ring.

Ben froze at her tousled dark hair, the usually neat wedge style sticking out in spikes, her green eyes without a smudge of makeup, her slim legs bare beneath a satin sleep shift that exposed the rounded tops of her breasts. He swallowed.

"Ben, it's after one." Then her gaze darkened. "Has something happened to the kids?"

"No," he said.

She stepped back, letting him inside. And put a hand to her heart. "I just had a terrible dream. Another one," she said, the hand moving over her eyes.

"I didn't wake you?"

"I was groggy but conscious. Thinking about making myself a milkshake. Would you like one?"

He made a face. "Watching my cholesterol," he said. "I've cut down on the beer and nuts at night, started eating more fruits and vegetables. I'm using Greg's weights." He looked around her foyer, not to examine Amy's brief attire too closely. "I've already lost three pounds. And part of my gut."

He shouldn't have said that. Her gaze shifted as his came back to her. She focused on his belly, and lower.

"A glass of lemonade, then? Orange juice?"

"Nothing, thanks."

With a shrug, Amy padded toward the kitchen. It was light and airy, hung with ferns, a garden indoors, and Ben always felt comfortable there, as comfortable as he could feel around Amy Stone. He had an alarming tendency to think of her in his bed.

"Was there something you wanted?" she said, splashing milk then dumping ice cream into the blender. She slammed the top on and punched buttons. The roar nearly drowned out her words. "Other than a quick roll in the hay, I mean, or a late-night swim without your clothes? Sorry, I don't care to join you."

"Amy." With a light hand on her arm, he turned her. "I want—"

"Yes, I can imagine." He caught a flash of wounded green eyes before she whirled away. "Ben, I think you'd better—"

A shrill squawk from nearby cut off her words. She wanted him to leave, though; he knew that much. He'd been crazy to come here, to think he could set things right. He wasn't even sure he wanted to. Hell, he didn't know what he wanted. He hadn't known since he'd shut Amy's mouth for her that morning in Tom's barnyard. Ben had started for the door when the squawk sounded again, followed by a whistle and some far-off, muffled words.

Amy hurried toward the sunroom off her kitchen.

"My police radio," she informed Ben, who had followed her. She fiddled with a few dials.

"Why doesn't that surprise me?" he said.

Then the message came through, loud and clear enough to chill his blood, and Ben watched the color leach from Amy's face.

Don't be a coward, Jessie thought. She laid her manuscript on the desktop. If Nick hadn't gone to bed yet, she'd drive over to see him. As he'd said, they weren't children now; like the plot of her book, the issues between them could be resolved. Somehow, they would work out their differences.

Her spirits lifting more at every thought, she glanced out her office window toward Tom Granby's farm. From this room, she could just glimpse the house. If the lights were still burning—

"Oh, dear God."

Jessie's heart slammed against her ribs. The instant she turned her head, she saw fire.

Gran's barn!

Aaron's barn, she thought, and flew down the stairs, pulse drumming, her feet barely touching the treads. Racing through the kitchen and out the back door, she called, "Greg! Heather!"

The last time she'd looked, Ben's son and Amy's daughter had been in the yard, in the old rope swing in her grandmother's huge maple tree, their arms and legs entwined, their mouths pressed tightly together.

Now the yard was empty, and the heat poured from the blazing barn. In the hot, unreal light, Jessie saw that the paddock next to the barn was empty, too. The gate stood open.

"Sunbeam!" she cried. The calf and its mother must be inside. Perhaps Greg and Heather had taken them in as a precaution in case the rain started early after all. *"Greg! Where are you? Heather!"*

There was no answer. Had they driven into town for burgers and fries without telling her?

"Oh, God," Jessie breathed, "please. Help!"

Wrestling Caroline's heavy rubber garden hose off the rack by the house, she twisted the faucet wide open. Jessie dragged the hose across the grass, stretching it to its full length, praying there were no new leaks. She had to save Aaron's barn, the animals.

Jessie had the hose spurting when she noticed Heather's car in the driveway, and her breath caught. Her heart pumped harder.

"Greg! Heather!"

A pickup truck skidded off the farm lane, plowing twin furrows through the yard, jerking to a stop. Two doors slammed but she didn't turn. She didn't have to look.

Nick grabbed the hose. As soon as her hands were free, Jessie started running toward the barn. "Pop called 911. The fire department's on the way." He shoved the hose at Tom. "Pop, turn it on full blast and play it on those doors. Jess, where's Greg?"

"In there," she said, sobbing, stumbling. "I think he's in there, Nick—with Heather! And the cows. We have to save them, Aaron's barn—"

In three strides Nick caught her. "Jess, for God's sake, stop!"

She struggled against his hold and he shook her, hard.

When their gazes met, Jessie's heartbeat paused. *Didn't I tell you that barn was a firetrap?* she expected him to say. But all she saw in Nick's eyes, his silence, for one heartstopped instant was regret.

"I didn't want this," he said, as if she blamed him for the fire. Then they heard screams and, thrusting her at Tom, he ran into the burning barn.

18

"*Nick!*"

Acrid smoke seared her lungs, clouds of it blinding her, as soon as Jessie pushed her way inside the barn. She heard a woman's voice cry out. From a nearby stall that she could have found in total darkness, she heard the crash and bump of terrified animals, the bellow of Sunbeam's mother. Burying her nose in the crook of her elbow, she put her head down and kept going.

"Jess, goddammit, get out of here!"

"I can help," she shouted.

"Greg!" he called.

"Up here." A hoarse male voice pleaded, "Get us down."

"The hayloft," Jessie said.

Nick stumbled toward the ladder but, peering up, apparently saw nothing. "Greg? Can you find the edge—" He broke off, coughing. "—the loft edge? That ladder's top rung sticks up enough to feel. Look for it."

Jessie stood by, helplessly. Heather's frightened cries sent shivers up her back, and the panicked lowing of cattle brought tears to her stinging eyes. "Nick?"

"Throw the bolt on that stall. Stand back and let the cows run. They'll see moonlight in the entrance."

She had to grope for the bolt. At the same instant her fingers found it, Sunbeam's mama threw herself against the wooden door, lodging the bolt tighter. "Stay back!" Jessie shouted. She flung out a hand, connecting with the cow's tender nose, sending the animal in a flurry to the far side of the stall.

Jessie fumbled the bolt.

Then she ran back toward the loft ladder, to Nick. "It's open," she said, her breath wheezing.

"Good, but this ladder's gone. The bottom half just cracked off." He muttered something about rotten wood, and heat.

"Get us down, Nick! Please!" Heather yelled.

Jessie looked up at the loft. And her heart stalled. Fire billowed at the farthest end, out the haymow window, creeped as she watched to the hayloft edge. Orange tongues of fire licked upward toward the barn ceiling.

"Heather! Come toward my voice," Nick commanded. "Greg, stay calm and help her onto the ladder. Can you see it?"

"Yeah, Nick." Greg's voice was barely controlled.

The old ladder had been bolted years before to the hayloft's broad floor beam, and Jessie prayed it would hold.

Nick said, "Okay, now turn her around onto that first rung. Heather, you come as far down the ladder as you can. When you feel empty air underneath you—" His voice a hoarse croak, he coughed. "I'll be there. Just put your feet anywhere, I'll do the rest."

When Heather tumbled into Nick's outstretched arms, nearly knocking him to the floor, Jessie could have breathed relief, but she could barely breathe at all now.

Whooshing and surging, crackling, snapping, the fire roared like a freight train.

"Get her outside!" Nick ordered Jessie, shoving Heather into her arms. "I'll bring Greg."

Ben was shouting his son's name even before he'd braked the Chevy in Jessie's yard. From the main road he and Amy had been able to see the flames and smoke, rising like some steel plant's exhaust plume into the night sky. His heart pounded triple time, his palms were sweaty. Over the years he'd seen barn fires like this—bonfires, the other volunteers called them—and he'd never seen one end except in disaster.

"Ben?" Amy clutched at his sleeve.

"Don't panic. That old barn was empty most of the time. On a night like this, even Jessie's cows are probably in the pasture." He slammed the gearshift into park and jumped out.

The news wasn't good. Ben turned away from Tom Granby, who was playing a gushing garden hose, one-handed, over the barn roof and into the haymow opening, and grasped Amy's shoulders. Her eyes were wild with fear.

"The kids?"

"Inside," he muttered, then had to restrain her. "Amy, don't! Nick and Jessie—the damn fools—are getting them out. Come on," he said, pulling her into his arms. He pushed her face against his shoulder. "Don't look. Don't think about it." He guided her away from the heat, the blazing light, to the dark shelter of Gran's maple tree. "Sit down here. They'll be out in a minute. Everything will be fine."

"I want my daughter!"

"Everything will be fine," he said, wishing he believed his own litany. Wishing he didn't have to leave her. But he had to help Nick. "I want my son," he murmured. Their animosity forgotten, he tipped her face up, looking deeply into her eyes. "I swear, everything will be all right."

Ben stumbled to his feet and headed for the barn.

Jessie hugged Heather close, the girl choking against her shoulder. Nick turned back to the loft, and in that instant, smoke enveloped him like an automobile's airbag, shutting off Jessie's view. "Nick—?"

"We'll be okay. Get out of here, Jess."

She and Heather, arms tight around each other, groped their way toward the open doors. From the distance behind them, Jessie could hear the sharp crack of wood. A loud thud, like that of a falling tree, made her heart jump. Looking back over her shoulder for Nick, she paused.

"Outside, Jessie," Heather croaked, dragging at her.

Then in the doorway they were gulping needle-sharp breaths of air that, although smoke-tinged, seemed to Jessie as clear and clean as glass. She had little chance to breathe. From behind a hard weight shoved into the small of her back, propelling her with

Heather the rest of the way into the yard, into the dark night, Jessie a step ahead of the others.

Ben's hard embrace threatened to crush her.

"Sweet Jesus, you're safe. You're safe," he said, giving her a quick hug. Then he hauled Heather into one arm, Greg into the other. With a cry, Amy Stone materialized from the darkness, surrounding her daughter and Ben's son, the four of them pressed tightly together in a circle.

"The beams are starting to go," Nick said at Jessie's heels. "The whole place will cave in on itself." He glanced toward the lane where Jessie, following his gaze, watched a stream of cars and pickups—Carran's volunteer firemen—and one red pumper speeding toward her grandmother's farm. "The fire department can stop its spread to the shed and the house, but the barn's gone, Jess."

For a second, she couldn't see why that mattered.

"I don't care. As long as the kids are safe and—"

Aaron's barn, she thought.

"I'll build you another one." Nick's hand lifted to her cheek, but Jessie turned away before he touched her.

"Nick, where are Sunbeam and her mama?"

"You threw the bolt, didn't you?"

"Yes, but . . ." She looked around the yard, ran toward the paddock. "They're not here!"

Nick was coughing again. "Maybe—" Bending over, hands on his thighs, he tried to clear his throat. "Maybe they headed over the hill toward Pop's."

"I don't think so." Jessie had a feeling. "I think they're still inside."

"Jess, you can't go back in there!"

But Jessie was running again. It wouldn't take

much. A slap on Sunbeam's rump, a tug at her mama's halter. She couldn't let them die.

"Jess!"

All around her, volunteer firemen set to work. Ben was snaking a huge flat hose from the town's one red fire truck to the haymow end of the barn. He didn't see her. Amy, standing off in the drive with both their children, called out, but Jessie didn't stop.

"Jess, dammit to hell!"

Nick reached for her arm, but Jessie evaded him, flashed past the two firemen in front of the barn doors, and shoved inside. Their shouts followed her. So did Nick.

"Jess, dammit, I could—"

"Help me!"

Stumbling toward the stall, she found its door wide open—and heard the panicked trampling of animals still inside.

"Sunbeam. Rosie," she called. "Come on, babies."

Nick edged past her into the stall. "Keep away from the door. They must have been too spooked to run." He stripped off his shirt, at the same time pushing against the dim, smoke-distorted shape of a large cow. "Move over, dammit."

Jessie could just make out Sunbeam's smaller form. She lay on the floor near her mother's legs, her body blocking the door.

"Oh," Jessie whispered, her voice breaking.

"Smoke inhalation." Nick wrapped his shirt around the cow's head, tying the sleeves to make a blindfold.

"Is she . . . dead?"

"I don't know," he said. "Come hold this cow's halter."

She didn't have to ask why. Nick tugged and heaved Sunbeam's inert body out of the way. "Now step outside and run for the door. I'll bring the cow."

"Nick, please," she said, not moving. "Don't leave her baby here. Please don't."

He coughed again. "I'll try. She's deadweight but I'll try." He whipped his belt from his pants, into her palm. "Use this if you have to."

She obeyed. But like Jessie, the mother cow didn't want to leave her baby. Hanging onto her halter, Jessie slapped at the cow's rump with Nick's leather belt.

Preoccupied with herding the cow toward the doors, she didn't hear the crack overhead; but she heard Nick's shout of pain. Jessie whirled, nearly wrenching her arm from its socket, and saw him fall, the heavy loft beam settling onto his body, as if in slow motion. The fall seemed to take forever.

"Nick!"

Jessie brought the leather belt down hard on the cow's back and she scooted, bellowing, for the door. Jessie ran back. Nick lay in the barn aisle, flat on his back, his hip and leg pinned by the broad wooden beam. Jessie tried but couldn't budge it.

Overhead the flames licked higher, spilled over the hayloft edge like bright orange curtains.

"Leave it, Jess!" he said raggedly. "Go get some of the men."

Tears streaming down her cheeks, Jessie crawled onto her knees, then stood. "I can't leave you."

"Dammit, go!"

Her legs felt numb, her chest ached. Time seemed to stand still. She took one last look at him and, with Nick's stifled grunts of pain in her ears, began groping toward the air, and moonlight. Toward help.

♦ ♦ ♦

Outside Ben squinted up at the burning loft. "Sonofabitch," he muttered. "This old barn's stood for at least a hundred and fifty years. Helluva way for it to go."

Then he looked down in time to step back as a maddened Guernsey cow hurtled from the inferno. Ben shouted to another volunteer to catch her, then turned back and saw Jessie in the barn doorway, holding her ribs and gasping for breath. Ben hurried toward her.

"Inside," she wheezed, "Nick's hurt," and then, "Sunbeam."

Tom lumbered around the corner of the barn, coiling a gurgling garden hose with his good hand. When he heard Nick's name Tom dropped the hose, but Ben saw his intention and blocked his way.

"Let me by, damn you!"

"Tom, you're in no shape—"

"Don't you tell me what I am." Tom gave him a hard shove.

"Jessie, take him—"

But dragging in air, Jessie fell to her knees, and Ben shouted for a paramedic. In that brief second Tom headed for the barn.

Swearing, Ben raced after him. Fire blasted through the open doorway, curled upward into the dark night. "Play some water on this door," Ben yelled. Then he ran past Tom.

Inside, Ben called out, "Nick? Nick!"

"Here."

"Jesus Christ."

"It's not the main loft beam, or I'd have lost my damn leg."

Ben crawled over the still form of a calf—Jessie's Sunbeam—to his friend. "It's okay, buddy. We'll get you out."

He heaved against the beam but couldn't budge it. Ben shouted back over his shoulder and a figure, silhouetted against the outdoor light, shuffled toward them.

"Tom, Christ, I told you—"

Tom Granby dropped to his knees. He studied Nick's leg, the fallen beam. "We can move it, the two of us," he said.

"You with one hand? The hell we—"

"Pop, don't strain yourself. You're in no condition to—"

"I'm fit as a country fiddle. Even if I wasn't, I'm near the end of my time anyway, and you're in no position to tell me what to do, city boy." Tom blinked. "Come on, Ben Pearce. Lend those lily white teacher's hands—"

As Tom started to lift the beam, Ben clamped a hard hand on the old man's gnarled arm.

"Help me, damn you! He's my son," Tom said, his eyes bright. "He's my only son."

Praying for Nick, Jessie hugged her arms to her knees. She'd tried to help, but Ben had called the paramedics, and before she could take a step toward the barn for a third time, she'd been lying on a stretcher with an oxygen mask clamped over her face. Nick, she thought again.

She'd assumed it would be easy. She would talk

sense to him, and they would mend their differences, the way Ben had wanted them to for years. Now, with her lungs cleared enough to breathe on her own, in the shelter of Gran's maple tree, beside Amy and Heather, Jessie closed her eyes, squeezing back tears. Nick's life was at stake and nothing else—nothing, not even Gran's farm or Aaron's barn—mattered.

"He'll be okay, Jessie," Amy murmured.

"Greg's dad went after him," Heather added. "Mr. Granby, and then two of the firemen."

"They'll be fine," Amy said.

Then Heather leaped to her feet, straining her eyes to see through the dark night. All around them, men shouted. And always, the fire writhed and spit like an angry snake.

Heather's tone was shrill. *"Where's Greg?"*

"Dad? Dad, you there?"

Ben's heart stopped. "Greg, for the love of—"

"Let me help. Nick helped me."

The task took five men: Ben and Greg, two firemen, and Tom Granby, who, once Nick's leg had been freed, insisted on cradling his son's shoulders in a one-armed embrace. "Nick," he murmured, "Nicky."

Her hand clamped around Heather's wrist, Jessie heard cries of triumph from the firemen, and the blood drained from her face in relief.

Heather pulled free, sprinting toward Greg.

Amy pelted across the yard through mud and water-slickened grass toward Ben.

Jessie ran toward Nick.

"I'm okay," he said, looking up at her from the same gurney Jessie had occupied.

"I thought I'd lost you," she whispered.

"Only if you want to."

But his face was white, and she hovered anxiously over him until the paramedics finished their examination.

"No broken bones," one said, "but plenty of soft-tissue damage. You'll have some pretty impressive bruises tomorrow."

"You'll need X rays to be sure about that leg," the other added. "Want a lift to the hospital?"

Nick sat up. "I hate sirens. Somebody here'll take me. Later."

Jessie made a sound. "Nick, I think you should go now."

Weakly, he smiled at her. "Later," he repeated. "But I love it when you make a fuss, Jess. Know what I really need right now? A hot cup of your coffee."

Muttering under her breath about men, Jessie huffed her way to the house. She didn't look back at the barn. In the kitchen she found Amy Stone with Heather, slicing sandwiches made from the remainder of the roast beef.

"I thought those firemen could use a pick-me-up," Amy said.

Heather grinned. "Mom just didn't think she could keep her hands off Mr. Pearce out there."

"You, young lady, have inherited your mother's mouth."

"Greg likes it," she murmured.

Amy groaned, but Jessie knew the banter was really relief that such joking could take place, that everyone was safe. Everyone but Sunbeam, Jessie thought. She hadn't been able to look toward Sun-beam's mama, huddled in the far corner of the pas-ture.

To keep her mind occupied, she started Nick's cof-fee brewing. Moments later the back door opened and Ben came in with Nick hobbling on one leg, his shoul-der jammed into Nick's armpit.

"Human crutch," Ben said, grinning. Soot black-ened his face, and his shirt had torn jaggedly at the shoulder seam. When he'd settled Nick at the kitchen table with coffee and a huge slice of Jessie's peach pie, he turned to Amy. Jessie couldn't miss the warm look he gave her. "Let me help you with that coffee. I'll carry the pot, you bring the tray of cups and spoons."

"Don't forget the napkins, Mom," Heather said, smugness in her tone.

Jessie stared after them.

"You remember when Ben was dating Beth?" Nick asked, stirring sugar into his coffee.

"Yes," Jessie said.

"Remember when he left town the summer night they eloped? And he didn't tell anybody? Me or you included?"

She thought a moment. "Yes, I think so. He said he had a date, but when Gran asked when he was com-ing home, he wouldn't say. You know Ben. He puffed himself up and acted angry, and I remember thinking he had something to hide."

"Yeah," Nick agreed. "He ran into me that night on his way down the lane. I was coming back from town. We said a few words, then he drove on—and the back of my neck started prickling. I know Ben," he said. "He was wearing the same look then as he did just now."

◆ ◆ ◆

Carrying his coffee, Ben walked Amy away from the
others. He'd left his car at the top end of the driveway,
keys in the ignition. It didn't matter here, because no
one this far from Carran was about to steal the Chevy.
But now he needed his keys.

"Where are we going, Ben?"

"You'll see."

At the car he opened his trunk. Reaching inside, he
pulled out the Burger King bag he'd bought earlier
that night; much earlier. Now the bag was freckled
with grease stains that made him shudder. "Here. For
you," he said.

"Two apple pies?"

"Packed in cardboard," he told her. "You might
need to heat them up in Jessie's microwave. One of
them's mine."

"Yours?"

He shuffled his feet. "Well, I figure I ought to learn
more about you and all . . ."

"All what, Ben?" Amy cocked her head. The glow
of firelight behind her turned her hair to copper, and
he wanted, badly, to slide his fingers through its
warmth.

He sipped at the coffee he didn't want.

"Speak," she said softly.

Setting the cup down, he wandered deeper into the
shadowy yard, and with the greasy bag clutched in
her hand as if it contained diamonds, Amy followed
him.

Ben spoke, finally, to Gran's maple tree. "Beth and
I got married young. We were married for nineteen
years. I never had another woman in that time, I never

needed one. Not even when we started growing apart."

"Ben." Her tone was exasperated.

"This isn't going to be a sonnet to my wife," he said. "But I need to say this. Beth and I had rubbed along like any other married couple for a lot of years. When she died, part of me died, too. But if she'd lived, I don't know what would have happened, Amy." He looked at her. "Maybe we'd have gone through a bad patch and come out all right. Maybe we'd have grown old together and she would have buried me first. Or maybe by now, we'd be separated, divorced. I doubt it, but who knows? All I know is . . ."

Silent, Amy touched his arm.

"I know," Ben said, his heart in his throat, "that when I wake up every morning, the first thing I think about is you." He moved, pulling her into his arms. "God, Amy. Tonight in that damn barn—"

"I know," she said. "I know. I was scared to death you wouldn't come out."

"I was scared to death I'd never have the chance to tell you, to open my mouth for once and say . . . I love you." He kissed her. Once, twice, a third time until he felt her compact body relax into his.

She looped her arms around his neck. The greasy bag bumped against his back. "I love you, too. I've loved you, Benjamin Pearce, since I was sixteen years old."

Pleasure shot through him at the words, but he felt he should explain. "Greg says I'm not easy to live with."

"Ancient history," Amy murmured.

So he kissed her again. "I'm self-righteous, a prude."

"Well, not at midnight, on the pond bank or upstairs, with me, in bed."

He groaned against her neck, nuzzling the soft
skin. "I wish we were there now, but Amy . . . I'm not
certain of everything. I don't know whether I can
change that much—"

"Don't talk it to death, Ben. You don't say much
but you're a good man. And once you get started
. . . Oh, damn. Maybe I was wrong and I'll have to
shut *your* mouth this time." She raised up into his next
kiss. "One thing." She dangled the greasy bag between them. "You call this roses?"

"Roses?"

"Jessie thought one night you'd bring me roses. As
a romantic gesture."

"She told me violets." Ben edged her deeper into
the tree's shelter. "You want romance? I'll show you
romance—"

"Dad?"

"Mom?"

Ben and Amy jerked apart an instant before
Heather and Greg ducked under the lowest branch of
the maple tree.

"What are you two guys doing?" Greg asked.
"Trying out Jessie's swing?"

"None of your business," Ben answered with a grin.

"Figure it out," Amy said.

Heather giggled. "They're fooling around."

Ben looked from her dancing eyes into Greg's,
swimming with laughter, then into Amy's, and his
grin widened.

"They've caught us," she said.

"Send 'em to the principal's office," Greg suggested.

"Study hall detention for a week." Heather's long brown hair gently teased Greg's cheek as she laid her head against his shoulder. "Or what about suspension?"

It felt good to laugh. Ben let the feeling build, the laughter rolling from him before he sobered. He could have lost all this tonight. He could have lost his son. They could have lost each other.

"Dad, can I tell you something?" Greg searched Ben's face. "You were right. And so was Nick, even Jessie in her way." Greg pulled Heather closer, his gaze going toward the barn. The roof had gone, and smoke poured into the sky. "I've been a selfish bas— plain selfish, Dad. But that's over. I want you to know that."

"Know what exactly?" Ben asked.

"That me and Heather—Heather and I—are going to . . . well, chill out," he said. "You know, cool things down. Try to stay mellow. I've been thinking of myself, of what I wanted." He looked at the young girl in his arms. "It won't happen again."

Ben's pulse kicked up. "What won't happen?"

"I won't lose control." Greg's tone was low. "Won't ever take her out in the barn again, or my car, or Jessie's swing."

"Greg," Heather murmured.

"It's my fault," he said, lifting tortured eyes to Ben. "Tonight, after we finished haying at Nick's, Heather and I came home with Jessie. Heather called her mom because it was late, but I talked her into staying longer. We . . . after a while, I had this idea that the rain Nick expected was blowing in early, so we put the cows in the barn and then . . ." He swallowed.

"We climbed up in the loft, Mr. Pearce." Heather's eyes, so like Amy's, were beseeching. "Nick told us it wasn't safe, but it looked okay. It was dark, though, and I kept hearing sounds."

"Mice scurrying," Greg supplied.

"But I thought maybe they were rats. I said we should get down and I should go home, but I didn't really want to." She glanced at Greg. "It's not all his fault. We'd been kissing a lot and . . . and it felt so good, that when Greg said we could bring up the Coleman lantern from below, I said okay."

"What happened with the lantern, Greg?" Ben asked.

"We were lying in the hay. I kicked it over—by accident—and the fire started." He looked miserably at Ben. "Jessie's barn burned down and Nick almost died . . ."

"My God," he said, "don't blame yourself. It's all right. You kids are safe, that's the important thing. I think you should tell Jessie and Nick about the lantern, apologize, but don't beat yourself up about this. It was only an accident."

Like Beth, he thought, and me. Looking at his son and Amy's daughter together, their arms tight around each other's waists, he felt his vision blur. Amy was right. He'd been younger than Greg when he had his "accident" with Beth, when they'd made the baby they had both loved with all their hearts.

Clamping a hand on Greg's neck, Ben drew him close. His eyes met Amy's, full of tears. She smiled mistily at him. "It's all right," she said.

And Ben forgave himself.

◆ ◆ ◆

Nick didn't want to let his leg stiffen up. So after nursing three cups of coffee—Jess even managed to burn that—he took advantage of her trip to the bathroom and limped outside. The night air smelled singed, too. It would take until morning for the fire to burn itself out, for the volunteers to leave. His talk with Jess would have to wait.

Nick didn't mind.

He thought he'd avoid confrontation at any cost just now. Especially if it didn't turn out right. Feeling reflective, he stood along the fence near the far end of the pasture until he heard his name, smelled aromatic tobacco and, turning, saw Tom. "You okay, Pop?"

"Right as spring rain on new-sprouted corn. I'm tougher'n those paramedic fellows. Tougher'n you, too," he said, glancing down at Nick's leg. "You hurtin' any?"

"Some."

Tom sucked on the forbidden pipe. "The doc give me some pain pills when I smashed my hand. You want me to get 'em for you?"

"No, thanks." Nick looked at his father. The old man stood several inches shorter than Nick, his spine bent a little now, but he was still a strong man in more ways than one. If you discounted the time bomb ticking away inside him. Nick was about to tell Tom to put the pipe away when he resigned himself to it; let him have his pleasures. "Why don't you go on home, though, Pop? You should rest, and there's nothing more anyone can do. The guys from Carran have ings under control."

"What about you?"

"'ll stick around. Jess said she'd drive me into
o get pictures of my leg." Wincing, he leaned

against the fence rail. "Guess I was lucky at that," he said. "Because of you."

"The Granbys take care of their own."

Nick smiled faintly. "You stubborn old cuss, I'm trying to say thanks for saving my life."

"Don't get dramatic." Tom gazed in the opposite direction, into the pasture.

"I promised Jess a new barn," Nick said after a moment.

"Better build it, then. Women take stock in the promises men make. I know your mother did. With talent like yours, the job should be a cinch."

Nick's head spun around.

"You heard me right," Tom said. "Talent. Brains. Vision. And a love for the land that I never saw before in you, Nicky. I didn't even know it was there, would have bet my farm it wasn't, until I looked at those old blueprints Jessie found this morning."

"They were just kid stuff. I never meant—"

"I know what you meant. What you had to do. But so do I." Tom kept staring at the field. "I think I'll take you up on that offer you keep makin'. To show me Charleston, South Carolina. I've wondered ever since you left here what kind of work you do. If those rough blueprints are any sign, I won't be disappointed. I like a man respects trees and open space and natural contours."

"Pop."

Tom tucked the pipe in his pocket. "I'll be ready," he said, his eyes meeting Nick's, "soon as we sell the farm."

◆ ◆ ◆

Walking from the house, Jessie skirted the smoldering barn, her gaze avoiding it, and picked her way across the wet grass. At the far end of the pasture, she found Nick with Tom.

"You escaped," she said. "Ready to go into town?"

"In a minute."

Jessie looked from Nick to his father. "Am I interrupting something?"

"Pop's selling out. His idea."

Her mouth dropped open, but before she could speak, Greg loped across the yard, calling out to Nick.

His stumbling apology included Jessie, but Nick answered.

"Accidents happen," he said. "Don't worry about it. As long as you and Heather are safe, that's what counts."

"That's what Dad said."

Jessie's eyes widened. "He did?"

"Then he kissed me and Heather and Amy Stone. What do you think, Jessie? If my girlfriend becomes my stepsister, too?"

"I say wonderful."

"Kinky," Nick said with a grin. Then he sobered. "But listen, Greg—and this has nothing to do with the fire—I can't keep you on at the farm." As he told Greg about the sale, Greg's eyes went bleak. "Once the corn's in, I'm afraid you're out of a job."

"Jeez, Mr. Granby"—he looked at Tom, who was studying something in the far pasture—"that's too bad. I know how much the farm means to you. I've only spent the summer there, but I'd stay forever if I could."

Jessie's throat tightened. Tom said nothing. Nick silent, and so did Greg. Six hundred acres, she thought. In Aaron Granby's time—the real Aaron Granby—Tom's farm and her grandmother's had been one. She hated to see even half of it sold, and when Ben got wind of Tom's plan, she'd have a real fight on her hands if she wanted to stay.

Maybe Ben and Nick would redo the old blueprints, but no matter how skillfully Nick designed a residential subdivision, Tom would hate the idea and so did she. Even if she didn't stay here, she didn't want to sell. It had been hard enough tonight, seeing Aaron's barn burn to the ground. Without Sunbeam, at least she wanted to see other Guernsey calves suckling their mothers in the pasture.

But Tom had debts, she knew, big ones. Nick couldn't keep paying them. And yet . . .

What if?

Her pulse thumped but she grinned. Her writer's imagination came in handy sometimes in real life, too. Jessie looked at Greg. "You really want to be a farmer?" she asked.

"I don't want to be anything else."

Like Aaron, Jessie thought. And he should have his chance.

"What if Tom didn't sell?" she said, her tone more excited with each word. "What if you stayed on there, and Ben and I leased our land to you as well? Tom could keep his house, you could live at Gran's. You'd have six hundred acres, more than enough to farm profitably. Tom could share profits and supervise until you learned all you need to know. What if—"

Greg, with hope in his eyes, let out a yell.

"It might work," Tom said. " 'Course I'd have to teach him from word one, beginning with how to tell a cow from a cornstalk . . ."

Jessie's breath hitched. "Nick?"

He hadn't said a word, and her spirits sank. It wasn't what he wanted, what he'd been wanting most of his life.

Still silent, Nick looked away. He'd had a long day, a hard one, but—except for the fire and his fight with Jess—gratifying. His hay was nearly in, and looked good. *His hay.* He'd given Tom a fine season and had come to understand his father's love for his land.

He'd waited years to hear his father offer to sell out, but now that he finally had what he wanted, he only felt hollow.

At Jess's words, he envisioned the fields full of grain, Caroline's house ringing with laughter, and maybe, one day, with the happy shouts of Greg and Heather's children. Or Jess's.

Nick turned around and found her watching him, her blue eyes dark, all but pleading. "All right," he said. "If Pop wants to stay, and Greg's willing to work his butt off, I've been thinking. I have another suggestion. A compromise."

Three pairs of eyes regarded him as if he walked on water. And as he spoke, Nick's own eagerness grew. He proposed selling off only part of Tom's land. "Like all farmers, Pop's been cash poor and land rich most of his life. We need to shift that balance. We could build a discreet executive community, expensive homes on large lots, low density. The profit would take care of Pop's debt, and there'd be plenty left for him and Greg to farm, say four hundred acres or more. I'll make sure you don't even see those houses from where you sit, Pop."

Greg gave another shout. "My dad doesn't need to sell everything he and Jessie own. He and Amy are gonna be okay—a dual-income couple, he said, part of the nineties."

Tom thumped Nick on the back. "Thanks, son."

Her eyes shining, Jess flowed into his arms, pressing her head against his chest, her arms around him. "Thank you, Nick."

Nick held her close, his throat tight, his eyes briefly closing. In the instant before she hugged him, he had seen what he'd been waiting for with Jess, too. The look he'd all but given up hoping to see again, that had made him curse himself in anger earlier that night; the look of trust he'd destroyed so long ago.

"Hell, don't thank me." He pointed a finger. "Thank that little thing scampering toward her mama. Who could even think of selling her relatives off our home place. Not me. What about you, Pop?"

"Not me," Tom murmured.

"Sunbeam!" Jess took off down the fence line and climbed into the pasture.

Taking his time, Nick said a few words to Greg and Tom, who headed for the house, then he joined her, the two of them stroking the calf's singed hide and its silky ears. "She took in too much smoke," he said, "but she'd been low to the ground, so she had enough air to keep breathing. Barely. One of the firemen carried her out."

"Oh, Nick, thank God. I couldn't even look at the pasture."

They were silent for another moment. He didn't know what her choice would be, but at last he had her trust. Maybe, if things didn't turn his way, that would have to be enough.

"Jess?"

She lifted her head, and Nick fought the urge to

look away from her brimming eyes. He met her gaze squarely.

"We have to talk," he said.

"We have to talk later," she corrected. With a final pat for Sunbeam, she straightened and took Nick's hand. "You have no business limping around on that leg—or climbing fences after me."

He grinned. "I'd climb anywhere after you."

"Well, do it later. Right now, Nicholas Granby, I'm taking you to see a doctor."

Crossing the pasture, Nick leaned on her more than he needed to just to feel the strength of Jess's embrace. "Anything you say, love."

19

Love, *he'd always* called her. Like Aaron with Elizabeth. Or should she say that Aaron was like Nick?

In the predawn darkness, in her bed, Jessie lay smiling, crying. She'd never imagined it was possible to do both at once, but tears trickled through her hair onto the rumpled pillow, and the smile—she envisioned it as beatific—spread across her mouth.

Earlier, she'd driven Nick into town for X rays and pain medication. On the way back he'd grown so quiet that Jessie assumed he'd fallen asleep, exhausted. When she pulled off the highway onto the farm lane, slowing at the foot of Tom's driveway, she glanced over and found Nick, his head rolled toward her on the seatback, intently staring. Noting that Tom's house was dark, she gave him an inquisitive lift of one eyebrow, but Nick only shook his head.

Jessie knew an opportunity when she met one. Without a word, she sent the BMW flying down the lane toward her grandmother's farm. By then, the firemen were packing up, and the barn lay in ruin. Avoiding it, Jessie led the way to Gran's back door, through the kitchen, and upstairs to her own bed-room.

She didn't turn on lights; she didn't suggest that Nick shower. She pulled the summer quilt to the end of the bed and helped Nick crawl onto the clean sheets with a heartfelt groan.

"Sleep," she whispered and, twitching the top sheet over him so he wouldn't catch a chill, started toward the door.

"Where are you going?"

She shrugged in the darkness. "Downstairs maybe. I might fix a cup of tea. Or into my office. I'm too wired to even think of falling asleep myself." She smiled ruefully. "Call me manic, but I think I'll watch the sunrise. Just shout if you need—"

"Come here," Nick said softly.

Jessie didn't think of refusing. Her heartbeat sud-denly loud in her ears, she walked to the old four-poster white spindle bed. Nick caught her hand, tugging her down onto the mattress. Then his arms went around her, tight and shaking, and he buried his face in the swell of her breasts. "God," he murmured, "I thought for sure I'd lost you."

"Only if you want to," Jessie said, as he had earlier. "Tonight—"

"Not just tonight. I mean lost you."

He lifted the T-shirt she'd put on before driving into town, nuzzling the fabric higher until she felt his mouth burn against her bare skin. Jessie leaned over him, cradling Nick to her chest, inhaling the remnants of smoke in his dark hair, finding the scent strangely arousing.

"Jess, I didn't mean to hurt you," he whispered. "Today when we quarreled, or years ago." He took a shuddering breath. "If I'd only told you then how I felt, what I wanted for us after you'd had a few more years to grow up, if I'd had the courage to talk to you—"

"If I could have listened," Jessie murmured. "Nick, we were in a different place then, a different time."

"And now?"

She kissed his forehead. "We're both here."

He sighed, then for long moments simply held her while Jessie stroked his hair as if comforting a child. Nick Granby, she thought. He'd always been so strong, stubborn, even at times high-handed, and she'd rarely seen Nick vulnerable. Maybe he'd seldom let her see that vulnerability until now.

"Lie down here," he finally said.

Her voice was husky. "Is that a proposition?"

"I wish."

Jessie slid lower, taking Nick into her arms this time, holding him close. She didn't know how long they'd lain there before she felt his breathing deepen and, drawing back, she saw that his eyes were closed. He needed sleep, even if that was the farthest thing from her own mind.

His X rays had been clear. He'd broken no bones, but the bruises went deep, and contusions marked his hip and thigh. Tonight he was numbed, even needy, but tomorrow he'd be sore.

Tonight Nick and Tom had made their peace.

What did the future hold for her and Nick?

All she knew was that they still wanted each other.

In spite of herself, Jessie had been half asleep when Nick, his eyes closed, reached for her.

"Rest," she said but couldn't resist pressing kisses

in his smoky hair, over his forehead, the tip of one ear. With a groan, Nick rolled onto his back and she followed, one leg thrown gently over his good one, her fingers swiftly unbuttoning his shirt, then her mouth scattering kisses across his bare collarbone.

"I'm glad Greg went home with Ben and Amy and Heather. Aren't you?" she said.

"God, yes."

"Are you sure you're up to this?"

"Nice choice of words, love." As Jessie sought his mouth with hers, she felt him grin. "I'm pretty dopey on that stuff they gave me at the hospital, but I'll try," he said, "because I want you so bad."

Nick's mouth was hot, his hands demanding. Swiftly he entered Jessie, both of them finding a rhythm that seemed at once ages old and brand-new. Jessie felt her body change, becoming soft and pliant, and the warm, familiar rush of sensation she'd always known in this house ran through her, over her, like the touch of Nick's hand.

"I'd do anything to have you," he murmured, his breathing harsh and shaken in her ear. "Give anything," he whispered.

And pushed her quickly to the edge.

"Just you," Jessie cried out and then, "Nick!"

In that instant she felt him spill into her, felt the warm sense of welcome become fulfillment, peace.

At the same time fierce and tender, their lovemaking had left her spent and boneless, but still awake. Now she lay beside him, Nick's head in the hollow of her throat, his lips, soft and open in sleep, against her skin, Jessie's hand entwined with his. Smiling, crying, she squeezed his fingers and felt Nick's unconscious grip tighten in response.

As the sky grew lighter in the east, Jessie sat up and eased her hand from Nick's. Months ago, outside this house, in her grandmother's raw spring garden, she had found flowers blooming and prayed, or at least hoped, for her own rebirth. Wiping her cheeks dry, Jessie realized she had just experienced it—in Nick's arms, in Aaron Granby's bedroom.

Slipping from bed, she padded across the hall to her office. Except for her unknown future with Nick, she had put her life back together, and now she knew what to do with Aaron's and Elizabeth's.

Jessie's fingers were clacking away at the keyboard when she glanced up, minutes or an hour later, and saw Nick leaning bare-chested, wearing jeans and boots, in her office doorway. He had showered, and his dark hair was wet, curling at the nape of his neck. Without a word she shut down the computer and went to him.

"Come," she said. "I want to tell you something. And I want to share the morning with you."

In the kitchen Nick made coffee—insisted on it— and they carried two steaming mugs out into the yard. Dew misted the grass beneath Jessie's sneakered feet and Nick's boots. A soft, warm breeze played through the orchard nearby, rustling leaves. Jessie sat on the ground and Nick, because of his injury, perched on Gran's swing under the old maple tree.

He dug his boot into the dirt, setting the swing gently moving.

"What's the secret?" he asked.

"Not a secret. The end of my book," Jessie sai

Nick stiffened.

"When Elizabeth asks Aaron to take her to town for their baby's birth, Aaron thinks he's lost her. That Elizabeth can never make the transition from her family to their marriage. That she'll cling to her old ways for the rest of their lives."

"He hitches up the sleigh," Nick said, "with a skittish horse."

Jessie nodded. "When the horse bolts, he and Elizabeth get thrown into a snowbank."

"And Aaron carries her home." Nick's voice was low. From the real Aaron's letter, he thought he knew how the story ended.

"He puts Elizabeth to bed and she seems all right, though chilled to the bone, but toward morning, wrapped in quilts and Aaron's arms"—Jessie glanced at Nick—"she starts labor."

"She must be terrified," he said. "Without her parents, her home, the security she loves."

"But with Aaron's help, Aaron's love, she delivers their baby."

"A son," Nick murmured, "who loses his mother."

Jessie shook her head. Taking both mugs, she set them down and turned to him. "Nick, I couldn't give them a sad ending. Besides, this is fiction—my own invention. Isn't it?"

"Yes."

"So after the baby comes, Aaron takes care of them both until Elizabeth regains her strength. To her surprise, she learns she's a quite capable young mother, and her baby thrives in Elizabeth's care—as Elizabeth ⌐es in Aaron's."

"She learns to trust herself," Nick said.

Yes." Kneeling, Jessie twined her arms around his

neck and kissed him lightly until he lifted his mouth and pulled her hands away.

"I'm glad you gave them a happy ending, Jess. But what about yourself?" Nick's eyes were dark. "What's your happy ending?"

She'd stopped believing in them. Until now.

"I fall in love," she said, "and marry and have beautiful children by a man I absolutely adore."

"And become an international, best-selling author." Nick's voice was low, husky. "Pretty damn perfect life you've envisioned there. Who's the lucky man, Jess?"

"You'll make me say it, won't you?"

"Damn right. It's not every day I get a proposal."

"Have it your way."

"Not always," he said. "I've learned that much. But in this case—"

"Will you marry me?"

Nick shook his head. " 'Will you marry me, Nicholas Granby?' " he repeated. "I want to make sure you know you have the right guy here."

"Oh, I'm sure." But Jessie said the words again because he seemed to need them. Then she added, "You'd better say yes, because if you don't, I'm getting on the first plane to Charleston after you. I'll get Rob and Alaina on my side, and Tani, have her mix up her strongest voodoo potion, and none of us will leave you alone until you—"

"Yes," Nick said, laughing, "yes," and wrapped her in his arms. The kiss was long, thorough, searching, and when Jessie raised her head at last, she could hardly breathe. Nick's dark, serious look stole the last oxygen from her lungs. "I love you, Jess. I'll make y happy this time."

"We'll make each other happy," she said. "Happy and sad and furious and joyful, sometimes all at once."

Nick took a deep breath. "So. The big question. Where do we live?"

Jessie frowned. "I do like Charleston, you know, your friends. And Delilah. I don't even sneeze there," Jessie said. "If you'd gone back without me, I'd have followed you."

"If you hadn't, I'd have come back for you. But last night I promised you a new barn. Pop says I'd better keep the promise."

She shook her head. "No, I think Sunbeam and her mama would be better off in Tom's barn. It's newer, fire-resistant."

Nick followed her gaze toward the still-smoldering embers of Aaron Granby's barn. "I can build you a safe barn, Jess. And still make it look just like the old one if you want. Hell, I've had enough practice with hurricane restoration work this year that I'm practically the world's expert on antiques, or the appearance thereof."

"I'm sure you are, but unless Greg needs a barn on this side of the fence, I'm inclined to let Aaron's go. It'll still be in my memory, Nick. Like the memories of growing up here, with Gran and my parents." She looked toward the hill and the small cemetery.

"You won't miss being close to . . . everything you loved?"

"They're in my heart, Nick. Where they belong."

He kissed one temple, then the other. "I think we [co]uld build the barn, fix the whole place up the way [it us]ed to be, and come back here for weekends, fam-[ily re]unions, to visit Pop."

"You do?" Jessie said so quickly that he laughed.

"I do, love."

It was a vow, and she took it as such.

"Maybe I shouldn't have given in so easily," Jessie said, "but I don't care where we live." She looked deeply into his dark eyes. "After last night, I know what you meant when you said that belonging isn't a matter of place. I thought then that you were just running away from your feelings about Tom and the farm—"

"I was, Jess."

"But you were right, too. Whenever I would think of Gran's house, of this farm, I'd remember the happiness, the warmth and love I felt here, but I didn't know why I'd been so happy. Why my life felt so centered then, so right for me." Jessie cradled his face in her hands. "You know why. You felt it, too, the first week I moved back here—when we took the tour of the house together—and last night when we made love. Didn't you?"

"Yes," he said. "I felt it, too."

"We belong together, Nick. Wherever we are, as long as we're together, that's all that matters." Her gaze held his. "Home isn't a place. It's the person you belong to, the person you love most."

"But you said—"

"I missed you, more than anyone else, Nick. For twelve years. I was always happy here because you were here then, too."

"Ah, Jess."

She heard the low tremor in his voice and thou he'd had enough. Getting up she held out a h "Come on," she said.

The morning lifted all around them, the su

in the blue sky, mare's-tail clouds floating high, birds flushing from the hedgerows on wings that fluttered like Jessie's heartbeat. She led Nick across her grandmother's yard, past the kitchen garden, trampled the night before by firemen and onlookers, then up the hill behind Aaron Granby's barn.

There, Jessie knelt at the gravesites of her parents and Gran and Caroline Pearce's husband. Nick pulled weeds around his mother's headstone. Then they paused at a pair of markers without inscription, the letters long since worn away by wind and rain.

"It could be," Jessie murmured.

"My great-great-great-grandfather and his wife, buried here?" Nick smiled softly. "The rest of our relatives are. I don't see why not. But it could just as easily be your imagination again, playing 'what if.' And right now, if you don't mind, I don't care to join you. My leg's stiffening up and my stomach's growling. I need a pain pill, and eggs Benedict—not necessarily in that order."

"I promise not to burn your eggs."

Going back down the hill, she felt certain Nick was leaning on her more than necessary, but Jessie didn't mind.

At the bottom of the hill, she stopped. "Do you really think you can rebuild this barn?" One wall was partially standing, and from Jessie's view, for one instant, she'd thought she was seeing things. That Aaron's barn still stood.

"Oh ye of little faith," Nick murmured. "If I could ᵇild Seaview's clubhouse to satisfy a bunch of angry ᵉʳvationists, I guess I can put up a pole barn."

ⁿ sorry," Jessie said, answering his smile. "I'm ᵤ can do anything you put your mind to."

"I always have." Limping, Nick followed her to the barn's entrance—or the place where it had been—and touched her arm in warning. "Watch out, that wood's still poker-hot. Don't burn yourself."

"I won't." Jessie jumped over a smoking beam. She looked down at the charred wooden floor, the burned hay that now resembled someone's frizzled perm. "But for the rest of my life, I'll be indebted to you for saving Greg and Heather, and Sunbeam and her mama—"

"I didn't save Sunbeam. The firemen did."

Nick grasped her shoulders just before Jessie barked her shin on a fallen beam, wedged against the stallside. At an angle, it made a triangle of the stall, the blackened floor, and the hayloft—most of which was gone.

"Jess, we shouldn't be in here. It's not safe."

"I won't stay." She looked down. "I just didn't want to dream about last night, have nightmares about this place. Remember when you and Ben graduated and I overheard you here, arguing about ag school?"

"You defended my passion for architecture. Sure, I remember."

"Those are the memories I want to keep."

"Me, too," Nick agreed. "Pop's place wasn't as bad as I wanted to think. And he's come a long way this summer, too, Jess, not just about me." He hooked an arm around her neck, kissing her briefly. "He's stronger, and his memory's almost a hundred percent again. He's excited about farming with Greg, and may have a surprise for him."

"What?" Jessie said.

"While you were getting your car keys to g

town for my X rays, one of the firemen mentioned a state program I hadn't heard about. I want to look into it for Pop.''

''What is it?''

''Farmland preservation. If a farm's really productive, the owner can offer development rights to the state, which then pays the farmer most of the difference between the land's value for agriculture and the money a developer might pay.'' Nick smiled. ''Then the farm itself can remain as it is in perpetuity. It's protected forever from development. Open space.''

''Nick, that's wonderful. Do you think—''

''We'll check it out. What happens in the next season or so with Greg might make the difference. I don't know what the guidelines really are. But you know, I think Pop just may be all right anyway. Until his first grandchild, or two or three, gets here.''

''I hope so.'' Jessie smiled at him. ''Is that a proposition?''

''A plan of intent,'' Nick said. ''Five-year plan. But the first phase might just be complete, say, around Seaview's opening next spring.''

''Maybe after breakfast we should implement it, then.''

''I like the way you think, famous lady writer.''

They had turned to go when a flash of bright metal caught Jessie's eye. At first she thought it might be part of Sunbeam's halter, a buckle or hasp.

''Careful, Jess. Whatever it is, it's hot.''

Buried in the rubble, the metal edge proved larger Jessie pulled it free. The fiery silver burned her ⁻ers, but she didn't cry out. The charred rag par-
⁻   wrapped around it felt somewhat cooler,

though still smoking, than the metal, and she gingerly cushioned the object. "Oh, Nick. Look."

By two fingers, Jessie lifted the old picture frame. Carrying it to the barn entrance, she wet the rag in a puddle and carefully wiped soot from the silver edges.

"Don't cut yourself," Nick said, hunkering beside her.

The silver had tarnished, the glass shattered long ago. But the image inside was still visible. Her heart thumping, Jessie stared at the sepia picture of two people: the blond man in stiff shirt collar, dark suit, and shiny shoes; the slender, dark-haired woman in a dress that might have been silk and lace. Yellow silk, Jessie thought.

"Who is it?" Nick asked.

Turning the picture over, she hardly needed the words written in now-faded ink, in a spidery, old-fashioned hand on the frame's backing. She'd seen these people before, but not in a photograph album or any of Amy Stone's historical documents; she'd seen them in her own imagination.

Her voice shaking, Jessie read aloud to Nick.

" 'Aaron and Elizabeth Granby, on their wedding day.' "

"Jesus," he murmured. "Did you know her name was really Elizabeth?"

Her throat had closed, and she had to swallow before she spoke again. "Amy found that letter from Aaron to his in-laws but not much more. She didn't have time to read everything in the file. I was going to spend time at the society myself, then . . ." She gestured around them. "No," she whispered. "I didn't know she was Elizabeth."

Still holding the picture, Jessie got to her feet. In the yard, she examined it again, while Nick stamped through the barn on some structural tour of his own. In the sunlight, noticing a small scrap of cloth caught in the frame, she gently tried to tug it free.

Nick came outside. "This barn must have been modernized—a little—sometime in the last fifty years or so. Probably by Caroline's husband. There's a false ceiling, or was, maybe meant as insulation, and when the hayloft collapsed, everything came down. The picture must have been in between the two ceilings, God knows for how long."

The cloth tore loose. It measured only an inch or so square, but when Jessie pulled, the frame backing dislodged. She drew it down, a fraction of an inch at a time, not to shred it. It was both brittle from age and now damp in spots from water sprayed on the fire. When she'd exposed the inside and the back of the wedding picture itself, Jessie drew in a sharp breath.

There, folded into quarters, she found a yellowed paper. Her eyes met Nick's. She hesitated, as if certain of what she'd found here, too.

"I love you, Nick," she murmured. "I always have."

And if home was the place she would share with him, so it had been for Elizabeth, here, with Aaron. Long ago, she thought, and now, love everlasting was the love of a good man.

For a moment longer their gazes held, and something passed between them again, like the warmth in Caroline Pearce's house.

Then Nick said, "I love you, Jess. Open it."

Her fingers shaking, she uncreased the faded paper, her lips lifting in a smile. She thought fleetingly of Greg's ghosts—then made a promise to herself, and Nick. They'd keep this scrap of Elizabeth's diary and this picture in its silver frame, a remembrance of another love, another time. Between them, she held the page dated, as Jessie had known it would be:

June 18, 1856

Aaron brought me to the farm today. No, Aaron brought me home. . . .

COMING NEXT MONTH

MORNING COMES SOFTLY by Debbie Macomber
A sweet, heartwarming, contemporary mail-order bride story. Travis Thompson, a rough-and-tough rancher, and Mary Warner, a shy librarian, have nothing in common. But when Travis finds himself the guardian of his orphaned nephew and niece, only one solution comes to his mind—to place an ad for a wife. "I relished every word, lived every scene, and shared in the laughter and tears of the characters."—Linda Lael Miller, bestselling author of *Daniel's Bride*

ECHOES AND ILLUSIONS by Kathy Lynn Emerson
A time-travel romance to treasure. A young woman finds echoes of the past in her present life in this spellbinding story, of which *Romantic Times* says, "a heady blend of romance, suspense and drama . . . a real page turner."

PHANTOM LOVER by Millie Criswell
In the turbulent period of the Revolutionary War, beautiful Danielle Sheridan must choose between the love of two different yet brave men—her gentle husband or her elusive Phantom Lover. "A hilarious, sensual, fast-paced romp."—Elaine Barbieri, author of *More Precious Than Gold*

ANGEL OF PASSAGE by Joan Avery
A riveting and passionate romance set during the Civil War. Rebecca Cunningham, the belle of Detroit society, works for the Underground Railroad, ferrying escaped slaves across the river to Canada. Captain Bradford Taylor has been sent by the government to capture the "Angel of Passage," unaware that she is the very woman with whom he has fallen in love.

JACARANDA BEND by Charlotte Douglas
A spine-tingling historical set on a Florida plantation. A beautiful Scotswoman finds herself falling in love with a man who may be capable of murder.

HEART SOUNDS by Michele Johns
A poignant love story set in nineteenth-century America. Louisa Halloan, nearly deaf from a gunpowder explosion, marries the man of her dreams. But while he lavishes her with gifts, he withholds the one thing she treasures most—his love.

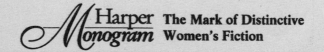

Harper Monogram The Mark of Distinctive Women's Fiction

ANALISE

Analise Caldwell was the reigning belle of New Orleans. Disguised as a Confederate soldier, Union major Mark Schaeffer captured the Rebel beauty's heart as part of his mission. Stunned by his deception, Analise swore never to yield to the caresses of this Yankee spy...until he delivered an ultimatum.

ROSEWOOD

Millicent Hayes had lived all her life amid the lush woodland of Emmetsville, Texas. Bound by her duty to her crippled brother, the dark-haired innocent had never known desire...until a handsome stranger moved in next door.

BONDS OF LOVE

Katherine Devereaux was a willful, defiant beauty who had yet to meet her match in any man—until the winds of war swept the Union innocent into the arms of Confederate Captain Matthew Hampton.

LIGHT AND SHADOW

The day nobleman Jason Somerville broke into her rooms and swept her away to his ancestral estate, Carolyn Mabry began living a dangerous charade. Posing as her twin sister, Jason's wife, Carolyn thought she was helping her gentle twin. Instead she found herself drawn to the man she had so seductively deceived.

CRYSTAL HEART

A seductive beauty, Lady Lettice Kenton swore never to give her heart to any man—until she met the rugged American rebel Charles Murdock. Together on a ship bound for America, they shared a perfect passion, but danger awaited them on the shores of Boston Harbor.